THE

LOST

CAUSES

THE

LOST

CAUSES

BY

JESSICA KOOSED ETTING

AND

ALYSSA EMBREE SCHWARTZ

KCP Loft is an imprint of Kids Can Press

First paperback edition 2018

Kids Can Press gratefully acknowledges the financial support of the Government
of Ontario, through the Ontario Media Development Corporation.

Published in Canada and the U.S. by Kids Can Press Ltd.
25 Dockside Drive, Toronto, ON M5A 0B5

Kids Can Press is a Corus Entertainment Inc. company

www.kidscanpress.com
www.kcploft.com

The text is set in Minion Pro and Avenir Black

Edited by Kate Egan
Designed by Emma Dolan
Cover photo courtesy of iStock.com/Pawel Gaul

Printed and bound in Altona, Manitoba, Canada in 6/2018 by Friesens Corp.

CM 17 0 9 8 7 6 5 4 3 2
CM PA 18 0 9 8 7 6 5 4 3 2 1

Library and Archives Canada Cataloguing in Publication

Etting, Jessica Koosed, author
The lost causes / written by Jessica Koosed Etting and
Alyssa Embree Schwartz.

ISBN 978-1-77138-844-3 (hardback)
ISBN 978-1-5253-0133-9 (softcover)

I. Schwartz, Alyssa Embree, author II. Title.

PZ7.E86Los 2017   j813'.6   C2016-906545-6

For Oliver, Sawyer, Archer, Theo and Gemma, our brightest lights

CHAPTER ONE

The Cedar Springs High campus looked Photoshopped that morning. Blue sky, zero clouds, birds strategically positioned on the lawn chirping their heads off. Even a few orange leaves drifted down from the treetops as if they were modeling for a fall advertising campaign.

"This weather sucks," Z Chapman grumbled to her boyfriend, Jared, who was sprawled next to her on the soccer field behind the school. This was the kind of day that made people feel they should be active and cheerful, two things Z despised. She preferred the weather to match her mood, permanently cloudy, like a mental version of Seattle.

She reached her arm above her, shielding her eyes from the sun, and crossed her spindly legs. Thanks to a growth spurt she'd had at thirteen, she was long limbed and twiggy, though her chest hadn't quite caught up. Not that she cared. A bra was just one less thing she had to put on under her daily wardrobe of a black camisole, black sweater, black pants and black combat boots. She liked that her pale skin looked almost translucent against the dark clothing and her raven hair, which at the moment was just barely visible with her short buzz cut.

"Have the cops come by your house again?" Jared asked as he downed the can of soda he always drank before first period.

"I don't know," Z answered indifferently. She closed her eyes, exhaustion pinning her body to the grass. Why couldn't they have one of those silent mornings where she could doze off instead of facing the effort of conversation?

Especially on this subject.

Last month, a woman had been brutally killed in her cabin, and though Z understood why it was still the talk of the town — single woman, no eyewitnesses, no leads, a seemingly random act of pure violence — that didn't mean she wanted to talk about it. Everywhere she went, people were murmuring about the Lily Carpenter murder, as if the killer was hiding in a stall in the girls' bathroom scoping out the next victim. Sure, it was possible, but panicking wasn't going to save anyone's life.

And because Lily Carpenter was found dead on some land Z's dad was trying to buy and develop, Jared brought up the murder constantly. As if that indirect link somehow made Z part of the story.

"I heard they still don't have a clue who did it," Jared said, absently ripping off threads from the bottom of his frayed cords. "No fingerprints, no motive, nothing."

"Yeah."

"I bet your dad's pretty upset."

"Yeah, he's pissed."

"I don't blame him. There's a murderer running around town and the cops have their heads up their asses."

Z shook her head, her eyes still closed. "That's not why he's pissed. His construction site is still a crime scene, so they won't let him build on it right now. Everything is being held up. And time is money, you know?"

Jared sat up, his voice rising with excitement. "I bet if your dad asks —"

"Can we please stop talking about the Lily Carpenter murder? It's boring."

"No it's not. It's crazy. Someone got killed," he said with a little too much enthusiasm, considering the subject. "You haven't lived here long enough. Stuff like this never happens in Cedar Springs."

Z pushed herself up on her elbows and raised an eyebrow at him. "Really? You do realize thousands of Native Americans were massacred here in the 1800s?"

"Well, yeah, but that was forever ago."

She flopped back down on the freshly cut grass, exposing the red star tattoo she'd gotten on her abdomen after reading *The Communist Manifesto* and trying not to dwell on the fact that Jared had the relative IQ of a couch. *He* might be shocked that something creepy happened here, but Z sure wasn't. She knew there was no way this tiny town was as placid as it seemed. People might think they were safe, tucked away where Colorado met New Mexico, but Z had been around long enough to know that nothing was ever as peaceful as it seemed. The school bell rang in the distance and she groaned. What she would give to ditch and hang out at Jared's house where it was empty and quiet, but Jared would never go for that. He was barely passing chem, and Z couldn't muster up the energy it would take to persuade him.

They ambled across the soccer field until they caught sight of a couple hooking up under the bleachers.

Jared pushed his unkempt hair out of his eyes to get a better look. "Is that …?"

Disgusted, Z narrowed her eyes at the couple. "He's such a cliché." Her twin brother, Scott, was too busy hooking up with Sabrina Ross to notice Z and Jared crossing the field.

Z gave them both a withering look as she passed. "Pathetic."

* * *

Sabrina heard Z's comment loud and clear, but she ignored it. She just had to focus on the end goal right now. "You are so hot," Scott murmured into her neck. With a Japanese mother and African-American father, Sabrina had always turned people's heads. When she was younger, it was because people were curious about what she "was." Now, people just thought she was hot. Sabrina didn't see it herself, but it was like her secret superpower, and every once in a while (like now), she let it work for her.

Scott moved his hands under her shirt toward the clasp of her bra, and she didn't bother stopping him. They had hooked up for the first time at a house party the weekend before, mostly due to the extra tab of ecstasy Sabrina had popped as soon as she felt the first one wearing off.

"Scott!"

Sabrina jumped at the high-pitched shriek coming from behind them. They whirled around to find it belonged to Emily Price, her face flushed with anger. She looked equal parts horrified and hurt, which could only mean one thing.

Scott had a girlfriend.

Sabrina strained to remember if she knew this about him. But how was she supposed to keep track of all the fleeting couplings at their high school?

"It's not what it looks like —" Scott began.

Emily shook her head, her ponytail whipping around behind her. "You're kidding me, right? Your hand was up her shirt!"

Scott reached for Emily, but she swatted him away.

"You know, I didn't believe your sister when she told me you were out here with … *her*." Emily spat out that last word as if it was burning her tongue. "It's so over."

As Emily huffed away, Sabrina briefly wondered if it was worth apologizing later. Hooking up with someone's boyfriend was a shady thing to do. But on the flip side, maybe this was the push Emily needed to show herself that she could do better than Scott. Or maybe Sabrina was just rationalizing her guilt away.

"I've got to go talk to her," Scott said, shaking his head. He sounded more annoyed than upset, which meant Sabrina still had a short window to get what she wanted.

She leaned casually against the bleachers. "Since you're leaving me high and dry here, maybe you have something to take the edge off."

If Scott realized he was being used, he didn't show it. Too much pride, Sabrina guessed. Typical guy. "I've got a few Vicodin but other than that I'm tapped out."

Sabrina's head tingled at the sound of that word. "Vicodin works."

Scott handed her three pills, two of which she swallowed dry as soon as he walked away. As she waited for her heart rate to slow down and that numb feeling to coat her skin, her thoughts wandered to Z, who had inexplicably caused this showdown. She tried to act so above it all with her buzz cut and "I don't give a crap" attitude. It was a sad attempt to veil how immature she was. Why would any girl want to screw over her brother like that?

Ten minutes later, though, the Vicodin had worked its dependable magic, and Scott, Emily and Z disappeared into the back of her mind, joining the hundreds of other things Sabrina refused to think about.

* * *

Andrew Foreman slogged into his math classroom, his oversize sweatshirt swallowing his skinny frame up as if it was feasting on his bones. He was tall and gangly and might have been basketball material if he'd ever shown a shred of physical coordination. But even the faint breeze that drifted through the classroom's open window almost toppled him over.

Head down, he told himself as he walked past the first row of desks, trying to avoid eye contact with his teacher. But Mr. Greenly made this impossible.

"Mr. Foreman, nice of you to show up today," Mr. Greenly said, pushing up his wire-rimmed glasses.

"I have a doctor's note," Andrew mumbled.

"Right," said Mr. Greenly, his thin lips settling into a smirk. "You always do."

A few students in the front row laughed, all in on the joke, and Andrew slunk to his seat in the back corner of the room.

As the clock struck 9:55, marking the beginning of third period, Mr. Greenly dimmed the lights and closed the blinds. He was one of those teachers who loved to teach by PowerPoint.

"Okay, today we're going to review solving two systems of linear inequalities by graphing and then move on to solving them by elimination."

He opened his first slide — a mess of letters and numbers that made Andrew realize just how far behind he was. He gripped his pencil tightly, jotting down everything Mr. Greenly said, though he didn't have a clue what it meant. Then he dropped the pencil as a sharp jolt ran up his left leg as if he was being jabbed with a poison-tipped needle. He instinctively grabbed his thigh to keep from crying out, and the pain subsided at his touch. Andrew patted his leg tentatively. He'd noticed it was a bit puffy the previous night, but he'd tried to convince himself it was nothing. Clearly, that was a mistake.

Another stinging jolt shot up Andrew's calf just as Mr. Greenly turned to him, eyes narrowed. "Mr. Foreman, at what point on the X-axis would the solution fall?"

A new throbbing sensation attacked Andrew in his chest.

"We're waiting …" Mr. Greenly said, tapping his pen on the desk.

The eyes of the entire class fell on Andrew. Usually that would've embarrassed the hell out of him, but he was in too much pain to care.

Chest pains like this were one of the major symptoms of a pulmonary embolism. Andrew's doctor swore he didn't have a blood clot when he'd seen her last week, complaining of poor circulation. She'd be sorry when she saw that not only did the clot exist, but it was already cutting off blood flow to his lungs.

"I'm sorry," Andrew sputtered, before jumping out of his seat and running from the room.

He rushed down the hall and made it down the stairwell, fighting through the bolts of pain in his leg as he reached the door to the nurse's office.

"I need an ambulance," Andrew said as he entered the small room, the antiseptic air burning his nose. "I have a blood clot in my left leg and it's causing a pulmonary embolism in my lungs."

Nurse Tammy looked blankly at him. "A pulmonary embolism? That's unusual," she commented, making no attempt to stand or help him.

Andrew was frantic. "I know! I may need emergency surgery! Why aren't you doing anything?"

"Because this is the sixth time you've requested an ambulance this month, Andrew," she replied.

He recoiled — he could've sworn it was only his third.

"After last time, your mother explicitly indicated that we not allow you to leave campus for incidents like this. You're costing her a fortune in ER bills."

Andrew bit his lip, upset but unsurprised.

His mother, along with everybody else, seemed convinced he'd been faking his illnesses for the last decade.

Nurse Tammy raised an eyebrow at him. "Well? Do you think you can make it back to class?"

* * *

Sabrina trudged down the hallway to get her books for her next-period class. The Vicodin she'd taken earlier that day was slowing her movements, forcing her out of sync with the rushing students all around her.

As she reached her locker, Sabrina's stomach tightened in annoyance. Peeking out of the top was the white cardstock she immediately recognized as the stationery of Dr. Pearl, the school psychologist. Sabrina scanned the note, which instructed her to skip her next class and meet in the Art Hall, room 113.

She got requests like this a few times every semester from Dr. Pearl, who'd flagged Sabrina as a student in need of psychological support back in ninth grade. Sabrina wasn't excited about sitting through another pointless session with the counselor, who would no doubt use passive therapy-speak to chastise her for whatever transgression had most recently been reported to the principal. (Dr. Pearl had stopped being sympathetic to Sabrina's family situation sometime around her third suspension for smoking marijuana on campus, which was also around the time Sabrina was told she'd need to repeat her junior year.) But anytime Dr. Pearl wanted to see you, it meant an excused absence from class, and it was worth hearing that woman's grating voice so she could skip the Spanish quiz she'd been too buzzed to study for the night before.

The Art Hall was an older, dilapidated building on the far end of campus, and the door creaked loudly as she opened it, the hallway dim and empty. Steven Chapman, Z and Scott's father, had successfully lobbied the school board to renovate this building into a cutting-edge technology, arts and media center, with the project breaking ground in the spring. In advance of the demolition, the school had moved the art classes to another area and stopped using the classrooms in this building altogether, something Sabrina had used to her benefit to get loaded a few weeks ago during lunch period. Could that be the purpose of this meeting? It would be *so* like Dr. Pearl to want to meet with Sabrina at the scene of the crime.

The building was chilly, in the way of a place that's long been vacant, and Sabrina pulled her jean jacket over her shoulders as she made her way down to room 113. It was the very last one in the hall, located next to an emergency exit door that led to the woods on the edge of campus.

She swung open the door.

But instead of Dr. Pearl, she found four students inside, sitting at hard metal desks arranged in a circle, each with a name card and a glass of water on it. Sabrina immediately recognized one of the students as Justin Diaz, the star of the football team. Then she frowned when she saw who was sitting next to him. Z, with a bored smirk on her face.

"What's going on?" Sabrina asked. Dr. Pearl always made an exaggerated point of keeping their sessions confidential. Had the brain haze from the Vicodin made her read the note wrong?

"Like *we* know," Justin replied.

On the other side of him sat a delicate blond girl, her name card identifying her as Gabby. She was staring straight ahead, tapping her tan ankle boots on the floor in a distinctive pattern. Two right, one left. One right, two left. The consistency of it was oddly hypnotic.

"Did you get a note from Dr. Pearl, too?" the final student asked her. Andrew, his name card read. He was a lanky guy, holding his leg as if he were in pain, his skinny body curled up in a chair. Like the toe-tapper, he seemed younger. Sabrina thought he might be that sophomore who was carted away in an ambulance last spring after some kind of asthma attack.

His cheeks reddened as Sabrina met his gaze. "Yup. I got a note," she told him.

She walked to the desk next to him and hesitantly sat down, taking off her jacket. Unlike the frosty hallway, the room was heated, its temperature almost too hot. Or maybe she was sweaty because she was coming off the Vicodin? Sabrina grabbed for the water on her desk, guzzling it down. "What do you think she wants us for?"

Z heaved a long sigh. "Isn't it obvious?"

"I don't know," Sabrina responded, her earlier irritation with Z flaring. "Do you think she wants to discuss your warped jealousy issues about your twin brother with all of us?"

"I doubt you could string enough words together to articulate an opinion on that," Z snapped.

"What is your problem with me?" Sabrina asked. "You don't even know me."

"Forget it," Z muttered.

Andrew cleared his throat. "Wait, what's obvious?" he asked Z.

"That Dr. Pearl has expanded her limited skill set from conducting rudimentary, inaccurate individual assessments to conducting one in a group setting. Maybe she thinks it will save her time."

Sabrina exhaled. Z was probably right about this being a group-therapy session. Sabrina didn't know about Andrew or Gabby, but Z seemed to have an array of psychological problems, and Justin, well ... she'd known him since elementary school. Everyone knew about his temper. The room remained quiet until Andrew began to cough.

"Are you okay?" Sabrina asked when he didn't stop.

Andrew took a swig of water and nodded.

"This room is dusty," he mumbled. "Maybe it's from the furnace. I bet they haven't turned it on in months and sometimes dust particles —"

"Dude, who cares?" said Justin, and Andrew scooted his chair back a few inches.

Z sighed. "Maybe if we all shut up, Dr. Pearl will finally show up and tell us what the hell we're doing here."

* * *

Ryan Nash sat in a nondescript white van, staring at a small television screen. He was absorbing every detail of the five students' interactions in real time, thanks to a tiny camera he'd embedded in the wall of the classroom.

He focused on Sabrina on the monitor, trying to ignore his nagging annoyance at being placed on this assignment. He observed the way Sabrina pretended not to see Z rolling her eyes at her, noting the underlying friction between them. He hadn't seen anything like that recorded in their files, but there were always nuances and quirks that emerged in person.

Patricia opened the side door of the van, slipping into the backseat. She wore a navy pantsuit that seemed too large for her narrow shoulders, though Nash couldn't tell if the jacket was the wrong size or if Patricia was simply the type of woman who didn't look right in a suit. He had yet to see one she appeared comfortable in.

"Everything is ready," she told him as she quickly scanned the screen. "Shall we?" Though she phrased it like a question, it wasn't. At fifty-five, she was over three decades older than Nash. She was the one with seniority, the one calling the shots. Despite her enthusiasm, Nash had a hard time believing this was going to work.

He nodded, but as he stepped outside the van, he couldn't help asking again. "You honestly think this is the best way?"

She paused, then said with absolute conviction, "I do. I know you're not a believer yet, but by the end of this, you will be."

CHAPTER TWO

Sabrina looked up when the door to room 113 opened, but two strangers greeted her instead of Dr. Pearl. The first was a thin woman with long, brown frizzy hair who immediately gave everyone a toothy smile. The second was a much younger guy, who remained near the door.

"Where's Dr. Pearl?" Andrew asked, echoing Sabrina's thoughts.

"I'm afraid she got detained, Andrew," the woman replied apologetically. Sabrina was about to ask how she even knew their names until she remembered the cards on the desks.

"Let's back up. Let me introduce myself. I'm Dr. Patricia Nichols, but no need for formalities. Please call me Patricia. And that's Nash over there by the door. We're clinical therapists. I'm actually an old colleague of Dr. Pearl's, and she recently called on me to begin a program here at Cedar Springs."

Sabrina sighed. Z was right.

"Dr. Pearl had planned to do a whole introduction, but a small student emergency popped up. I told her we could proceed without her until she's available." Patricia paused, as if expecting an interjection, and Andrew immediately shot his hand up. "Yes, Andrew?"

"Can we turn the heat down?" he asked.

Patricia nodded. "We've been trying. There seems to be something wrong with the system. I know it's an old building …"

"But I might have a pulmonary embolism. And I definitely have asthma that could require serious attention at any time —"

"We're aware of that, Andrew," Nash cut in curtly.

Sabrina turned toward Nash, really seeing his face for the first time since he'd entered the room. Recognition flashed through her entire body. It was *him*.

It had been a Monday, almost two weeks ago, when he'd walked into the Sonic Burger where she worked after school. She heard the door open but didn't look over because she was in the middle of grabbing an order of fries for a customer who'd complained that his first batch was soggy.

When she finished getting the fries out and punching in the voiding codes, she finally looked up at the guy waiting at the register, his green eyes, five-day stubble and jet-black lashes causing an unfamiliar tsunami-size wave of attraction to crash over her.

"Can I help you?" she'd squeaked, her heart beating quickly.

And when he'd glanced up at her, about to speak, he paused, a look of surprise in his eyes. As if he was seeing some part of Sabrina that she didn't even know existed. They stood like that, in silence, for what was probably five seconds but felt like five hours, before Nash cleared his throat.

"I'll just take a number-four combo."

"Okay, coming right up." She tried to think of something more to say — she just wanted to be in his presence a little longer — but he turned and sat at a table, tugging his gray beanie down and gazing out the window.

When his order came up, Sabrina picked up the tray and walked toward his table. Usually she was supposed to just call out the number, but she wanted one more chance to talk to him. She checked out her reflection in the small mirror by the takeout window, cringing at the sight of the dumb hat she was forced to wear.

"Here you go," she said as she reached his table, her heartbeat again intensifying. She couldn't remember ever feeling like this before. It was like a chemical reaction — for once without the actual chemicals. But it was more than that. It was a feeling like this person was inevitable.

"Do you live around here?" she asked. It was a lame question, but she couldn't let him get away.

"What?" he answered, his look instantly guarded.

"I just … haven't seen you before," Sabrina sputtered. "Not that I know every single person who walks through. I mean …" What did she mean? "Anyway, the point is, if you're new to Cedar Springs, I could show you around a little bit." She quickly scribbled her phone number on the receipt before she lost her nerve.

"Oh. I'll keep that in mind," he replied, the intensity of his deep voice almost making her knees buckle.

She'd waited several days for him to call or text. But by the weekend, she'd realized it was hopeless and retreated into a two-day drug-fueled bender.

Now, she couldn't tear her eyes away from him. *What is he doing here?* He was in a deep blue V-neck, his dark hair more apparent without the gray beanie from before. That was probably why she hadn't recognized him straightaway.

Nash turned to her, caught her eye and raised a single eyebrow. She looked away, her cheeks hot. She'd somehow deluded herself into thinking they'd had a real connection, and now here she was, sitting like a child at a desk, and it turned out he was some kind of *therapist*?

Maybe his visit to Sonic hadn't even been an accident. Maybe he'd been scoping her out for this therapy session ahead of time. Or maybe that was paranoid thinking. There were just three fast-food joints in

Cedar Springs, so he was bound to go into at least one of them. It was probably just a coincidence.

She looked back to see he was still watching her. But this time Sabrina knew it was clinical observation, nothing more.

"Why don't we begin?" Patricia said. "What is this meeting about, exactly? To put it simply, we're beginning a weekly group-therapy program designed to help you overcome your issues and move forward in life." Z raised an eyebrow at the group — she'd guessed correctly. "We've found peer support to be incredibly effective. Through role play, memory games, trust-building exercises and other therapeutic activities, you'll see that this is a safe place for you all to share whatever is holding you back."

Sabrina wished she'd opted to take that Spanish quiz.

"I've had success with programs like this at several other schools in the county. When I contacted Dr. Pearl about implementing one here, she suggested the five of you as terrific candidates." Though she tried to couch it as a compliment, Sabrina wasn't fooled. Being the first person the school shrink thought needed heavy-duty therapy was nothing to be proud of.

"What the hell issues do I have?" Justin blurted, his forehead dotted with tiny beads of sweat. "It's not like I'm like *her*." He pointed at Gabby, who ducked her head lower as a result of the attention, though her feet continued their rhythmic tapping.

"Did you not just get in a physical altercation with a student last week?" Nash asked. He meant the cafeteria brawl Justin had instigated last Tuesday, where he threw an entire table and half a dozen metal chairs at the captain of the soccer team.

"Lots of guys fight." Justin narrowed his eyes at him. "And why should I listen to you? How old are you? My age?"

Sabrina leaned forward. She *was* curious to hear how old Nash was. He didn't look much older than she was, so maybe he was a grad student or something. *Off-limits*, she reminded herself. *Never going to happen.*

"Justin, the fact that you have what could be categorized as a sociopathic proclivity toward violence should come as no surprise to you," Nash responded coolly. "Now, does anyone else feel the need to interrupt or can we move on?" Sabrina stayed silent. She knew what the others in the room probably already thought of her. She didn't need Nash to open it up for a group discussion.

Patricia took a deep breath. "There is one thing that qualified the five of you for this program. As different as you are, you all have one underlying similarity."

The room went quiet.

"You've all been dismissed," Patricia said, her tone incredulous, as if to express her exasperation with those who had judged them that way. "Your school files indicate that you've been deemed lost causes by everyone around you. People have given up trying to help. Your teachers, your fellow students, even your parents." This wasn't new information to Sabrina, but it still stung to hear someone say the words aloud.

"That's not true," Andrew managed to say before a hacking cough overtook him again.

Z shrugged and took a gulp of water. "Sounds accurate to me."

"What do you mean, our parents gave up on us?" Gabby asked softly, the first words she'd uttered since entering the room, her blue eyes wide and innocent. She reminded Sabrina of the American Girl doll she used to play with when she was little.

Nash spoke, a new note of empathy in his voice. "We sent them all letters about this program a week ago. Actually, we sent them to a dozen or so students' parents. We explained the program and why we thought you might benefit from it. The success stories we've had. Some parents called us right away, desperate to get their children into the program. Others called and chewed us out, claiming their kids didn't need help. Do you want to know what your parents had in common?"

No one responded.

"They were the only ones who didn't reply at all."

Sabrina looked up, finally making eye contact with the others. For one brief second, they were all united in their anger and shame.

"That's how we chose you all."

Patricia jumped in quickly. "But we don't happen to agree with your parents or anyone else. That's why we're doing this. We want to prove them wrong. Nash and I refuse to give up on you. We can help you — we've done it before. All you need is a little extra support from us and from each other. We believe in you." Patricia tapped her hand on the desk for emphasis. "And we want you to believe in each other."

For a split second, Sabrina allowed herself to wonder if this program could actually work. She guessed by the way Gabby was leaning forward in her chair that she was wondering the same thing. It wasn't as if Sabrina enjoyed that every thought she had was blurry and she could barely remember what she'd done the day before. It hadn't always been like this for her. Caught in the endless cycle of chasing the next high. But how was doing trust falls with a bunch of fellow losers going to fix her?

"You'll notice a contact list with all of your phone numbers on your desks in case you want to connect with each other before we meet again," Patricia continued. "I have a feeling that in the next few days you'll need one another. Truly, this program could give you all a new purpose in life."

Need each other how? Sabrina now felt validated in her skepticism. The vague platitudes Patricia was spewing didn't sound any different from the run-of-the-mill group-therapy programs that Dr. Pearl had emailed Sabrina about a few years ago.

"Well, I for one don't give a crap," Justin announced, getting up from his desk and striding toward the door.

"Justin, please sit down," Patricia said in that firm but calm tone that therapists were famous for.

Justin didn't break stride. "I'd rather sit through algebra than talk to you freaks. And that's saying a lot."

With that, he slammed the door, the sound reverberating in the room.

When neither Nash nor Patricia went after him, Sabrina said, "Wait, we can just leave?"

"I'd rather you didn't," Patricia said evenly. "But we are seeking *willing* participants. I can't hold you here and force you to talk to us."

Sabrina hopped up just as the others scrambled to stand as well. No one wanted to be the last one left.

Z slithered out first, with Gabby shortly behind her, painstakingly plotting each step to the door.

"I'm sorry," Andrew muttered, limping. "But I really don't have any psychological issues, anyway. If you were medical doctors, I might be interested."

Sabrina shot Nash one last look, hoping it came across as composed, though her hands were already shaking as she fumbled for the last Vicodin in her jacket pocket. It didn't surprise her that her mother hadn't replied to Patricia's letter. But she thought her dad would've cared enough to mention it, at least. She pressed her lips together, forcing herself not to think about it until after the fuzzy numbing agent could work its magic on her again.

* * *

Ten minutes later, Nash surveyed the circle of vacant desks, the empty glasses of water all that remained as proof they were ever there. "You think that worked?" he asked Patricia skeptically.

"It worked," she replied, collecting the name cards and handing them to Nash.

"Because we're losing time every day that we could be using more efficiently to —"

"Have faith," Patricia interrupted, before she walked out of the room as well.

Nash would rather have answers than faith, but he kept that thought to himself as he silently began shredding the name cards one by one.

CHAPTER THREE

Gabby Dahl had pushed the failed therapy meeting out of her head by the time she entered the locker room for last-period PE. When there were so many more pressing issues, it was easy to squeeze everything nonessential out of her brain.

As it was, she had just begun washing her hands when the sixth-period warning bell rang. She only had five minutes or she'd be marked late yet again. She was already in danger of receiving a failing grade, which boggled her parents' minds. "How do you fail a class like PE?" Gabby had overheard her father grumble to her mother with a resigned sigh. He couldn't conceal his disappointment anymore.

She let the water run for exactly fifteen more seconds before turning it off and grabbing three paper towels, wiping each finger with precision.

Satisfied, she began counting the twenty-seven steps to her locker, taking care to avoid the cracks in the aging cement floor, her eyes catching sight of her reflection in the full-length mirror that lined the wall. She was smaller than most girls her age, with so much blond hair that it was easy to hide behind it.

She reached her gym locker, tapped on it three times and twirled in the combination, opening the dilapidated metal door, then shutting it quickly. She'd have to do this five more times, assuming of course that nothing went wrong, before she could leave her locker open and begin to change.

A few feet away, a group of girls were clustered at the end of the wooden bench.

"My parents have been so freaked out. They didn't even want to let me go to the football game last weekend," Hannah Phelps said, pulling on her socks. As Gabby slammed her locker shut for the second time, she wondered if Hannah remembered that she'd ever been friends with Gabby. It all felt so long ago.

"I know," Emily Price agreed. "Mine want to drive me everywhere. I mean, I get it. I don't want to end up like poor Lily. I'm scared to go anywhere by myself right now. But I wish they'd catch this guy already so my curfew could go back to midnight."

Gabby shivered at the mention of Lily Carpenter's recent murder in her cabin on the edge of the Arapahoe Woods. Gabby had been stunned when she'd initially heard that the sweet woman known around town for her handmade cedar-scented candles had been shot point-blank. She'd visited Lily's stall at the farmers' market more than a few times and always noticed how calm and patient Lily was, even when Gabby had to count her dollar bills eight times before handing her the money. Who would murder someone like that, and for seemingly no reason?

Despite the admittedly loose connection Gabby had with Lily, she couldn't help feeling affected by her murder, hoping for justice for such a nice person. She read every article she could about the case, and by this point she'd heard every theory out there. Did Lily's murder have something to do with Steven Chapman, who wanted to buy her land to build a commercial development? Or was she the victim of a transient — some kind of serial killer popping in and out of towns targeting single women? Or was the murderer someone homegrown, a Cedar Springs resident, now eager for his next victim? It was the latter option that was freaking out most of the town, Gabby included. Everyone's parents had been vigilant lately, buying high-tech alarm systems, instituting neighborhood watches and new curfews. Not that Gabby needed to worry about that. It had been years since she had anywhere to be after school, returning straight home at exactly 3:47 each day. Her memories of long practices at the ice rink and slumber parties with friends had mostly faded away.

The final bell rang.

Gabby willed herself to stay calm. She couldn't let the stress of the bell get to her. If she could just make it to the hallway quickly, she might have a shot at getting to class on time. But the maze of complicated cracks near the entrance of the locker room formed a particularly challenging gauntlet for her.

Luckily, the outer corridor floor was covered with wide black-and-white linoleum squares that required fewer acrobatic feats than the locker room did.

As she leaped between the white squares, she could almost taste the relief in her mouth, the gym door just feet away. Then several members of the football team emerged from the boys' locker room in workout gear, including Justin, the brawny guy who had stormed out of that therapy group.

As they spilled into the hall, they jostled Gabby, knocking her firmly into a black square.

This couldn't be happening.

But if any of the guys realized the disaster they'd caused, they didn't let on. Not one of them looked back as Gabby began her retreat to the locker room.

* * *

Justin Diaz was having a crappy day.

First, some idiot took forever to load his bike on the bus, which made him get a tardy demerit first period. If that wasn't bad enough, while he was rushing to get to class, he bumped into Mr. Wincott, who spilled hot coffee all over Justin's shirt. If hitting a teacher wasn't an offense that would get him expelled, Justin would've punched that half-assed apology right off Wincott's face.

Then he'd had to deal with that dumb therapy meeting. In what world was it supposed to be surprising to Justin that his mother had given up on him? He'd known that since before kindergarten.

And now he was late for weight training, thanks to his half-deaf English teacher who kept droning on about *Tender Is the Night* because she didn't hear the bell ring.

But his irritation peaked when he entered the stale aired weight room and saw that tight end Adam Dodson had beaten him to the leg-curl machine. Everyone knew Justin liked to start on that machine.

With clenched fists, Justin maneuvered past his other teammates and approached the rack of dumbbells instead. He effortlessly picked up some heavy weights and began a series of bicep curls, his annoyance fueling every rep.

"Hey, man," his buddy Greg Hindenberg — Hindy — groaned as he struggled through a curl, his shaggy blond hair plastered to his face.

Hindy was a foot shorter than Justin, like most players on the team. Justin had always been the tallest and strongest in his grade, the kind of kid other parents thought was a sixth-grader when he was just in third grade. His size was intimidating as hell on the football field and one of the reasons he made such a kick-ass tackle.

Justin nodded at Hindy, then looked back at Adam, who was still hogging the leg-curl machine. Finally, after an agonizingly long ten minutes, Adam rose and Justin quickly turned to rerack his weights.

But he wasn't fast enough. Their quarterback, Mike Silvestri, slipped onto the machine and was already adjusting the settings. The heat rose in Justin's cheeks as he approached Silvestri and stood over him aggressively.

"I was getting ready to use that," Justin said.

Silvestri shrugged. "Too bad, man. You can go after me."

Silvestri might be quarterback, but everyone knew this team wouldn't be undefeated without Justin.

"I don't think so," Justin snapped. He didn't move.

Silvestri stood to look at him.

"What's your problem?" he asked. "Can't you just wait your turn?"

Fury funneled through Justin's body and he drew back his fist, connecting it with Silvestri's jaw. It was only one hit, but the release made his entire body feel lighter. For a brief moment, he was taken back to the meeting earlier that day. *Sociopathic proclivity to violence,* they'd said.

More like *constantly surrounded by idiots who need to be taught a lesson.*

He raised his fist again, to throw an extra punch for good measure, but he felt two bear-size hands on his shoulders, pulling him away.

"Justin! That's enough!" Coach Brandt, the team's defensive coordinator, ordered. With a muscular lumberjack build, Coach Brandt was probably the only guy in the room with the pure strength to take him on.

He dragged Justin toward the small office attached to the weight room and closed the door once they were both inside.

"Sit down," Coach Brandt said calmly. Unlike the other coaches, he never lost his temper. "What was that about?"

Justin shrugged noncommittally. "Silvestri's been drunk with power ever since he became starting QB."

"So you punched him in the face? Come on, you know you can't lose it like that," Coach Brandt responded evenly. "Even if it's true."

Justin allowed himself a hint of a smile.

Coach Brandt settled into the tattered black leather chair across from Justin, his forehead creased in concern. "Anything else on your mind? Everything okay at home?"

He asked it casually, but Justin knew what he was getting at. Coach Brandt had just come on staff over the summer, but the tale of Justin's crappy life had already made its way to him.

"Yeah," Justin mumbled quickly.

"You know, I didn't have a great relationship with my parents. My dad left, traded us in for a new family and never even bothered to —"

"Everything's fine," Justin interrupted. Though he was mildly intrigued by the revelation that Coach Brandt had grown up without his dad around either, Justin was aware that he'd be expected to reciprocate and share his own feelings. And that wasn't going to happen. "Can I go now?"

CHAPTER FOUR

On Monday morning Z awoke in the oversize four-poster canopy bed (chosen by her mother) with a shrill ringing in her ears.

Then, in an instant, it all went clear and silent.

I wonder if I could convince Mom and Dad to buy me a yacht.

Z shook her head forcefully and everything went back to normal. Her eyes darted around the room as she wondered what had just happened. Why had that question crossed her mind? She hadn't asked her parents to buy her anything since she was nine and they'd denied her request for a boa constrictor. And a yacht? It was a symbol of exactly the kind of bourgeois consumerist culture she detested.

It was still bothering her as she slipped into her usual all-black ensemble, her only jewelry an armful of wristbands from the music clubs she'd been to with Jared. She topped it off with a frayed black hoodie she'd had for years, so broken-in and comfortable that it was like wearing a favorite blanket. She still wasn't used to the chilly mornings in Colorado — their last house had been in southern Florida, where the temperature rarely dipped below seventy.

Once she'd laced up her black combat boots, she stepped into the long, arched hallway that ran across the second story of their massive, ornate French Baroque–inspired home, filled with antiques her mother had sourced from Europe. Every time Z's family moved, her mother decided on a new theme for the next house.

Z took a right at the fork in the hallway, toward the back staircase. Though this route was a longer path to the kitchen, it allowed her to avoid passing Scott's room. The fact that they shared a womb for nine months did not provide the sort of tight bond one might expect. Scott and Z were opposites on every level. For years, Z's father loved to tell the story about when he'd gotten her and Scott matching mini-BMW convertibles for their third birthday. Scott had jumped into the car right away, zooming around the manicured lawns of their historic home in Connecticut. Z had given the car a withering look and proceeded to play with the box it came in, pretending it was a house. "One of them already loves the finer things in life and the other wants to live like a hobo in a box on the freeway," her father would tell everyone who came over. Z often wondered if she and Scott really had been born polar opposites or if comments like those had set up their differences for life, each playing the expected part. Not that it mattered. The damage had been done and Z could barely stand to be in the same room with him.

When she stepped into the cafeteria-size stone-gray kitchen, though, she realized that Scott was already there. He was lounging on one of the kitchen stools, his feet propped up on the enormous granite center island as if house rules didn't apply to him.

Their father sat at the large round breakfast table, the *Wall Street Journal* in his hands, devouring a ham and cheese omelet that Louise, their housekeeper, had made for him.

"Good morning, Zelda," he said, his voice booming. Usually, by this point in the morning he was already at the construction site of whatever shopping mall complex he was currently developing. But the mess of red tape resulting from Lily Carpenter's murder was forcing him to be idle, something completely foreign to him. Z had heard him screaming on the phone at his lawyers just the night before, though you couldn't tell he had a care in the world this morning. That was the thing about her father. He could be affable, charismatic, even gregarious. But he could also change on a dime.

Z made her way over to the espresso machine (perhaps the one extravagance she appreciated) and began grinding beans, only half tuning in to the conversation her father and brother were having.

"It doesn't make sense this year, Scott," her dad said.

"But, Dad, you could probably use it as a write-off somehow. At least the fuel could be."

Something about what he said jolted Z's subconscious. "What are you talking about?" she asked.

"Scott's trying to talk me into buying a yacht," her father responded, opening up the business section.

The hairs on the back of Z's neck suddenly shot up. The thought she'd had earlier wasn't hers at all.

It was Scott's.

* * *

Andrew approached the door to math class later that day, almost overcome by nausea. He had a feeling it wasn't a flu bug or intestinal virus causing his queasiness, though. In fact, he'd been remarkably pain-free this morning. His leg had stopped throbbing in the middle of the night, and the chest palpitations that plagued him yesterday were gone. At least for now.

He was pretty sure the nausea was all due to his trepidation at entering Mr. Greenly's classroom. What barbs would Mr. Greenly publicly hurl his way today? Each day, Andrew told himself that it wasn't possible for Greenly to shame him any more than he already had. And every day, he was proven wrong. Because Mr. Greenly, like everyone else apparently, had already given up on Andrew.

Andrew could still remember the year, even the month, when everything fell apart. Fourth grade, April. Of course, he'd been sick before then. There had been the four-week itching spell in second grade that left his skin pink and raw. In third grade, he'd caught a record five cold viruses, each of them blending into the next, leaving him bedridden for most of the winter. But he'd always been able to catch up with the other kids in his class. Maybe it was because they weren't learning anything too challenging in second grade, or maybe his teachers just felt sorry for him, the kid whose father died of a heart attack when he was just three years old.

But in fourth grade, it all changed. Andrew had taken a fall off a playground swing, which developed into chronic lower back pain that made it impossible for him to sit or concentrate. During his hiatus from school, Ms. Strandquist, a sweet teacher who looked like Snow White come to life, had begun teaching fractions to the class. And when Andrew finally returned, no matter how hard he tried to make sense of the tricky numbers, he couldn't force his brain to understand them. Ms. Strandquist had tried to help him at first. She'd even taken him aside during recess, convinced he just needed a little extra attention. But eventually, as his absences piled up, she lost hope and stopped trying. Was that the first time he'd been deemed a lost cause? It certainly wasn't the last.

Every year from that point on, it was the same — from the first moment he walked into class at the start of September, he was already behind because he'd never really mastered what he was supposed to learn the year before. Certain teachers were crueler than others, calling his inadequacies to the attention of the entire class, and Mr. Greenly was clearly in that category, zeroing in on Andrew from the first day and never missing a chance to mock him. In Andrew's opinion, it seemed like a total waste of class time, but no one ever called Mr. Greenly on it.

Andrew slouched toward his desk, and Mr. Greenly gave him a squinty-eyed sneer from behind his glasses. "Mr. Foreman, thank you for gracing us with your presence. I hope you can manage to stay in class today." A few students snickered, and Mr. Greenly allowed himself a small smile. "I'd like to know how you think you're going to pass the test tomorrow, considering all the material you've missed?" He snaked through the desks toward Andrew. "Particularly since you've done nothing to try and make the work up."

Andrew was silent, wiping his now-clammy hands on his pants. The unfairness stung him — he knew he had it in him to perform better than he did. It wasn't his fault his body wouldn't cooperate.

"Are you hoping it just miraculously clicks into place?" Greenly asked.

Andrew didn't have an answer, so he kept his eyes planted on the desk, aware of the teacher hovering over him, when suddenly the bell rang.

"Very well," Mr. Greenly said, giving up on Andrew for the moment and returning to the front of the room. "Let's get on with our review. We'll start with solving systems of equations by substitution."

He dimmed the lights, and the first set of problems from his PowerPoint lit up the dry-erase board.

Andrew looked up, ready for the usual feeling of confusion to wash over him, but instead the equations practically sang to him.

If he solved for y in the second equation, then plugged that value into the first equation, he could find the values for both x and y. He didn't even need a piece of scratch paper. The logic was so clear that he could do the problem in his head. He felt his hand float into the air, like a balloon filling with helium.

Mr. Greenly looked up with an exaggerated sigh as everyone else in the room scribbled notes, attempting to solve for x or y. "No, Foreman. You cannot leave class to go to the nurse."

"I have the answer," Andrew blurted out. "X is seventeen and y is twenty-six." He wasn't even worried. He knew it was right. He knew it in his bones. The only confusing part was why he'd never seen it before.

"That is … correct," Mr. Greenly replied, flabbergasted. Andrew flushed with pride and Mr. Greenly narrowed his eyes. "What would you do if I added a third equation?"

He wrote out the three equations on the board as the class watched in silence.

Fern Gordon, the resident front-row Goody Two-shoes, shot her hand up. "I thought we weren't doing three equations until next week —"

"I'd just like to see how well versed Andrew is," Mr. Greenly interrupted. "Since this is suddenly so easy for him." He made air quotes as he said it, as if suggesting Andrew had cheated.

Andrew studied the board, again not writing anything, the variables easily moving around in his head.

"X is fourteen, y is twenty-three and z is four."

Mr. Greenly folded his arms. "Incorrect. Z is *negative* four."

Andrew scanned the equations on the board. "Check your math, Mr. Greenly. I think you forgot to apply the negative-one multiplication to both sides of the equation."

Mr. Greenly looked down at his notes, his face reddening as he realized his error. The class began to whisper, looking back at Andrew, who relaxed in his seat, extending his long legs into the aisle.

Mr. Greenly walked toward him now. "What's going on here?"

Andrew flashed him a quick, crooked grin. "I guess it just miraculously clicked into place."

* * *

Z walked through the hallways with Jared after school, unable to concentrate on a single thing he was saying, her mind attempting to make sense of what had happened so far that day.

Though the incident that morning with Scott and the yacht idea had been eerie, she'd been trying to write it off as twin telepathy, a concept she'd read about once. She and Scott had never had that kind of bond before, but what else could account for the coincidence?

Then at lunch, right when Z had expunged the incident from her brain, the ringing in her ears returned and nearly knocked her out of her chair.

If I don't throw up this pizza in the next five minutes, it'll digest right into my thighs and I'll never fit into my costume.

Z's head shot up from her veggie burger and her eyes darted around until they landed at the table across from her, filled with theater kids. It felt as if she was watching in slow motion as willowy Lindsey Singer put down the crust of her pizza and excused herself from the table.

What could this be? Why was it happening? Was she really hearing other people's thoughts? Was it all in her head somehow? An early sign of schizophrenia?

But the current of new energy surging through her felt positive, a stark contrast to the hopeless, dead-weight feeling she usually lugged around. She liked it. As much as Z liked anything.

"So do you want to right now?" Jared asked, pushing a piece of tangled hair behind his ear.

"Uh, no," Z replied. She had no idea what Jared was talking about, but whatever it was, she had no interest. She had to figure out what the hell was happening to her, and she definitely wasn't going to discuss it with Jared. He'd think she was insane. Which she very well might have been. But she wanted to decide that for herself.

A group of students pushed open the double doors at the end of the corridor, guffawing as they spilled into the hallway, mock tackling one another. Z rolled her eyes when she saw her brother was at the center of it all. As usual.

But then the ringing began. *Scott Chapman is sooo hot. I want him so bad.*

Z.'s stomach convulsed and she almost threw up on the scuffed white floors of Cedar Springs High. She obviously didn't think her own brother was hot, but that didn't make it any less repulsive to have the thought invade her mind.

Jared looked at her oddly. "Are you okay?"

"I've got to go," she stammered, turning abruptly and striding away from him. Luckily he didn't try to follow.

She rounded the corner, almost knocking over a short freshman boy, when she caught sight of Gabby Dahl standing in the sophomore hall in front of her locker, looking bewildered.

Z hadn't considered mentioning her mind reading, or whatever it was, to the other four students who had been summoned to that group-therapy session last week. The other losers. But as soon as she saw Gabby, Patricia's words echoed in her head. *I have a feeling that in the next few days you'll need one another.*

Could that pointless meeting have something to do with this? It was the only thing out of the ordinary that had happened in the past few days, the only deviation from Z's regular schedule of avoiding her family, listening to music with Jared and waiting for the high school years to pass.

Z changed course in the hallway and headed toward Gabby. Was there a chance she was experiencing the same thing Z was? It was a long shot, but Z was desperate.

"Gabby," Z said breathlessly. Gabby almost jumped, startled by the intrusion. The two had never spoken before, though of course Z had noticed her. Who hadn't? That was part of what made Gabby the perfect person for Z to talk to. It wasn't as excruciating for Z to expose her newfound condition to Gabby, when she herself had so many issues and was hardly in a position to judge.

"Hey," Gabby said softly. If she thought it was odd that Z was casually swinging by her locker, she didn't let on. It was almost as if she'd been expecting Z.

"Hey," Z began, unsure of where to begin. *Might as well jump in headfirst.* "Is anything … um, strange, happening to you?" Z's heart rate accelerated as she waited for the answer. If it was no, Z would be forced to acknowledge that she had some major problem that was probably going to get worse.

Gabby bit her lip, as if she was debating whether to be honest.

"You can tell me," Z prodded her.

Gabby nodded. "Yes."

Z took a deep breath. She wasn't going crazy. "We need to talk."

Gabby surveyed the crowded hallway. "Not here."

CHAPTER FIVE

Gabby followed Z into the wooded area behind the school. There was a makeshift trail often used by the Cedar Springs cross-country team, but Z quickly veered off that path, passing an empty creek bed where the school stoners congregated. Gabby had never ventured this deep into the trees before, part of her actually believing all the local ghost stories about these woods. Now, though, it wasn't ghosts that scared her. It was the murderer on the loose. As the foliage thickened around them, she couldn't help thinking of Lily Carpenter killed in her cabin deep in the woods without a soul nearby to help her. But as nervous as it made her, she really wanted to talk to Z — and they couldn't at school.

Z weaved left and right around massive trees, pine needles crunching under her feet. As Gabby scrambled to keep up, she realized she had stopped counting her steps. But instead of being seized with panic, she kept moving. She waited for the awful thoughts to surface, the ones that always arrived and told her *something bad would happen* if she didn't do things just so. But right now, nothing happened.

She'd have to add it to the ever-growing list of unexplainable strange things going on that day.

They reached a group of cedars nestled around a rock configuration, and Z stopped, perching her long body on top of a boulder. The leaves overhead blocked the day's sunlight, and Gabby shivered in the cool air.

"So it starts with the loud ringing in my ears," Z began, her eyes piercing Gabby's. "And then it's like I have a thought. But it's not *my* thought. Right? Is that how it happens for you, too?"

Gabby frowned, confused. "What do you mean? Whose thought is it?"

"Someone else's. Like this morning it was my brother's. Other times I'm not sure." Z frowned. "I thought you said this was happening to you, too."

Gabby shook her head. "Not like that. I'm not hearing things." She looked up at Z, afraid what it would sound like when she said it out loud. "I'm *seeing* things."

Z sat up straighter, her eyes widening. "Like what?"

Gabby paused, trying to find the right words to describe what had happened, but it was hard to explain fully when she didn't even understand it herself. "Let me see if I can do it again. I'm not sure it will work, but …"

Gabby walked to the boulder where Z sat and crouched down, pressing her hands firmly onto Z's black canvas messenger bag. She closed her eyes, waiting for the sensation from earlier to come over her, but nothing happened.

"What are you doing?" Z asked impatiently.

"Let me try with something else," Gabby murmured, growing frustrated. She wasn't sure exactly how to make it, whatever *it* was, happen again. "Can I open your bag for a second?"

Z nodded and Gabby began rifling through its contents. She took out Z's chemistry textbook and fanned through the pages. Nothing. "I *know* it happened before." Suddenly something occurred to her. "Maybe something you're wearing?"

Gabby tentatively reached out to touch the worn edge of Z's black hoodie. The second her fingers touched the soft fabric, her eyes fluttered shut.

The vision was hazy at first, but Gabby could hear the music. Pounding. Raging. As she closed her eyes tighter, the image became more vivid, almost cinematic. There was a thin teenage girl, maybe fourteen, sitting on a queen-size wrought-iron bed in the same black hoodie. A younger Z, before the buzz cut, holding a small bottle of pills in her hand. The room was like something out of a magazine, decorated in soft blues and grays, in direct contrast to the harsh music. In the corner of the room, there was a large glass-fronted cabinet full of eerie Victorian dolls staring out, their eyes wide. Z unscrewed the bottle, the tip of the Washington Monument peeking through the window behind her, and dumped twenty pills onto her nightstand. She paused for a moment, then scooped up a handful and downed them with a few sips of water. Then she scooped up another handful and downed them. And another. Finally, she lay back on the bed and closed her eyes. That's where the vision ended, fading to black like the end of a film.

Gabby opened her eyes, her heart racing.

Though she wanted to believe the vision was a product of her imagination, part of her already knew she'd just witnessed a private moment from Z's life.

"Did something happen?" Z looked at her. "What is it?"

"I saw something," Gabby told her. "It was just a blip. A vision of you."

"Of me?"

"Yes. You were younger — it must have been a few years ago. In Washington, D.C."

Z looked at her in surprise. "We used to live there."

Gabby nodded, less surprised. The vision had been too vivid not to be real. The question was why it had happened at all.

"You were sitting on a bed in a blue-and-gray room. And there were a bunch of old dolls ..."

"That's what my room looked like then," Z confirmed. "My mom's decorator convinced her those creepy dolls were perfect for a girl's room. I was always petrified they were going to come to life and chop me into a million pieces."

"That's exactly what they looked like," Gabby agreed.

"So ... you just *saw* that? Like a vision?" Z looked at her with new-found curiosity.

"Yeah. Kind of like I was watching a movie."

"What else did you see?"

"That was it," Gabby said quickly. She couldn't bring herself to say that she'd watched Z's suicide attempt.

"But this happened to you before, too? The same way?"

Gabby nodded, the words bubbling up quickly now after being locked inside her all day. "This morning. I was in the science hall, walking to class, and I almost tripped on a scarf on the floor. I picked it up and I had this ... vision, like I had with you. First it was kind of fuzzy, but then I could tell I was in the middle of Kohl's, the one near here, in the Brooks Center, holding the same scarf. But when I looked in the mirror, it wasn't me. It was Hannah Phelps."

"Who's Hannah Phelps?" Z asked, chewing her nails.

"A girl in my grade." Gabby left out the part about Hannah being one of her former best friends. Or the fact that she used to spend all her precious few free afternoons at that exact mall with Hannah. "Anyway, just now I was more of a distant observer. But earlier it was like I was watching from Hannah's point of view, like I was in her body. And then both times, after a few seconds, the scene just faded away."

"And you know for sure it was her scarf?"

"Yeah. I saw her in the cafeteria later and gave it back to her. I told her I'd seen her wearing it earlier that day." Hannah had easily bought the explanation and Gabby had almost believed it herself.

Almost.

"What do you think is happening to us?" Gabby asked. "Do you think we're both just ..."

"Going insane?" Z finished, and Gabby was relieved that she didn't have to say the words herself. "Coincidentally, at the same time? I don't know ..."

"This has never happened to you before?" Gabby asked.

"Never. I've had a lot of crazy thoughts, but they've always been my own."

Z and Gabby's eyes locked in the solidarity that comes from thinking the same thing at the same time.

"Do you think anyone else in that group-therapy meeting is having the same thing happen to them?" Gabby asked in a voice she barely recognized as her own.

Z looked at her seriously. "I don't know, but we need to find out."

* * *

That evening, Sabrina took her time washing the dishes in her family's small kitchen. The cream-colored tiles, dark wood cabinets and faded burgundy wallpaper were in desperate need of an update, but her mother was hardly in a position to tackle a redecorating project. The house used to be cozy and warm, the smell of her mother's Japanese *dashi* broth mingling with the intoxicating scent of her father's favorite tri-tip. However, in the past six years, no matter how many candles Sabrina lit or windows she opened to let in the air, it never seemed to blow away the scent of staleness. Of sadness. She eyed the cedar-and-cinnamon–scented candle that she'd bought last Christmas from Lily Carpenter, the woman who had been inexplicably murdered.

Ever since, Sabrina had been oddly wary about lighting it, as if it would somehow spread misfortune.

She turned her attention back to the dishes, rinsing another plate under the hot water. Though she'd given up on taking care of her parents, she still found washing the dishes cathartic. When her brother, Anthony, was still alive, cleaning up after dinner had been one of their joint chores. He would bring all the dishes to the sink, she would wipe down the table and then together they would rinse and dry. They used the time to really talk, the running water drowning out their conversation so their parents couldn't hear. Anthony told her about the leather jacket that Angie, the first girl he had ever *really* liked, gave him for Valentine's Day. She told him about her idiot fifth-grade teacher who made her stay in the classroom while they were dissecting a squid, even though it made Sabrina throw up and everyone teased her the rest of the day. They were five years apart, but Anthony had always treated Sabrina like an equal.

She and her parents hadn't sat down for a meal together since that drunk driver barreled into Anthony's car head-on six years ago. But Sabrina still did this chore every single day. It wasn't just because her parents seemed incapable of doing the simplest tasks. It was because the activity kept her close to her brother.

She scraped off a plate, setting aside the scraps for Rocket, their German shepherd, who was almost as ignored by her parents as Sabrina was. But she suddenly stopped when she realized something odd. Usually by this point in the night, the acute emptiness of her house would have sent her digging into her bag to take the Klonopin she'd tucked in there earlier. But for some reason, her desire to self-medicate had been dimmed. Actually, it was nonexistent.

She was so distracted by that realization that she didn't hear her father enter. Doug Ross had the same tall frame as Sabrina, and though he was handsome, the strain of the past few years had etched so many new lines on his ebony skin that he looked a decade older than he really was.

"I'm going back to the office for a bit," he told her as he passed by, not waiting for or expecting a response. For the past two years, the house had become more like a storage unit to him. He'd stop by briefly between work and meeting the women he used to distract him from his home life. Did he think she didn't know?

"Sure you are," Sabrina shot back sarcastically.

Sabrina's comment surprised her as much as it did her father, who looked at her as though she was speaking another language. Sabrina never questioned or commented on her father's erratic comings and goings, having long ago accepted her circumstances, the sharp detour their lives had all taken after the night of Anthony's accident. Her father hadn't wanted Anthony to go out to the party that night. Her mother, who used to be sweet and funny and vivacious, thought he should go. And from the moment the police officer showed up at their door at two in the morning, resentment and blame began tearing their marriage apart. It wasn't easy to have a father with one foot out the door and a mother who self-medicated until she was practically comatose. Sabrina thought she'd reached a place of detached observation with the whole situation, though. That therapy meeting must have unearthed a repressed wave of anger she didn't realize she was still carrying around.

Her father jostled his car keys. "Sabrina, why are you picking a fight with me?"

"I just don't know why you bother coming home at all," Sabrina replied. She'd wondered that for years, but it was something she'd pushed to the back of her mind and refused to think about.

"Do we have to discuss this now?" her father snapped.

"Forget it," she answered quietly.

"I'm late," her father said, and then he walked out.

As the door rattled behind him, Sabrina's phone vibrated with a text. She was surprised to see it was from Gabby, that girl with the unsettling OCD. And it wasn't just for her — it was for the entire group that had been summoned to the therapy session.

It's Gabby. Need 2 meet. Flagpole b4 school. Important.

What could Gabby possibly think was so urgent? Instead of replying, Sabrina picked up the last dirty plate. She was about to turn on the hot water when a cold blast of air hit her so hard that she shivered. She looked down at her arms and was hit with another cool wave, covering her in goose bumps that felt like scales on her arms. She glanced at the two windows above the sink. Closed and locked. The cold didn't feel like a gust of wind anyway. It felt as though someone was concentrating a massive blast of air conditioning directly on her body.

She moved toward the kitchen table to grab her sweatshirt, when the three lightbulbs over the table began to flicker, followed by three popping noises. The bulbs had all blown out, one right after the other.

Now shivering in the darkness, Sabrina felt something else.

She wasn't alone.

Her heart started beating so fast that it was painful.

She heard him before she saw him.

"Hey, Beanie."

There was only one person in the world who called her Beanie. Anthony. Her brother.

Her dead brother.

She fumbled for the flashlight on her phone. But before she could tap it on, she saw something that ripped the air out of her lungs.

Her brother was standing before her, his skin still flawless, almost glowing. His charcoal eyes bored into hers.

"You need to be careful, Beanie," he said.

She opened her mouth to try to respond, but the words were stuck in her throat.

And then, just as suddenly as he'd appeared, he was gone.

CHAPTER SIX

Justin walked briskly through the bustle of students the next morning, toward the flagpole in the center of campus. He scowled when he spotted the others assembled underneath its looming presence.

The five of them had never interacted at school before that worthless therapy meeting, which Justin had forgotten about until the text from Gabby last night jolted his memory. He was planning on strolling right by the flagpole and ignoring them, but the sight of Gabby made him slow his pace. There was something different about her today.

When he was a few feet away, she looked up and caught his eye. And then it hit him. When she wasn't doing any of her weird murmuring or tapping, she was really hot. Way hotter than any of the Cedar Springs High cheerleaders.

He might as well see why she wanted to meet.

"Hey," he said, giving her a grin and joining the group.

But instead of smiling back, she turned away. Instantly embarrassed, Justin wiped the smile off his face. That wasn't the type of reaction from girls he was used to. "So what's up, Gabby? Why did you text us?" he added. He made it clear they were wasting his time.

"Did it happen to you, too?" Z asked him, not bothering to wait for Gabby.

They were all staring at him. He glowered back. "What are you talking about?"

It was as if they had all hit the mute button until Sabrina spoke up. "Last night I saw my dead brother in my kitchen."

Justin scoffed. "Yeah, drugs make you hallucinate, Sabrina. You should be used to that feeling by now." From what he'd heard around school, her purse could give any pharmacy some major competition.

"I wasn't on anything," she snapped back. "And I'm still not."

"Something happened to me, too," Andrew piped up.

Justin rolled his eyes. "Big surprise. Isn't an ambulance here every week for you?"

"No," Andrew retorted. "Not an illness. It's like I have quantum perception all of a sudden. If I really focus on something, my brain reaches this level that's beyond genius."

Justin was about to remark on what he thought was *actually* wrong with Andrew's brain, but Z spoke up. "All of us have felt some of our other … problems lessening, too."

"Good for you. I didn't have any to start with." Justin's agitation was increasing by the second.

Z gave him a hard stare suggesting she didn't believe him. "You seriously haven't experienced anything weird in the past few days?"

Justin turned to Gabby, who was laser-focused on this conversation.

"You can tell us, Justin," she said softly.

"Tell you what? Did you see a dead guy, too?" Justin ignored the icy look from Sabrina.

"No," Gabby replied, reddening now that he was staring at her. "But I can … see things." She swallowed. "Things that happened to other people."

"Why the hell are you freaks telling me this?" Justin growled, shoving his hands in his pockets. Gabby flinched, which made him feel slightly guilty but not enough to apologize.

"Because it started happening after that therapy meeting," Sabrina answered impatiently. "But we barely spoke to those people ... I don't get it. How could they have done anything to us?"

Z scuffed the dirt with her boot. "Maybe it was hypnosis."

"And we don't remember any of it?" Sabrina questioned.

"That's the point of hypnosis," Z huffed.

Justin shook his head in disbelief. Did these psychos seriously believe they'd been hypnotized?

"What else could it be?" Z asked. "It wasn't like they gave us a pill or something."

Andrew's eyes bugged out of his head. "I bet they put something in that water they gave us! In those glasses on the desks. It's the only reasonable explanation. And that room was so hot I drank my entire glass. Did you guys?"

Sabrina nodded quickly. "I know I did."

"Me, too," Gabby added. "Just a few sips, but it was so hot I needed to."

Z's eyes were closed, as if she was trying to think back. "I'm almost positive I did."

They all turned to Justin. "Yeah, I did. So what?"

"Maybe they put some kind of experimental hallucinogen in the water," Sabrina said. Justin smirked. She'd be the one to know.

"We should talk to Dr. Pearl," Andrew said. "She's the one who left us those notes. She's the one who knows who Patricia and Nash are. We have to tell Dr. Pearl what they did."

Sabrina turned to Andrew. "Wait a second. If it was the water, why isn't anything happening to Justin?"

Their eyes shifted back to him and he threw his arms up, peeved. "Because nothing is happening to any of you guys! You think those two shrinks drugged us? If you really did have these special abilities, you'd be able to read my mind or listen to my thoughts and know I'm telling the truth!"

"Maybe I can." Z cocked her head, as if trying to hear some sound in the distance. After a beat, she frowned. "Well, it doesn't exactly work on command."

This had to be some kind of practical joke. He wondered if Hindy or the other guys on the team put them up to it. Just what he needed, to be lumped together with this collection of freaks.

He pivoted on his heel as he saw a group of cheerleaders approaching. That group was more his speed. "I'm out of here." He couldn't get away fast enough.

CHAPTER SEVEN

Five minutes later, Z was trekking up the staircase with Andrew, Sabrina and Gabby to the second floor, where Dr. Pearl's office was tucked away with the other administrative offices. Z had never been here before, thank God. It was one benefit of having your father donate a dump truck full of money to the school board. When they enrolled her, Z's parents told the principal that Z had a psychologist on call if she were to need one, so seeing Dr. Pearl wouldn't be necessary. She'd heard her mother refer to Dr. Pearl as a "low-budget shrink," and her mother despised anything on sale. Now it turned out her mom could be right for once. This low-budget shrink might have poisoned her daughter.

When they reached the office, the door was ajar and Dr. Pearl's voice drifted out to the hallway. "I think I can get away for a few hours next weekend —"

Suddenly, she paused and turned to the doorway, glancing through the slight gap to see the four of them congregated in the hall.

"I'll call you right back," she muttered into the phone before hanging up.

Z and the others crowded into her office, as small, dreary and windowless as Z had expected. If you weren't depressed before a visit to Dr. Pearl, you certainly would be afterward.

"Good morning, everybody," Dr. Pearl chirped. She raked her hand through her short hair as she took in the group before her, seemingly unfazed. "How can I help you?"

"What did you do to us?" Z snapped before anyone else had the chance to answer.

"Excuse me?" Dr. Pearl straightened up in her chair.

Sabrina shot Z an annoyed look. "We need to talk to you about that group-therapy session," she said, sounding less pissed off than Z, which in turn only annoyed Z more. When did Sabrina become the moral authority of the group?

"Group therapy? What are you talking about?" Dr. Pearl appeared genuinely confused.

"Last Thursday," Andrew told her. "We each got summoned by you to a group-therapy session. You left us all notes in our lockers. The four of us and Justin Diaz."

Z's instincts were already clocking something very wrong. "They said you had a student emergency and couldn't come —"

Dr. Pearl cut her off. "Who's 'they'?"

"The people running the therapy program," Sabrina replied. "A young guy named Nash. And an older woman … what was her name again?"

"Patricia," said Andrew. "Dr. Patricia Nichols."

Dr. Pearl stared at the ceiling for a moment.

"Let me be clear," Dr. Pearl said. "I did not give anyone notes last Thursday. I wasn't here that day. I had a countywide conference scheduled off campus. I wasn't even in Cedar Springs."

Z looked at the others. If Dr. Pearl hadn't authorized Patricia and Nash to begin the program, then who had?

"We need to find out who those people were," Z said, hating that a hint of desperation had entered her voice. "They sent us all notes from you.

And really weird things have been happening since we met with them."

Dr. Pearl crossed her arms. "Okay, this alleged note you all received —"

"It wasn't 'alleged.' It was real," Andrew insisted.

"Wait — I think I still have it." Sabrina fished through her bag until she produced the note, creased and slightly torn from sitting under a pile of textbooks.

Dr. Pearl read it dubiously.

"Someone must have stolen some of my stationery ..." Dr. Pearl said, raising an accusatory eyebrow at them all, her eyes settling on Z. Z bit her tongue. Convincing the school shrink that she wasn't a klepto wasn't the point right now.

"You think *we* did this?" Andrew asked incredulously. "Someone put these in our lockers. Why would we make this up?"

Dr. Pearl swiveled back toward her computer. "I think I have an idea."

She clicked on the keyboard for a few seconds, then scanned the screen.

"Uh-huh ..." She clicked her mouse again. "Uh-huh ... uh-huh ... and yes." Finally, she looked at them again. "That's what I thought."

"What?" Z asked, her heart already sinking.

"I just checked the attendance record. All four of you have an unexcused absence last Thursday. I'll give you points for creativity. But if you're looking for a way out of detention, I'm sorry, it's not happening. Z, this is your fourth unexcused absence this month, which means you'll be suspended for at least a day."

Z ignored the irony that the punishment for skipping class was to be granted an entire day off school. "Think about it, Dr. Pearl. The reason we *were* all absent at the exact same period is because we all went to this therapy session."

"We really did get these notes," Gabby finally said.

Dr. Pearl gave a half sigh as she looked at Gabby, a bit of sympathy filling her dark brown eyes. "Well, then, someone may have been playing a joke on you, Gabby. And if that was the case, I'm sorry. If you get a note like this again, come directly to me."

As she turned back to her computer, signaling that the meeting was officially over, the ringing in Z's ears began.

These kids have really gone off the deep end this time.

"Dr. Pearl —" Andrew began, but Z cut him off.

"Let's go. This is pointless." She looked contemptuously at Dr. Pearl. "Some therapist. She's given up on us, too."

CHAPTER EIGHT

Justin knew he was procrastinating as he stood at the door of the refrigerator and studied its meager contents. He opened the cracked plastic fruit drawer, which had been out of alignment ever since they'd gotten the fridge at a garage sale a few years ago. There was one apple left, so he grabbed it, ignoring the fact that his mother would give him a hard time about finishing the last piece of fruit. He bit into it and immediately recoiled at the mealy taste of a rotten apple. He wouldn't be having a snack after all.

He plopped down at the kitchen table and glared at the copy of *Tender Is the Night* that he was supposed to be reading. It was almost midnight and he still had six chapters to go if he wanted to pull at least a C on his English test tomorrow — which he needed to do if he had any hope for a football scholarship. Florida State, his top choice, was sending scouts in the next few weeks, but he needed at least a 2.0 to qualify. It was impossible to focus, though. Every time he picked the book up, his brain rewound to that stupid prank at the flagpole with those weirdos trying to convince him they were psychic.

Gabby's involvement in the prank, or whatever it was, kept tripping him up. It didn't seem as if practical jokes were really her thing. What explanation was left, though?

His head shot up when he heard keys rattling in the door. Even though the apartment felt like a cubbyhole, he wouldn't be able to make it to his closet-size room fast enough to escape his mother coming home. Two nights ago, after clubbing with her girlfriends, she'd drunkenly told Justin she'd wanted to have an abortion when she found out she was pregnant with him, but she didn't have the money.

"You forget how to use a key, baby?" Justin heard a muffled male voice say just as the door opened. His mother burst out laughing, as if that was the funniest joke she'd heard in her entire life.

Great. Not only was his mother tipsy, but she'd also brought a random guy home. They entered the apartment like a tornado, bumping into the couch by the door and carelessly casting off jackets and shoes in every direction. Carla looked tired. She always looked tired, even when she'd gotten a full night's sleep. Her long, dark wavy hair was stuck with sweat to the sides of her face, and her eye makeup was smudged. She must have gone out dancing again.

Then Carla caught sight of Justin. "What are you still doing up?"

"Homework," Justin grumbled.

"You want a beer, Travis?" Carla asked her new friend.

Travis was pushing forty, but he looked like a high schooler in ripped jeans and Converse.

"Sure thing," he answered with a slight Southern twang.

Justin grabbed his book off the table so he wouldn't have to be part of this awkward scene. Unfortunately, Travis's skinny frame was blocking the door to Justin's bedroom.

"Aren't you gonna say what's up, *ese*?" Travis asked him with a lopsided grin. This guy was whiter than snow, yet somehow found it perfectly acceptable to use Spanish slang. It made Justin want to punch that grin off his face.

Travis tried to make his scrawny presence larger in the doorway so Justin couldn't get by.

"I said, aren't you going to say —"

"I heard you," Justin said. They were the same height and only inches from each other. Justin could smell the beer on Travis's breath. Why hadn't he punched this guy yet? He waited for the attack reflex to move his arms for him, but his clenched fists stayed right by his side.

"You ain't got no love for me, *papi*?" Travis asked, feigning offense.

"Travis is trying to be nice, Justin," Carla called from the fridge, where she pulled out two beers. Not that either of them needed more alcohol.

"Yeah," Travis said in a low voice only Justin could hear. "I bet your mama gets real *caliente* in the sack when I'm nice."

Justin blinked as the anger flared from his eyeballs to his fingertips. The next thing he knew, Travis was flying through the open doorway, where he slammed into Justin's bedroom wall and crumpled to the floor like a rag doll.

"What the hell, Justin!" Carla screamed, dropping the beers and running over to Travis.

Travis glared at Justin as he got to his feet unsteadily. "I don't need this crap from a little punk."

He slammed the door on his way out. Carla threw Justin a look of fury and ran after him. Justin stared after them, too shocked to move.

He was absolutely positive that he hadn't laid a hand on Travis.

Once Justin was alone in his room, he sent out a text to Gabby, Sabrina, Andrew and Z. It was only three words.

You were right.

CHAPTER NINE

The storefront of Cytology, Inc., was located in a nondescript building on the main highway, formerly home to an insurance office. Though Sabrina had driven by it many times since it appeared several weeks ago, the name was just vague enough that she had never questioned what it was.

Until now.

Sabrina, Gabby, Justin, Z and Andrew walked from the small four-spot parking lot to the front door and tried to peek through the closed blinds. "Are you sure this is it?" Sabrina asked.

"This is the address she sent," Andrew confirmed, looking down at his phone. Patricia had sent the group a cryptic email early that morning saying she had a feeling they were looking for answers and to meet at this exact time after school.

Sabrina had been bombarded by a series of emotions ever since. It had been a long time since she'd experienced true feelings without an anesthetizing filter.

Shock was the first, gut-level emotion that had coursed through her. Patricia and Nash *did* have something to do with what had been happening to them all. As inevitable as it had seemed that they were involved, it was still surprising to have it confirmed, however veiled and cryptic.

The shock had quickly given way to anger by mid-morning. What gave Patricia and Nash the right to just *experiment* on them ... or whatever this was? How many breaches of therapeutic etiquette had they committed? No way this was allowed.

She had a special supply of anger reserved for Nash, whose deceit she felt even more acutely. How could she have thought she had a connection with him?

But the strongest emotion running through her when they reached the doors of Cytology was her hunger for answers. An intense desire to understand what was happening. What exactly had Patricia and Nash done to them? The hallucinogen in the water theory was the only one Sabrina could come up with. But why? And how did it allow her to go cold turkey off all drugs and feel fine? Better than fine. Exactly as she'd wished to feel for years.

Justin jammed the red button beside the door several times. A second later, Patricia's voice crackled over the intercom. "Come in."

The door buzzed open.

"Let's go," Justin said, jostling Sabrina as he pushed past her.

Sabrina followed him into a darkened, empty room containing a dismal setup seemingly left behind by the insurance company.

But in the back, behind the last cubicle, was a single locked door with a complex alarm keypad system next to it that looked completely out of place. Was that an alarm to keep other people out ... or to keep the five of them in?

Before she could hesitate, the door swung open as they reached it, revealing a large room with a gleaming maple table at its center. A dozen plush executive chairs surrounded it, facing a large drop-down optical-projection screen.

What was this place? It didn't look like any therapist's office she'd ever seen.

Two enclosed offices with automated glass doors stood on opposite sides of the room, each furnished with the most sophisticated computer equipment on the market. Nash sat in one office and didn't look up from his computer when they entered, while Patricia emerged from the other, smoothing down her wrinkled gray suit.

"Hello, again," she greeted them, her eyes shining brightly. "I'm sure you all have a lot of questions —"

"What did you guys do to us?" Sabrina asked, unable to contain herself.

"And who the hell *are* you?" Justin jumped in. "Dr. Pearl's never even heard of you."

Patricia put her hands up disarmingly. "I understand the confusion. That's why we called you here. There is an explanation for this. For all of this. Everything will become clear."

She motioned for the group to sit down around the table as Nash stepped out and joined them. He sat next to Patricia at the head of the table, and Sabrina ignored the nervous flip-flop her stomach performed as she looked at him.

"Let's cut to the chase," Patricia said, setting her forearms on the table once the five were all seated. "At this point, you're all experiencing what could be classified as psychic phenomena, correct?"

Sabrina nodded tentatively, still unsure how much they should reveal to Patricia and Nash just yet.

"Psychic? Like fortune-teller crap? That's not what I'm having," Justin scoffed.

"It's a scientific label," Patricia said. "We'll see if it's accurate. Why don't we discuss what you've each been experiencing and then we'll explain further?" She took the brief second of silence as acquiescence. "Gabby?"

Gabby blushed, but Patricia gave her an encouraging nod.

"Uh, well … I can see certain things that happened in the past."

"Retrocognition," Patricia replied, as if what Gabby said was totally normal.

"But I think it only happens if I touch an object," Gabby added. "I touch the object, and then I have a vision about it and whatever's happening around it."

"With retrocognition, it's like you're tapping into the energy of the object," Patricia explained, scribbling furiously in the Moleskine journal laid in front of her. "How about you, Andrew?"

"It's like my brain has been liberated," Andrew told them, at the edge of his seat. "Anything with logic, numbers, sequences. It's all very clear to me now."

"Interesting …" Patricia said, smiling as she jotted something down. She eagerly turned to Z. "Zelda? Oh, sorry, Z?"

"I've been hearing people's thoughts," Z volunteered. "I don't always know whose they are, though."

"Clairaudience," Patricia confirmed, putting a name to it. "Justin? How about you?"

He tipped back in his chair so far that Sabrina thought he was going to tip over. "I was staring at some d-bag my mom brought home and then he flew across the room." He cracked a small smile. "Unfortunately he was fine."

"How were you feeling right before it happened?" Patricia asked.

"Pissed. Like I wanted to throw him across the room."

"Psychokinesis," Patricia replied, studying Justin as if he was under a microscope.

"Psycho-what?" Justin asked, defensiveness already creeping into his voice. His jaw set, and Sabrina wondered if objects were going to start flying around the conference room.

"Psychokinesis. The ability to manipulate matter through your mind. Has it happened again since?"

Justin shook his head. "I actually tried a couple of times this morning with a book. Just to see if I could move it across a desk. Nada."

"Psychokinesis requires more mental strength than almost any other clairvoyant ability, so it can be more difficult to summon," Patricia explained without looking up, scribbling even more notes.

It was Sabrina's turn. Nash arched an eyebrow at her. "How about you, Sabrina?"

"I saw my brother," she replied, looking him straight in the eye. "My dead brother." She deliberately kept her eyes on him, challenging him for an explanation. Because it hadn't escaped her notice that so far they hadn't gotten one.

"Have you seen any others yet?" he asked.

"Others? Like other … ghosts?" Would other ghosts besides her brother now be appearing to her out of the blue? The thought hadn't occurred to her before. "I mean, are ghosts even a real thing?"

"You already saw one, did you not?" Nash answered unhelpfully.

"Yeah," she replied, irritated. "But is this real? How is any of this happening? Why is it happening? I thought we were here to get answers."

Nash looked at Patricia and she cleared her throat.

"You're right. As you can obviously tell, this program is different than we initially let on," Patricia said. Justin snorted at the understatement. "For one thing, Nash and I are not psychologists."

While the others gaped, Sabrina wasn't that surprised. They'd lied about so much, so why not that? *Maybe Nash isn't off-limits, after all.* She pushed the embarrassing thought below the surface, reminding herself that he was a liar — and that Z might be able to hear what she was thinking.

"If you're not shrinks, then what is this?" Z asked. Sabrina leaned forward. It was a good question. Who were they? Doctors? Researchers?

Nash's eyes swept across the group. "We work for the FBI."

It was the last thing Sabrina had expected to hear, and this time she joined the group in speechless shock.

"What do you mean?" Z finally sputtered.

"We work within a covert section of the FBI's national security branch," Nash clarified. "We're based out of the bureau's Albuquerque field office, but we moved up to Cedar Springs several weeks ago for this assignment." Sabrina was reminded again of that afternoon in Sonic. He must have just arrived in town. Nash was an FBI agent. *Completely off-limits.*

"While you were in the classroom with us that day, you each ingested a chemical compound that caused these changes within you. In the water," Patricia explained.

"I knew that's how you did it," Andrew said.

"You really *did* drug us …" Sabrina smarted at the violation. It didn't matter that she'd spent years ingesting drugs of her own accord. This one had been given without her consent. "How is that legal?"

"If we're talking about the FBI, they don't care about legality," Z said authoritatively. "They have a whole department devoted to shutting people who've seen UFOs up."

"Let's back up before anyone gets panicked, please," Patricia continued. "Part of our division at the FBI deals with developing new drugs. But not just any drugs. My department's mission is to develop drugs for a purpose. Drugs that assist the bureau in solving crimes or that further aid our quest for justice here and abroad. My own background is in neuroscience and biochemistry. The compound you ingested was a special project of mine. A serum that unlocks the brain. That gives you access to psychic abilities you might not naturally be able to access. It took my previous partner and me many years to create it and synthesize it to perfection."

"Then why are you using it like some kind of superpower Zoloft on us?" Z asked.

Patricia looked slightly ruffled, even with the smile on her face. "That's not exactly what we're doing, though the side benefit of this compound is that it neutralizes emotional responses in the temporal lobe. That's why all of you should've noticed some of the issues you'd previously been dealing with have lessened to an extent, correct?"

Sabrina looked around the table as the others nodded. Was that the trade-off? Patricia and Nash drugged them against their will but for good reason? Part of her could admit that the consequences hadn't been all bad. She'd forgotten how exhilarating it felt to be clearheaded, to have the full working capacity of her brain. And as weird and eerie as it was to see Anthony, the idea of seeing him again — maybe even getting to speak to him — was compelling.

That didn't take away the fact that this had been done to them against their will, though. And without their full understanding of the consequences. Nash had already hinted at seeing other ghosts. Sabrina had a suspicion those spirits might not be quite as friendly as Anthony.

She spoke up, trying to put it all together. "I don't understand. The cost of fixing our old issues is to replace them with new, weird issues?"

"I don't think this is an issue," Andrew chirped from his spot beside her. "Not for me. I don't feel sick all the time and I'm a genius. It's way better."

Patricia's eyes twinkled as she looked across the table at him. "I was hoping some of you would see it that way. We don't view what's happening to you as a set of problems, either. We see them as a set of assets. This is not a punishment. Some people would give everything for these kinds of skills."

Sabrina doubted there were long lines of people willing to trade in their own free will for the chance to see ghosts. Though Andrew was nodding in enthusiastic agreement with Patricia, the others seemed to share Sabrina's doubts.

"Maybe other people would want these skills," Gabby said diplomatically. "But how do you know we did?"

Justin nodded swiftly. "Right. You drafted us against our will."

"And you still haven't told us why," Sabrina pointed out. "If it's not about fixing our problems, why did you do this to us?"

"Fair enough," Patricia conceded. "We didn't give you the serum just to alleviate some of your issues. There's something we're asking for in return. You all were chosen for a reason. This town was selected for a reason, too."

Justin scoffed in surprise. "Why would anyone choose this town for anything?"

"As you are all aware, there was a murder in this area a few weeks ago on the edge of the Arapahoe Woods. A woman named Lily Carpenter. And the killer is still at large."

"Probably long gone," Justin responded. "I heard it was some out-of-town bum who needed cash and whacked her for it."

"That's just what the cops want you to think because they can't admit there might be a serial killer on the loose," Z said.

"I heard it was something to do with that guy who wanted to turn her house into a mall," Andrew said, reddening when he realized a second too late that the guy was Z's father.

"All theories with no evidence to back them up," Patricia said. "Most people do not have all the facts. Lily Carpenter was actually a former FBI agent."

Sabrina looked up in surprise. The quiet woman who sold homemade candles was an FBI agent? Sabrina had assumed she was a nature-loving hippie type. Never in a million years would she have guessed she was in the FBI. Then again, how much could you ever tell about someone from the outside?

"But why aren't they saying that she was an FBI —" Andrew began and Nash cut him off.

"Not everything has been made public."

"Lily wasn't just any FBI agent," Patricia added. "Before she left the bureau years ago, she was my original partner. She created the serum with me."

"The serum you just gave us?" Sabrina asked. She was totally confused.

"Yes," Patricia replied. "The night she was killed, a cache of serum was stolen from her safe."

Andrew was suddenly suspicious. "How did you manage to give us this serum if it was already stolen?"

Sabrina flashed him an impressed look, grateful to have his new-found powers of deduction on her side.

"We had the serum stored in multiple places. Being one of the chemists involved originally, Lily had a sizable cache in her own locked safe. I kept the rest. The night she was killed, Lily's serum was stolen from her safe."

"And *that's* why she was killed?" Andrew asked. "So someone could steal the serum?" Patricia nodded gravely and Sabrina finally understood what Patricia had meant earlier. When she said some people would give anything for these skills. To someone out there, this serum Sabrina had just ingested was so valuable that it was worth killing for. Not that she had any idea why.

"The perpetrator used Lily's code to open the safe in her home. Though a gunshot wound killed her, her body was also covered in fresh third-degree burns." Another detail that had been left out of the papers. "We believe those burns were a torture tactic. So the perpetrator could find out where she was hiding the serum and get the code to her safe."

"Whoever killed Lily Carpenter has that serum," Nash interjected. "They must be found. Immediately. Because having this compound in the wrong person's hands would be catastrophic."

Sabrina's stomach tightened. "I thought you said there was nothing wrong with this drug. 'Synthesized to perfection.' Now it's a catastrophe?"

"This was a drug created for good, if used correctly," Patricia replied. "But a person who has no clue how to administer the serum ... that's a different story."

"Or a person who intends to use the serum for the wrong reasons," Nash added. "A person who wants to exploit it to do harm. To commit crimes. To claim power. Not to mention, this serum is classified. If we don't find out who has it, they could expose it. Or worse, clone it and distribute it at large."

Andrew's eyes widened. "Or they could sell it to our enemies. Create an army with heightened abilities, always one step ahead of us."

"Exactly. You can't imagine how much people would pay for a weapon like this," Nash continued. "Imagine our enemies with Z's ability. They could be listening to our thoughts right now."

It was a terrifying prospect, and Sabrina realized there were probably many more.

"That's why it's extremely important that we find out who did this to Lily so we can get the serum back in FBI hands," Patricia said. "As of now, we've only reached dead ends. We have no leads to speak of." She leaned forward in anticipation, her gaze intent on the five of them. "That's why we decided to turn to something less traditional."

Sabrina saw something click in Andrew's eyes.

"You want us to help you solve this case," Andrew concluded. "Armed with our new abilities. Use the serum to find the serum."

Sabrina thought he was nuts until she saw Patricia and Nash both nodding.

"He's right?" Z asked, as stunned as Sabrina.

"Yes," Patricia said. She was silent for a moment, letting the concept sink in. When she spoke again, her voice was lower, more solemn. "We recognize this is unorthodox. The FBI does employ psychics on cases from time to time, but we've never attempted this before. It may not work and we'll have to accept that. But the FBI decided the stakes of this case are high enough. That's how important it is. We need to find out who killed Lily Carpenter and get the serum back."

Questions erupted in Sabrina's brain like fireworks. "Why didn't you all just take the serum yourselves? Wouldn't it make more sense to use it on trained FBI agents and not a bunch of teenagers?"

"Believe me, we tried," Patricia responded. "On adults, the drug causes no pronounced results. But there's something to the fact that a younger brain is still developing, the synapse growth accelerating at a higher rate than a mature adult's, that allows the drug to take hold. This seems to be the 'magic window' when the drug operates most effectively."

Gabby nervously twisted her hair to the side of her neck. "You said this was classified. So our parents don't know anything about this?"

"They can't," Patricia said. "Those letters we told you we sent out about the group-therapy program — the ones they didn't respond to — that was the extent of our communication with them."

"And they can't even be traced back to you anyway, I'm sure," Z noted.

"Correct. Because they cannot know," Nash replied. "The five of you cannot tell them about this. In fact, you can't tell anybody. Not your friends, not your siblings, not a teacher, nobody. Everything we've explained today is classified information and it must stay that way."

Sabrina couldn't remember the last time someone had trusted her with anything.

"What if we do tell?" Justin asked defiantly.

Z sighed. "Like anyone would believe you. If you tell someone you're moving people across rooms with your mind, they'll just think you started taking steroids."

Justin glared at Z. "Like anyone would believe you either. They'd probably just think you became a schizo."

"Like anyone would believe any of us," Gabby said, her hushed tone instantly commanding the group's attention. "That's why they picked us. That letter they sent out — that's how they vetted us. Who had parents, a family, that would care the least? Who were the biggest lost causes? Even if we told our parents, it's not like they'd care. They already think we're crazy. We went to Dr. Pearl to ask her about the meeting and she thought we were making the whole thing up."

"She's right," Sabrina concluded, thinking of her own parents. The five of them were trapped any way they looked at the situation. But for some reason, that thought didn't anger her as much as it had earlier.

Patricia surveyed the group slowly before she began to speak. "What we said to you in that classroom was true. Others might have given up on you, but we do believe in you. We wouldn't have done this otherwise. We wouldn't have taken such a big risk. You guys are tired of people underestimating you. Of disregarding you. We want to take you seriously. Here's your opportunity on a silver platter."

Sabrina wavered. There was no doubt they'd been used. But they weren't being recklessly experimented on. They were being used for something important.

"No offense, but why should we help you guys?" Justin interjected. "You drugged us. We didn't sign up for this."

"Who cares?" Andrew said. "Seriously, what was so great about our lives before this? What are we all honestly giving up?"

Nothing. There was nothing great in Sabrina's life to give up. The few interactions the five of them had had in the last few days were the most engaging ones she'd had with anyone in years.

"There's no way what we're giving up is better than what we're getting in return. I'm only seeing an upside," Andrew said.

Justin sucked in his breath sharply. "Speak for yourself, loser. My life was fine before this." He turned his dark eyes to Patricia and Nash. "I might not get anyone to believe me, but that doesn't mean I have to help you."

"If you don't want to help, there is a simple solution," Patricia offered mildly. "There is an antidote to this compound. An antibody I can inject that neutralizes it. We wanted to let you experience the effects of the compound firsthand so you could make an informed decision, but if you don't want to help with the case, we can reverse what's happened to you at any moment."

"And the antidote makes everything go back to normal?" Justin asked, though the edge in his voice had softened, as if now that he knew this newfound ability could disappear, he was rethinking whether he was angry.

"Yes. You will all go back to exactly how you were before," Patricia replied. She added with emphasis, "Exactly."

"Issues and all," Sabrina said, and Patricia nodded.

There it was. The choice Sabrina hadn't been given before was now hers. The options were stark opposites. She could go back to being the addict dismissed by everyone. To being the girl people didn't trust to string together a coherent sentence. Or she could stay this new version of herself, a girl trusted with a secret. Sure, they only picked her because she was considered a lost cause by everyone around her. But she could still use this as a chance to prove everyone else wrong. To do something of actual value. To make up for all the years she'd wasted.

"What happens with the antidote if this actually works and we find the serum?" Z asked. "Are you going to force us to take it?"

"No," Patricia answered. Sabrina felt a burst of relief that confirmed everything she'd already been feeling about the antidote. "It will always be your choice whether you want to take it or not."

Sabrina leaned forward tentatively. "So can you tell us how any of this would work? Us helping you to solve the case and find the rest of the serum?" Sabrina asked. Quickly, she added, "I'm not saying yes for sure. I'm just curious."

Patricia raised an eyebrow at the group. "It might be easier for us to *show* you how it would work."

* * *

Patricia didn't specify where they were ultimately headed, but Z was still putting one combat boot in front of the other, walking toward Nash's van in the parking lot with the others. Maybe it was morbid curiosity pushing her forward. Or maybe it was the idea of being on the inside of the biggest story in Cedar Springs. Half the town was convinced that a serial killer was camping out in the woods, waiting for his next victim. If they only knew it was so much bigger than that.

And so much worse.

How do you beat a foreign army who can move bodies with their minds? Or who can figure out the other side's strategy through just one vision?

"Are you sure about this?" Gabby whispered as she sidled up to Z. "Don't you think it's dangerous to get involved in a murder case?"

The danger factor hadn't crossed Z's mind. At least not in that way. "Probably. But if some psycho has the serum, we're still in danger even if we don't go along with this."

"I don't know ..." Gabby said, her forehead creasing with worry. "Maybe I should ask for the antidote."

"Why don't you come with us and then decide afterward if you want it?" Z suggested. "That's what I'm going to do."

Gabby exhaled, relieved not to have to make the decision. "Okay. That's a good idea."

Z followed her into the van and Nash pulled out of the parking lot. Z rubbed a hand over the soft fuzz of her hair, contemplating the antidote herself. Did she want to go back to feeling … empty? It wasn't as though she'd spent the last two days thinking about rainbows and unicorns, but her new world did feel a little like someone had turned up the brightness on a computer screen. Would it be so bad to hear people's thoughts occasionally? It was kind of like heightened eavesdropping. Now that she understood why it was happening, it didn't seem such a bad exchange. Provided that Patricia and Nash were telling the truth, which, of course, she could never know. Government agencies were famous for their secrecy.

Even now, she had no clue where they were headed. Patricia just said that once they got there, they'd all have a chance to test out their new abilities and see how using them could lead to finding the serum.

Andrew's voice broke through her thoughts. He leaned forward toward Patricia. "How is the serum able to do this to us? Scientifically speaking."

"Great question." Patricia twisted her body around to face them. "We all possess a range of mental powers we're usually not aware of. The primary compound in this serum, like that in many drugs, opens the channels within your brain that you're not typically able to use. LSD, for example, activates the serotonin receptors to allow for heightened perception."

Z's ears perked up. Every antidepressant she'd ever been prescribed claimed to increase her serotonin levels, but none of them worked. Until now.

Patricia continued, her eyes sparkling as if she could talk about this subject for hours. "Our compound operates on the so-called 'psychic neurons' of the prefrontal cortex of your brain. When this area is stimulated, abilities are elevated, which allows for clairaudience, clairvoyance, psychometry, precognition, telepathy … all versions of what some would call a sixth sense. Individuals with natural talent in this arena — I'm not talking palm readers, but people with true, inherent telepathic gifts — are able to stimulate this neuron naturally. This compound mimics that ability, though it works differently on different people."

"That's why we're not experiencing the same things," Andrew noted.

"Why don't you recruit real psychics to help you instead — people who naturally have the gift?" Sabrina asked.

"The FBI does employ psychics now and again to help with a case that's gone cold," Patricia answered. "But they're not always reliable. This serum should be a much more effective way to derive those skills. It's almost like creating an infallible psychic."

"Are you a chemist, too, Nash?" Andrew asked.

"No," Nash answered.

Justin eyed Nash curiously. "So are you, like, the muscle?"

"No."

When he didn't elaborate, Patricia added, "Nash is a special agent in the counterterrorism unit." *And not much of a talker,* Z thought. "Like I said before, the missing serum is a national security threat."

The pavement ended and Nash turned off the wooded rural road onto a dirt path.

"Are you going to tell us where we're going right now or are we supposed to use our superpowers to guess?" Justin grumbled.

When the van finally stopped, Nash looked at their faces in the rearview mirror. "We're here."

Z recognized the place from the photographs in the newspaper.

It was Lily Carpenter's cabin.

Patricia and Nash had brought them to the crime scene.

CHAPTER TEN

Sabrina climbed out of the van with the others and looked up at the dark clouds hanging above Lily Carpenter's small cabin. They were making it no secret that they'd be releasing their fury in the form of a thunderstorm within the next few hours.

"Detectives have been through the house several times, but the cabin is basically as it was when Lily was found," Nash told them as he and Patricia led them up the wooden steps to the front door.

Patricia turned to face them. "As I've told you, we've reached a dead end. That's why you're here. I'm hoping your arsenal of skills will expose a lead the rest of us can't see. Because if we don't find the serum soon, Lily's murder will be just the beginning of the damage. We don't have any more time to waste."

Sabrina was the first one to duck under the crime-scene tape and enter the cabin. Excitement was the wrong word to describe how she was feeling, but it wasn't too far off. She'd forgotten how much she loved that burst of energy right before she was about to tackle a challenge. She used to be the girl who would never pick "truth" over "dare" because she couldn't imagine any scenario she would back away from.

Patricia and Nash had given her this feeling back, and all they were asking in return was to help them solve a murder that could affect the security of the country, of the world, even. It suddenly didn't seem like too much to ask as she entered the cabin fully alert with anticipation. Was it possible she would see something — or somebody — that blew the case wide open today?

She gazed around the cozy living room, which was devoid of any sign of a crime except for the faded chalk outline of Lily's body in the center. Several black-and-white landscape prints of what appeared to be the early American West hung on the walls, and a mammoth gray stone fireplace took up a large portion of the room. A worn-in small sofa was positioned in front of it with a basket full of books, newspapers and magazines nearby. Lily probably spent many winter evenings holed up in this exact spot, reading while the fire roared before her.

It was odd, though. The sofa was the only piece of furniture in the room. Yes, it was a small space, but another chair could've easily fit. Nash had said everything had been left untouched, so they wouldn't have removed anything. Did Lily never have visitors? Or did she not want them?

The back of the room opened up to the kitchen, where Lily had set up her candle-making operation. Boxes of wax chips sat on the floor, double-boiler pots filled the stovetop and bags of handpicked cedar, lavender and honeysuckle were arranged neatly on the table. A crate of completed candles was set next to the back door. Any signs that Lily had been in the FBI, or was even a chemist, were absent, except for the meticulous way she had alphabetically categorized her herbs and essential oils.

Nash crossed the room until he was standing next to the chalk outline. "The positioning of Lily's body indicates the murder occurred here in the living room. There were no fingerprints and no blood in the house except hers. Fibers throughout the house indicated DNA of four different people, but none of them were in our system. We don't yet know who the DNA belongs to."

"And there's no telling when those four people were here or if any of them were involved with her murder," Patricia explained. "For all we know, one of the hairs we found was left by a repairman months ago."

"One of the only things the investigators were able to confirm is that she was shot at close range right here," Nash said.

"Execution-style. That's what it said online," Justin added.

A shiver went up Sabrina's spine as she looked back to the chalk outline. Lily had been killed just inches from where she now stood. When Sabrina looked closer, she saw the spots on the wood floor still faintly stained with blood.

"I also mentioned the burn marks earlier," Patricia said. "They were found all over Lily's arms, legs and abdomen. Third- and fourth-degree burns that penetrated every layer of the skin. Some areas on her arms were black and charred." Her voice quavered slightly as if she was reliving her friend's pain.

Sabrina looked back up from the floor. Poor Lily's final moments had been full of excruciating pain and terror.

"Do you think they used one of her candles to burn her?" Andrew asked. "Or heated wax?"

"It's possible, though there's no evidence to suggest that," Nash replied. "It also could've been from some kind of blowtorch, given the intensity of the burns, but we haven't been able to conclude exactly what the perp used."

"Or perps," Patricia added. "We can't rule out the possibility that there was more than one person involved."

Patricia hadn't been exaggerating about having no leads, Sabrina thought. Whoever killed Lily knew how to cover his tracks.

"How many people even knew this serum existed?" Andrew asked, his eyes darting around the room. It was like you could see his brain moving in hyper-drive. "Doesn't that narrow down the suspect list?"

"By our count, less than ten," Patricia answered. "With most of them currently working at the FBI, already interrogated and completely cleared of suspicion. The few who have retired or quit the FBI were also questioned."

"What if they told other people? Did you track them, too?" Andrew asked.

"All of the agents who knew about the scrum said they did not disclose their classified knowledge to anyone outside the case," Nash replied.

"But you didn't interview Lily," Sabrina said. "She could've told someone."

"I don't think so," Patricia replied. "She knew what we were dealing with. She didn't want this in the wrong hands any more than I did." Nash looked a little less sure.

Sabrina walked over to a framed picture on the mantel. It was of Lily on the beach with her arms wrapped around a man, both of them beaming at the camera. It grabbed Sabrina's attention because it was the only personal photo in the entire room. "What about this guy?"

Gabby plucked the frame off the mantel, then inhaled sharply, and her eyes rolled back in her head.

"Gabby! Are you okay?" Sabrina reached out to her grab her in case she fainted.

Patricia stuck her hand out to block Sabrina. "She's fine."

"Really? How is *that* fine?"

Z gave Sabrina a knowing look. "Relax. I've seen her do it before. She's having a vision."

Sabrina couldn't take her eyes off Gabby, who stood rigidly still, her face expressionless except for her fluttering eyelids. After less than a minute, Gabby's eyes popped open and her body relaxed, like a statue coming to life. "That man in the photo is Lily's husband. I just saw them on the beach on their honeymoon."

Patricia frowned. "Actually, Robert is her ex-husband now."

"An ex-husband whose picture she keeps on her mantel?" Z smirked. "Kind of a bizarre decorating choice, right?"

Andrew agreed with a nod. "Has he been ruled out as a suspect?"

"Yes," Patricia said, with a hint of disappointment. "He was on a plane from Denver to New York that day." She pursed her lips as if she wished she could eliminate this little fact.

"Did they have kids?" Gabby asked.

Patricia hesitated. "No." Out of the corner of Sabrina's eye, she saw a questioning look cross Z's face. Had she heard Patricia's thought? Or someone else's?

"But he knew about the serum?" Andrew asked.

Nash nodded. "He was adamant he never told anyone about it." Now it was Patricia who didn't look as sure.

"This is a good time to discuss what we *do* know about Lily Carpenter," Nash continued. "She moved into this cabin three years ago, after her father died and left it to her. Before that she lived in several locations throughout the Southwest. This was the most settled she'd been in the ten years since she resigned from the FBI."

"Why did she move around so much?" Sabrina asked. "Did it have anything to do with why she left the FBI?"

Patricia shook her head. "No, she'd just had enough. The pressure was getting to her. She'd never had much leisure time. She enjoyed having the ability to travel freely."

Sabrina was formulating another question, when a foul odor entered her nostrils so powerfully that she lost her train of thought. "What is that smell?"

"What smell?" Justin asked. The rest of them were staring at her blankly.

How could they not smell that? It was as if she'd just put her nose directly into a dumpster. But it wasn't only the smell. There was a sudden chill in the air, too.

Out of nowhere, she started to hear a faint knocking sound like shoes tapping across the wooden floorboards. But when she looked around, no one was moving.

Sabrina suddenly felt the presence of another body.

A split second later, Lily Carpenter wrapped her long fingers tightly around Sabrina's wrist.

CHAPTER ELEVEN

If Anthony had looked as if he was being lit from within when Sabrina saw him, Lily appeared to be standing in the shadows, in stark contrast to the beaming woman in the photo. Everything about her, from the color of her cheeks to the color of her dress, was faded and dull. The only vibrant part of Lily was her fierce gaze, which had the same intensity as her grip on Sabrina's wrist.

She couldn't tear her eyes from Lily's.

"I know ..." Lily's breath was choppy and labored as she whispered to Sabrina. She blinked rapidly, as though saying the words was agonizing. "I know why they want it."

Before Sabrina could ask her whom and what she was talking about, Lily was gone. When Sabrina looked down at her wrist, there were red marks from where Lily's fingers had dug into her skin. She stared at them in disbelief as they slowly faded, her body pumping more adrenaline than she'd ever felt with any drug.

Everyone was watching her. Especially Nash.

"What just happened?" Patricia asked, practically jumping out of her skin.

"I saw Lily," Sabrina told them. She felt nervous, out of breath. "Lily was right in front of me. Actually *touching* me. I could feel it."

Gabby wrapped her arms around herself, her eyes darting around the room as though a spirit was about to reach out and grab her, too. "That sounds terrifying."

"It happened too fast to be terrifying," Sabrina replied honestly, though her heart rate still hadn't returned to normal.

"Did she say anything?" Patricia asked, glancing at the spot as if Lily was still right there, perhaps wishing she was the one with the ability to see her.

"Yes. She said, 'I know why they want it.'"

"Want what? The serum?" Andrew asked her.

"I don't know," Sabrina replied, suddenly a bit disappointed that she hadn't been able to glean more information.

"It's definitely possible she was talking about the serum," Patricia responded.

"She said, 'I know why *they* want it.' Maybe she's trying to tell us that more than one person did this to her," Andrew suggested. "You did say that the DNA of multiple people was found here. Maybe that's what she wanted us to know."

Sabrina brightened. Maybe she'd gotten more information than she realized. "That's true."

"Or maybe she was referring to whoever was buying the serum from the murderer. She knows why they would want it," Patricia added.

"Wouldn't it have been easier if she just told you who whacked her?" Justin asked. "Then we could solve this thing and be out of here. Case closed."

"Yeah, obviously, but … maybe she couldn't say much more," Sabrina said, remembering how Lily had fought to get the words out. "It was like talking was a huge struggle." Thinking about it suddenly made her feel dizzy. Or maybe there wasn't enough air in this cabin.

"That makes sense," Patricia agreed. "According to the mediums I've worked with through the FBI, it takes an abundant amount of energy for a spirit to bridge both sides. That one statement probably was all she could get out."

"If that was the only thing she could say, it must be important," Andrew pointed out.

"My thought exactly," Patricia responded. Her eyes were glowing. "I think you all should take a look around the rest of the cabin. You don't necessarily have full control of your abilities yet, which means that something could hit you at any time."

Was Patricia insinuating there might be a point where they could control their abilities? When Sabrina could seek out a ghost?

"The safe where Lily kept the serum is in the closet in her bedroom," Patricia continued. "That might be a good place to start."

While the others made a beeline back there, Sabrina slipped out the back door. The cool air instantly made her feel less dizzy, though her heart was still pounding erratically.

She settled herself on the steps, experiencing the same feeling she used to have after riding a rollercoaster — nervous and scared while she was on it, but back in line to do it again the second the ride was over. Was she ready for this to be her reality? Rollercoasters were fun every once in a while. You wouldn't want to ride one forever. Was seeing ghosts something she wanted to deal with all the time?

And yet ... the serum had given her a second chance. If she decided to take the antidote, would she be digging into her personal drug stash the second she got home?

The door creaked open behind her. She knew it was Nash before she saw him.

Get a hold of yourself, Sabrina.

"Patricia wanted to make sure you hadn't taken off," he said shortly. "Nothing new to report, I assume?"

"I just needed a minute."

Nash observed her clinically as he leaned against the stair railing. "Are you having second thoughts about this?"

She looked up. "Not exactly ... It's more complicated than that."

"Situations only get complicated if you let them."

"You didn't know me before."

"I don't know you now."

She flinched at his blatant dismissal of her. She thought she saw a glimmer of regret behind his eyes, but when she searched for it again, his expression was back to inscrutable.

Nash sat down next to her, and she could feel the heat radiating from his body. They stared silently at the empty space in front of them. There were no other cabins in sight. Z's father had already demolished them to prepare for his luxury lakefront condominiums. All that was left standing now were the large clusters of fir trees.

Nash finally spoke. "I imagine seeing these ghosts must be difficult for you."

Sabrina raised an eyebrow. "Are we pretending you're a shrink again?"

It seemed like that he wanted to hide it, but a small smile momentarily escaped his lips.

"I didn't even play with Ouija boards when I was younger," Sabrina said.

"Because they scared you?"

"No, because I thought they were dumb." If only Sabrina could tell her younger self she should practice with them. "And the truth is, people are a lot scarier than ghosts."

An undecipherable expression crossed his face, though he remained staring out to the woods in front of them.

"I just wish Lily had said something a little less cryptic," Sabrina added quietly, more to herself than to Nash.

"Did your brother say anything to you?"

"He told me to be careful."

He finally looked at her, his eyes on hers, and the intensity took her breath away, just like that first time she'd seen him at Sonic. She felt completely exposed, but the last thing she wanted was for him to look away.

Nash said, "Your brother's right. You should be careful."

Then the door opened and the rest of the group began to pile outside. Nash cleared his throat and abruptly stood, the moment between them dissolving.

* * *

Justin walked purposefully to the shed outside of Lily's cabin. He, Z, Gabby and Andrew had already poked around Lily's small bedroom to see if anything jumped out at them, the pressure rising as Patricia watched from the doorway. Gabby had touched a few small items — a bedside candle, a few shirts hanging in the closet — but nothing had given her a vision.

When Patricia suggested they might have more luck outside, Justin welcomed the change of scenery. It was better than poking around some dead lady's bedroom like a perv. He'd immediately zeroed in on the small shed twenty yards away from the house. Maybe he'd be able to find something in there that no one else had seen yet. Even though Justin hadn't decided about taking the antidote, seeing the others in action definitely tapped into his competitive streak. He didn't want to be the only one without some sort of discovery today.

As he opened the door to the shed, though, he saw that the only thing there was fishing equipment. Tons of it. He'd never seen a chick who was so into fishing before. Could it be a clue of some sort?

"Look at all this stuff," he said. "Maybe Lily told her fishing buddies about the serum and one of them took it."

"That was her father's equipment," Nash countered. "From what we've learned, Lily had never been fishing around here."

Yeah, most of the fishing equipment was dirty and rusted. Justin's big clue was a bust. Gabby glided up next to him and peeked inside the shed, picking up one of the fishing rods. She must not have been able to get a vision from it, though, because she quickly put it back.

Her hair was down today, not in the ponytail she usually wore. It made her look even hotter.

Then Z snorted.

"Did you hear something, Z?" Patricia asked eagerly.

"Yeah. Someone here thinks Gabby looks even hotter when she wears her hair like that."

Justin flushed. He'd completely forgotten about Z's ability. Not cool. He wanted to shoot her a back-off look, but he didn't want to give himself away.

"Anything of relevance, Z?" Nash asked.

"Nope."

"This thing looks like it could be a weapon," Justin said, holding up a strange contraption resembling a large measuring tape with four chains attached to the bottom. He didn't really think it was relevant — he just wanted to distract everyone from Z's announcement.

"That's a lure catcher," Andrew said. "You slip it on to your fishing line and the chains snag the ends of the fishing lure."

"Of course you're a fishing geek," Justin said and tossed the contraption back in the shed.

"I'm not," Andrew said. "But my uncle loves it. He talks about it all the time and I always tune it out … But I guess I can access things in my brain now that never registered before. How awesome is that?"

"That is pretty awesome, Andrew," Gabby said, smiling up at him.

Justin could no longer hold back a massive eye roll. Was Andrew actually impressing Gabby with his fishing Wikipedia crap?

"You picked a pretty good lab partner, huh, Gabby?" Andrew said, cocky as hell.

Was Andrew going to spend the whole time in science class hitting on Gabby? Justin wondered. He probably had a bunch of dumb pickup lines about the periodic table or whatever. Would Gabby ever be into Andrew? No way.

"And now someone thinks Andrew is annoying," Z reported.

"I'll take credit for that one," Justin said. He was going to have to watch his thoughts around this girl.

Andrew was standing at the top of the steps, probably so he could be above everyone else who wasn't as smart as he was, Justin thought. If he didn't shut up, Justin was going to shove that antidote down his throat to make him stop.

"I'm not scared of you anymore, Justin," Andrew replied, puffing his chest out. "Everybody knows brain beats brawn every time."

Justin thought he heard a few chuckles, but he couldn't tell who was responsible. His annoyance at Andrew quickly bubbled into rage as he stared him down.

Then Andrew yelped.

The top step had suddenly collapsed under his feet. He clawed at the banister, managing to jump down the four remaining steps and hit the ground just in time. The entire set of steps were completely obliterated, as if a cyclone had ripped them apart, leaving pieces of broken wood lying in piles where they had stood.

"Holy crap, I just did that," Justin whispered.

CHAPTER TWELVE

Gabby looked back and forth between Justin and what used to be the porch steps until about ten seconds earlier. How had he done that much damage without touching anything?

Justin unclenched his fists, looking surprised himself. Gabby knew he was famous for his temper. He was going to have to get it under control because sending people flying across rooms and demolishing porches was going to look awfully conspicuous after a while.

A glint of light near Andrew caught Gabby's eye. Something in the dirt where the steps once stood. "What is that?" she asked, walking toward it.

Andrew looked down at his feet and picked up a delicate rose-gold bracelet. As he handed it to Gabby, she felt a flutter of nerves in her stomach. The same ones she used to feel right before she skated onto the ice for a competition. It was that panicky anticipation that comes with wondering whether, with everyone watching, you're going to be able to deliver something you *know* you can do when you're alone.

She fingered the thin links, her anxiety growing, until her eyelids suddenly began to shut as if two magnets were between them …

A blond woman in her early twenties tapped her bright red nails on the check-in counter of a motel, the rose-gold bracelet on her wrist. Her skin had an orange hue, like someone who had spent too much time on a tanning bed.

"Welcome to the Belvedere Inn. Do you have a room preference?" the front desk clerk asked, not bothering to hide her boredom. The name tag drooping off her shirt read, LORRAINE.

"Whatever you got that's nice. And clean," the woman answered as she shook out her hair from a tight ponytail. She leaned forward, her ample cleavage exposed. "I'm meeting this guy. Not really my type, but he seems different from the other guys who come in and hit on me while they order. Usually they're all sleazeballs, you know?"

"I hear ya," Lorraine said, perking up. "I got two kids by one of those sleazeballs. Room 304 is open. I just need a credit card to hold."

The woman smoothed down her polyester black miniskirt. "Yeah, sure." She smiled, though her eyes remained cold, her sharp nose casting a harshness over her entire face. "But don't charge it. This guy is definitely going to pay. You should've seen the tip he gave me tonight."

She grabbed her phone off the counter and clicked on it before dropping it into a large black leather purse. As she fished around for her wallet, a silver glint caught Gabby's eye. It took her a second to realize it was a gun.

Gabby's eyes snapped open as the vision ended.

Feeling a little woozy, she tripped over the rubble from the stairs. She was surprised to find Justin by her side, catching her right before she face-planted into the dirt.

"Are you okay?" His arm remained around her waist as she caught her balance.

"Yeah," she answered, still shaken from her vision. "Thank you."

"What did you see, Gabby?" Patricia asked.

"Almost as soon as I touched the bracelet, I went into this vision where I could see a woman wearing it." The words tumbled out quickly. She was nervous that her memory would evaporate if she didn't get it all out, the way a dream did soon after you first woke up.

"Lily?" Patricia asked expectantly.

"No, definitely not. She was much younger. She was checking in to a motel. The Belvedere Inn. And she was getting a room so she could, um …" Gabby fidgeted. "So she could … meet someone. A man. To … you know …"

"Bone?" Z asked, saving Gabby the embarrassment of having to spell it out.

"I think so." Gabby paused. "But she had a gun in her purse."

The whole group went silent. Even Nash seemed electrified by this new development.

"What else can you tell us?" Patricia asked.

"I think she worked at a restaurant. Maybe as a waitress or a bartender or something. She said most guys who come in are sleazeballs, but this guy she was meeting was different. She didn't say the name of the restaurant, though."

"It's most likely close to the motel," Nash suggested.

Another thing struck Gabby. "I saw the date on her phone when she clicked it. September 8."

Patricia and Nash exchanged a look.

"September 8 was just two days before Lily was killed and the serum was taken," Nash said. "That means the bracelet got here within a day or two of the murder, if not that day."

Gabby looked up at him in surprise. "Do you think the woman that I saw is the person who took the serum?"

"What if she stole it and was racing out of here so fast that the bracelet slipped off her wrist on the way out?" Andrew speculated. "Fell between the steps before she even noticed it was gone. And even if she did realize she'd lost it under there, she couldn't get to it easily. She probably figured no one would ever see it."

"Those are all possibilities," Nash said. "But even if this woman has nothing to do with the serum or the murder, this bracelet still places her here at Lily's cabin within the time frame of the murder, and that's important. She's the only person we've found who had any kind of contact with Lily in the days before she died."

"This is exactly why I brought you here," Patricia said excitedly. "I knew you would find something in one hour that no one else could find in a month."

Gabby was still afraid, but something else was making her heart thump. Excitement. And it wasn't just her own. She could see it on the others' faces, too.

"This is probably a good time to discuss one last matter," Patricia continued. "Is there anyone who would like to bow out now and take that antidote? Because this is your chance."

Gabby had forgotten all about the antidote. When Patricia had first mentioned it at Cytology, Gabby was positive she wanted it. How could she not? She'd just learned that two FBI agents had drugged her without her knowledge and left her with an ability that she still didn't understand. But now her feelings had shifted. She was exhilarated by the vision she'd just had and the possibility that she had changed the entire course of the investigation. And if she was injected with the antidote, wouldn't it mean her OCD would come back?

She looked around the circle at the others. Maybe they were thinking the same thing, because not a single one of them raised a hand.

CHAPTER THIRTEEN

The rain beat on the windshield as Z turned in to the subdivision where Gabby lived, trying to avoid skidding. Since they'd left the cabin, it had begun to storm and now it was pouring so hard that Gabby could barely see a few feet ahead.

"It's the one at the end of the block," Gabby said, pointing to a split-level house almost identical to all the others on the street.

Z pulled her Range Rover into the driveway.

"I guess I'll … see you soon?" Gabby said tentatively. After what they had all just gone through together, Gabby couldn't help feeling a connection to Z, but it had been a long time since she'd really had a friend.

"Yup," Z answered, then gave Gabby a serious look. "And you're right. You definitely got us the biggest lead of the day."

"I didn't say —"

"I eavesdropped on your brain." She gave Gabby an expectant look.

Gabby *had* had that thought in the car, but it didn't sound nearly as conceited in her head as it sounded coming out of Z's mouth. Gabby had just been proud of herself that she found something useful for the case.

"It wasn't on purpose," Z backtracked, seeing the look on Gabby's face. "I just can't really control this thing yet. But seriously, it was a great lead. Whatever you like to do to celebrate, you should go do it tonight."

"Homework?" Gabby said, half smiling.

Z groaned. "Me, too. The FBI should give us a 'get out of school free' pass for this. How are we supposed to concentrate on homework when we're doing something a million times more important?"

Gabby was thinking the same thing. Patricia said they needed to sit tight for at least the next twenty-four hours while the FBI lab tested the bracelet to see if there was any physical evidence on it. But Gabby couldn't turn off her thoughts for the next twenty-four hours about what had happened at the Cytology office and the cabin.

"Maybe you can get a vision of all the homework answers," Z quipped.

Gabby laughed and got out of the car. She zipped up her jacket, the image of the bracelet so etched in her mind that she barely felt the torrent of rain pouring down on her.

She slipped her key into the lock and immediately heard her father call out. "Who's there?" There was a surprising edge to his voice.

"Just me," Gabby said.

Her parents looked up at her in shock. They were at the dining room table with her younger sister, Nadia, surrounded by flyers, markers and poster board.

"You're just getting home now?" Her dad glanced at her mother for an explanation.

"I didn't realize she wasn't here," her mom said. "When I got back from gymnastics with Nadia, I just assumed she was in her room."

Not that Gabby could blame them. Usually she did come home at precisely 3:47 each day, retreating to the sanctuary of her bedroom where she could perform her rituals without Nadia's prying eyes or the disheartened stares of her parents. After more than a year of attempting to "cure" her with possible solutions from fruitless drug regimens to hypnotherapists, they'd ultimately given up.

Now, they were expecting an explanation.

"I ... uh," Gabby faltered. Thankfully, her eight-year-old sister piped up.

"We're making posters for Twinkie," Nadia announced, dressed in her leotard and track pants. She pulled out a red permanent marker and meticulously outlined the photo of a cat in the middle of the poster.

Nadia's beloved mackerel tabby had gone missing two days earlier, sending her parents into a level of stress they normally reserved for Nadia's gymnastics meets. The same kind of stress they used to have over Gabby's ice-skating competitions.

"So where were you?" her mother prodded.

"Just ... doing homework at the library." Gabby was surprised at how easily the lie rolled off her tongue.

Both her parents were stunned into silence. She braced herself for the additional questions and wished she had planned some kind of explanation for her sudden change in behavior.

"I think we're going to find Twinkie tomorrow," her little sister said, immediately drawing her parents' attention back.

"Sweetie, even if we don't find Twinkie right away, it's important you don't let it ruin your mental preparation for the meet on Friday," her mother said.

Gabby's father nodded seriously. "We need those scores to be in the top fifteen percent."

"Do you think it's worth it to do a session with Frank?" her mother wondered. Because every fourth-grader needed a sports psychologist.

It was the first time in almost two years that she'd come home at a time *other* than exactly 3:47, and her parents had already moved on. The lack of interest was a new low, even for them.

Gabby walked to the staircase. She'd always thought if she could just get better, if she could shake off the tentacles of her OCD, her parents would begin to care about her again. That things would go back to the way they used to be. But now she was realizing that they didn't forgive weakness. She should have remembered that from her figure-skating days. The competitions where Gabby did well, placing somewhere in the top three, meant she could look out at the crowds and see her mom beaming proudly. When she'd emerge after the medals were handed out, her parents would wrap her into tight hugs, and her father would always suggest stopping for ice cream on the way home.

All the fawning made it that much worse when she didn't place.

Her mom and dad weren't monsters. They didn't yell at her from the stands or scream on the way to the car like some of the other ice-skating parents. But the gaping absence of affection was almost worse. As if she had ceased to be their daughter. In fact, once her mother had even said as much. After a meet where Gabby had fallen right in the middle of her first combination, a rookie mistake to say the least, her mother had looked at her through the rearview mirror in the car and insisted, "That wasn't my daughter out there today. Gabby Dahl has known how to stick a single axel since she was six."

Gabby knew her mother was trying to make her feel better. Acting as though some alien had momentarily inhabited Gabby's body was supposed to give her confidence for the next time. *She* wasn't the one who had fallen. It was an impostor's fault. Instead, all Gabby had heard was that she wasn't their daughter. She hadn't performed well enough to earn that connection. A few weeks later, the OCD had started, with small compulsions at first, building slowly and steadily, until it had finally overtaken her life.

And now, even though she'd made such an obvious stride by deviating from her routine, her parents still wanted nothing to do with her. Now that her veneer of perfection had been shattered by years of odd behavior, her parents would always see Gabby as damaged goods, irredeemable, not worth the number of gym meets and billable hours it would take away from them to try again. The realization stung more than she thought it would. She imagined telling her parents that she was working with the FBI. They wouldn't believe her — that much was for sure. But would they even care?

Gabby shut the door to her small pink-and-white room filled with old skating trophies and the novels she ingested like candy. For the last few years, reading had been her only escape, the only time she felt free from OCD.

A Tree Grows in Brooklyn, which she was rereading for the third time, beckoned from her nightstand, but after the long afternoon at Cytology and the cabin, Gabby still had hours of homework to do. She flipped open her chemistry textbook to the page on acid-based reactions. Now that she didn't have to focus on highlighting sentences in multiples of three, studying was going to take half the time. She tried to focus on her chemistry book. Acid-based reactions. Acid-based reactions. She read the three words over and over until she came to a definitive conclusion.

Who cared about acid-based reactions?

An unfamiliar sound jolted Gabby away from chemistry: her cell phone. She'd barely used it before the past few days. She pulled it from the side pocket of her backpack to find the caller ID read JUSTIN.

"Hello," she answered, hoping her voice didn't sound as nervous as she felt. Back in junior high, she'd spent hours on the phone with her friends, giggling about boys they liked and whatever happened at school that day. But now the only person she could really count as a "friend" at school was Ali Hanuman, whose parents didn't allow her to socialize after school hours lest she stray from her path to becoming valedictorian.

"Uh, Gabby … hey …" Justin said.

"Hey."

Justin cleared his throat. "I think I might have dialed you by accident."

Gabby was surprised to feel a burst of disappointment. "Oh, okay, then."

"But, uh ... since I have you on the phone, how are you? With everything that happened this afternoon. Are you okay?"

"Oh yeah, I'm fine." The vision she'd had was haunting her, but otherwise ... yeah. "I'm still kind of in shock with everything else, though. It's hard for me to believe this is really happening."

"Me, too," Justin admitted. "It's kind of cool, but kind of ..."

"Crazy," Gabby supplied.

"Gotta go, bye," Justin abruptly announced. As the phone beeped in Gabby's ear, indicating the call had ended, she wondered if she'd somehow said the wrong thing.

She was starting to think she would never finish her chemistry when her phone beeped.

Sorry. My mom just got home. Had to deal.

Was she supposed to text something back? She didn't want him to think she was ignoring him.

After a few false starts, Gabby settled on *OK*.

It was probably the lamest text message in the history of texts, but at least it was a reply.

Her phone beeped almost instantaneously. *I'll see you tomorrow.*

A full smile spread across her face. *Sounds good.*

CHAPTER FOURTEEN

Patricia wasn't usually an early riser, but this morning she found herself pacing around the tiny living room of her rented apartment well before five o'clock, willing the phone to ring with an update from the Albuquerque field office. Though she'd sent the bracelet they found at Lily's cabin to the techs just the day before, she was anxious to hear back about the forensic results.

Lily had come to her in a dream again last night. Luckily, it was one of the better ones. She and Lily were laughing together in their old lab, Lily's blond hair glistening under the fluorescent lights. They'd spent hundreds of late evenings there together, breaking only when Robert would stop by to drop off a takeout dinner for them. It didn't feel like work when they were feeding off each other's energy, one of them always saying exactly what the other one was just thinking. That was the friend Patricia preferred to remember. Lily before her life turned upside down. Before the mess with Sam. Before she'd left the FBI, abandoning Patricia. Before she'd taken up residence in Cedar Springs, letting her scientific brilliance languish while she pursued a life of simple crafts. Patricia knew her candles had been a local favorite, but Lily was a genius. She was wasting her talent.

A dream analyst would probably say Patricia kept having these dreams because she had unresolved feelings about Lily's death. That she was feeling guilty. Well, of course she was. She and Lily had once been inseparable. As the only two female chemists in their entire division, they were initially drawn together by their gender, sharing the frustrating stories of professors who had underestimated their abilities. But they also shared a drive to innovate. Lily was the only person at the FBI who didn't think Patricia was too intense in the lab because Lily was the same way. How could you be too intense when you were responsible for creating chemical compounds that could be tools for justice and change the world? The serum certainly hadn't happened overnight, of course. In fact, it was a byproduct of something else she and Lily had been developing — a drug for the FBI that would allow people to access repressed memories after witnessing a crime. After several dozen trials, Patricia and Lily found there was one consistent side effect: extrasensory clairvoyant bursts. That's what gave them the idea to construct a new drug with those side effects as the primary goal. It could help with missing persons cases, cold cases, anything that had reached a dead end. They isolated the compound causing the clairvoyant side effects, and after months in the lab, barely sleeping, barely speaking with anyone else, they finally did it.

And Lily had been tortured and murdered by someone who wanted to get his hands on their work.

Patricia owed it to Lily to find out who was responsible. Not just because of her remorse over the fact that she and Lily hadn't spoken in years. Or her survivor's guilt after Lily's murder. But because she knew that Lily would have wanted Patricia to do every single thing in her power to get the serum back.

Patricia left her apartment at seven, only to find that Nash had beaten her to Cytology. She nodded at him, impressed that a twenty-two-year-old had such a strong work ethic. But considering who his father was, Nash probably felt he had to prove himself twice as much as anyone else. Patricia knew Nash had blazed an unconventional path to the FBI — testing off the charts as a child and developing a natural athleticism not usually found in tandem with an extraordinary analytical mind. Given the initial incident that had put him on the FBI's radar, it was no wonder he'd been tracked by the bureau and recruited right out of high school.

She walked into her glass-enclosed office and returned to her notes from the cabin. She wasn't sure how the waitress wearing the bracelet in Gabby's vision fit in with the case. She could have been Lily's friend or Lily's enemy. Either way, at least they now had some kind of lead. Patricia believed in her serum more than anyone, but even she was surprised by how well the five teens had performed right out of the gate.

Suddenly, her computer rang with a video call from Carl Plouffe, her supervisor at the bureau.

The knots in her stomach tightened. *Please have the results for the bracelet.*

"Carl," she answered crisply as his pale face filled the screen.

"Patricia. Any other progress to inform me of?" Plouffe asked.

Patricia tried not to snap. "Not in the last twelve hours. We've been waiting for your analysis of the bracelet we found."

"For God's sake, Patricia, the world doesn't stop while you wait for evidence to be examined," he said. "We can't waste any time."

Carl Plouffe was more worried about his trajectory toward the top of the FBI than the fact that there was a murderer running loose with a covert mind-altering serum. He wanted Patricia to solve the case so he could get the credit.

"I'm concerned you're not fully grasping the gravity of this situation," he continued, glaring at her from the screen.

"Of course I am."

"Then why didn't you destroy that serum like you were supposed to?"

Patricia did her best to suppress a scream. There was no point getting trapped in this conversation again. Yes, she and Lily had been asked to destroy the serum ten years prior when Carl and the new administration had come in, part of an organizational overhaul that took out several of Patricia's former supervisors. She couldn't fathom why they would have wanted to destroy something of such value. "Dangerous," the paper pushers at the top of the FBI hierarchy had called the serum, exposing their fear of anything in the clairvoyant realm. They also didn't see the point if they couldn't use it on adult FBI agents. Despite all her and Lily's tinkering, there was no getting around the fact that the serum was effective only on younger, developing brains. But after all the years of difficult work, they were just supposed to throw the serum away because their new supervisors lacked imagination?

Instead, she and Lily divided up the serum, each securing her own cache off FBI premises. Lily had left the bureau shortly after that, but Patricia had always held out hope that a new field office director, one with more vision, would finally see the power behind the serum and hail its return.

"I don't think I can apologize any more," Patricia replied tersely. After Lily was killed, Patricia had decided that the potential consequences of the serum being stolen were too monumental to deal with on her own. There was no telling what kind of death and destruction could potentially come next. A domestic terrorist group able to use their psychic abilities to wreak havoc and stay a step ahead of the law. A foreign guerrilla movement or any other group who wanted to use the serum for their own gain. The serum could cause a national or an international emergency. Patricia knew more than anyone the allure of the extrasensory … and how valuable a tool it could be.

"Do you need more resources?" Plouffe asked. "Anything to put an end to this disaster."

"I don't need anyone else," Patricia replied. "Ryan Nash has proven tremendously helpful." It was the truth. Regardless of his storied back-ground, she'd been skeptical at first that someone so young had been assigned to the case. However, their working relationship had quickly fallen into place.

Plouffe cracked his knuckles. "Okay. Well, we did run the bracelet found at the crime scene."

He'd had the forensic results this entire conversation and he waited to reprimand her for five minutes before telling her?

"There were no fingerprints we could identify … but we did find traces of blood."

Patricia leaned forward.

"The blood belonged to two different people, we believe. One was unidentified. Not in our database."

"And the other?"

"A ninety-nine percent match to Lily Carpenter."

*　*　*

Nash could see Patricia talking to Plouffe as he sat at his desk, running searches on restaurants and bars within a five-mile radius of the Bel vedere Inn, the motel the waitress in Gabby's vision had visited.

He himself had spoken to Plouffe on only one occasion — the day he had been recruited. But he had a suspicion that Plouffe was always watching him from behind the scenes, that he was the one who had signed off on the series of difficult but plum assignments Nash had re-ceived over the last few years, despite his young age. Maybe he was just testing him, but Nash was always determined to rise to the occasion.

He stopped typing for a second to massage his rotator cuff, his right arm slightly sore from rebuilding the steps that Justin had blown to pieces at Lily's cabin. It was important that the police not notice the difference in their crime scene. The cops were aware that the FBI was conducting its own investigation into Lily's murder, but the flow of intelligence was not exactly a two-way street. Director Plouffe had chosen not to inform the police about the serum since it's very existence was classified. The sore shoulder was worth it, however. That bracelet was the first solid clue they'd had in weeks … if you could call a psychic vision "solid," something Nash was still wrestling with.

When he'd first been assigned to the case, he'd been doubtful that Patricia's plan would work. Their afternoon at the cabin had forced him to reassess. Gabby's "vision" was so specific that it was hard to dismiss. But he couldn't accept these new clues at face value yet, either. He was still interested in finding tangible evidence. Would Lily's cryptic statement to Sabrina somehow begin to make sense? Could they actually find the waitress Gabby had "seen"?

The door to Patricia's office opened and she emerged with bright eyes. Was that a smile he detected?

"They found Lily's blood on the waitress's bracelet."

It was an even bigger lead than they'd thought. Nash's skepticism was fading by the second.

"Did you notice any blood around the area where it was found last night?" Patricia asked.

Nash shook his head. He'd done a sweep of the space before he rebuilt the steps but came up with nothing. "None. The blood must have gotten on the bracelet inside the house." He turned over the possibilities in his mind. "Maybe the waitress from Gabby's vision was wearing the bracelet while she tortured and killed Lily — alone or with a partner. Then she wiped the site clean of any signs she'd been there, but the bracelet fell off as she exited. Like Andrew suggested, it could have slipped off her wrist and through the steps while she was running away."

"There's also the possibility the woman *wasn't* there during the murder. That she was at Lily's house for another reason and lost the bracelet then."

"But why would the bracelet have Lily's blood on it if there was no other blood around the steps?" Something nagged at him, though, another option in the back of his mind. He looked up at Patricia. "I suppose she could've shown up *after* the murder. Seen the body, somehow made contact with some of the blood, got spooked, left without saying a word. Or maybe even *during* the murder. Saw something. Got away."

"We need to find her. See what she knows."

"Easier said than done. Is Plouffe sending up more bodies to help?" Nash asked.

"No, he's not." Patricia didn't elaborate.

Nash frowned. Usually when an investigation began to heat up, additional manpower was assigned. Did that mean Patricia and Plouffe planned to rely solely on the newest members of the team? As much as he appreciated the new leads, a big portion of his job was to keep their five assets safe — and it was suddenly becoming apparent to him how hard that would be with such minimal backup.

"Who knows what that guy thinks," Patricia said. It was clear there was no love lost between Patricia and Director Plouffe. "Call the five of them in. I have their next assignment."

CHAPTER FIFTEEN

On a typical Thursday late afternoon, Sabrina would either be stuck at Sonic, where she'd make sure she was high enough to endure the monotony of the job, or stuck at home, where she'd make sure she was high enough to endure the sinking feeling of loneliness that greeted her as soon as she opened her front door.

But today was not a typical Thursday.

Instead of either of those things, she was sitting across from Andrew in the bar area of a restaurant in Falcon Rock, stone-cold sober and sipping an iced tea. It was their first official assignment since the cabin, though there wasn't much for Sabrina to do. This one was all about Gabby.

They'd received urgent texts from Patricia a few hours earlier, telling them to meet at Cytology immediately after school. As soon as they were all around the conference table, Patricia explained what she needed from them. Lily's blood had been found on the bracelet they discovered at the cabin. Finding the woman from Gabby's vision had become top priority.

"We need to identify this waitress as quickly as possible," Patricia told them gravely. "Unfortunately, we couldn't get her name through the Belvedere Inn, the motel Gabby saw the waitress checking in to. They never ran credit cards for that room on the date Gabby gave us, so the waitress and the man she was meeting must have ended up paying with cash. The motel doesn't keep records of guests' names unless they pay with a card."

"What about the man? Shouldn't we be checking him out, too?" Sabrina asked. She hadn't stopped trying to make sense of what Lily said to her in the cabin. *I know why they want it.* Who were "they"? Were they the waitress and the man she hooked up with at the motel? Could they have worked together to kill Lily for the serum?

"All we have to go on so far is Gabby's vision," Patricia said. "And she saw the woman, not the man. Finding her is the priority right now."

"I've put together a list of restaurants near the motel — any of them could be her workplace. We need you to check out these spots today if possible," Nash instructed. "It's been several weeks since Lily was killed, so we can't be sure if this woman still works at the same place, but let's hope she does."

Now Sabrina and the other four were at the third restaurant on Nash's list, and though Gabby hadn't seen anyone who resembled the waitress from her vision, Sabrina remained optimistic. After the way they'd managed to generate such a big lead at the cabin, she was eager to see what they could do next.

Gabby was conducting a sweep of the billiard area with Justin, who had taken it upon himself to stay by her side, mumbling something about how she might need his help. Z was roaming around by herself, listening in for any thoughts that could help them. And Sabrina was parked at a table with Andrew in the bar area, watching the incredibly depressing landscape of patrons, mostly disheveled middle-aged men sitting alone. The bartender was by far the youngest person in there, besides the five of them who looked incredibly out of place.

"You ever been here? To Falcon Rock, I mean," Andrew asked.

"Once," Sabrina answered. It was only a forty-minute drive from Cedar Springs, but the town of Falcon Rock couldn't have been more different. Cedar Springs was woodsy and charming with rolling grass fields and picturesque hiking trails, while Falcon Rock was right off the highway, the run-down homes and trailers visible from the exit ramp. Sabrina had a blurry memory of buying Percocet out there once, then throwing up in a dumpster behind a Popeyes. Not one of her finer moments.

"It's a little … *délabré*."

"A little what?"

"Decrepit. I was bored last night, so I decided to learn French." Andrew said it casually, but he couldn't suppress his grin. "The book I downloaded said it would take three months, but I pretty much had it down after three hours."

It was fascinating to see the difference between the Andrew she'd first met in that classroom and the confident genius sitting across from her now.

"That's amazing, Andrew. How fast can you read now?"

"I can read a five-hundred-page book in about a half hour. I couldn't decide between French or German, but I downloaded a German book, too, so maybe I'll try that one tonight."

"French was a good call. Much sexier language."

Andrew blushed from one ear to the other. Sabrina had a feeling he didn't have much experience talking to girls.

"Boning," Z said as she slipped into the chair next to Andrew. "That's what all these old dudes are thinking about. Boning their waitresses. Pathetic."

"You're lucky you could at least hear something," Sabrina said. "I haven't seen any ghosts since Lily at the cabin."

"Maybe you need to concentrate on something specific to see them.

Like something directly related to them. That's what I've seen mediums do in movies," Andrew suggested.

"Maybe," Sabrina agreed, filing that suggestion away to try later.

The bartender walked over to their table, his eyes all over Sabrina.

"Let me get you another iced tea. A girl who looks like you shouldn't have to go thirsty," he said with a grin.

Z's disapproving snort practically echoed through the restaurant.

Not that it deterred this guy. "Or I can get you something stronger. Let me guess, you're" — he looked her up and down — "a tequila girl, right?"

"Actually I'm underage. Another iced tea would be great," Sabrina answered curtly. She didn't want to give this guy any ideas.

"Coming right up. I'm Toby, by the way." He winked and walked away. Clearly he wasn't a pro at taking hints.

"What's wrong, Sabrina? Not your type?" Z asked. "If he has a girlfriend, would that make him more attractive?"

Was that why Z was always so rude to her? Because of Scott?

"Look, Z, I was using your brother for drugs," Sabrina told her candidly.

Andrew shifted in his chair uncomfortably, as though he wanted to bolt from this confrontation, but now that she'd started, Sabrina wanted to get it all out. "He had access to pills I wanted, so I hooked up with him. I didn't know he had a girlfriend. But to be honest, if I had known I probably wouldn't have cared. It was a mistake and it wasn't the worst thing I've ever done to get drugs or get money for drugs."

Sabrina's speech seemed to shut Z up. But only for a second.

"What *was* the worst thing you've done?" Z asked, her curiosity slightly defrosting the chill in her voice.

Andrew awkwardly cleared his throat. "You don't have to tell us, Sabrina."

It was only a week earlier that she had sat in a room with the others, mortified at the idea they would find out her secrets. All the horrible things she'd done over the past few years. Now, these were the only people she felt she could trust. "It's a toss-up between pawning my grandmother's wedding ring and stealing money from a sleeping homeless guy."

"Whoa," Andrew said quietly. "That's grim."

Z flashed Sabrina a quick smile. "I still think hooking up with my brother is worse." Sabrina laughed.

"One iced tea on the house for *Sabrina*, who hopefully won't leave without giving me her number," Toby interrupted, setting the drink in front of her. He must have overheard Z or Andrew saying her name.

"I don't think so, *Toby*," Sabrina said with a tight-lipped smile. "But thank you for the drink."

"My pleasure." He finally left them alone.

"Do lines like that ever work?" Andrew asked.

"No," Sabrina replied.

She was about to take a sip of the iced tea when Z's hands flew across the table and snatched it away. "Don't drink that!"

Sabrina looked up at her in surprise.

"He put something in it."

"What do you mean?" Andrew asked anxiously. "Like" — he lowered his voice — "a roofie?"

Z nodded. "Yeah. *A few sips of that and you won't remember you weren't interested.* That's what was going through his head when he gave it to you."

Sabrina's stomach turned at the thought of what could've happened. "Oh my God. Thanks, Z."

"Should we call the cops?" Andrew asked.

He whipped out his cell phone, but Sabrina shook her head. "I don't think we should draw any attention to the fact that we're here. We can call them anonymously later. So he can't do that to anyone else."

"It sucks, but she's right," Z agreed solemnly just as Gabby and Justin walked up to the table.

"She's not here," Gabby told them. "I guess we should go to the next place on Nash's list."

Sabrina, Z and Andrew were already halfway out the door.

*   *   *

As they walked down the block to the next restaurant on Nash's list, Justin covertly glanced at Gabby. Her hair was down again today, and he wondered if maybe it was due to the fact that she knew *someone* had liked it the day before at Lily's cabin. Did she realize it was him and not Andrew?

His phone buzzed with a text from Coach Brandt. *I got permission to open the weight room early tomorrow morning. See you then.* To Justin the subtext was crystal clear. *You sucked at practice today and need to do everything you can before the game tomorrow night.* He sighed.

"What's wrong?" Gabby asked. Justin wasn't used to people picking up on his moods. Unless, of course, it was anger — in which case, people generally knew to give him a wide berth.

"I had a crappy practice today and now Coach is on my case to do an extra weight-training session."

"Just because of one bad practice?"

"More than one," he admitted. He'd been a walking disaster on the field all week, and he couldn't figure out why he was suddenly sucking so badly. "It's like I can barely get my body moving. Guys are slipping through my fingers."

Gabby thought about it. "You must be a little distracted with all this ..."

"Maybe." Being undercover for the FBI could do that to a guy.

"It's thrown my concentration off, too," Gabby told him. "I can barely get through my homework."

Could it be that simple? That he just needed to focus a bit more?

He looked back at Gabby and debated asking her to come to the game the following night. He'd never asked a girl to a game before, and now he imagined what it would be like, looking up and finding her in the stands between plays. After this week, though, maybe it wasn't a good idea. He didn't want to risk her seeing a crapfest on the field.

They reached the Tipsy Tavern, a ramshackle restaurant wedged next to a 7-Eleven. As the others stepped in, Z pulled Justin aside with a knowing look. "Why don't you just ask her out, already? If not to your football game, something else?"

Justin looked around to see if Gabby or any of the others had heard her, but luckily they were already inside and out of earshot. He turned back to Z, annoyed. "You've got to get out of my head."

"I know," Z agreed. "It's not that interesting a place to be."

"Then why do you keep coming back for more?" He gave her a long look. "It's not cool. How would you like it?"

Z reluctantly sighed. "All right. I get it. I'll *try*," she promised.

"Try hard," Justin told her, before he entered the restaurant. The Tipsy Tavern was different from the geezer-infested craphole they just left. It was loud and packed, mostly with people in their twenties who needed to blow off some serious steam after work, by the looks of it. There were guys and girls doing shots, playing drunken games of darts and making out sloppily, almost on top of their burgers and fries.

The group fell into the same pattern they had at the last place. Sabrina took her post at a table while Andrew followed her there like a pathetic puppy dog. Z walked toward the back of the restaurant to do her mental eavesdropping thing, and he and Gabby went the other way, trying to look casual as she examined everyone.

A blond waitress emerged from behind the bar and he nudged Gabby. "Is that her?"

Gabby shook her head. "No. The woman in the vision was a little younger, I think."

They made their way to the back room of the restaurant, which housed another bar and was much less crowded. Two waitresses were serving, one blonde and one redhead. Justin looked at Gabby hopefully.

"No," she finally said. "It's neither of them. What if she was wearing a wig at the motel? Or she changed her hair color? I don't know if I'd recognize her."

"We still have one more restaurant to go," he responded, his upbeat tone sounding foreign even to him. He felt the need to pump Gabby up, though. She was starting to wilt.

Just as he was about to motion to the others that they could leave, he felt Gabby's nails dig into his wrist. Her eyes were on a hard-looking woman coming out of the kitchen, her large black purse slung over her shoulder, keys dangling from her red fingertips.

"That's her," Gabby said. They watched as she waved to the bartender.

"I'm out," the woman said brusquely.

"You're off already, Sadie?" the bartender answered, sounding annoyed. "I thought you were on till nine."

"Nope," she said. "You're on your own." The chip on her shoulder was so big that Justin could almost see it as she headed for the door.

"Should we follow her?" Justin asked.

"Nash and Patricia just said we should identify her. And now we know her name."

Justin nodded. If he had been by himself, he probably would've done it anyway, but Gabby was a rule follower and he didn't want to push her.

They both realized at the same time that her hand was still wrapped around his wrist. She quickly pulled her hand away, embarrassed, but he could still feel the warmth of her touch as they joined the others.

"Sorry, guys. I don't have anything to report," Z said. "Except that guy over there by the darts asked me if I would buzz off his hair like mine."

Andrew made a face. "That's so creepy."

Z shrugged. "I would've done it. But he didn't have a razor on him." Z suddenly noticed Gabby's smile. "Did you find her?"

* * *

Justin slung his jacket over his shoulders as the group walked into the cool fall night. It had worked. They'd actually managed to find the waitress from Gabby's vision. He was pretty sure they were all feeling the same mix of awe and excitement.

Andrew said exactly what Justin was thinking. "The five of us have gotten further on this case than the cops or the FBI."

"Not bad for a group of lost causes," Z noted wryly.

Sabrina smiled. "Tell me about it. If being a lost cause means solving a murder faster than the FBI —"

"And saving humanity —" Gabby chimed in.

"Then that's who we are," Sabrina finished.

"A hundred percent," Justin agreed. He looked down the line at the group — the other Lost Causes — and felt a grin sweep over his face. He hadn't even wanted to be seen with them the other morning at the flagpole, and now he realized they were people he actually kind of liked being around.

"Anyone want to grab some dinner on the way home?" he asked. "There's an awesome burrito stand halfway between here and Cedar Springs." It was the first time they'd all be hanging out voluntarily ... not as part of a mission or assignment.

For a split second, Justin wondered if maybe he'd misjudged the warm, fuzzy vibe among them all, but then Sabrina spoke up. "I'm in! Let's do it."

CHAPTER SIXTEEN

"Listen to this," Jared said to Z, playing a song for her on his laptop. They were sitting side by side at the massive kitchen island at Z's house, picking at the remains of a plate of pizza bagels. It was the only thing Jared knew how to make in an oven, but they were always baked to perfection.

Z listened to the melancholy beat of the song, the near whisper of the singer's voice rising with the guitar riff behind him.

"I don't know, it's kind of depressing," she said honestly.

Jared cocked his head at her. "Since when is anything too depressing for you?"

It was a good point. Z wasn't used to not feeling dark all the time. Until now, life had always felt as though she was trying to walk up the down escalator. She still didn't know if she could fully trust Patricia and Nash yet (after all, they'd introduced themselves by secretly drugging her), but getting to see who she was without the depression was worth it so far. When was the last time she'd actually wanted to get out of bed in the morning?

"No, I mean, I like it. Obviously."

He smiled. "I knew you would."

Good. She'd saved it. It wasn't that difficult to keep the secret about the serum from Jared — they didn't really get into deep personal conversations. Sometimes Jared felt more like a golden retriever than a boyfriend. Someone who was just inexplicably happy to hang out with her at all times. When she'd overheard Jared calling her his girlfriend a few months ago, she hadn't argued the point. It wasn't as if she was dating anyone else, and she knew he didn't expect her to do typical girlfriend things like have dinner with his parents, show public affection or go to prom. Instead they saw bands together a few times a week, something they totally bonded over. If there was one thing Jared knew, it was music. Every genre, every sound.

"Tell me what you think of this," he said as he clicked on another song. "I'm kind of obsessed with it."

As a male falsetto burst from the computer against a choppy beat, Scott strolled into the kitchen in his gym clothes.

"Whoever this guy is, he sounds like a drowning cat," Scott said, nodding toward the laptop.

Jared laughed and Z shot him an annoyed look.

"What?" Jared said with a shrug.

Scott grabbed a bottle of water from the fridge. "I'm going for a run," he said to no one in particular.

"It's supposed to rain," Jared said to him.

"It's always supposed to rain in this crappy town," Scott muttered as he walked out.

Z turned to Jared. "Why are you so nice to him when he's so rude all the time?"

"I don't know. Haven't you ever heard of killing someone with kindness?"

"I've heard of killing someone," Z mumbled.

* * *

A few hours later, she climbed into bed, wriggling uncomfortably beneath her comforter. Now that Jared wasn't there to distract her, she couldn't avoid thinking about tomorrow, already feeling nervous.

She was supposed to meet Nash outside an apartment in Falcon Rock in the morning. It belonged to Sadie Webb, the waitress from the Tipsy Tavern Gabby had seen in her vision, whose bracelet had somehow made it to Lily's cabin. Z probably wouldn't have to say anything tomorrow, but she was still anxious. Her sole purpose was to listen to what Sadie said and act as a human lie detector. Maybe Sadie would bring them one step closer to finding out what had happened to Lily.

As Z stared at the ornate light fixture on her ceiling, she finally zeroed in on the source of her nerves. The fear of failure. It would be the first time she was meeting Nash alone, without the rest of the group, the other Lost Causes, as they'd named themselves that night in Falcon Rock. Without the others around, the burden of pulling through with the next lead would be solely on her. And that was nerve-racking. For years, Z had managed to evade feeling the pressure to succeed. If nothing mattered, then you couldn't ever really fail. Tonight, though, she felt the weight that came with actually wanting to accomplish something — and the accompanying self-doubt. What if she couldn't hear Sadie's thoughts while Nash was questioning her? So far she'd only conjured up her ability at random moments. She had no idea how to make it work on command. What if she couldn't deliver? Besides knowing the sky-high stakes of moving the case forward, Z didn't want to let down the other Lost Causes, who would no doubt be keenly waiting to hear how she fared on her solo assignment.

It proved to be a sleepless night, and with only an hour left until she needed to leave, she dragged herself downstairs to the kitchen for some caffeine.

She was sipping her triple espresso, an untouched bagel in front of her, when she heard the quiet tapping of footsteps on marble floor. She grimaced as her mother swept into the room, her post-facial skin tight and glowing. Nicole Chapman hadn't grown up with money, but she wore it comfortably like a second skin. She made her way to the fridge and pulled out a Perrier.

"Good morning, Zelda."

Z cringed as she always did when her mother called her by her real name. She and her brother had been named after F. Scott and Zelda Fitzgerald, a couple famous for their dramatically dysfunctional relationship. Though her mother had never bothered to read *The Great Gatsby*, she had apparently been collecting 1920s flapper dresses at the time of the twins' birth, so she found the names chic. Her parents could hardly blame Z for turning out depressed after naming her for a woman who lived her last years in a psychiatric hospital. Not to mention the fact that there was something sick and incestuous about naming a brother and sister after a married couple.

"It's getting crisp out there. After a year in Florida, I almost forgot what fall looks like," her mother said more to herself than to Z. They could go days without having a direct conversation. Z always told herself it was because her mother was superficial, living in her own two-dimensional world. Was it actually because her mother had long given up on her? Though her parents had provided Z with beautiful cars to drive, luxurious homes to sleep in and credit cards she refused to use, they'd also given her nothing. They didn't care when she was depressed. And they certainly hadn't noticed that she was now happier. (Not even when she'd laughed — *laughed* — at a kitten GIF the other night.) If nothing else, they were consistent in their lack of ability to muster interest in their daughter.

Z got up and tossed her bagel in the trash, finally accepting the fact that she was too nervous to eat it. Just as she was about to walk out of the kitchen, the ringing in her ears stopped her dead in her tracks.

I wonder if she saw Steven come home last night.

Z looked at her mother, who was leaning over the counter on her elbows, absently flipping through *Veranda* magazine. She'd always wondered about her parents' relationship, which appeared flawless in public. It was hard, even for Z, who lived with them, to get a read on where they stood with each other for real. Sometimes it seemed that the only people who really knew her father were the people who did business with him.

"Where was Dad last night?"

Her mother's head shot up. "Excuse me?"

"Where did Dad go last night?" Z asked again, trying to sound more casual this time.

"You'll have to ask him, I never heard him come home." She gave Z a withering look, as if Steven's odd hours were somehow Z's fault, and huffed out of the kitchen.

* * *

Nash was already waiting for Z when she pulled into the designated spot a block away from Sadie's apartment building. He was leaning against the white van in gray pants and a black long-sleeved shirt, and could easily have been mistaken for a college student. The residential street was deserted except for a man raking the leaves off his front lawn as if each one was personally insulting him.

"Are you ready?" Nash asked.

Z nodded, but there was one thing she needed to do first. She pulled a slip of paper out of her back pocket and handed it to Nash.

He unfolded it, reading what Z had scrawled on it. "What's this?"

"The name of the bartender who tried to roofie Sabrina."

Nash kept his eyes on the paper.

"You are an FBI agent," she reminded him. "I don't want that to happen to anyone else." It was the least she could do, considering she now had the energy to care about justice being served.

"Noted." Nash folded the paper and put it into his pocket. "Let's go."

Z tried to keep up with his brisk pace as they approached the apartment building.

"This woman could be dangerous, right?" Aside from Sadie's bracelet, which had Lily Carpenter's blood on it, there was the fact, Z remembered, that Sadie seemed to be in the habit of carrying a gun.

"She could be," Nash said. "That's what you're here to find out."

Z tried to ignore the implicit pressure he'd just put on her. "Fine. But wouldn't it make more sense to bring her into the office for questioning?"

"People tend to clam up under those circumstances. Or worse, lawyer up."

"How are you going to explain why I'm here?" She was aware she sounded like Jared when he bombarded her with a million questions, but the fourth espresso she'd had on the way had left her more jittery than she'd realized.

"Just follow my lead."

Sadie Webb's address was a neglected four-story apartment building that hadn't had any major renovations done since the eighties. The pale yellow stucco was faded and peeling, and the clothes strewn haphazardly across several of the balconies gave the dingy building its only pop of color.

When they reached the entrance door, Nash punched a combination of numbers into the keypad outside. The door made a loud buzzing sound and the lock unclicked. Z didn't even ask how he knew the combination.

She was practically twitching with self-doubt as they entered the building. What was she doing here? Why were Patricia and Nash so sure she was up for this task, when Z herself was far from convinced?

"What if I hear your thoughts instead of hers?" she asked Nash.

"You won't hear my thoughts."

"How do you know that?"

"Because I won't let you."

Z raised an eyebrow. She was not exactly an open book, but Nash was like an impenetrable vault. Was it because he was in the FBI and trained to subvert his thoughts? Or was it more than that? Did he have his own secrets to hide?

The elevator had a yellow Out of Order sign taped to the doors, so they climbed the four flights of stairs to Sadie's apartment. It was hard to keep up with Nash's long strides because the soles of her combat boots kept sticking to whatever had been recently spilled in the stairwell. With each step, she became more anxious, but it was pointless to continue asking Nash questions. She wasn't going to get any real answers from him and he certainly wasn't going to give her a pep talk. When they reached apartment 4D, Nash rapped on the door purposefully. He tried again when no one opened the door after a few moments. Z strained to hear footsteps on the other side of the door, but it was difficult with the techno music blasting from a neighbor's apartment.

"Do you have a weapon?" Z whispered, not sure what she wanted the answer to be.

"I do."

Just then the door opened with the chain attached, and the woman Gabby had described from her vision peered out at them suspiciously.

"Who are you?" she asked. "What do you want?"

"I need to ask you a few questions, Ms. Webb," Nash answered.

"You a cop?"

Nash showed her his badge. She scrutinized it with a practiced eye, as if this was not the first law enforcement official to show up unannounced at her door.

"FBI, huh?" Sadie glanced at something or someone behind her in the apartment. Z willed herself to hear what Sadie was thinking, but all she heard was her own heart beating. Was there someone else in the apartment? Was Sadie sending some sort of signal? "You've got five minutes, then I've got to go to work."

The door closed loudly, then the chain rattled and it opened again.

"Come on in," Sadie said in an overly enthusiastic voice dripping with sarcasm. She took a good look at Z for the first time and studied her so harshly that Z looked away. "Who's she?"

"She's a spiritual adviser to the FBI," Nash told her.

"Spiritual adviser? Like a psychic?"

Z wasn't sure how to answer. Luckily, Nash replied for her. "Something like that." He stepped into the apartment. "Didn't you say you had to get to work soon?"

The apartment wasn't just clean, it was immaculate, without a particle of dust. The faint scent of lemon and cleaning solution suggested the small living room and adjoining kitchen had been freshly scrubbed down. Had Sadie washed important evidence away? There were only two small windows, but the shades were drawn, making it a little hard to see.

Z sat next to Nash on the brown velour couch, her hands clasped on her lap. Sadie perched on the end of the matching armchair across from them as if to say she wasn't bothering to take the time to get comfortable.

"How do you know Lily Carpenter?" Nash asked directly.

"Who's that?" Sadie asked. Z strained to hear something, anything, praying for the ringing in her ears to consume her.

Nash held up a photograph of Lily on his phone.

Sadie squinted. "Isn't she the one who got popped? I've seen her on the news, but I don't know her or anything."

Nash gave Z a quick look, but she could only shrug. Nothing was coming to her.

"Does this look familiar to you?" Nash held up a plastic bag containing the rose-gold bracelet.

Sadie nearly dove off the armchair, trying to grab it. "Where did you find it? I thought that bastard stole it!"

Nash's posture was alert, like a guard dog's when first hearing the sound of an intruder. "What bastard?"

Sadie avoided the question, keeping her eyes firmly planted on the bracelet. "I want that back. It was the only thing my piece-of-crap father ever bought me before he croaked."

"If it belongs to you, then I'm sure you can explain how it ended up at a crime scene. It's evidence in a murder investigation."

Sadie crossed her arms over her chest. "A murder investigation? I don't know anything about that. I haven't seen that bracelet in weeks."

"What happened to it?"

"I … I … lost it."

It didn't take a psychic to know she was lying. Z had to find a way to hear her. Patricia had told them the serum heightened abilities that were already within them. If there was any way this was going to work, Z had to trust that and ignore all her inner noise.

Z breathed in the lemon-scented air, then slowly exhaled on the count of three. Her mother's yoga instructor said that helped clear the mind. She tuned out the sound of her beating heart and forced the bass from the techno music next door to melt into the walls. She heard Nash ask Sadie another question, but she focused all of her senses on Sadie's mind. She took another deep breath, the techno music now almost feeling hypnotic. The ringing in her ears erupted so loudly that she winced.

If he did that to me at the motel, who knows what he'd do if I gave the feds his name. He'd probably kill me.

"… but I can't help you if I don't know anything," Sadie was saying indignantly to Nash when Z snapped out of her trance-like state.

"We know what he did to you at the motel," Z said quietly. Nash glanced at her, expressionless. Now he was the one following her lead.

Sadie stiffened. "How the hell did you find out about that?"

Z exhaled and the ringing began again.

It's not like I went to the cops. It must've been that stupid cow at the front desk. She was looking at the bruises funny.

"The front desk clerk told us," Z said. This was easier than she'd thought it could be.

Sadie groaned. "It was my own damn fault. I shouldn't have gone there with some jerk I didn't know …"

He didn't look like a guy who was going to punch a girl in the face.

Z felt sheltered and small, with a burst of empathy for this woman. It was an unfamiliar feeling.

Nash shifted his weight on the couch. "And is this the man you met at the motel?"

He pulled out a paper from his back pocket, unfolding it as he placed it on the coffee table, revealing a zoomed-in grainy image of Sadie Webb and a man. Nash and Patricia hadn't mentioned anything about a photo.

Sadie glared at him. "How did you —"

"This is a street-cam photo from outside the Tipsy Tavern the night you met him."

They must have pulled photos from that night after Gabby identified Sadie. Z tried not to look too eager as she peered at the photo. The man was young, no more than thirty, and unquestionably attractive, though in an edgy way, with a beard and long brown hair to his shoulders. He looked as though he'd be at home riding in a motorcycle gang or playing bass in a death-metal band.

His arm was slung around Sadie and his lips were curled into a sinister smile. Or maybe Z was just projecting. Soon after this photo was taken, he'd assaulted Sadie in their motel room. Was he already thinking about it at that point? Relishing the thought of how his fist would shatter her cheek?

"That's him," Sadie said, a little of her earlier resistance chipping away.

"And he stole your bracelet that night?" Nash confirmed.

"He knocked me out, and when I woke up a few hours later, my bracelet and wallet were gone." Z winced, picturing Sadie lying unconscious on the floor while this man ripped the bracelet off her wrist.

"Was that all he took?" Nash asked.

Sadie hesitated. "My gun, too." She sighed. "If I'd gotten to it faster, none of this would've happened."

"What type of gun was it?"

"I was just about to register it, if that's why you're asking," she answered defensively. "It was a .357 Magnum."

Something flickered in Nash's eyes.

"I need the man's name," Nash said, leaning forward.

Sadie shrugged. "I don't know it. He made this big deal about no names and no job talk. I thought it was sexy at the time."

Nash eyed her skeptically. "Do you remember if he paid you at the restaurant with a credit card?"

"Cash."

Z glanced at Nash, expecting him to leave. They needed the name, and she didn't know it. But Nash just kept staring Sadie down, not moving a muscle. A tactic he'd learned in FBI training?

A second later the ringing nearly blasted out Z's eardrums.

I don't care how long this guy looks at me like that, I'm not telling him I saw that psycho's license when he paid. Devon Warner. I'll never forget that creep's name.

Devon Warner.

Z had gotten the name herself.

"Well, thanks for your time," Z blurted, standing up. Nash instantly stood to leave as well. He knew Z had what they needed.

And it was just in time because, as soon as they stepped out of the apartment, Z's nose started gushing blood.

CHAPTER SEVENTEEN

"You know if there's anything you want to talk about, I'm here," Coach Brandt told Justin as he leaned his massive frame back in his desk chair.

"Yeah, cool, thanks," Justin responded quickly, hoping that would end this meeting faster. He was embarrassed and frustrated in front of Coach Brandt after stinking up the field the entire game last Friday. He'd been waiting for Coach Brandt to grab him after the game, but it would be Coach's style to want Justin to cool off and think things through over the weekend. The only thing Justin had come up with was confusion. He couldn't understand why what used to be easy for him, natural even, now seemed to be slipping between his fingers. Even Gabby's earlier explanation — that he was distracted by the investigation — didn't totally make sense, because he thought he had managed to block all that out as soon as the game clock started Friday night.

"It just seemed like you were ... a little ineffective on the field during the game," Coach Brandt prodded. That was putting it mildly.

"At least we won," Justin said lamely. Luckily, their kicker had pulled out a thirty-five-yard field goal with just seconds left in the game.

Coach Brandt didn't seem to care. "I'm on your side here, Justin. I want you to be as good as you can. If there's anything going on in your personal life, I'm here to help."

Sure. Well, the FBI tricked me into drinking some weird serum, and if I concentrate hard enough, I can lift your desk off the floor without moving a muscle.

"I know I've been off lately," Justin began, attempting to cut off any more questions about his personal life, "but I'm good now. I'm going to kill it in the next game." And he meant it. He was already planning on doing an extra weight-training session every day until then and staying after practice to run drills. If he had to set the case aside, so be it.

"I hope so," Coach Brandt said. "Because the Florida State scout just confirmed he'll be at the game in two weeks."

Justin's stomach dropped. Florida State was his first choice. Not only could he play football there if they awarded him a scholarship, but he'd get the hell out of Cedar Springs, across the country and away from his mother. Last year, that scout told Coach he was keeping an eye on Justin because their starting tight end was graduating. It wasn't as if his mom was going to help him pay for college. She'd told him a week earlier that he needed to get a job on the weekends so he could finally "be a man" and start paying for his own groceries.

"All right, then. I guess that's it," Coach Brandt said in that same disappointed tone. "Just remember, I want you to get this scholarship as much as you do."

Justin seriously doubted that.

* * *

When Justin left the meeting with Coach Brandt, Hindy was waiting for him in the hallway. Luckily he could tell that Justin had no interest in recapping his meeting with Coach Brandt as they walked toward the senior lockers. Instead, Hindy went on and on about a party he wanted to go to at Colorado State. Justin couldn't focus on anything, though, except the possibility that he was throwing his entire life away.

"… but I think sorority girls want something more classy like champagne. What do you think?" Hindy was asking.

"Yeah, sure," Justin responded, not even pretending to be interested in what he was talking about.

"I know you're pissed off, but everyone has a few bad games."

"I'm not pissed off," Justin said, knowing he kind of sounded pissed off.

"You've just been MIA lately. Silvestri said he saw you hanging out with that weird chick with the buzz cut. Tell me you're not hooking up with that freak."

"What if I was?" Justin said, glaring at him.

"It'd be cool." Hindy raised his arms in surrender.

Z drove Justin crazy with her conspiracy theories and trustafarian attitude, as if having truckloads of money was the world's biggest burden. But he had way more in common with Z than he did with Hindy. Hindy, whose mom and dad practically erupted into applause every time he entered the room, didn't know what it did to you to have your parents write you off. Or what it felt like not to be able to trust anybody but yourself. Z did. If Hindy was insulting Z, it almost felt like a direct attack on Justin, too.

"You can invite the hairless girl to party with us if you want," Hindy offered.

They were almost at his locker when Justin suddenly perked up. Gabby was standing right next to it. She started pulling the straps of her backpack down as if she suddenly wasn't sure what to do with her hands.

"Uh, hi," Justin said when they reached her, trying to make his body language less awkward than his voice. He could feel Hindy's nosy, gossip-hungry eyes on them.

"Hi," said Gabby.

"I'll see you later, man," Justin said, dismissing Hindy.

"Aren't you coming to lunch?" Hindy countered. Couldn't he just get the hint to take off?

"I'll catch up with you."

"All right, dude, whatever," Hindy mumbled. He finally walked away.

"Did something happen with that Devon Warner guy?" Justin asked her quietly, after making sure no one else was within earshot. As soon as Z was on her way home from Sadie's apartment, she'd texted all of them what happened. She sounded pretty stoked that she'd found out the name of the guy who'd stolen the bracelet. They all had responded with pretty much every celebratory emoji on the planet. Devon Warner had stolen Sadie's bracelet two days before Lily's murder, which meant he was probably the one who dropped it at the cabin. He could be Lily's killer and the one who had the serum. Z had gotten another amazing lead. Justin could tell himself all he wanted that he could quit the case and focus on football, but it wasn't going to be easy. He'd never been a part of anything except a football team, and this was so much bigger. But solving the case wasn't going to get him a Florida State scholarship.

"I haven't heard anything," Gabby responded. She suddenly looked uncertain. "I wanted to talk to you about something else."

Three cheerleaders passed by, interrupting them.

"Hi, Justin," they said in unison, their arms linked as if they were glued to one another. Justin couldn't believe he used to think they were hot. Compared with Gabby, they were about as attractive as his ancient physics teacher.

Justin ignored them and turned to Gabby. "Let's go somewhere quiet."

* * *

They parked themselves on a stone bench in the courtyard behind the school. People rarely used it except for in the spring, when the cool teachers sometimes held class out there. But with the temperature dropping, it was deserted except for Justin and Gabby. Justin wished he'd grabbed his coat, but he didn't want to look like a wuss and go in and get it now.

"So what's up?" he asked curiously.

"I've been thinking about your football problem," she responded. He was surprised. A good kind of surprised. "Do you think it has something to do with … what's happening to us?"

He shrugged. "You mean being distracted?"

"No, I meant …" She lowered her voice even though there was no one else around. "Because of the serum."

"What do you mean?"

"Not that I really knew you then or anything, but haven't your, uh, past problems mostly gone away?"

He realized she was talking about his violent temper and he felt embarrassed. Even when punching out assclown Nick Preston onstage in the middle of an all-school pep rally, Justin had always worn his fury like a badge of pride. It was a not-so-subtle warning to others to stay away or else. Since he'd taken the serum, the anger seemed to have simmered off him. Sure, he still got annoyed. But the deep, instinctive rage that made him not just inflict violence but *relish* violence … that was nowhere to be found.

"I'm not as angry as I used to be," he admitted.

"That's exactly what I mean. What if that was what made you so great on the football field?"

He couldn't believe that had never crossed his mind before. "You're right. Jesus. The reason I suck is because I don't *need* to pummel everyone like I used to."

Gabby exhaled as if she'd been nervous.

"Do you think I should ask Patricia for the antidote?" Just saying the words deflated him. A tiny, menacing thought lingered in the back of his head, though. *What if that still didn't work?*

"Maybe you don't have to." Her eyes were smiling. "I have an idea."

"What is it?" he asked, trying not to sound too desperate.

"Well, it's kind of cheating, but not exactly."

"I'm not juicing, if that's what you're thinking."

She looked horrified. "What? No, not that. What if you used your psychokinesis on the football field? To move the players?"

"Move them?"

"You know, out of the way. Or you could tackle them just by looking at them. I mean, you'd have to really practice so you don't hurt anyone. But I think you could do it."

It was definitely better than choking in front of the Florida State scout in a few weeks. Or getting Patricia to inject him with the antidote. "That's pretty genius. I have a game on Friday, so if I start sucking like last time, I'll give it a try." If it worked and he was back to himself on the field, that meant he could focus on the case *and* play football.

She smiled sweetly. "It seems unfair that you have to decide between feeling good or playing football. The rest of us don't have to do that."

Justin had never wanted to kiss a girl this badly in his life. But he'd also never been less sure of himself. "Thanks, Gabby. Who knows? I might still have a shot at Florida State."

"Is that your first choice?"

"Yeah. It's the farthest school from my mom where I can still play football."

"What about your dad?"

Justin hesitated. He'd never told a girl anything about his personal life. "I don't know where he is. He bailed like a week after I was born. My mom said I cried all the time and it drove him crazy."

Gabby's eyes widened. "She blamed it on you?"

He didn't want to admit he still carried it around. Instead, he just shrugged. "Yeah, I don't think I've cried since, though."

She saw right through him. "Come on. That's not true. Not even during a movie?"

"Nope."

"What about *Braveheart*? Don't all guys cry during that movie?"

Justin shook his head. "Nah. Mel Gibson had it coming to him."

"*Bambi*? *Dumbo*? *E.T.*?"

"Never saw them. My mom only watched movies she wanted to watch when I was little. I've seen *Steel Magnolias* thirty times. And no, didn't shed a tear."

Gabby raised an eyebrow. "*The Blind Side*?"

Crap. She had him.

CHAPTER EIGHTEEN

That night, Sabrina stood in her kitchen, washing the few dishes that remained in the sink a little more vigorously than necessary.

When Z had texted everyone about her discovery, Sabrina couldn't help feeling a tiny bit jealous. Z had delivered a huge clue. They had a name now. Devon Warner. They knew he had taken Sadie's bracelet and gun from her after he knocked her out in the motel room.

Had he been the one to take the bracelet to Lily's house? Did he use Sadie's gun to kill Lily?

This case seemed to be moving quickly now, and Sabrina was still coming up blank in seeing any other spirits. She was starting to worry that the serum had somehow worn off. Was it less potent for her than for the others because she was the oldest? Or maybe it was because she had taken so many drugs before. If she didn't perform, would she be kicked off the team?

Andrew had suggested that she concentrate on something specifically related to the ghost she was trying to conjure up. She'd tried rummaging through some newspaper articles about Lily earlier, hoping it would spark something. She'd even done a little online research that afternoon on paranormal sightings to see if there were any tips she could follow. But she still had no luck.

As she finished the dishes, she wondered if maybe trying to summon Anthony again would be easier than Lily. He wouldn't necessarily help with the case, but she'd been longing to see him again. She wanted to make sure he was okay. To tell him she loved him. And to ask him what he meant when he'd said, *"Be careful, Beanie."*

Her online research into the supernatural realm suggested that spirits were often all-seeing, aware of everything going on among the living they visited. So was Anthony warning her about some new specific imminent danger he could see coming her way … something to do with this case? Or was the warning more general, or about something else entirely? Could he have merely been cautioning her to stop numbing her body with drugs?

That was the problem. Even when Sabrina *could* see these spirits, they spoke to her in a cryptic way that was impossible to pin down. The same thing had happened with Lily. When she'd said, *I know why they want it*, there was no guarantee she was even talking about the serum. She could have been musing about why people wanted her candles!

Suddenly, she heard a rustling behind her. Her back stiffened for a moment — could it be Anthony? She waited for cool air to blast over her or for the lights to begin flickering like last time, but nothing happened. She turned around, realizing it was probably just Rocket begging for scraps but was surprised to find her mother on one of her rare expeditions outside her bedroom. She was so frail and haunted in her thin nightgown that she might as well have been a ghost.

"Sabrina, it's you," her mother said, as she shuffled by to get a glass of water. Christine Ross was still a beautiful woman, even with the vacant stare she wore whenever she was awake. Her thick, dark hair resembled Sabrina's, though it was usually tangled, the effort of brushing it too much for her to handle.

"Yeah, it's me, Mom," Sabrina sighed. Who else would it be?

She stepped aside so her mother could fill her glass at the sink, each movement sluggish and heavy as though she was moving her limbs through mud. Sabrina gnawed the inside of her cheek, silently begging her mother to hurry up so she could get back to trying to summon Anthony. People always talked about wanting something so badly that you could taste it. That used to make sense to Sabrina. When she'd lust after a pill, she could literally feel the bitter, chemical tang on her tongue moments before it was even in her hands. But her desire to talk to Anthony had bypassed her taste buds and gone straight to her heart.

When Christine finally turned the water off, she took a long sip, then looked up at Sabrina.

"Oh, I just spoke to Anthony a few minutes ago, honey."

"What?" Sabrina asked. Had she heard right?

Her mother shook her head, mildly disappointed. "I'm afraid your brother isn't very happy."

"What do you mean? What did he say?" Her mother had claimed to have spoken to Anthony before, but Sabrina always dismissed it as the drugs talking. Her mother was on a cocktail of medications no sane doctor would approve of mixing.

But now Sabrina saw it in a different light. What if it actually *was* the drugs talking? Patricia had told them certain drugs had the ability to open up channels in your brain, to stimulate dormant senses.

What if her mother was telling the truth?

Christine shivered and narrowed her eyes. "You need to be careful, Sabrina."

"Careful of what?" Sabrina asked, clutching the edge of the counter. "What do you mean?"

Christine opened her mouth, then closed it, as if she'd thought better of speaking.

"Mom, please," Sabrina begged, but she knew it would do no good. The moment was over as quickly and strangely as it had begun.

* * *

Sabrina gazed out the window from the last row of English lit the next day, still preoccupied with figuring out some way to unlock her abilities. If she could just see Lily again, maybe she'd be able to expand on what she'd told Sabrina the first time. *I know why they want it.* Could Devon Warner be part of the "they" Lily Carpenter had been referring to? And if so, who was his partner in crime?

"Sabrina."

Mr. Wincott was standing beside her, a concerned look on his face. He was one of the youngest teachers on staff at Cedar Springs. Not so coincidentally, he was also the one most of Sabrina's classmates were infatuated with, his witty observations sending them into fits of giggles from their front-row seats. What bothered Sabrina, though, was how much Mr. Wincott got off on it.

"Are you okay?" he asked. Like Sabrina, he was a "halfer," but in his case half Chinese and half British. He'd once tried to discuss their commonality with Sabrina, but she'd been too hungover at the time to add any significant opinion. His posh accent was yet another reason he'd attained hot-teacher status.

She looked around to see the rest of the class had already begun packing up. The bell must have rung.

"Yeah," she said. "Just a little distracted."

He followed her into the hallway.

"How's the school year going so far, Sabrina?" he asked. He had a way of seeing into people, which made Sabrina feel the need to blush.

"Fine. Nothing special," Sabrina lied.

As they approached her locker, Sabrina saw Z standing next to it, waiting. It felt like a lifetime ago that Z had ratted out her and Scott, though it had only been a few weeks ago.

"Zelda," Mr. Wincott said. "Fancy meeting you here."

"Is it really that hard to believe?" Z drawled, smart aleck that she was. "We're all forced to be here the entire day, aren't we?"

Mr. Wincott nodded, faintly amused. "That we are." He raised an eyebrow at her. "You missed our adviser meeting this morning." All the Cedar Springs High students were assigned faculty advisers. Sabrina's, Mr. Manzetti, or "Sweaty Manzetti" as everyone called him behind his back, had given up on scheduling meetings in the middle of last year since Sabrina never bothered showing up.

Z shrugged. "I wasn't feeling well."

"Glad to see you've made such a quick recovery," he replied cheekily, and Sabrina suppressed a smile.

Mr. Wincott looked from Sabrina to Z as if he was trying to work out how the two of them were friends, then shook his head. "Always a pleasure, ladies," he said breezily before he continued down the hall.

"Have you spoken to Nash?" Z asked, once Mr. Wincott was a reasonable distance away.

"No, why?" Sabrina replied. Z gave her a funny look. Was it possible Z had heard her thoughts about Nash at some point? Sabrina made a mental note to be more carefully guarded.

"Don't you think it's weird that I told him Devon Warner's name three days ago and we haven't heard anything since?" She gave Sabrina a look implying that she felt it was, indeed, very strange. But Sabrina knew better than to get too caught up in Z's conspiracy theories. On the ride to Falcon Rock, she had heard Z expound ideas on JFK's assassination, OJ's guilt and whether a man had actually walked on the moon.

"I don't know," Sabrina said as she took her Spanish book out of her locker. "I mean, yeah, I've been waiting to hear from them. But I guess I just figured they'd call us when they need us. It's not like we're actually in the FBI. They don't owe us an explanation."

"They're the ones who drugged us against our will, so yeah, they kind of do."

Instead of going down that road, Sabrina decided to change the subject. "I have a question for you." She slammed her locker shut. "When you were at Sadie Webb's apartment, how did you make yourself hear her thoughts? How did you summon it?"

They began walking toward the exit of the building, dodging the other students and keeping their voices low.

"I don't know. I guess I just blocked out all the other noise and it happened."

It was the opposite of what Andrew had suggested. But Andrew's advice hadn't really panned out.

"It was that easy?" Sabrina asked.

Z hesitated. "I wouldn't call it easy. I think it made my nose bleed."

"Really? Has that happened before?" Sabrina asked, concerned because she could tell Z was trying to play it as no big deal.

"No." Z was quiet for a moment, then added, "But it could've been that chick's apartment. It smelled like she lit an ammonia candle in there."

Before Sabrina could ask another question, Z spotted Gabby ahead of them and called out for her. Gabby smiled shyly and waited for them to catch up.

"Have you heard from Patricia or Nash?" Z asked Gabby.

"No, why? Did something happen?"

"Nothing they've told us," Z answered. "But it's hard to believe they haven't found out more about Devon Warner. Think about it. He's a violent psychopath who stole Sadie's gun and her bracelet, which ended up at Lily's cabin with her blood on it. He's got to be our guy. But they're just keeping us on the sidelines."

"We don't know that for sure," Sabrina interjected, a new theory forming in her mind. "What if Devon is just a middleman. He could've stolen the gun and bracelet from Sadie and sold them for a few bucks to someone else — maybe the *real* killer."

Z cocked her head, unconvinced. "Maybe. Regardless, he's our one lead and we need to find him. But we're just sitting here pretending things are normal. I called Patricia yesterday and she never called me back. Nash and Patricia aren't telling us everything, I just know it."

"They could be getting their facts together before they fill us in …" Sabrina said. It did bother her slightly that Patricia had never returned Z's phone call.

"What did Nash say after you told him the guy's name was Devon Warner? Or, more importantly, what did he think?" Gabby asked.

Sabrina sighed. If only she had the ability to tap into Nash's brain.

"Nada. And it wasn't for lack of trying. There's something off with him."

Gabby agreed. "I know. He's so serious."

"Yeah, and when I tried to hear what he was thinking when we left Sadie's apartment, it was like I heard white noise instead," Z said, taking off toward the parking lot. "Maybe he's undergone Navy SEAL training or something. They teach them all kinds of Jedi mind tricks so they won't give anything up if they're ever tortured for information."

"Probably," Sabrina agreed. Somehow none of this surprised her.

"When Patricia didn't call me back last night, I realized we've been way too naive, trusting everything they say, even though this whole thing started as a lie in that fake therapy meeting," Z said. "So why are we so quick to take them at their word now?"

Sabrina suddenly felt as innocent as Gabby. She'd been so caught up in the adventure of it all — and the magnetic pull she felt toward Nash — that it never occurred to her not to trust him.

"I think we should look into Devon Warner ourselves," Z announced.

"I don't know if that's a good idea," Gabby said quickly. "It could be dangerous." They both looked to Sabrina at the same time.

"Why don't we give it one or two more days?" Sabrina finally said. Z's theories might actually have some merit this time, but that didn't mean she was ready to go rogue. "If they don't contact us by then, we check out Devon Warner ourselves."

* * *

Later that afternoon, Sabrina unearthed her running shoes from the back of her closet and wiped off the thick layer of dust that had accumulated on them.

She whistled for Rocket, who ran over when he saw Sabrina wielding the leash. The houses on her street backed up to the dense wooded forest of the Cedar Springs nature reserve. Sabrina used to run the trails all the time, but she hadn't been out there for years.

She surprised herself when she took off like a bullet on the wooded path behind her house, the orange and red leaves crunching underneath her pounding feet. But it was the only idea Sabrina had left for how to "block all the noise out" as Z had managed to do at Sadie's apartment. At this point, she was willing to try anything. Sabrina had never had much luck with meditation or even yoga. The harder she worked at silencing her mind, the more it spun out of control.

Wasn't that why she started with drugs in the first place? For the first few years after Anthony's death, she'd carried the weight of her pain around while figuring out how to take care of herself. Sabrina handled the pressure and sadness and forging of signatures and grocery buying all while managing to do well in school. She'd become a bit of a loner in the process, not wanting to invite anyone over to her house for fear they would discover she was basically an orphan. But even that was okay with her. She had a few satellite friends at school and that was good enough.

And then on her sixteenth birthday, she decided to go to a party. She figured she deserved to go out and celebrate since her parents hadn't acknowledged her birthday with so much as a card. It was only a few seconds after she took that hit off the bong that she felt as if someone was giving her brain an amazing massage. Some people did drugs to feel *something*. Sabrina did them to feel *nothing*.

She reached a fork in the running path and stopped, out of breath. She'd done it — completely zoned out while she ran. Except she hadn't realized how fast she'd been going, and now she couldn't figure out how to get back to where she started.

The sun was setting, and even with sweat dripping down her forehead, Sabrina felt chilled from the drop in temperature. She looked around for familiar landmarks. Nothing. Rocket peered up at her expectantly, his tongue hanging out the side of his mouth.

Sabrina closed her eyes and tried to retrace her steps.

As soon as she opened them, a cold blast of air hit her and her skin began to crawl.

It's happening again.

Someone was coming. And something told her it wasn't Anthony or Lily.

Her breath — coming out in short, anxious spurts — formed tiny clouds of fog in front of her. She could hear the sounds of faint whispers and Rocket's ears went up, his hair on end. He could feel it, too.

And then she saw the ghost.

Standing in front of her was a teenage girl, her skin glowing the way Anthony's had. She was close enough to reach out and touch. The girl was sopping wet from head to toe, water dripping from her long black hair, off her rumpled purple dress and onto her muddy bare feet.

She opened her mouth to say something, when Rocket began aggressively lunging for her.

The girl quickly vanished. Rocket took off — spooked — and the leash was wrapped so tightly around Sabrina's wrist that he yanked her along with him.

"Rocket, stop!" she commanded as she tried to keep up. Her screams were swallowed by the wind, and she became vaguely aware that her feet were sinking into the ground. Rocket had gone off the path. Without the sun and with only a sliver of the moon, she could barely see in front of her.

She had no idea whether they were going the right way or falling deeper into the woods, but she didn't have a choice in the matter. Rocket wasn't slowing down.

"Rocket!" She tripped over some stones and tumbled to the ground face-first. Something jabbed into her leg and a sharp pain shot up her body. She didn't have time to register how badly she was hurt, though. Rocket dragged her through the dirt and debris. She managed to spring up, her arms and legs now caked with mud, as the dog propelled her forward again.

There was a dim glow through the trees fifty feet in front of her. A street lamp. Sabrina broke out of the woods and found herself at the end of her street. Rocket knew where he was going, thank God. The relief gave her the last burst of energy she needed to make it all the way home. She threw open her front door and sank to the ground, gasping, trying to breathe through the stifling air of her own home.

Who was that girl? Was she related to Lily Carpenter somehow? She looked to be about Sabrina's age. Was that the age she was when she died?

Just when she'd almost caught her breath, there was a banging on the door. She jumped to her feet, her heart racing again.

"Sabrina? Are you there?"

Nash.

She opened the door. "What are you doing here?"

"Jesus, are you okay?" he said without any formal greeting as he entered the house. How did he know what had just happened?

"What do you mean?" she asked, instantly guarded.

"You're bleeding."

She looked down to see what he was talking about, and the color drained from her face. There was a gash on her left leg so deep that it was spurting like a geyser and blood had puddled on the floor underneath her feet.

"What happened?" he asked, looking closer. "Were you in the woods?"

She nodded. "I was running and I tripped ..." She tried to steady herself, but a whoosh of dizziness overpowered her and she swayed. Nash scooped her up before she hit the ground.

"Breathe," he commanded as he walked toward her bathroom. "We need to clean that."

Now she was even more light-headed, but not because of her leg. The sudden physical contact with Nash overwhelmed her. His arms felt as strong and chiseled as they looked and his body radiated heat like a furnace against her. The closest they'd come to actually touching before was when he sat next to her outside of Lily's cabin. But now she was so close that she could smell the spicy, oaky scent of his aftershave. Was this what the term "animal attraction" meant?

Her cheeks suddenly reddened. What if Nash could tell she was smelling him? Oh God. He must be able to smell her. She was muddy and sweaty and probably stunk like the inside of her running shoes.

He sat her down on the edge of the tub and reality set back in — along with a searing pain where the gash on her leg was. It throbbed so much that she couldn't believe she hadn't felt it before. Nash placed a damp towel right below her knee.

"You don't have to do this," she told him. Helpless wasn't comfortable on her. "I can clean it myself."

"You know how to properly disinfect and wrap a puncture wound so it heals correctly?"

"I can look it up."

"Since I'm already here, how about I just do it?"

"What *are* you doing here?" she asked, suddenly aware that this was seriously weird.

Nash hesitated for just a beat before he dug a small bottle out of his pocket. Pepper spray. "I came to give this to you."

"I don't think that works on ghosts," Sabrina said.

"It works better on aggressive bartenders."

She looked up and saw there was no humor in his eyes. "Z told you."

"You didn't think it was worth *mentioning* that someone tried to assault you?" His eyes flashed with anger.

"I'm sorry." She hated that she felt like a girl being chastised by her parents. Even worse, she realized in all the commotion of the past few days, she'd never called and reported that guy to the police. "I was planning to report him. I just —"

"It's handled." He didn't explain what that might mean. "Just keep this with you from now on."

He cleaned off the debris from the wound with some rubbing alcohol he'd found under her sink. "You must have been running pretty fast." She could only nod.

He locked eyes with her, his large hands completely wrapped around her leg. "The stinging will be over in a second. Hang on."

"I'm fine."

He patted her leg dry, then pressed the towel over the gash. "Something sharp cut into your leg. Probably the end of a branch."

The stinging finally subsided enough for Sabrina to remember her conversation with Z. "Hey, have you found Devon Warner yet?"

"No." He repositioned the towel. "But I think we're getting close. We're a few days away from needing your assistance again."

Maybe Z was getting in her head, but Nash's vague answer annoyed her. How were they supposed to help if they were being kept at arm's length? Had Nash and Patricia given up on them, too?

"Give me your hands," Nash instructed.

She held out both hands in front of her. He wiped off the thick layer of dried mud on them, then carefully inspected them for scrapes. As soon as he had touched her hands, she felt her entire body ignite again as if it had been lit with a match. There was no use fighting it. And her mind and body were too exhausted to try. His face was inches from hers, and for the first time, she saw the small gold flecks that outlined his blazing green irises. He looked up and caught her staring at him.

"Were you scoping me out that day at Sonic? For the FBI?" she asked, forcing herself not to look away.

"Scoping you out?"

"Doing recon or whatever you call it. Gathering information on me for Patricia."

"Maybe I just wanted a burger."

"You don't strike me as the fast-food type."

He looked back up sharply. "You don't strike me as the type who doesn't know the answer to that question."

So he was there to scope her out. "What did you see?"

Nash concentrated on securing the bandage. "Everything."

He'd seen her drunk, high, probably partying with people she'd never see again. Until she needed another fix. But that wasn't who she was anymore. "You know everything about me, but I don't know anything about you."

"What do you want to know?"

This caught her off guard. "Where do I start? I don't even know if Nash is your first name or your last name."

"Last."

"So what's your first name?"

He paused. "Ryan."

"How old are you?"

"Twenty-two." Only a few years older than Sabrina.

"What else should I know?" she asked.

"I kept your number. In case you weren't chosen." He stood up abruptly before Sabrina could even relish this tiny piece of information. "Tell me what happened in the woods."

Back to business.

"I went for a run and got turned around, so I stopped for a second to figure out where I was." It was such a short time ago, but it already felt blurry. Like something that happened to someone else. "And then there was this —"

She stopped, the breath knocked out of her.

The teenage girl from the woods was standing right behind Nash, staring at Sabrina.

The girl raised a thin finger to her lips.

"Shhhhh."

Sabrina heard Nash say something, but his voice was muffled, as though it was being filtered through a tunnel. She couldn't take her eyes off the ghostly girl. This time, Sabrina could see something in the girl's almond-shaped eyes. Urgency, yes. But something else, too ... compassion.

The girl looked at Nash, then she whispered something that took Sabrina a second to process.

"You can't trust them."

The girl was gone as quickly as she'd appeared, and Sabrina was left staring at the empty spot behind Nash.

"Sabrina? What's going on? Are you okay?"

"Nothing. I ... I ..." she trailed off lamely. Sabrina couldn't explain it, but there was something protective about this girl's presence. Something she trusted. But how could Sabrina believe this girl over Nash?

Nash's confusion immediately turned to frustration. "Sabrina, whatever you saw, you need to tell me."

Sabrina bristled at his commanding tone. She'd done it again — gotten caught up in her feelings for Nash and let them cloud her judgment. Z's words echoed in her ears, in chorus with the girl's. They had no reason to trust Nash and Patricia.

"Are you telling *me* everything?" she challenged.

His expression barely changed, but the energy in the room shifted to something adversarial. Nash's eyes bored into hers, but he didn't say anything except, "Your leg should heal fine now. I'll show myself out."

Eventually Sabrina stood up, wobbly on her feet. She limped into her bedroom, sat down on her bed and grabbed her phone. She had to tell someone about this.

"What's up?" Z said, answering on the first ring.

Sabrina took a deep breath. "I agree. We should look into Devon Warner ourselves."

CHAPTER NINETEEN

"We don't have to go in there," Gabby said for the third time. She shifted in her seat in the back row of Z's Range Rover, the chill of the night air slipping through the partially open windows. For the last hour, the five of them had been huddled together in the car, parked on the outskirts of Falcon Rock, watching the second-floor corner window of an apartment building down the block. "What if that's not even the right place?"

"I'm positive that's it," Andrew replied from his seat next to her. "I didn't even have to hack anything to find this out. All I needed to do was go on Spokeo. It's the only address for a Devon Warner in this area."

Devon Warner's apartment building was in an even more bleak area than the motel and restaurant had been, on a run-down street that boasted three liquor stores, but no working streetlights.

When the group began their drive here tonight, Gabby had gotten swept up in their nervous excitement. It felt liberating to be out at night, doing something totally unexpected. But now that she was there, she was just plain nervous. Anything could happen on this dark, desolate street. It was so different from the last time they were all crammed in

Z's car on the way to Falcon Rock. That was for an actual assignment from Patricia and Nash with a clear-cut goal. Now that the five of them had decided to take matters into their own hands, they had to come up with their own plan of attack.

"I say we go into the apartment now. He could come back any second. We're just wasting time," Sabrina said. Gabby wasn't surprised that Sabrina was pushing them to go in. Sabrina had told them about the ghost and what she'd said to her. *You can't trust them.* Now Sabrina was just like Z, aggressive and suspicious. Maybe even more so.

Sabrina had volunteered to enter the building as soon as they'd arrived, just for some early reconnaissance.

"He's not home," she reported when she came back to the car. She'd knocked on the door, received no answer and heard no sounds from inside. Since then, the window had remained dark.

"We'll be quick," she urged them all now. "Let's go in, see what we can find out about this guy. Who is he? How did he know about the serum?"

Gabby shook her head nervously. "We don't even know if Devon Warner did know about the serum."

"Gabby, he took Sadie's gun and bracelet. The bracelet that ended up with Lily's blood all over it," Sabrina reminded her. "He was at the scene of the crime. Chances are he knew about the serum."

"But didn't you say he could've been a middleman? I think we should wait. Just scope out the place from out here. Nash said he'd let us know when they needed us."

Z gave Gabby a pitying look.

Gabby's eyes flitted to the dark window again. "Don't you think that if it's as easy to find this place as Andrew said, then Nash and Patricia have probably already been here —"

"Which makes me wonder why we haven't," Z broke in. "We can find out things they can't. Remember what happened at Lily's cabin?"

"It's just … something doesn't feel right here," Gabby countered. She wished she could articulate it better.

"Of course something isn't right here. There's three guys doing crack fifty yards away and Devon Warner could come back at any second to find us all," Z replied.

"I know it's a little risky, Gabby," Sabrina admitted.

The understatement of the year, Gabby thought. At best Devon Warner was a guy who knocked out women for fun and a few dollars. At worst he was a murderer.

"But you know what could happen if the serum gets into the wrong hands. This is worth the risk. We need some answers." Her eyes locked with Z's, and Gabby realized they were totally on the same page.

"Maybe you could stay in the car," Justin told Gabby quietly, his eyes focused on the car console. Since they'd arrived, he'd been testing his ability to move the heating dial psychokinetically, with limited success.

"No, she can't," Andrew piped up from the other side. "Gabby needs to be up there. She's the one who has visions. If she sees the right thing, she could solve the whole case."

"Answers could be only a few minutes away," Z reminded her.

Despite the danger, Gabby could admit that this part was tempting.

"I don't want to force you to go, though, Gabby," Sabrina said, softening. "If you feel that strongly, then we'll respect it. Going into Devon's apartment should be a unanimous decision."

The others nodded, which Gabby appreciated. But Z had touched a nerve. Gabby did want answers. She shouldn't let her personal fear get in the way.

"Okay," she said. "I'll do it." A look of relief spread across their faces.

"I'll go with you," Justin told her. "Nothing will happen to you, I promise." He sounded so sure that Gabby almost believed him.

* * *

A few moments later, she was following Justin up the graffiti-covered stairwell. The rest of the group would stay in the car a bit longer to avoid being too conspicuous.

Gabby reached the second-story hall, which had a thin, stained carpet. Before she knew what she was doing, she reached down to touch a large brown mark on the carpet and was instantly transported.

Blood. Fresh blood splattering everywhere, the sounds of someone in pain suddenly in Gabby's ears. Then she could see two girls with stringy hair and wiry frames but almost superhuman strength kicking a third one who lay on the floor, clutching her ribs. Again and again and again, they kicked her head and body, the girl on the floor begging them to stop, while the perpetrators laughed.

"You okay?" Justin asked, bringing her out of the vision.

"Yeah," she lied, keeping her eyes firmly forward, avoiding the other telltale stains. *Don't look, don't touch.* She didn't want to know what other sordid secrets were hidden in this filthy place.

A light flickered at the end of the corridor, above the door to apartment 204.

"I'm going to knock one more time," Justin whispered. "Just in case."

Gabby wondered if he was even scared.

The knocking was met by silence. Justin looked at her. "Should I …?"

"I guess so," she replied, though every bone in her body was telling her to turn back.

"I honestly don't know how much control I have. I don't want to rip the whole door out," he said in a low voice.

"Maybe you could just focus on sliding the lock over. See this part here …" Gabby slipped her hand on the brass knob, then found it turned easily under her hand. "Wait — it's not even locked."

She allowed the door to open, revealing the small, dark apartment. Her heart was beating at triple speed.

"Let me double-check he's not here," Justin whispered, taking the lead as they quickly shut the door behind them. The place was tiny, with a hallway leading to just one bedroom and bathroom off a main living and kitchen area. Justin was able to check it out within a few moments.

"I think we're clear. No one's here."

Gabby should've been relieved, but the feeling in her gut just intensified. *Something isn't right.*

"Do you want to look around in the other rooms? See if you get a vibe off anything? I'll stand by the door, just in case."

Gabby wasn't thrilled at the prospect of going through the apartment alone, but it was smarter to have Justin standing guard.

She entered the small beige bathroom and nudged open the vanity drawer to reveal a mess of soaps and shaving creams. She sorted through it, her palms clammy as she looked for anything that could contain the serum. Then she took a deep breath and opened the medicine cabinet.

It was empty except for a dozen orange prescription bottles lined up on the top shelf. Gabby pulled one down, reading the label. Valium. She was about to put it back when she caught sight of the name on the prescription label. Her hands started to shake.

Lily Carpenter.

CHAPTER TWENTY

Nash waited in the shadows of the darkened alley.

He had been there twenty minutes already, and if the person he was waiting for didn't come soon, he'd be forced to leave.

He'd give it five more minutes.

His thoughts shifted to Sabrina. Not many people could surprise him, but he had a hard time getting a clear read on her. He was still frustrated by what had transpired the night before. Clearly, she'd seen something — or someone — in the woods while she was running. And she seemed spooked all over again the second he asked her about it. What was she not telling him? He shouldn't have left her house so quickly. He knew that. If he'd been less reactive, waited, given her some time, she might have told him the truth.

Suddenly, he heard the back door swing open. A broad-shouldered guy in a white T-shirt exited, carrying a crate full of empty bottles on his shoulder. It was the bartender who'd tried to drug Sabrina.

Toby.

It took all of Nash's self-control to stop himself from hurtling straight toward him and bashing him into the brick wall.

Instead, he moved silently through the darkness as Toby dumped the bottles in the bin. When Toby turned back, Nash was right in his face.

Toby puffed his chest out. "What's your problem, man? Back off."

He tried to shove past Nash. Toby was arrogant enough to think he was still in control.

Nash kept his body steady. Toby couldn't move even a fraction of an inch.

"What the hell? Back off, dude." Toby tried to shove Nash again, but this time Nash shoved back, sending Toby stumbling against the trash cans.

Toby's eyes narrowed. "You messed with the wrong guy." He made a fist and took a swing. Nash easily dodged the jab and returned with a right hook of his own. When it connected with Toby's jaw, the shattering sound echoed through the alley.

Toby recoiled and Nash shoved an elbow against his throat, backing him to the wall. That was when Toby realized how outmatched he really was.

"Take whatever you want. I have, like, eighty bucks in my wallet," Toby said.

"I don't want your money," Nash said in a low, calm voice. "I want you to stay away from Sabrina."

"Sabrina?" Toby blinked a few times. "That girl who came in the other day? Nothing happened, bro. I swear."

"I know what you did."

Toby looked as if he was going to protest but then saw Nash's face.

"Is that what you do every time a girl doesn't want to go home with you?"

"I'm sorry. It was a mistake." He was almost crying now.

Nash pressed his elbow in harder. "If you ever slip a drug into someone's drink — anyone's — I will know and I will be back." Nash held his gaze for a moment, tightening his grip. "Nod your head if you understand."

Toby nodded weakly and Nash removed his elbow. "Get out of here," he instructed.

Toby quickly scurried back into the bar before Nash made a fast exit from the alley himself. He had to make one more stop before this night could be over.

CHAPTER TWENTY-ONE

Gabby watched as Z pulled down the rest of the prescription bottles from Devon Warner's medicine cabinet. The rest of the group had joined her and Justin in the apartment after he had texted them that it was all clear.

"Xanax, Effexor, Ambien," Z said, inspecting the labels. "These meds are all for different things — anti-anxiety, depression, sleeping pills. And every single one is prescribed to Lily Carpenter."

"What kind of doctor prescribes so many pills all at once?" Gabby wondered.

Z pulled the rest of the bottles down from the shelf. "Looks like it wasn't just one doctor. They're all prescribed by different ones, but around the same time. I guess Lily was a doctor shopper."

Gabby's impression of Lily kept getting fuzzier. Maybe she was being ignorant, but she never imagined the woman who sold her two pine-scented Christmas candles last year was so mentally unstable that she needed an arsenal of drugs. And wasn't "doctor shopping" against the law?

"Do you think Devon took these from her house that night?" Gabby asked Z. "It's definitely proof he was there." The bracelet was proof, too, but all the intelligence they'd gleaned from it had come from Gabby's vision and Z's superhearing. This was the first piece of solid proof they'd come across that Devon and Lily were, indeed, connected.

"It's proof he was there … or that she was here," Z replied thoughtfully. "I mean, what if Lily slept over here a lot? Like if her and Devon were dating … who knows what secrets she might have told him then."

Gabby frowned, the scenario feeling wrong to her. "Isn't she a lot older than him?"

"Maybe he liked that."

While Z continued her inspection, Gabby entered the bedroom tentatively.

Devon's bed was unmade, a navy blue comforter lying in a jumbled mess of sheets near the end of the mattress. As odd as Lily's cabin had been, Gabby couldn't imagine a mature professional woman like Lily spending the night here. A solitary nightstand stood beside the bed, only a lamp and an alarm clock on top. An oak dresser was against the wall, the top devoid of framed photos or anything personal.

The one thing Devon seemed to take pride in was the tall bookshelf in the corner of his bedroom, overflowing with hardback and paperback books. She ran her finger along the book spines: everything from Tolstoy and Shakespeare to Franzen and Rowling. The pages were worn and dog-eared, as if they'd been read over and over, as Gabby often did with her collection. It was the library of a book lover, the last thing she expected to find here. It was hard to imagine Devon as anything other than a man who had beat up Sadie Webb, stole from her and maybe murdered someone else.

Gabby held her breath as she opened the top drawer of the bureau, wondering if she should call Z in for moral support. Who knew what she'd find in there? A bloody knife? A severed head? To her relief, it was just dozens of balled-up socks. Should she try to touch them? She hesitated, but nothing came of it. She was about to close the drawer when something stopped her. She listened to her instincts.

She reached in again, and this time, her fingers caught something leathery in the back corner. Gabby pulled the drawer all the way out to find three wallets, all creased and seemingly used but empty. Two were men's wallets made of black leather, but the third was daintier, a robin's-egg blue. It had to belong to a woman.

Gabby picked it up and the involuntary spasm began immediately, her eyes fluttering. *Sweat.* It was still dark and hazy, but the first thing she sensed was the acidic smell of hot sweat clinging to a body. Voices swirled around her, so close, too close. She felt confined, claustrophobic. So crammed in that she could barely move her arms.

Her eyes fluttered, but Gabby pressed her fingers more firmly on the wallet, willing herself to stay in the vision.

She was on a bus. She knew it before she could see it. Within a few seconds, the darkness had begun to dissipate and the picture unfolded around her. A crowded bus at rush hour.

She knew instinctively she was in Devon Warner's body. Next to him stood a young guy, eighteen or nineteen, with broad shoulders and a shaved head, clicking shut a flip phone. The landscape looked unfamiliar to Gabby, but a few billboards caught her eye, one advertising the University Medical Center of El Paso. She was in Texas?

"You ready?" the guy asked Devon. It appeared they were friends.

She could feel Devon's muscles tensing. *Something's about to happen.*

Then the bus lurched to a stop, and Devon stumbled into a woman next to him. "Sorry," he said, before heading to the exit door.

Suddenly, the vision jumped forward a few minutes, disorienting Gabby. Devon was running down a street; she could feel his heart pounding. The teenage guy from the bus sprinted next to him. They rounded a corner, the two of them slowing to enter an alley, before Devon slouched and began to vomit.

"Gabby …"

Z's voice took Gabby out of the vision for good.

"Are you okay? It sounded like you were gagging."

"Was I?" Gabby was surprised, but when she put her hand to her stomach, she felt it contracting as if she had been retching herself. She held up the wallet for Z. "He stole this wallet. From a lady on a bus."

"He took the bracelet from that waitress, too. Maybe he's a kleptomaniac."

"Maybe …" Gabby said, but something about that answer didn't fit. She'd spent a long time researching mental illnesses when her OCD had first taken hold. Kleptomania was a compulsion, too, possibly even a variant of obsessive-compulsive disorder. But this wasn't a compulsion for Devon, Gabby was pretty sure. It had felt like pure, scorching desperation.

"No. He's not a kleptomaniac," Gabby said firmly. "He's not doing it for the rush. He needs the money … I have a feeling what I just saw happened a long time ago, though."

"Why do you say that?"

Gabby paused, letting the details of the vision come back to her. "The billboards." Z looked at her for more. "Out the window, I saw some billboards. One was for *Ratatouille* — that movie with the rat chef. That came out when we were kids, right?"

"You guys! Come here!" Sabrina called from outside the room, interrupting.

Gabby and Z found the others gathered in the tiny hallway by an open closet.

"I found a safe in here," Sabrina said, peeking out of the closet. "A tiny one under the carpet."

"How did you think to do that?" Z asked, impressed.

Sabrina shrugged. "The edge of the carpet was already coming up a little. I pulled it back and there it was. It's bolted in pretty good, though."

"Yeah, it is," Justin said as he crouched down, trying to lift it up. "I don't think we can move it without some kind of electric screwdriver or something. If I try to move it with my mind, I might blow a hole in the floor."

"Do you think you can just open it?" Sabrina asked him. "Undo the lock with your mind?"

"Maybe …" Justin said, leaning back. Gabby clicked her tongue nervously, her inner radar growing stronger again. *Get out while you can.*

"You guys, we should go," Gabby pleaded. "It's already been a while."

"If the serum is anywhere in this apartment, it's probably in the safe," Sabrina said. "Two more minutes and then I promise we'll go. Andrew, stand by the window as lookout."

Andrew moved quickly to the small kitchen, standing behind the faded sheet that served as a curtain.

"Let's see if I can make this happen." Justin focused on the safe door. For several long beats, it was completely silent, nothing happening.

Gabby bit her lip, the knot in her stomach growing to the size of a grapefruit. But before she said anything, she heard a scraping sound from the lock, metal against metal, the latch unlocking.

"You did it," she said, astounded. Justin looked pretty shocked himself.

They huddled in the cramped space to get a closer look as Justin pulled open the safe door all the way. There was no vial of serum in the small velvet-lined safe. There was just one thing.

A small silver handgun.

Justin reached out to touch it, but before he could lay a finger on it, a creaking noise from the living room stopped them all in their tracks.

It sounded as if someone had just walked through the front door.

The footsteps crossed the apartment quickly. Gabby tried to control her breathing. Justin stood up in the closet, flexing his body, preparing to attack.

"Who's there?" a gruff, familiar voice called out.

Nash.

"Just us," Gabby croaked in relief.

Nash entered the hallway. Though his face bore its usual impenetrable expression, there was anger in his eyes. "What the hell? I could've killed you."

Gabby swallowed. There was a pistol in his right hand. His knuckles were bruised and caked with blood. Where had he just come from?

"Way to look out, Andrew," Justin grumbled.

Andrew defended himself. "I swear, he came out of nowhere."

"What are you guys doing here?" Nash asked.

The five of them shared an uncertain glance.

"We got Devon's address," Sabrina said, taking the lead. "We figured we'd take a look."

Nash glared. "Without telling us? Do you know how much danger you all put yourselves in?"

I do, Gabby wanted to shout.

"But why haven't you told us about this place?" Z asked.

"Because I've been conducting surveillance and collecting evidence for the last two days. It appears Devon Warner hasn't been back to his apartment for at least a week. We wanted to make sure there was no immediate danger before we brought you in. I came back tonight to grab a safe I discovered last time and then we were going to call you all." He stopped, as if he suddenly knew why they were huddled around the closet. "I see you found the safe, too."

They nodded and he pulled a drill from his black backpack. "You want to let me at it?"

"We managed to open it up ourselves," Z said. "Or Justin did."

"With what?" Nash asked.

Justin shrugged. "My brain."

Even through Nash's annoyance at finding them there, Gabby could tell he was grudgingly impressed. Nash kneeled at the safe and carefully examined the gun. "It's a .357 Magnum."

"What does that mean?" Justin asked.

"It's the same type of gun Devon stole from Sadie Webb," Andrew said.

Nash paused, as if debating what he was about to reveal.

"What is it?" Z prodded him.

"It's also the same type of gun used to kill Lily Carpenter."

* * *

Later, as they trudged down the dark street toward Z's car, the eerie feeling returned to Gabby, even more strongly than before. It was a prickly sensation, a taste in her mouth.

But finally she was able to recognize what it was.

It wasn't fear. It was the distinct feeling of being *watched*. And someone had been doing it all night.

CHAPTER TWENTY-TWO

The hallways of Cedar Springs High were beginning to empty, ten minutes after the final bell.

As Andrew waded through a group of lacrosse players playfully jousting with their sticks in the hall, he almost felt he was part of the hubbub. No, the serum hadn't improved his athletic ability, but that didn't matter. Because he actually had a place to go after school — and it had nothing to do with the case. After their intense evening at Devon Warner's apartment last night, where they'd found the same type of gun used to kill Lily Carpenter, it seemed even more certain that Devon was their guy. As embarrassing as it was to get caught like that at the apartment by Nash, Andrew preferred to look at it as a learning experience. The five of them learned that when Patricia and Nash didn't inform them of every single detail, it was because they were trying to keep them safe. And Patricia and Nash learned that the Lost Causes were perhaps more capable than they even imagined. Andrew saw the look on Nash's face when he realized Justin cracked the safe open with his eyes.

Nash was running tests on the gun, and today, Andrew was trying something else entirely.

"Andrew! Hey!" Eric MacNamar said, welcoming him with a high five as Andrew stepped into one of the math classrooms.

When Andrew had first seen the flyer advertising for new Mathletes last week, he ignored it the way he ignored all the club and group notices that appeared on the bulletin board outside the cafeteria. But he'd passed by the meeting on his way out of school yesterday, heard them discussing parametric equations and found himself pulled in. He stayed for the entire meeting and even agreed to return today.

He'd debated if he would really do it. Yet here he was.

"I'm so glad you came back!" Ali Hanuman exclaimed. That was a huge compliment, coming from her. She'd been at the top of their grade the last two years and now *she* was the one excited to have Andrew on the team? Andrew grinned. People didn't usually greet him so warmly. Was this what it was like to be Justin? Why that guy didn't have a permanent smile on his face was beyond him.

"Hello again, Andrew," Ms. O'Reilly called out from beside the dry-erase board. Andrew had been terrified of her in geometry last year, but now he flashed her an easy smile.

"Are you officially joining the team?" she asked.

"I think so." Andrew still had commitments to Nash and Patricia, but there was no reason to let his skills go to waste during his time off.

"Fantastic," Ms. O'Reilly replied as she projected a string of equations on the board. "We have a qualifying meet coming up in two weeks. If we're going to get through to regionals, we need each member to be on point. Today let's try some problems from the individual round at last year's semifinals."

She passed out scratch paper to the group and everyone got to work. These questions were much harder than anything they were doing in Greenly's class, but Andrew had the answers within fifteen minutes.

"First again today?" said Krissy, a senior. "No way."

Ms. O'Reilly reviewed Andrew's page, shaking her head in astonishment. "Very impressive, Andrew. You've come a long way in a year."

He made a mental note to wait a few more minutes next time. Nash had warned them to fly under the radar.

Ali said, "You do that at these meets, and we're going to nationals."

Eric nodded vigorously. "Crested Butte can suck it."

When the meeting ended an hour later, Andrew was dreaming of leading his team to the national championship. The winners even got to go to the White House to meet the president. Who else in Cedar Springs got to do that?

All thoughts of what he would say to the president vanished when he saw Nash in the doorway.

"Hello," Ms. O'Reilly said, noticing Nash at the same time. "Can I help you?" She quickly raked her hand through her hair, flashing a smile.

"Hey, there," Nash replied. "I'm Andrew's cousin. Here to pick him up. Flew in from Massachusetts yesterday." He had effortlessly adopted a Boston accent and taken on a charming persona Andrew had never seen from Nash before. If it was possible for a woman to melt in a guy's gaze, Andrew was seeing it before his very eyes.

"It's so nice to meet you," Ms. O'Reilly gushed. "Your younger cousin here is quite the mathematician. I've never seen someone solve deductive reasoning questions so fast."

"Is that so?" He cocked his head at Andrew. "Let's go, buddy. You can tell me all about it in the car."

As he and Nash walked through the empty courtyard, Nash said, "Way to fly under the radar."

Andrew rolled his eyes. "Please. It's not like anyone would ever guess that it's because an FBI agent drugged me with a serum that suddenly made me a genius."

Nash shrugged. "You're probably right about that."

"What are you even here for?" Andrew asked.

"You'll see."

*   *   *

Nash led Andrew to the white van parked several blocks from school on an empty street near the woods. Patricia was up front, tapping away on a laptop until Andrew entered the car.

"He was in a Mathletes meeting," Nash said. He slid into the driver's seat, though he didn't turn the engine on. Patricia pressed her lips together, hiding a smile.

"What's going on?" Andrew asked. Every other time he'd met with them, the other four had been there, too.

"We need your help," Patricia replied.

"Where's everyone else?"

"We haven't called them yet," said Nash. "Hopefully your friends will be patient this time."

"We felt we could use *your* help the most right now, Andrew," Patricia explained. Andrew actually felt a surge of pride.

"Sure," he said. "What do you need?"

"Devon Warner hasn't returned to his apartment in a week and I doubt he will anytime soon, if he ever does," Nash told him. "Our initial ballistics tests show that the gun found in the safe appears to be the exact one used to kill Lily Carpenter. At this point, Devon Warner is our prime suspect."

Andrew couldn't believe it. Their work had actually led the FBI to something real. Maybe Devon hadn't been back to the apartment because he had the serum and was now on the run. It was frightening to think that whatever plan he had for the serum might already be in motion.

"As I see it, the timeline plays out like this. We know the guy's a thief. When he shows up to Lily's house, he has the bracelet he'd stolen

167

from Sadie Webb — two days earlier — in his pocket," Nash said. "So he tortures Lily, steals the serum and kills her with the gun he stole from Sadie. Then as he's leaving, the bracelet falls out of his pocket."

"Why take the bracelet with him?" Andrew asked.

"It's almost as good as cash. And he was about to go on the run with the serum," said Nash.

"Then after he stole the serum, he returns home to put the gun away in his safe?" Andrew asked dubiously.

"Maybe he needed to change course on the fly," Nash suggested. "He returns home with the gun, some of the prescriptions he stole from Lily —"

"Z thought maybe Lily was the one who brought those prescription bottles to his apartment. Like they were dating or something."

Patricia shook her head. "I sincerely doubt that. But we are still looking into possible connections between Lily and Devon. So far, we've come up with nothing. It's more likely he stole the bottles from her home at the time of the murder. Those are worth several hundred dollars on the street."

"She was really on all that medication?" Andrew didn't know much about FBI recruiting, but mental illness didn't seem to be an ideal trait.

Patricia paused. "Lily had some family issues she was dealing with."

Andrew shifted in his seat. "So how can I help?"

"We need to find out who Devon Warner is and where he has gone," Nash said. "How did he discover the serum? What was his connection to Lily? Was he working with someone else?"

Andrew thought back to what Lily had said to Sabrina in the cabin. *I know why they want it.*

"We want you to pull every piece of cyber-information you can find on him," Nash continued. "In case anything relevant somehow escaped my notice." The way he said it, Andrew could tell he thought that was impossible. Patricia gave Andrew a quick wink and he suppressed a grin.

She opened a file folder to reveal a photo of a man and woman on the street. "This is a street cam photo pulled from outside the Tipsy Tavern on the night Devon Warner left with Sadie Webb." This had to be the photo Nash showed Z at Sadie's apartment.

Devon was well illuminated by the streetlight above him, his muscular build apparent even at a distance. He was dressed in jeans and a black leather jacket, his arm around Sadie.

"We have a whole sequence of photos that shows them leaving the bar together. Sadie got into her car to drive to the motel while Devon walked down the street to the liquor store. Here's another image from outside the store. He bought a twelve-pack of beer that he brought back to the room."

Patricia flipped through to the next page. "This is the lease agreement for the apartment in Falcon Rock that you all went to. Devon signed a year's lease five months ago. There's a social security number on there, which may prove helpful when you go through the federal search databases."

Andrew nodded, slightly overwhelmed. "Federal search databases?" Patricia looked at Nash.

"I'll give you some passwords," Nash said gruffly. "See what you can find."

* * *

Three hours later, Andrew was on the cyber-trail of Devon Warner from the small desktop computer in his room. If you typed most people's names into Google, a few hits would come up right away. A Facebook or Instagram page. Maybe an article from a local paper or a white pages listing. But "Devon Warner Falcon Rock" had brought up nothing like that, nor had any of the other dozens of search parameters Andrew had thought of.

He clicked out of the Internet browser, feeling nervous. It was time to go deeper. His pulse quickened with excitement. He'd been itching for an assignment like this where he could really let his new analytical abilities loose. Maybe when this case was over, he could ask Patricia about becoming an FBI analyst after he graduated. With all his illnesses, he never had an answer to the "what do you want to be when you grow up" question. But if he could do this kind of thing all day and actually get paid for it, it would be a dream job.

He opened the Colorado Department of Motor Vehicles database, using the passwords Nash provided. It took him a few minutes to run the search query. Finally images began popping up on the screen, one by one, until a total of three driver's licenses came up. Each belonged to a different Devon Warner.

His eyes darted between the street-cam photo Patricia gave him and the driver's license images, trying to find the match. One Devon Warner was in his late teens, making him way too young. One was African American and a good foot shorter. But the final image — the most recently procured license — belonged to the Devon Warner in question. Even though it was immediately obvious by the way the photos matched — Devon had a beard and long brown hair parted in the middle, just as he did in the street-cam photo — Andrew confirmed that the social security number matched the one Patricia had given him.

Devon obtained the license five months ago, the same time he'd rented the apartment in Falcon Rock. He didn't own a vehicle, though it appeared he rented one whenever he needed. His license had been scanned several times at the local Enterprise franchise.

What next?

Andrew could pull up a credit report on Warner using the social security number. He could see which credit cards he had in his name and if Devon had used them recently. If he had, that could suggest where he was hiding. Nash had probably gone through the records himself, but it was worth another try. Wasn't that what Patricia wanted of him? To find something Nash had missed?

A slight throbbing had erupted behind his eyes, and Andrew massaged his temples with his fingers. He'd had a few headaches, varying in magnitude, over the last few days. He wasn't sure if it was all the screen time he'd been logging, or if it was, somehow, a side effect of his sudden brain power, all the synapses suddenly firing so rapidly that they literally made his head hurt. Of course, there was another option, too … that the pain in his head right now was all imagined. But he couldn't let himself believe that one. Patricia said their old symptoms would go away. Everyone else's had.

He took a gulp of water and shifted his focus to the credit reports. Unsurprisingly, Devon had no credit cards. No bank accounts either.

He continued down the report. Before Falcon Rock, Devon's last listed address was in Homer, Alaska, where he'd seemingly been for two years. Before that, there were two addresses in North Dakota. Clearly, Devon Warner was a big fan of cold weather.

A pattern jumped out at Andrew as he studied the report. In Alaska and North Dakota, Devon had lived more of a life. He had bank accounts, credit cards, even a car lease. But he had none of those things since moving to Colorado. In fact, he'd closed all of his previous accounts. Was he running from something — or someone — in Alaska?

"Hey, Hype." Andrew swiveled to see his older sister, Morgan, at the door. Hype was short for "hypochondriac," the not-so-clever nickname she had given him several years ago.

"What are you doing here?" he asked, minimizing the browser window in what he hoped was a nonchalant fashion. His sister was a freshman at Colorado State Pueblo, and she'd made a big production over the fact that she wasn't going to be coming home every weekend.

"The piece-of-crap washing machine in our dorm broke. I need my uniform cleaned by tomorrow morning." Unlike Andrew, Morgan had actually used her tall and lanky genes to her advantage, as the outside hitter on her college volleyball team.

"So, what were you so busy hiding on your computer?" she asked, raising an eyebrow at him. So much for nonchalance.

"Nothing."

Morgan rolled her eyes. "I bet I could guess. Looking up your newest symptoms on WebMD."

"I don't have any symptoms right now," Andrew retorted before realizing that was exactly the wrong way to shut Morgan up.

"Really? There's nothing bothering you? Not one thing?"

The look of disbelief on her face was so blatant that Andrew declined to mention the headache that had just flared up. "Nope. I feel great."

She looked at him for a long moment, her close-set tawny eyes a mirror image of his. "That's amazing." Her face was still etched with shock, but there was something else there, too … was it *happiness*? Was she actually relieved that he was feeling better? His gaze drifted toward a Batman snow globe on his desk. Morgan was the one who'd given it to him, after debilitating stomach cramps had landed him in the hospital for five days. She'd even used three weeks of her own allowance to buy it for him. Back then, Morgan used to muster sympathy for him. But as time passed, something had shifted in her — the sense of duty morphing into deep resentment. Andrew doubted he'd had a real conversation with her in years. "So how did this amazing recovery happen?" Morgan asked. "Medical marijuana or something?"

Andrew shrugged. "Something like that." A slight smile tugged at his lips. Patricia *did* say the serum operated like a drug.

"And what are you looking at that's so secret?" she asked, and before he could stop her, she grabbed the mouse, reawakening his screen. Straight to the Colorado DMV page.

Crap.

"What the …" Morgan trailed off, her confusion slowly turning to excitement. "No way. Are you making fake IDs?"

"Uh, yeah," Andrew replied, grateful for the out. "You, uh, caught me." He flashed Morgan a conspiratorial grin.

"Can you make me one?" she asked. "This guy from my dorm promised he was going to get me one, but he totally flaked."

Could he actually pull it off?

"Ah … sure." He'd figure it out somehow. It couldn't be that difficult.

"Awesome." She gave his shoulders a quick squeeze. "Thank you."

She was almost out the door when she turned back. "Oh, but don't do a Colorado one for me. It's harder for bouncers to tell a fake if you use an out-of-state ID that they don't see a lot. Like Maine or Alaska or something."

Alaska.

The wheels in Andrew's head were already turning before the door had shut behind her.

He hadn't looked up Devon's driver's license from Alaska, where he lived just before Falcon Rock. It might tell him more about Devon's life up there, maybe give him another lead.

He typed the name into the Alaska DMV database. There was just one Devon Warner in the state, and his social security number matched the one Patricia had given him. Andrew clicked on the name, waiting for a few seconds as the image loaded up on the screen.

Devon was clean-shaven in this license photo, and his hair was shorter, just grazing his cheeks.

Andrew was going to double-check the address on the license when something caught his eye. He zoomed in on Devon's photo on the Colorado license, then zoomed in to the photo on the Alaska license. He placed the images side by side on his screen.

Something was off. The man in the Alaska photo had the same

wide-set eyes as the man in the Colorado photo. But they didn't have the hazel undertones. The nose bridge was slightly thinner. And above the left eye, on the Colorado ID, there was a thin red scar. It looked old, maybe left over from a childhood fall.

But the scar was nowhere to be found on the Alaska ID.

Andrew's stomach dipped as he suddenly understood why the Devon Warners in these two IDs looked different.

Because they weren't the same person.

CHAPTER TWENTY-THREE

"It's called ghosting," Nash explained to the Lost Causes seated around the maple table at Cytology. Sabrina glanced between the two images projected side by side on the screen behind him. One was a photo from Devon Warner's Alaska driver's license and the other from Devon Warner's Colorado license. Andrew had already explained how they were actually two different men. The question now was how that was even possible.

"Ghosting is a specific form of identity theft," Nash explained, his eyes grazing the room. Sabrina couldn't quite meet his eye. She still felt sheepish about the way things had played out between them all at Devon's apartment. Nash had only been looking out for their safety by keeping them out of there. It made sense when she thought about it logically. Why would the FBI bring five teenagers into a potential murderer's home unless they could vouch for their safety as much as possible? Sabrina was annoyed she'd let Z's frenzied worrying create so much doubt in her.

And yet … she couldn't forget the warning she'd received from the ghost, either.

You can't trust them.

Was it possible she was putting too much stock in what this girl whispered to her? Sabrina had no idea who the girl was or how she possibly fit in to any of this. Sabrina wasn't even sure if the girl *did* fit into the story. What Sabrina did know, though, was that Patricia and Nash seemed as intent on solving this case as the five of them were. Maybe it was time to start trusting them more than a ghost.

Sabrina caught Nash watching her and she immediately straightened up. His knuckles were still a mess, as they had been at Devon's apartment. No one had dared to ask him, but she wondered what had happened. Not that she was holding her breath she'd get an answer.

"This is the original Devon Warner," Nash said, pointing to the man on the Alaska ID. "Up until about nine months ago, he was living in Alaska, working on an oil rig. Then, according to his former boss — I spoke to him this morning — one day he just disappeared. Never showed up to work. No forwarding address. No goodbye."

Z frowned. "Did they report him missing?"

Nash shook his head. "They figured he'd just moved on to the next job. It's pretty common on the rigs. It's hard hours. Long periods of time away from your family. People get burnt out. Sometimes they even flip out.

"The day before Devon left, there was a small explosion on board. No one was seriously injured, but it spooked a lot of the guys. A few men besides Devon skipped work the next day, too. And then a month later, Devon Warner pops up in Colorado. Same social security number. But it's a completely different person."

"How can that be?" Gabby asked.

Patricia broke in. "That's how ghosting works. The man in the Alaska ID, the original Devon Warner who went missing, must have died or he would have surfaced by now. Murdered, most likely. And then this man, the Falcon Rock Devon Warner, whatever his name really is, just stepped in and took his place. Assumed his identity. He's probably the one who killed him in the first place."

"He killed him to get a clean identity?" Sabrina asked, trying to make sure she was following.

Andrew nodded. "That was obviously valuable to him. Once he took over the Devon Warner identity, he managed to erase whoever he was before, whatever record he had. He's been living here with a blank slate for five months."

That meant the guy they were after could literally be anybody. A former FBI agent, a criminal, a member of a foreign government ... the possibilities were endless. Many people could put the serum to good use.

"Why do you think he picked Devon Warner as his new identity?" Z wondered.

"Usually the ghoster picks a person around the same age and with a similar build so they can easily take over the ID," Patricia explained. "As you see from the photos, these two men weren't identical, but they resembled each other enough to pass through undetected at what was probably a busy DMV office. Especially with the beard shaved off, it's difficult to tell."

Sabrina's head was spinning. "So what does this mean?"

"It means we need you all to help us figure out two things," Nash said. "First, who is this man?" He pointed to the Colorado ID photo of Devon Warner. "We know he assaulted Sadie. We know he had the gun used to kill Lily in his apartment. But who was he before he assumed this identity? Was he someone with an FBI connection? Is that how he knew about this serum? Is he a gun for hire? What criminal history did he have in his old life?"

He stood up and began pacing. "Second, where has he escaped to? Has he shed this identity already and assumed another one? Or is he just lying low?"

Sabrina looked around the room and wondered if the others felt as overwhelmed as she did.

"Whenever you find anything, no matter how small, you let us know." Nash's eyes found Sabrina's. Did he know she was keeping something from him? She looked down quickly. "We're dealing with someone who is very dangerous. No charging into places without us. Be careful and keep your eyes open. We'll reconvene here tomorrow to see if we've made any progress. You guys should get to school — first bell is in fifteen minutes."

Patricia and the others filed out of the room, but Sabrina hung back with Nash. She wasn't sure what she wanted to say, but she didn't like the weird vibe between them.

"Did you need something, Sabrina?" he asked coldly. His detached expression made him seem like a completely different person than the one who had lifted her off the ground and into his arms just days ago.

"I'm sorry that I didn't tell you we were going to Devon's apartment." The words tumbled out of her mouth, unplanned.

He looked as if he expected her to say more.

"It seemed like you were mad at me," she added.

"It's my job to ensure your safety. Don't make it hard for me to do my job. That's it."

Strictly business. Sabrina flushed, though she knew she shouldn't have been surprised. With her foray into Devon Warner's apartment, she'd suddenly turned herself into a petulant child in his eyes, a problem to be dealt with.

"It won't happen again," Sabrina replied.

"I appreciate that." He raised an expectant eyebrow at her. "Now that we've agreed to full disclosure, are you ready to tell me what really happened in the woods?"

She paused. All she wanted was this tension between them to go away, but something still held her back from telling him about the girl in the woods. Even if Sabrina wasn't sure whether she trusted her.

Nash's stare was firm. "So, is that a no?"

She didn't like the edge in his voice — or his hypocrisy. It wasn't as though Nash divulged every detail of his life either. The double standard was starting to annoy her.

"I don't know," she answered combatively. "Do you want to tell me what happened to your hand?" He followed her gaze to his bruised knuckles. "If you're set on full disclosure, then you won't have a problem telling me."

"Sure." He didn't even blink. "I met up with my friend Toby. The bartender."

Sabrina was caught off guard. And not just because he'd called her bluff. He'd beaten up the guy who slipped something into her drink in Falcon Rock.

"Don't look so surprised. When I told you I'd take care of it, I meant it."

He locked his eyes on her and she saw a flicker of vulnerability in them. He wasn't exactly tearing down the wall he'd built between them, but it was as if he'd knocked a few bricks out. "Thank you," she finally said.

He turned back to his computer, effectively dismissing her. "You don't have to thank me," he said brusquely. "I wasn't going to let a serial rapist just roam around."

"Right," Sabrina muttered, her cheeks flaming. This had nothing to do with her. It was just another part of Nash's job. Law enforcement. "Sorry to add another thing to your plate."

Sabrina walked quickly to her car without turning back.

Frustrated, she jabbed her key into the ignition.

And then she screamed.

It was the girl from the woods again. She was in the passenger seat, but there wasn't a chill in the air this time. Just a radiant warmth enveloping them both.

"What's your name —" Sabrina started. Before she could get an answer, the girl disappeared.

"No! Don't go!" Sabrina shouted desperately, her heart slamming against her chest.

She put her head against the steering wheel and tried to regain control of her breathing. When it finally returned to normal, she glanced over at the passenger seat again. There was still no sign of the girl.

But the seat was sopping wet.

CHAPTER TWENTY-FOUR

Gabby sat across the table from Andrew at the school library, trying to pay attention to his third attempt at explaining molecular mass.

Even through the worst of her OCD, she had always managed to be an above-average student. Once she got through her rituals, she could settle in and focus on the task at hand. But that was back when she had hours of time every afternoon and evening. Now she was so busy that reading assignments were piling up and math problem sets were left half done.

Luckily, Andrew had been sitting next to her when Dr. Fields mentioned the upcoming exam Gabby had completely forgotten about. All it took was one look at Gabby's panicked face for Andrew to offer to get her up to speed. The problem was, her mind kept wandering to the Lily Carpenter case and what she could do to help find Devon Warner, a man who tried on and shed identities like winter coats. With someone that skillfully evasive who could vanish without a trace, Gabby knew the best shot the FBI had at generating any kind of lead was through one of the Lost Causes. She had been carrying one of Lily's prescription bottles around with her since she'd found it in his apartment, trying at various points to see if it would "speak" to her. She hoped it might give her a glimpse into who Devon Warner really was. But she hadn't gotten a single vision from the bottle.

"I guarantee you he's going to ask about that lab we did in class," Andrew said. "Do you have your report for that?"

Gabby flipped through her binder. "I feel like maybe I didn't finish it?"

"Okay, well, the main takeaway from the lab was about calculating molar mass. So molecular mass is the mass of one molecule, while molar mass is the mass of one mole in a molecule."

While Andrew spoke, he also typed on his laptop, one activity having no impact on the other. He wasn't like her dad, who insisted that he *was* listening while his eyes never left the screen of his iPhone and then remembered nothing about the conversation.

His stomach rumbled. "I'm starving. I'm going to get something from the vending machine. You want anything?"

"Maybe some chocolate," Gabby said. If she was going to get through this, she needed some energy.

"Speaking of which, there's a good chemistry question. What's the molar mass of candy?"

"Huh?"

Andrew blew the hair away from his forehead as he scribbled on a piece of paper, "CaNdY."

Gabby met his eyes and saw he was smiling, a big un-self-conscious smile where you could picture exactly what he had looked like as a seven-year-old. "Is that real?" she asked.

"Yup. Calcium, neodymium and yttrium." Gabby wondered if there was anything Andrew didn't know at this point. "Remember what I told you about calculating the molar mass. Try to see if you can do it on your own before I come back."

Gabby was overcome with appreciation. "Thanks for this, Andrew. I would be lost without you right now."

"What are friends for?" he said casually, but it made Gabby wonder. How long had it been since any of them truly had a friend they could count on? She'd forgotten the feeling of belonging that came with friendship. She was feeling less and less like a lost cause.

She started in on the equation, checking back to the periodic table. Then her phone beeped with a text from Justin.

She blushed before she'd even opened it. Gabby found herself thinking about Justin at odd moments of the day. Even seeing his name on group texts made her happy. She liked to imagine where he was when the two of them were reading the same words.

So … she'd developed a slight crush on him. Though *crush* seemed like the wrong word. Crush was what she used to have back in fifth grade. Back then, she'd invite over her three best friends, the "A-list team" they called themselves, and discuss for hours who had crushes on whom, making MASH lists for whom to marry. But of course, that was just silly. Gabby couldn't remember actually *liking* any of those boys. With Justin, it was different.

Hey. I've got a game 2nite if you want to come. Trying your idea if I start sucking like I did in the last game.

He was inviting her out, though Gabby knew better than to get too excited. Someone as popular as Justin probably invited tons of people to come to his games. Still, it had to mean something that he'd liked her suggestion to use psychokinesis on the field.

Another text came quickly.

Unless you already have plans. In which case, don't worry about it.

Her only other plans were going home and listening to her parents obsess over her sister's upcoming meets and their relief that Twinkie the cat was safe at home. Maybe Twinkie ran away in the first place because he was afraid Gabby's parents would pressure him into doing cat shows.

Gabby knew that when you liked a guy, you were supposed to banter and be witty and flirty with your texts. She always overheard girls at lunch discussing what the perfect response to a *What's up* text should be. Gabby must not have been listening hard enough because she had no clue how to jazz up her reply. After a few minutes, with some worry that Justin would text back to rescind the offer, she quickly tapped out a response.

Sure. I'll see you there.

A second later, he answered. *I'll be on the field, but yeah. I'm number 25.*

Even with a simple reply, she'd made a mistake. But she could picture him smiling when he read it, amused by her cluelessness.

She briefly debated texting again, but all she could come up with was *Cool* and then maybe Justin would feel obligated to write something back and she'd again be left with the question of what to say next. Better to just leave it for now. For a second, she wished she had her own gaggle of girlfriends to get her text etiquette up to snuff. Could she ask Sabrina and Z for help with something like that? Z's texts were probably cryptic, loaded with Marxist quotes. Sabrina seemed to have a snappy answer for everything, though. Texts probably flowed right from her brain to her fingertips. Maybe if Gabby got up the courage to ask her, she could help out the same way Andrew was helping her with chemistry.

Suddenly, Gabby thought of something. Had Justin invited only her or had he asked everyone else to come to the game, too?

She looked across the desk, wondering if Andrew had gotten a text from Justin about the game. Was that his phone under his notebook?

Gabby reached for it and accidentally knocked over her backpack. The prescription bottle she'd been toting around with her spilled out along with a handful of pens and pencils.

Quickly, she grabbed the bottle before it could roll off the table and into the hands of the study group at the nearest table. Gabby had no idea how she'd explain coming into possession of medications prescribed to the most famous murder victim Cedar Springs had ever had.

Her eyes caught on Lily's name as she put the bottle back in her bag. What had led her to seek out these medications? What had she been covering behind her smile? Not only had poor Lily died in pain but she'd lived in pain, too. With those thoughts burning in her mind, Gabby was jolted into a vision.

The colors overtook her first. Tangerine orange melded with grapefruit pink and vibrant purple, the colors swirling together like a melting Popsicle.

It was a sunset, Gabby slowly realized. Set against craggy baked-red rocks that were dotted with small shrubs and cacti.

But the sky's warmth couldn't dispel the chill below.

Lily was sitting on a blanket, her long hair covering her face as she cried uncontrollably. The harsh sound clashed with the eerie silence around her.

A small picnic dinner and water were laid out next to her, though they hadn't been touched.

But Gabby understood.

This was no park.

They were in a cemetery.

Lily's body shook as her deep, unrestrained bawling continued, her heaving sobs echoing through the otherwise quiet graveyard.

Finally, Lily dug into her bag, fumbling for the orange prescription bottle, then washed down the pill with the small thermos of water beside her.

When her tears subsided, Lily placed her hand on the headstone, her fingers tracing the engraved letters slowly.

Samantha Hope Carpenter. Beloved Daughter.

Whose life had lasted only eight years.

"I'm sorry," Lily whispered, her voice husky and raw. "I'm sorry."

When Gabby faded out of the vision, her own cheeks were soaked in salty tears.

* * *

Gabby's knowledge of high school football games pretty much came from watching *Friday Night Lights* with her parents years earlier. They loved the show, no doubt due to the town's obsession with the athletic accomplishments of its children.

The Cedar Springs High football game was almost that intense, as the Cedar Springs Bulldogs faced their rival, the Wildcats, the only team who beat them last year. Practically the whole school was packed into the bleachers, and many people had painted their faces blue and white. Gabby saw her friend Ali Hanuman, whom she would have expected to be home studying for their chem exam, sitting a few rows over and waving a blue pom-pom. The whole world had been going to these games except Gabby.

"Thanks for coming with me," Gabby said to Sabrina when they settled into the bleachers. Apparently Justin had not texted their whole group about the game (not that that meant anything), but the idea of arriving alone was so terrifying that she'd asked Sabrina to go with her.

"No problem," Sabrina replied as the Wildcats broke out of their huddle for the first play of the game. "It's nice to have a distraction and do something normal."

Sabrina gave Gabby's shoulder a squeeze. They'd made a pact not to discuss Devon Warner or Lily Carpenter or anything else about the case here. It was a welcome relief because Gabby had been driving herself crazy analyzing the vision of Lily crying at what seemed to be her daughter's grave. Patricia had told them in the cabin that Lily didn't have children. The vision seemed to prove otherwise, which, of course, convinced Z that they'd finally caught Patricia in an outright lie and they needed to call her on it immediately.

Gabby and the others thought there was a much more reasonable explanation. Yes, Patricia told them that Lily didn't have kids, but technically that was true. According to the small gravestone Gabby saw, Lily's daughter died more than ten years ago. It made sense that Patricia didn't want to overwhelm them with every detail of Lily's past if it didn't directly affect the case. But was Gabby being naive not to consider Z's point of view?

Suddenly the crowd went nuts, and Sabrina and Gabby leaped to their feet to join them. One of the players on the opposing team had just caught the ball and was sprinting down the field with half the crowd rooting for a tackle and the other half cheering for a touchdown. The sprinter was almost to the end zone, but he'd have to go through Justin first.

"Come on, Diaz!" a student exclaimed from behind her. "Destroy him!"

Justin was poised and ready at the end zone. Gabby clutched Sabrina's arm, surprised by how nervous she was for him. He tucked his head down and hurled himself toward the guy with the ball, ready to steamroll him, but the runner twirled to the side, shaking Justin away like a fly and blowing past him into the end zone for a touchdown. The fans of the opposing team went crazy, high-fiving and fist-pumping while the Bulldogs fans sank into their seats.

"Get your head out of your ass, Justin!" a woman screamed loudly from the front row. Even ten rows back, Gabby knew it was his mother, who apparently liked to bask in the glow of celebrity that came from being the star player's mom … even if she didn't act like his mother any other time. An unexpected surge of protectiveness made Gabby want to strangle her.

"That's weird," Sabrina said. "Justin never misses a tackle like that. I've never been to a game sober, but he's usually a one-man wrecking ball."

"It must be hard to make every tackle," Gabby replied casually. She hadn't told Sabrina about her suggestion to Justin to use his new powers on the field because she wasn't sure if he was actually going to do it. He'd said he'd only try it out if he "started sucking like in the last game." As Gabby watched him pick himself up off the ground, looking at the end zone in disbelief, she figured that play probably qualified.

She waited impatiently while the Bulldogs were on offense and Justin and the rest of the defensive team were on the bench. As soon as Justin stood up to take the field again, he looked up to the bleachers as if he was searching for something. Butterflies erupted in Gabby's stomach when she realized the something he was searching for was her. His eyes found hers and he nodded, his way of telling Gabby he was going to try her idea. She smiled and nodded back, wishing he had Z's power. Then he could hear her think: *You're going to be great.*

"What was that look?" Sabrina asked, bringing Gabby back to reality.

"What look?"

"The one Justin just gave you."

"Oh, I don't know. I think he was just saying hi." Sabrina looked at her skeptically. Had Justin told Sabrina about Gabby's idea?

"You really don't know, do you?" Sabrina asked.

"Know what?"

"Justin was the one who had that thought about you at the cabin. The one about your hair."

Gabby had completely forgotten about that. "Really? How do you know?"

"Justin likes you, Gabby. It's pretty obvious."

"It is?" A momentary thrill circled through her, only to be replaced by fear. How was she supposed to talk to him now? She could barely handle texts.

Sabrina laughed. "I wish I was recording your reaction to this. It's hilarious." But she patted Gabby's arm reassuringly, too. "Don't over-think it."

Down on the field, the teams reassembled and the snap of the ball echoed up to the bleachers. The quarterback for the opposing team dropped back, searching for an open receiver, when Justin began driving through tackles to get to him. He made sure to at least place his hands on the players, but Gabby could tell it was his mind doing all the work. He reached the quarterback in seconds, sacking him before he could get rid of the ball.

The Bulldogs fans started chanting Justin's name. Gabby tried to catch his eye again, but he was too surrounded by high-fives to see her.

* * *

The rest of the game went by in a victorious blur for Justin. Whoever had the ball, he managed to bring down. Plus he was able to get down the field even faster because he was using mental — not physical — strength to make every tackle.

Justin had always dominated games, but it had never felt like this. His tackles used to come from the angriest place inside him, and when the opposing player went down, there was only a split second of calm before the rage came back. Almost every game ended with the team rallied around him, but he had never enjoyed it. When you're angry all the time, even celebrating feels like crap.

But this time when the clock ran down and the scoreboard lit up with the Bulldogs' 45–7 victory, he couldn't wipe the massive grin off his face. He wasn't going to choke in front of the Florida State scout *and* he wasn't going to have to use the antidote or quit the case.

It all happened at once — the crowd rushing the field, the ice-cold Gatorade dumped on top of him, flying through the air as the fans hoisted him up on their shoulders, even a bear hug from Coach

Brandt. Justin tried to break free of all of it, though, because there was only one person he wanted to see. He just hoped she hadn't left already.

He pushed his way through the crowded field, random people high-fiving him and patting him on the back along the way. He thought he spotted her at the end of the field and was headed in that direction when Hindy got in his face.

"Diaz! You were on fire!" Hindy screamed. "We've got to celebrate, man!" Justin just nodded, trying to see past him to where he thought he saw Gabby. Hindy was still talking when Justin spotted her again and he practically shoved Hindy out of the way. She was standing with Sabrina by the Bulldogs bench, craning her neck — maybe she was looking for him, too. He had the urge to bulldoze all these people out of the way with psychokinesis so he could get to her faster, but instead he pushed through the crowd until he finally reached her.

She lit up when she saw him. "Justin! Great —"

She was probably going to say "game," but Justin didn't wait to find out. Instead, he grabbed her hand, pulled her in to him and kissed her.

CHAPTER TWENTY-FIVE

Z wound her way down the back staircase of her house that night on her way to the kitchen. She'd gotten Gabby's text about her vision of Lily at her daughter's grave, and hours later, it was still bothering her.

There were usually several text chains a day among the group. Some were funny, like the one when Sabrina had them convinced for over an hour that Tupac asked her to solve his murder. Some asked for help, like Justin's request that Z listen in for the questions on his English lit test the following week. And some were actually about the case, like this one about Lily's daughter.

Why did Patricia think the Lost Causes didn't need to know about her? There's no way she and Nash could think it wasn't relevant to the case. What if Lily was part of a grieving parents support group and Devon targeted her through that? What else were Patricia and Nash not telling them? How were they supposed to work on the case if they were partly in the dark?

Z knew she had a tendency to read into things more deeply than others. Her very first psychiatrist had told her parents when she was four that she had trust issues with authority figures, something every psychiatrist after him echoed. But Z had never viewed this as a problem. What was wrong with questioning people you were supposed to trust only because they were older? Her paralyzing depression might have disintegrated with the serum, but her belief that trust had to be earned remained. And Patricia and Nash hadn't earned it.

Z could admit she was wrong about going to Devon's apartment alone, but Gabby's vision of the cemetery provided solid proof that Patricia had lied to them. Why was Z the only one who seemed concerned about this? The five of them had texted back and forth after Gabby told them about her vision, and the consensus (minus Z) was that Patricia must have a good reason why she didn't mention Lily's daughter. Justin had even texted before his game, *Don't make this Devon's apartment 2.0, Z.* Andrew was the only one who was partially on her side, but that was mainly because he loved playing devil's advocate, telling them once that it was like giving his super-brain a workout. The most she could do was get them to agree to bring it up at the Cytology meeting the next day.

Z's stomach growled, refusing to be ignored. When she reached the bottom of the staircase, Scott was standing there. She could hear the exasperated voices of their parents coming from the kitchen.

"What are you doing?" Z asked.

"Shhh," he said. "I'm trying to hear how long this fight is going to last so I can ask Dad for the keys to the Bentley. If he's pissed off, he might say no." Z didn't bother asking Scott why his Porsche Cayenne wouldn't cut it tonight. She assumed it was about impressing a girl.

"All I'm saying is it's illegal!" Nicole exclaimed.

"What's illegal?" Z whispered to Scott.

"She keeps seeing some guy driving by and sitting in his van right outside the house. She thinks it's one of the reporters looking for a new angle."

No wonder her mother was so amped up. The second Z's father had been put on the suspect short list for Lily Carpenter's murder, Nicole had taken it as a personal affront to her social status. The first thing she asked Steven was if the police were going to freeze their assets or try to cancel their American Express Black Card.

Z would never admit it to anyone, but when she'd first heard about the murder, it didn't seem completely impossible that her father had been involved, considering that screaming match he'd had with Lily the day before her murder. Every other resident of the area that Steven planned to demolish for his new condominium complex had taken the generous buyout he'd offered without putting up much of a fight. But Lily had refused to sell her cabin. Several construction workers recounted in their police statements that Lily had said she'd sell the cabin "over her dead body," and Steven had angrily replied, "Don't tempt me."

Nothing enraged him more than someone standing in the way of a lucrative business deal. Z didn't think he was capable of the torturing and killing, but she wouldn't put it past him to order someone else to do it. Now that she knew Lily's murder was all about the serum and not the land she was living on, she felt a *twinge* of guilt about her earlier suspicions.

"You don't think it pisses me off, too? They've written five false stories about me. Five!" Steven bellowed. "I've got investors in Russia who will pull out tomorrow if they catch wind of this. But my hands are tied here."

"It's practically stalking!"

"You might be out here for a while," Z told Scott as she sauntered into the kitchen. Her parents didn't acknowledge her presence.

Nicole sank into an armchair at the head of the kitchen table as if she was carrying the weight of the world on her shoulders. "I just don't understand why they're still harassing us like this."

"Because some liberal jackass at the paper hates anyone with money and won't let the story die," Steven snapped. "Probably thinks he's going to win a Pulitzer with this pathetic attempt at journalism."

The throbbing vein on Steven's forehead looked as if it was about to burst. For a split second, Z wondered if he did know something he wasn't telling the cops.

Then she remembered her mother's thought from the other day. Nicole had no idea where Steven had been the night before or what he'd been up to.

That could be innocent enough. Who knew what kind of extracurricular activities her father was hiding from her mother? Just because he'd taken off for a few hours didn't mean he was hiding something about Lily's murder.

"If the guy approaches the gates, I'll have words with him," Steven said as he punched something into his phone. "But I can't do anything when he's out in his van. I haven't even seen him."

Nicole scoffed. "Well, I have. Several times."

Z was about to leave with the leftover pizza she'd grabbed when she stopped short.

A van.

"What color was it, Mom?"

Nicole looked at Z as though she'd totally forgotten her daughter was in the kitchen. "What color was what?"

"The van."

"White, I think."

A white van driving by the house several times a day? Could it have been Nash? Was he keeping tabs on them? It made a lot more sense than a reporter swinging by every few hours.

"Have you caught him on the cameras?" Z asked. They had an extensive security system with several cameras positioned around the perimeter of the house. It was always the first thing their father had installed when they moved in somewhere new.

Her mother gave her an irritated look. "No. It's like he knows where they are. And when I pulled up to the gate last night, he was there, but he sped off the second he saw me."

"Did you get a good look at him?"

"He had dark hair. He was probably in his twenties or thirties, but he drove off so fast that it was a blur."

It had to have been Nash. Z bristled at the violation of her privacy. Even if it was for their so-called protection, Nash could've at least told them he was watching them. She might not have cared so much if it wasn't for the timing. First Lily's daughter, now this. These small details Patricia and Nash consistently left out made her nervous.

Z wanted to solve this case with every bone in her body. She understood how destructive the serum could be in the wrong hands and in the last few days had found herself checking the news app on her phone, afraid of what she would see. That there would be an unexplainable mass killing or terrorist attack where it was only obvious to those assigned to this case that the person who stole the serum was responsible for it.

But that fear wasn't the only thing driving her forward.

Z had asked Patricia when all of this started if the five of them would be forced to inject the antidote if they solved the case. Patricia had answered that it was up to them — it was their choice. But Z hadn't thought to ask about the alternative. What happened if they *didn't* solve the case? Whose choice was it then? Would they strip her of her newfound ability so the only things she'd wake up to the next day were bleakness and depression? It was a question she wasn't sure she wanted answered.

She got back up to her room and debated whether to text the others about the van. They already thought she was reading too much into Gabby's vision, though, so maybe it was better to wait. When her phone beeped with a text from Nash an hour later, it confirmed her decision.

Reminder of meeting tomorrow 8 a.m.

She'd bring up Nash's stalking then. One way or another, she was going to get Patricia and Nash to start telling them the truth. And did Nash really need to send out a reminder? As if any of them would forget they had a meeting about how to stop a psychopathic murderer and save the freaking world.

CHAPTER TWENTY-SIX

"First of all, you're lucky my parents didn't call the cops on you," Z snapped at Nash before Sabrina had even taken her seat at the conference table. The cops? What was Z accusing Nash of now, Sabrina wondered.

"What are you talking about, Z?" Justin asked, equally confused. Sabrina glanced over at Nash to see his reaction, but he was stone-faced, as usual. After their last conversation or argument, or whatever that was, she had finally accepted that he and she might have had a connection at one point, but it wasn't one Nash wanted to explore. Too bad she still had to force herself to tear her eyes away from him.

When Sabrina looked back at Z, she was glaring at Nash, her arms folded across her chest defiantly. "You're watching us."

"What do you mean we're watching you?" Nash asked. Why did the black T-shirts he always wore have to seem specifically designed to make him look hotter? *Focus*, she reminded herself.

"A white van keeps cruising by my house," Z answered. "My parents assumed it was a reporter stalking my dad, but that doesn't make any sense. It's obviously you keeping tabs on us. Ever since we went rogue at Devon's apartment."

Nash was still unruffled. "Let me get this straight. You think we're watching you because you saw a white van drive by your house? The most common color passenger van out there, which is why I rented it in the first place?"

Z looked a little less certain, but she nodded anyway. "Yeah, but it wasn't just that. The guy drives by only at really weird hours. And my mom said he always makes sure to park just out of range of our security cameras so he doesn't show up on the video feed. I doubt some random reporter would be that tech savvy about a security system."

Something shifted in Nash. "Did you get a license plate?"

"No, I never saw the van myself."

"Was it a man driving? A woman?" The way Nash's jaw tensed made Sabrina nervous.

Z also must've picked up on the serious note in Nash's voice because she suddenly lost the attitude. "A guy in his twenties or thirties. My mom could never get a good look at him because he sped off when he saw her."

"So it wasn't you, Nash?" Gabby asked, threading her fingers together nervously.

"No."

"The other night …" Gabby started. Then she stopped herself.

Z practically pounced. "The other night, what?"

"I had this strong sensation someone was watching us. I don't know. I didn't say anything because it was just a feeling, but it could be connected to this van."

Andrew was typing furiously on his laptop. "I knew it," he announced, looking up from his screen. "Devon Warner's ID was swiped three times at Enterprise over the past year. Every time he rented a white Chevrolet Express cargo van. He rented one a month ago and still hasn't returned it."

The room went silent. "So Devon Warner is stalking Z? How would he know about her?" Sabrina finally asked, fear creeping into her voice no matter how much she tried to swallow it.

"What if he was watching us that night at his apartment and started following us?" Andrew wondered.

Patricia held her hand up. "I think we need to calm down. Let's not get hysterical. We don't know for sure that it was Devon Warner in that van."

"But we don't know for sure that it wasn't," Nash pointed out. "We've had an APB out on that van since we started looking into Devon and haven't had a hit yet. If he's still driving the car, it's likely he changed the plates out a while ago. All of you need to keep your eyes open and be careful. If something feels wrong, just assume it is and call us. Especially if you see this van."

Sabrina nodded along with the others. She didn't want to get spooked when they didn't have proof either way, but for once she was thankful for Z's conspiracy theories. Maybe she just had the wrong conspirator this time.

"And just to be clear, Z," Patricia said, annoyance in her voice for the first time. "We have no reason to spy on you. We're on the same side here."

"Then why didn't you tell us that Lily had a daughter?" Z asked.

Here we go again, Sabrina thought.

She expected Patricia to finally lose it on Z, but instead she paled. "What are you talking about?"

Z nudged Gabby. Gabby hesitated but started talking after the second nudge. "I had a vision about Lily." Her voice quavered and Justin moved his chair closer to her. "She was visiting her daughter's grave."

"When we asked you at the cabin if Lily had kids, you said no," Z responded, her voice one degree away from triumphant.

Patricia cleared her throat. "You're right. I didn't tell you that Lily had a daughter. Sam. She was found dead just after her eighth birthday."

"How did she die?" Gabby asked.

"And how do you know it doesn't have to do with the case?" Z had to add.

"It does have to do with the case, but not in the way you think." Patricia breathed deeply. "Lily's daughter is the reason we created the serum in the first place."

Sabrina was now utterly confused. Even Andrew looked lost.

Patricia started at the beginning. "Sam disappeared a little over ten years ago when she was only eight. She was riding her bike home from a friend's house, and she never made it back."

"What happened?" Sabrina asked, even though there was a part of her that didn't want to hear the answer.

"She was abducted. Vanished without a trace. There were the usual alleged sightings that happen with missing persons cases but none we could confirm. We had search parties going for weeks. Lily used every resource she had through the FBI. The chances of finding a missing child go down exponentially every day, but she tried to hold out hope. We all did.

"We ran out of leads quickly. There was literally nothing left. That's when Lily thought to ask for help from a psychic who'd done great work for the FBI before. Lily gave her some of Sam's clothes and belongings and took her to the last place Sam was seen, but she wasn't able to give us anything concrete. A few minor leads that led nowhere, nothing more. Lily was starting to fall apart." Sabrina knew firsthand what something like that would do to a parent, though she wondered if Lily had it even worse than her own family. It destroyed Sabrina's mom and dad when that drunk driver killed Anthony, but at least they knew what happened to him. Not knowing would be much worse, an impossible limbo where mourning felt like giving up, but staying hopeful felt like fooling yourself.

Patricia looked down into her coffee mug. "We'd developed the serum already but hadn't tested it yet. When the psychic didn't give us anything substantial, Lily insisted on ingesting the serum herself. As I told you before, the adult brain doesn't absorb it in a way that makes the compound effective. We didn't know that at the time, though, and we conducted trial after trial trying to figure out what the problem was. We ran out of time. We never got to use it. Sam's body was found by hikers in a remote area of the Sandia Mountains." Patricia paused for a moment. "Lily resigned shortly afterward. We divvied up our portions of the serum at that point, as well."

Sabrina finally understood why Lily had quit her job and retreated to that cabin alone in the woods. "Did they ever find out who did it?" she couldn't help but ask. Did Lily get the closure that may have come with that?

Patricia nodded, her face darkening. "He was caught a few years later. A handyman who had worked around Lily's neighborhood at the time of Sam's disappearance. The police caught him attempting to kidnap another young girl outside of Albuquerque and his fingerprints matched those found on Sam — and, sadly, numerous other victims."

Sabrina swallowed, imagining the horrors endured by those poor girls and the brutalizing pain their families had been forced to suffer through. She looked up and found Nash watching her, an inscrutable expression on his face. He quickly turned his gaze back to Patricia.

"I'm sorry I didn't inform you of all this before," she told the group. "I didn't want Lily's past to distract you from the more relevant details of this case. But when I told you this serum was created for good, I meant it."

Justin gave Z an "I told you so" look and Z rolled her eyes. "I was right that it had to do with the case," Z snapped.

"Which is exactly what we should be talking about right now," Nash said, walking to the projector screen. "We are fairly certain Devon Warner killed Lily Carpenter. We have the bracelet that places him there. The gun found at his apartment was used to kill her. But that means nothing if we can't catch up to him somehow. We know he left Falcon Rock at least a week ago. Where did he go? The more days the serum is out of our possession, the more damage it can do. The only question is how much. We still have no idea if he plans to use it for his own agenda or sell it to someone else."

As Patricia eagerly launched into ideas for generating leads, Sabrina felt something brush her arm. The sudden contact gave her the chills. She looked down and saw the goose bumps popping up.

Was someone else here? She waited for the horrible smell or the lights to flicker, but nothing happened. She was about to dismiss the sensation when the whispering started. It was a low voice that sounded as if it was coming from nowhere and everywhere, but she couldn't make out the words.

Then someone yanked her hair so hard that she almost fell out of her chair. He finally showed himself, appearing right next to Nash.

With the beard and long, shaggy brown hair parted down the middle, she knew exactly who it was.

Devon Warner.

And she was the only one who could see him. No wonder they hadn't been able to find him.

Apparently he — like Lily Carpenter — was dead.

They'd been chasing a ghost.

He was even more shadowy than Lily, looking as if he was standing underneath a rain cloud, his eyes like two pools of blackness.

A putrid sulfur smell overtook her nose as the whispering started again. This time she could finally make out the words.

"'Nature teaches beasts to know their friends.'"

Devon was saying it over and over as if he was programmed on repeat.

"What does that mean?" Sabrina fumbled, afraid he would disappear before she got any answers.

"'Nature teaches beasts to know their friends.'"

"What happened to you?" Sabrina practically shouted over him.

He stopped mid-sentence and his lips curled into a snarl. "The Springs."

He vanished, but the smell lingered. Sabrina blinked slowly, letting everything sink in before she turned to the group staring at her, jaws dropped, even Nash. She couldn't imagine what that exchange had looked like from the outside.

She sat down, trying to slow her quickly beating heart.

"Are you okay?" Nash asked, his eyes boring into hers in a way that only made her heart beat faster.

"I'm fine," she managed. "But you guys aren't going to believe this ..."

"Try us," Z deadpanned.

"I just saw Devon Warner."

The impact registered on each of their faces, one by one. If Devon Warner was dead, who the hell had killed him? And what did it have to do with Lily Carpenter?

Gabby gasped. "If he's dead ..."

"Then who has the serum?" Justin completed her thought.

Everyone started talking at once, but Patricia cut them off. "Did he say anything, Sabrina?"

"Yes." She closed her eyes to recall it exactly. "'Nature teaches beasts to know their friends.' He said it over and over. Then he said, 'The Springs.'"

"'Nature teaches beasts to know their friends.' That's a Shakespeare quote!" Andrew exclaimed. "It's from *Coriolanus*. I skimmed it last year and got a D on the summary test, but I can recite the whole play now!"

"Devon Warner is quoting Shakespeare?" Justin asked incredulously. "Am I the only one who finds that weird?"

"He did have all those books in his apartment," Gabby reminded them.

"So what does the quote mean?" Sabrina asked impatiently.

"It means animals are taught the difference between friends and enemies through their experiences in nature," Andrew answered, going into teacher mode. "A lamb instinctively knows not to go near a wolf because it'll get eaten. But if for some reason a lamb tested this out and approached a wolf, nature would teach him the hard way that a wolf isn't his friend. In the play, Coriolanus knows how to be both the lamb and the wolf."

Justin scowled. "Can you nerd out a little more and tell us what the hell that has to do with Devon?"

"Devon could think he's both a killer and a victim," Patricia said gravely.

"Or that someone he thought was a lamb turned out to be a wolf," Nash suggested. "Maybe a friend stabbed him in the back."

"What was the other thing he said?" Z asked.

Sabrina ran through the encounter again in her head. "'The Springs.' He has to mean the Pikes Peak springs, right?" They were the springs their town was named after, located near the top of the Pikes Peak mountain range. They'd completely dried up a decade ago, as temperatures got warmer and the snow packs in the mountains melted faster. But everyone still referred to the dusty remnants as the Springs.

"Maybe someone stabbed Devon in the back at the Springs," Justin said. "There could still be evidence. Like the knife. I mean, it wasn't very long ago, right, if he killed Lily?"

"Nash meant that someone stabbed him in the back *metaphorically*," Andrew retorted. "Not with an actual knife."

Gabby perked up. "Wait, Justin could be right," she said. "No one goes to the Springs anymore. That could've been where Devon was murdered. It would be the perfect place to hide a body."

Nash was already on his feet. "There's only one way to find out."

CHAPTER TWENTY-SEVEN

It took over an hour to get all the way up to the Springs, thanks to the most winding road Andrew had ever been on. The only reason he was able to hold his motion sickness back was that Sabrina was next to him, completely unfazed by the nauseating twists and turns. He didn't want to embarrass himself in front of her. Justin was tough, but Andrew thought Sabrina was probably the strongest of them all.

They piled out of the van and scattered around the area, searching for something, even though they weren't sure what that something was. Andrew had seen pictures of what the Springs used to look like, but it was hard to believe the dry, cracked dirt underneath his feet had once been a pool the size of a football field.

He planted himself near a bed of twenty or so large rocks. Could Devon or his killer have hidden something underneath one? Andrew held his breath and picked one up.

Nothing but dirt underneath.

As he lifted another heavy rock, it occurred to him that a rock like this could've been used as a weapon, too. What if whoever killed Devon hit him over the head with a rock to knock him out? Andrew picked up one rock after another, bracing himself for a bloodstained one. He picked up the last rock and a lizard jumped out from beneath it, scaring him half to death.

"Did you find something?" Nash was suddenly right behind him. How did he get there so fast?

"I thought I saw something, but, um, turned out it was nothing." *Good save*, Andrew told himself.

He ditched Nash and chose a new location, which he estimated to have been the center of the pool before it dried up. He roamed around between the small succulents that had sprung up over the years and started to question if coming here was a smart idea. What if Devon wasn't talking about this place? The Springs could have been anything. A restaurant, a book, a last name. None of them had found anything remotely suspicious yet.

Andrew swatted at a fly that buzzed around him as if it was mocking his lack of progress. As soon as that one left him alone, a few others zipped around his face, as though the first fly had called all his friends over. Andrew pushed them away and strode toward another pile of rocks. He'd rather deal with lizards than flies. But the more steps he took, the more flies he encountered. The buzzing kept getting louder and louder until he reached a spot where there must have been hundreds of flies. They were all circling around the same area.

A thought suddenly occurred to him. *Flies congregate near dead bodies.*

There wasn't a dead body on top of the dirt, but maybe there was a dead body buried underneath. "Guys! Over here!"

The group rushed over at once.

"The ground's been disturbed," Nash said, unperturbed by the flies buzzing in his face. "There's something buried under here." Andrew felt nauseated again when Nash went to grab a shovel.

"Wait," Justin instructed. "Stand back. This'll be faster."

It was hard not to be impressed as Justin stared at the dirt and separated it into two huge clumps like Moses parting the Red Sea.

Andrew smelled the body before he saw it. In fact, all their hands immediately flew up to cover their noses. Then they looked down into the grave. Even though his face was now a greenish-blue color, it was definitely Devon Warner's, or whatever his real name was.

"Guess that dude in the white van really was a reporter," Justin said to Z. "'Cause this corpse definitely wasn't driving it." Z was breathing into her sweatshirt and couldn't reply.

"We need to see if the serum is on him," Patricia said, not missing a beat. "It's obviously a long shot, but we need to check."

Nash pulled out gloves and jumped into the grave without flinching. *Show-off*, Andrew thought. He could barely look at the body. Gabby almost had her back to it.

"There's nothing," Nash said, after going through Devon's pockets. "Not even a wallet."

"How long do you think he's been dead?" Andrew asked, his voice nasal because he was trying not to breathe in that putrid smell.

"I'd guess four or five days," Nash answered. "But we won't know for sure until we talk to the medical examiner."

"What do you think happened? Do you think someone killed *him* for the serum?" Sabrina asked.

"It could've been a deal gone wrong," Andrew replied. "We know Devon was desperate for cash. He could've been trying to sell the serum to someone — and instead the guy just killed him for it."

"Or what if Devon was more like a hit man?" Sabrina asked. "Somebody else paid him to kill Lily and steal the serum, and then once the job was done, he killed Devon, too. No loose ends."

Z, who looked more fascinated than disgusted by the corpse, said, "How can we be positive his death is related to Lily and the serum at all? It seemed like he had a bad temper, after what he did to

Sadie. Maybe he just crossed the wrong dude and got killed for it."

"I don't think so," Nash said. He lifted up Devon's shirt so they all could see what was underneath.

Burn marks. They were all over Devon's stomach in the same shape and pattern as the strange ones that had been found on Lily.

Justin's eyes went wide. "I'm confused. I thought Devon was the one who burned Lily. Now someone did the same thing to him?"

"Maybe Devon and whoever did this to him were both at Lily's cabin that day," Nash answered. "Working together to murder Lily and then steal the serum. So the same person who did this to Lily could've also done it to Devon."

Sabrina nodded. "Remember what Lily said to me? 'I know why *they* want it.'"

"Right," Andrew agreed. "Devon and his killer could've started out as a team, as friends. That's why Devon said, 'Nature teaches beasts to know their friends.'"

"And once they had the serum, Devon's killer stabbed him in the back. *Metaphorically*," Justin said, making a point to mock Andrew.

Andrew ignored him because he'd actually been thinking the same thing. "Exactly. Devon's friend could have tortured and killed him the same way they did Lily Carpenter so he could keep the serum for himself. If their plan was to sell it to the highest bidder, killing Devon meant not having to split the money."

"So where do we think the serum is now, then?" Gabby asked, finally finding her voice.

"It's possible Devon managed to hide it somewhere, but I think it's much more likely that whoever killed him took it," Nash answered, effortlessly pulling himself up and out of the grave. "That's who we need to find now. We couldn't find any connection between Devon and the FBI or Lily. But his killer could be the link."

They were getting closer, but Andrew hoped they weren't running out of time now that there was such a huge new development. Whoever had the serum was either going to exploit it for his own gain or sell it off to someone with an even worse plan in mind. It was up to them to get to the serum back before he could do either.

Patricia gripped her hands together so tightly that her knuckles were white. "We'll have the FBI scour this entire scene for evidence to see if Devon's killer left anything behind that we can trace. And once we get the fingerprints from the body, maybe we'll get lucky."

"When you're done doing that stuff to the body," Gabby said, practically gagging, "can you give me that shirt Devon's wearing? Maybe I can get a vision from it. It might be wishful thinking, but it's worth a try."

"Better yet, maybe you'll see who killed him," Z added. Andrew was electrified by that thought.

"As soon as the medical examiner takes a look at the body, we'll get you the shirt, Gabby," Nash said.

Gabby nodded nervously and Andrew gave her an encouraging smile.

Patricia stared at the corpse as if she was willing it to supply answers. "Every second matters now. The more hands this serum moves between, the less chance we have of finding it."

CHAPTER TWENTY-EIGHT

Sabrina took out a batch of fries from the fryer and filled up two tall chocolate milkshakes. After the morning of firsts she'd had — first experience with a ghost manhandling her, first time seeing a dead body — the normalcy of her late-afternoon shift at Sonic felt oddly comforting. It was better than sitting by the phone waiting to hear back about what the FBI field techs had discovered.

"I'm taking my five," she announced to Paul, who nodded from his perch at the drive-through window.

She carried the tray to the back corner where Gabby sat half reading a history textbook.

"I come bearing snacks," Sabrina said, sliding into the seat across from her.

Gabby nibbled at a fry before putting it down. "I'm sorry. I can't. I have no appetite after this morning."

Gabby had been more shaken than anyone after they'd found Devon's body. She'd decided to come to Sonic with Sabrina so she wouldn't have to be alone in her house since her parents were in Denver with Gabby's little sister for a weekend-long gymnastics meet.

"Are you leaning toward A or B?" Sabrina asked. They had two working theories about Devon's murder now.

Theory A was that Devon was a hired hand. Whoever had paid him to kill Lily and get the serum had then killed Devon once he had the serum in his own hands.

Theory B asserted that Devon and someone else had been in on it together from the start. A friend. Then after they killed Lily together, that person had killed Devon. Betrayed him.

In either case, that was the person who probably had the serum and who they now needed to find.

"I think B," Gabby replied. "It makes more sense with that quote 'Nature teaches beasts to know their friends.' I don't know, though." She shivered and pulled her jacket over her shoulders.

"Are you going to be okay?" Sabrina asked, concerned. They needed Gabby more than ever now. It was important that she didn't crack under the pressure.

"I'm fine," Gabby said. Just then, her phone rang loudly and she jumped. Sabrina raised an eyebrow at her.

"It startled me. I'm fine." She looked down at the phone. "It's Nash."

Sabrina took a sip of her milkshake and watched the color leaving Gabby's face.

"I didn't realize it would be so fast," Gabby stammered into the phone. She paused for a while, listening to Nash, before adding, "No, no, I want to do it."

She hung up, visibly shaken.

"What is it?" Sabrina asked.

"The FBI fast-tracked the shirt through evidence." Sabrina thought DNA testing usually took months, not hours. However, considering someone could be creating an army of psychic killing machines right now, she guessed the lab did what it needed to do.

"Did they find anything?"

Gabby nodded. "They found a few hairs on Devon's shirt that weren't his. They tested them and got a DNA hit."

"A hit?"

"The DNA from these hairs discovered on Devon's body matched DNA found at Lily's cabin. "

"So whoever killed Devon was at Lily's cabin, too," Sabrina replied. It seemed that theory B was shaping up to be the correct one. Devon and a partner plotted to kill Lily and steal the serum, and that person ended up double-crossing Devon.

"Exactly. Nash said they couldn't be certain this person was there during the murder, but it seems likely that he and Devon were in on it together."

Sabrina nodded, wondering why Nash had called only Gabby with this information. As if reading her mind, Gabby added, "He said he'd send out a message to the rest of you guys soon, but he wanted to give me Devon's shirt as soon as possible."

If Gabby could catch a vision from it, she might see Devon's killer's face — the face of the person most likely to have the serum now. It would be the biggest lead they'd had yet.

"Do you want me to go with you?" Sabrina asked, noticing how nervous Gabby seemed. "I can take you to Cytology to get it."

"Nash said he'll drop it off at my house."

"The same house you didn't want to be in alone? I'll go with you."

Gabby looked relieved but only for half a second. "What about work?"

"I'll tell Paul something came up," Sabrina said confidently, though she was aware he was annoyed that she'd dropped a few shifts this week. But who cared? This was infinitely more important, the chance to help Gabby so they could get the next — maybe even final — puzzle piece they needed to find the serum. How could cranking out trays of fries compare to that?

Gabby's phone beeped. "Hold on," she said, looking down. A small smile crossed her lips.

"Justin?" Sabrina guessed.

Gabby nodded. "He said he can come meet me at my house. He finished watching his game tapes early." She gave Sabrina a relieved smile before she paused. "But if you still want to come, too, that would be great. I don't want you to think I'm picking him over you or something … I just figured it's not worth you getting in trouble over, if your boss is going to get mad …"

Sabrina decided to let Gabby out of her misery. "Gabs, it's okay. Go with Justin."

* * *

Sabrina finished her shift without much excitement.

"See you later," she said to Paul as she grabbed her purse from the employee lockers.

"I'm glad you could make it today," he replied with a little attitude.

"I'm sorry. Things have been a little crazy —"

"Sure. Two hamburgers and a large Coke."

It was impossible to have a conversation with Paul when he was on the drive-through headset. Sabrina flashed him an apologetic smile and he waved her off.

She unlocked her car and checked the passenger seat, as she always did since seeing the ghostly girl right there, but the seat was empty. As she drove out of the Sonic parking lot and onto the main highway, she began to wonder why the girl had visited her not once but twice. Did she have anything to do with this case? Or were her appearances completely unrelated? Sabrina had told the others about her last sighting, and they didn't have a clue what to make of it either, but she still couldn't bring herself to mention it to Nash and Patricia. As much as she tried to downplay its meaning, the girl's warning echoed in her head whenever she thought about telling them.

You can't trust them.

Sabrina cruised forward, debating whether to go home or swing by Gabby's for moral support, when she noticed a vehicle remaining steadily two cars back from her in her rearview mirror.

A white van.

Okay, there were plenty of white vans on the road. Nash had said so himself. Just because Z's mom had reported one outside her house — and Devon Warner had once rented one — didn't necessarily mean anything. Not to mention that Devon was sitting in an FBI morgue.

She focused on the road, deciding she'd swing by Gabby's just to see how she was doing. Her thoughts turned back to the DNA discovery. If the person who'd killed Devon had the serum now, what was his connection to Lily? Was it possibly someone from her past who knew about the serum and had come back to steal it? And what about her ex-husband? Even if the ex had an airtight alibi, it didn't mean that he might not have divulged information. Could they be sure he was telling the truth when he said he'd never mentioned the serum to anyone? There were too many possibilities but not enough clues. They needed a breakthrough if they were going to solve this and they needed it fast. Sabrina's head buzzed with the same anticipation she'd felt at Lily's cabin when it all began. But the feeling was much more intense now. She couldn't have realized then how badly she would want to solve this. The serum had given Sabrina her life back. She didn't want others to lose theirs because of it.

Her eyes darted back to the rearview mirror.

The white van was still there. Exactly two vehicles behind her.

You're being paranoid, she told herself. *You've been hanging out with Z too much.*

Still, it wouldn't hurt just to confirm she wasn't being followed.

Sabrina quickly made a turn off the main highway onto Cedar Creek Road. The white van did, too. She squinted, trying to see if she could make out a face in the driver's seat, but it was too dark.

She turned toward Main Street, Cedar Springs' "downtown." The white van followed.

Suddenly, she had a thought. Was it possible it was Nash? It didn't make sense that he'd be following her — didn't he have enough on his mind right now, sifting through FBI evidence? She figured she'd call him just in case.

He picked up after one ring.

"Where are you?" Sabrina asked.

"Cytology." Just as she'd thought. "Why? Did Gabby have a vision?"

Sabrina checked the mirror again. The van had crept a little closer, allowing only one car between them now. Did he want her to know he was there?

"No … there's a white van following me."

"Where are you?" His words were quick and calm.

"Approaching Main." She had an idea. "I'm going to lead him to you at Cytology."

"No," he replied firmly. "You're not bait, Sabrina. I'm coming to you now. Stay on lit roads and keep your phone on so I can track you."

"What if he drives away? I'm going to see if I can at least get a look at his license plate."

"Don't try anything. I'll be there within five."

Sabrina kept checking the mirror as she drove. Maybe if she slowed down she could lure him closer. Get part of the plate, at least. She sank her foot on to the brake pedal.

The car behind her got annoyed and swerved into the other lane, speeding by. The van hung back, though, maintaining the distance.

Sabrina braked again, narrowing the gap once more, and stared into her rearview mirror. It was too dark to make out a face, but she connected with two dark flashes in the reflection. Eyes. Did he realize she was on to him?

She sped up slightly, trying to remain inconspicuous. But when she dared to look back again, the van was turning left onto Grand.

He knew she'd noticed him and he was ditching her.

She couldn't let him get away before Nash arrived. This guy was clearly keeping tabs on the Lost Causes, and they needed to know why. She sped up to the next street and hung a left, too. When she reached the first intersection, she inched out and looked both ways.

Yes. There, down the road to the left, the white van was speeding away. Sabrina turned onto the road, a few cars between her and the van.

If she just got a little closer, she'd be able see the license plate. And if she drove up beside him, she might catch sight of his face. There was no time to come up with a different plan.

She jammed the gas pedal. But he must have noticed because suddenly the van accelerated, too.

He shot up fifty yards in a half second before swerving around the car in front of him. Now Sabrina knew for sure the van was suspicious. Why else would he be driving like a lunatic to keep her from catching up?

She followed the van, ignoring the honking horns beside her. Soon the van was hemmed in by a slow-moving VW Bug and a large truck.

This was her chance. Sabrina sped up, closing the distance.

The van was riding the Bug's tail so hard that it finally got the hint and pulled over to let him through.

The van hurtled forward, but Sabrina was right on its heels now. It was still too dark to see the license plate, but with a few more inches her headlights would catch it.

He sped into the next intersection. But right as she was attempting to make out the letters and numbers, he took a sharp right turn. Sabrina was going too fast to stop — she was already in the intersection.

She turned her head to the side for one last attempt to see the license plate number, and she could've sworn she saw a small flame erupt in the car. Had he hit something? Was his car on fire? That was the last thought she had before her body was rocked by the deep impact of a metal-on-metal collision.

And then everything fell into darkness.

CHAPTER TWENTY-NINE

"There's a good concert coming up next Thursday," Jared said as he flipped through music on his phone. He was lounging on the overstuffed chair in Z's bedroom that night while she watched an episode of *Seinfeld* on her laptop. She'd never seen the show before, but she was actually enjoying it. She'd even chuckled a few times. Which was a miracle, considering her anxiety an hour ago when Gabby texted that she'd gotten Devon's shirt.

Now Z was waiting on pins and needles to see if a vision would come to Gabby. After the third time she'd texted Gabby *Anything?* Justin had politely told her and the rest of them to back off. Z had turned on the *Seinfeld* episode to keep herself from checking her phone every five seconds. Jared didn't seem to notice anything was up.

"So should I get tickets?" Jared asked.

"Huh?" It was getting hard to stay focused when she was around Jared. He was part of a completely different life, and she wasn't sure how he fit into this one. Or *if* he fit into this one. She was trying to sound like her old self around him as much as she could, but she thought at least her boyfriend would be able to see a subtle difference. She was watching *Seinfeld*, for God's sake.

"To the concert. On Thursday."

"Right. Uh, maybe." Who knew what she'd be doing that night?

"Okay. Let me know," he said casually. It was at least the fourth music event Z had turned down in the past two weeks. Was there ever going to be a point when he started asking questions?

Z's finger hovered over the mouse to start another episode when the ringing in her ears made her freeze.

I gotta find that cool electric blues song I heard the other day. Z would love it.

Jared's thought. Z's stomach did a nervous little flip.

It was the first time this had happened, and it felt a little wrong — but kind of exhilarating. And interesting. He was sitting here thinking about a song that would make her happy. That was sweet.

Getting a glimpse into his mind was strangely addictive, though, now that she had heard that one thought. She tuned every sound out in the room until her ears started vibrating again.

Man, I'm hungry. They never have good food at this house. Maybe I should leave and go grab a burger. Z couldn't argue with him there. Her mother was notoriously stingy on buying snacks. Probably because she got full from a glass of cucumber water.

Now that Z was attuned, Jared's next thought came to her quickly.

Then again, if I stay a little longer, I might get to see Scott in his boxers. Or maybe even out of his boxers. In the shower …

Z's mouth dropped open. "What did you just say?"

Jared looked up from his phone. "I didn't say anything."

Of course he hadn't. He'd thought it. Z watched him, flabbergasted, as he went back to scrolling through his music.

Jared wanted to see Scott naked.

Her boyfriend had a thing for her twin brother.

This was not happening.

She tried to recall any warning signs that he was into Scott.

Suddenly, random flashbacks started pounding her like a hailstorm. The fact that Jared insisted on going swimming when Scott was in the pool. How Jared consistently lingered in the kitchen when Scott was there and made awkward small talk. *Oh God.* The time in the school hallway when she heard that thought about Scott being hot and she'd assumed it was one of the dumb cheerleaders. It was her own boyfriend!

"You should go," she told him, slamming her computer shut. Had he seriously been using her this whole time? She cringed when she considered that he might have been thinking of Scott even when he was hooking up with her.

"Yeah, it's getting late," he answered, standing up.

"No, I mean … this isn't working, Jared."

"Wait, what?" He was looking at her as if she was crazy. "What happened in the last five minutes that made it not work?"

As annoyed as she was, she wasn't going to embarrass him. Clearly he had some issues he needed to work out. "I think deep down you know we should break up."

There was no way he realized she was on to his secret, but something made him nod amenably, once again reminding her of a golden retriever. Although at least golden retrievers were loyal.

"You're probably right," he finally muttered. Then his face scrunched up in concern. "Hey, your nose is bleeding."

It seemed like the least important thing in the world right now. "I'm fine. Don't worry about it."

Jared slunk out of her room. As Z reached for a tissue to wipe the blood from her nose, she looked back at her phone. Still nothing from Gabby. Z started typing a text to Sabrina instead.

FYI, my taste in guys sucks worse than yours. Have I got a story for you.

She waited a minute for the telltale dots to appear, showing that

Sabrina was typing a response. After a moment, Z realized Sabrina hadn't even weighed in on the earlier text chain. Maybe she was stuck at Sonic and couldn't look at her phone.

Call me when you can. Or come on over. I'll be up for a while.

Somehow, hanging out with Sabrina had started to sound like a fun way to pass an evening.

CHAPTER THIRTY

Darkness swirled around Sabrina.

The first thing she was aware of was the smell. Smoky and acrid, like an extinguished campfire.

She opened her eyes slowly.

She was in her car, lodged between the seat and her airbag, the front of her car burst open, cold air attacking her.

She blinked a few times.

"Sabrina!"

Nash. Could it really be him? Memory fragments fought their way into her brain. *The white van.* She'd called Nash. He had planned to catch up with her.

"Sabrina!" There was no mistaking it now. It was Nash's voice. She tilted her head to the side and saw his face through the broken passenger window, though his expression was less assured than she'd ever seen it. She tried to respond but was finding it hard to catch her breath.

Nash swung the door open, glass particles crackling onto the pavement. "I've got you." He moved his hands around her, unbuckled the seat belt and scooped her out of the car.

As he carried her across the street, Sabrina looked around, growing more aware of her surroundings. Of what had happened.

Her car had spun out and was facing the wrong direction, the entire front hood bashed in, the windshield shattered. A small green SUV was also stalled in the center of the intersection, its front smashed up like a pancake.

A man ran up to them. He looked like a young dad. "Is she going to be all right? I didn't even see her!"

The driver of the other car.

Nash gave him a steely look. "You're lucky you didn't kill her."

Sabrina wanted to protest — it hadn't been all this guy's fault. But her head was hurting and it was too difficult to get the words out.

Nash placed her down on the strip of grass alongside the road, his arms still propping her up.

Her breathing had regulated slightly. She looked back up at Nash, expecting to find anger in his eyes. She'd done the direct opposite of what he'd told her to do. Again.

But as he hovered over her, she could see only fear in his face. "Are you okay?" he asked. She nodded, and that seemed to reassure him.

"Say something," he urged. His fist was covered in fresh, bloody cuts.

"Are *you* okay?" she asked.

Nash followed her gaze to his hands, then made a noise, his body shaking slightly. For a second, Sabrina was worried and then she realized … he was *laughing*. She'd never heard him do that before.

"What?" she asked weakly.

"Seriously? You're asking me if *I'm* okay?"

"You're bleeding," Sabrina said sheepishly.

"This is nothing. I punched the side window out to unlock the car."

She raised a hand to her forehead and grimaced.

"That's where the airbag hit you."

He looked back to the cars. "It looks like he was making a left and bashed the front of your car. You were lucky, Sabrina. Another few inches and ..."

He looked away, letting the sentence hang.

"It was a yellow light," Sabrina remembered. "I was right behind him ..."

"Behind that guy? How?"

"No. Behind the white van. And then it got away." She had a brief flashback to the last thing she had seen ... some kind of flame erupting in the van. Could she have really seen that? It seemed unlikely now.

"You were chasing the white van?" Nash spoke slowly, as if he didn't know whether to believe her or examine her for brain damage. "I thought *he* was following you."

Oh, of course. Nash wasn't upset with her because he didn't know what really happened.

Sabrina took a breath. "I was scared I was going to lose him. I think he knew that I'd noticed him. I figured if I could just keep him in sight until you got here — or get a license plate number — it would be worth it. But then he turned so quickly and I lost him."

"Dammit, Sabrina," Nash snapped.

"I know. I'm sorry. I was trying to stay on him as best I could, but he was going so fast —"

"You think I'm upset because the guy got away?"

Just then, a traffic cop arrived on his motorcycle.

"We'll talk about it later," Nash said quietly.

"What should I tell the officer?" Sabrina asked, suddenly nervous.

"The truth. Minus the white van."

A half hour passed as the police officer spoke to both her and the man who hit her, and tow trucks came to haul the vehicles away.

"Do you want to go to the hospital, miss?" the officer asked her. "I can have an ambulance pick you up if your friend can't take you." He looked at Nash.

Sabrina shook her head. "I think I'm okay." Her face was sore and bruised from the airbag and she had a nasty case of whiplash already setting in. But she didn't need the ER.

"Let's just double-check for a concussion, then." The officer grabbed a small flashlight from his belt. "Follow the light."

Sabrina obeyed, flicking her eyes back and forth as he moved the flashlight. Satisfied, he shut it off.

"No concussion."

Nash raised a skeptical eyebrow. "How can you be so sure?"

"I'm fine," Sabrina insisted. "Just shaken up."

"Let's get you home," Nash said, steering Sabrina away from the officer. When they were out of earshot, he added, "I don't trust that meter maid. I want to check you out myself."

Sabrina frowned. "I don't want to go home." The thought of going back to the small, stale house with her parents right now felt unbearably depressing.

"Then let's go to my place. If you have a concussion, you need to be watched. I'll feel safer with you there anyway."

The one upside to having parents who could not care less about where she was? She didn't need to check in with anyone after a car accident or even bother going home.

Nash was suddenly watching her carefully. "Is it okay with you if we go to my place?"

They both knew they were crossing a line. And they were both pretending it wasn't a big deal. That it was only about staying safe. Sabrina nodded, maybe a bit too enthusiastically.

Nash gave her a small smile. "Okay, then."

* * *

Sabrina wasn't surprised to find Nash's short-term rental was neat and sparse. A black couch took up most of the living room, a few books stacked neatly on an end table. It reminded her of a college dorm room, which wasn't that strange considering how young he was.

"Come," he said, leading her onto the couch. His fingers gently probed her head. "Does that hurt?" he asked.

"Not really," Sabrina said. "I have a little headache, though. And my neck is hurting."

He got up and rummaged in the small kitchen.

"Have you checked if everyone else is okay?" Sabrina asked. "What if he left me just to go to one of the others?" She cursed herself for not thinking of it earlier.

"They're fine. I talked to Patricia while you were with the officer. We've checked in with everyone. Nothing out of the ordinary."

"What if he decides to get more aggressive? Or goes to one of their houses tonight? I'm pretty sure he was waiting for me to get off my shift at Sonic. Should we call the police? I know they can't know about all this, but maybe there's a way …"

"Sabrina, we have infinitely more resources than the police. Believe me. If I thought they could help, I'd call them, but we don't need to. Patricia is handling it. We're going to start monitoring your houses."

"But what if everyone's not at home? I think Andrew has a Mathlete thing tomorrow —"

"We know," Nash answered, softening without sounding condescending as he walked back to her with a bottle of ibuprofen, a glass of water and a heating pad. "Put this on your shoulders."

Sabrina slipped the pad onto her neck and shoulders, the warmth relieving the stiffness that was setting in. He sat down next to her. "Don't worry. The FBI is on it. It's my job to make sure this guy, whoever he is, doesn't get near you or any of the others again."

"Who do you think it was?"

Nash sighed. "I'm not sure. It might not even be related to our case."

"The van was definitely trying to get away from me. The driver didn't want me to see him. Or her, I guess."

Nash paused, as if he didn't like what he was about to say. "We know the white van Devon Warner rented was never returned."

"What does that mean?" She met his eyes and instantly understood. "You think whoever killed Devon took his van. And that person was the one following me tonight."

"I hope not. But yes, that's a … strong possibility."

Sabrina tried to connect the dots in her aching head. Devon had conspired with someone — a friend? — to kill Lily. That person double-crossed Devon and killed him to keep the serum for himself and do God-knows-what with it. And now, if he was driving Devon's van, he was the one who followed her. The one who had been driving by Z's house. But why? How had he found them? And what did he want from them? Did he know they were looking for the serum?

Her heating pad slipped off, and Nash picked it up. "Turn around." She assumed he was going to return the pad to her, but then she felt his hands start to knead her shoulders.

"Is that okay?" he asked. "You'll feel better tomorrow if we get some of the knots out now." It was another line they were crossing. And another attempt to pretend they weren't.

"It's good." The tension she'd been holding in her body for the last few hours melted away.

"Tell me if it's too much pressure." His fingers nimbly pressed into the flesh of her neck, and her body temperature shot up as though she'd just stepped into a sauna.

"Sabrina, you need to be careful," he said in a low voice. "Promise me. I don't want you chasing after this guy. Whatever possessed you to do that —"

"What would you have done if you were me?" Sabrina interjected. "Just let the guy go? I couldn't. I was so close to seeing his face."

Nash didn't reply right away. When he spoke, his voice was serious. "And you could have gotten yourself killed doing it. Whoever he is, he's extremely dangerous. Promise me this won't happen again."

"I can't," Sabrina said. "Not if I'm being honest. I keep thinking about all the sick and twisted things he could do with the serum. If I got that close to him again, I'd do the same thing."

Nash was silent, though his hands continued working into her shoulder blades.

"I'm sorry. I know I'm making your job harder again," she added.

He turned her to face him, planting his gaze on Sabrina so fiercely that her whole body shivered. "You think that's really what I'm worried about."

"You're … not the easiest guy to understand," she answered honestly.

"Has it ever occurred to you that I don't want anything to happen to you?" Their faces were just inches apart. Sabrina's pulse raced.

"I don't know," she breathed.

"Let me lay it out for you. If something happened to you, I would be destroyed."

He suddenly brought his hand up to her cheek, and before she had time to analyze what was happening, he was kissing her. Softly at first, then with more urgency. She'd never kissed anyone like this before. His fingers were in her hair, on her face, grasping her hips. She brought her hands under his shirt, bringing him closer, pressing her body against his, the intensity almost too much to handle.

"Sabrina …" Nash murmured into her neck, igniting a chill down her body.

"Don't stop," Sabrina urged, breathless.

"We can't," he said, but his lips found hers again, his arms wrapped around her shoulders until he pulled away. She brought her lips back toward his, but after a beat he pulled away again.

"We can't," he repeated more firmly, his breath still coming fast.
"Why not?"

Nash looked at her, their bodies still enmeshed. "It's wrong on so many levels. If anyone ever found out —"

"I wouldn't say anything."

He shook his head with a rueful smile. "I'm sorry. Believe me. I really am." Suddenly, he stood up. "You should get to sleep. Let me show you where the bed is. I'll stay on the couch."

He led her back to the bedroom, equally as sparse as the front room. "You can stay in here," Sabrina said, feeling guilty for usurping his bed and secretly hoping he'd change his mind. "Nothing has to happen."

Nash's eyes raked over her again. "Let's not test that, shall we?"

He propped up the pillows and handed her a shirt from his drawer. "Is this okay to sleep in?"

Sabrina nodded wordlessly.

He stopped at the door. "Let me know if you need anything, okay? Don't worry about waking me."

Sabrina nodded again and nestled into the soft sheets, tinged faintly with the scent of Nash's shampoo. It was only once she closed her eyes and began to dream that the girl from the woods, her almond eyes urgent, began swirling around in her unconscious, her words echoing.

You can't trust them.

CHAPTER THIRTY-ONE

"I should try again," Gabby said. It was almost midnight, and she and Justin were sitting on top of her comforter, Devon's red-and-black flannel shirt in the middle of them.

"Are you sure? You just tried five minutes ago. Maybe you need a break," Justin replied.

When she didn't have a vision the first few times, she wasn't too discouraged. The same thing had happened with Lily's prescription bottle before she finally saw something. But then she got the text about Sabrina's accident and the urgency became even clearer.

"I need to keep trying. We have to find this guy. After what happened to Sabrina —"

"We'll find him. But you're putting way too much pressure on yourself." Justin was trying to hide his anxiety for Gabby's sake, but what happened to Sabrina had rattled him, too. With Gabby's parents out of town, he refused to leave her house that night and he kept glancing out the window every few minutes. He never said why, but they both knew he was looking for the white van.

Justin stood up, presumably on another excursion to the window, but he tripped over an overstuffed box of Gabby's trophies beside the bed.

"Are these all from ice-skating?" he asked, picking up one of the dusty gold-colored statues. "You've got so many in here, you could fill a museum."

"I just packed them up," she answered. "I'm finally going to throw them out. I should've done it years ago."

She was surprised yet relieved to find she had zero emotional attachment to those trophies when she'd thrown them in the box the night before. They just reminded her of giving up everything for her parents' approval and then her subsequent fall from grace when the trophies stopped coming. Throwing them out felt like a final act of liberation from her OCD — and from that girl she had let herself become for way too long.

"You think you'll ever skate again?"

"Maybe just for fun. I hated those competitions." She'd never said that out loud to anyone, but confiding in Justin was as easy as saying it to herself. "I want to find something else I really like now."

"Besides me?" Justin said, grinning.

Her cheeks burned pink as she smiled. "Yes, besides you."

"So what else do you like to do?" he asked with such intense curiosity that it made her realize just how much she liked him.

Gabby considered it for a minute. "I used to love creative writing. But I had so many rules for myself when the OCD started that it was too stressful to keep up with it. The only things I could manage to write were papers for school." All the short stories she'd written were in an untouched folder on her computer. She remembered trying to finish one a few years ago, but she hadn't been able to write a sentence without going over it a dozen times.

"Well, if you want to start back with it, you've got some pretty great material from the last two weeks," Justin said.

He was right. But it was only a good story if it had a good ending.

She eyed Devon's shirt. Maybe now that Justin had distracted her for a few minutes a vision would come. She picked the shirt up, clinging to the worn piece of fabric like a lifeline. She closed her eyes.

Nothing.

When she opened them, Justin could easily read her frustration.

"You've got to relax. You're psyching yourself out, Gabs. You're too in your head," he said. He grabbed a stuffed bear off her shelf and started tossing it in the air like a ball. "This happens all the time in football. Coach Brandt always says, 'Keep your focus away from the uncontrollables.'"

"Uncontrollables?"

"All the things that are out of your hands. Like when I'm on the field, I can't control the crowd, or the outcome of the game, or who the coach puts in."

"And I can't control when my visions come."

He sat back down next to her. "Exactly. So focus on something else. You can control your thoughts. Think about something other than having a vision and maybe it'll come to you."

"How do I do that, though? If I'm not thinking about having a vision, I'm thinking about what happened to Sabrina and then I immediately think about how I need to have a vision again." She sounded as frantic as she felt.

"Lie down, close your eyes and go to your happy place," Justin instructed. "Then in ten minutes, you can try again with the shirt. I'm not letting you try again until you relax."

Maybe he was right. She lay down and let her head sink into the pillow. Where was her happy place?

Justin moved closer and brushed back a jumble of her hair that had fallen over her eyes. The sweetness of the gesture — a sweetness she never saw him bestow upon anyone else but her — incited an eruption of butterflies in her stomach. Before she knew what she was doing, she'd pulled him closer and pressed her lips onto his. Nothing in her life had ever felt as good as kissing Justin. She grabbed him, pulling his body on top of hers, and for a split-second, he stopped kissing her. The look in his eyes suggested Gabby's sudden brazenness had surprised him as much as it had her. But then he was kissing her again. She shivered with a desire she hadn't known she was capable of.

Her hands reached for his shirt, about to pull it off, when her phone buzzed loudly next to her, jarring them both. She forced herself to pull away to glance at the text. It was from Z requesting a vision status update and it instantly brought Gabby back to reality.

"We should stop," she whispered, finding it difficult to speak. The only thing better than Justin kissing her, was a shirtless Justin kissing her. But she had to refocus. "You said I can try again for a vision after I relax for ten minutes, right?"

"Did I say that? I think I meant we should do *this* for ten minutes instead."

She grinned, then planted her hands next to her sides to keep from pulling him back on top of her. "I think I can relax now."

"Well, that makes one of us," he grumbled, but then smiled and kissed her forehead. "You can do this, Gabs. Go to your happy place and I bet in a few minutes you'll be relaxed enough to try for a vision again."

She closed her eyes. Her happy place was easy to find. He was sitting right next to her.

* * *

A few hours later, she woke up with a start. When did she fall asleep? She sat up and tried to get her bearings. The room was bathed in early morning light. Her attempt to not focus on the uncontrollables must have worked better than she expected. Justin was asleep next to her, and she was actually grateful her parents had left her alone in the house. They probably wouldn't even notice if a guy slept over. When they left for Denver, all they said to Gabby was to remember to set the alarm.

She reached across the bed for her phone to see what time it was, but her fingers grazed Devon's shirt instead. As soon as her hand touched the worn flannel, she was no longer in her body. She was in Devon Warner's body, at last.

She was lying on the ground, outside, in the darkness, gasping for air. She could feel his body was freezing cold, yet at the same time, it was burning. What was that smell? It was like rancid beef.

And then she realized what it was. Devon's body was on fire.

She felt her fingers, Devon's fingers, claw at the dirt, trying to sit up. It was useless, though. Devon wasn't going anywhere. He was on the edge of consciousness.

She froze when she saw a man coming toward her. It had to be Devon's killer. She couldn't make out his face because he was too far away.

Stay awake, Devon. Please don't pass out.

She strained her eyes to see the figure, but Devon's eyelids were so heavy … She willed him not to shut his eyes. The second he did, she was afraid it would be the last time.

The figure stepped toward her just as her eyelids fluttered closed. She felt the man reach into Devon's pocket and pull something out. It had to be the serum. Devon couldn't move and he was panting, trying to say something. He finally managed to whisper to the man who was inches from his face. "'Nature teaches beasts to know their friends.' You were my only one."

"I'm sorry it had to end like this," the man replied.

Open your eyes, Devon. Open your eyes.

Just as the man turned, Devon's eyes opened. The man was walking away, but Gabby tried to memorize as many details as she could. He was wearing faded jeans and a green windbreaker. And just as she'd thought, he was holding the large vial of serum in his right hand.

She took a breath, Devon Warner's last breath.

Her body shot straight up and her eyes popped open. She was gasping for air.

She knew that green windbreaker.

She'd seen it a million times at school. It was the jacket all the teachers had received after a school-wide retreat over the summer.

Whoever killed Devon Warner was a faculty member at Cedar Springs High.

CHAPTER THIRTY-TWO

Nash's hands flew over the keyboard, trying to keep pace with the mounting theories in his head. Even after several years with the FBI, he felt a need to prove himself. No one ever mentioned it explicitly, but the shadow of his father loomed large. Luckily, it was also what motivated him.

He'd sprung into action the second the call came in from Gabby. The green windbreaker could be their big break. After he dropped Sabrina off at home, he went straight to Cytology to vet the Cedar Springs High faculty. He'd barely moved for the past six hours.

They needed to narrow down the list of faculty suspects before the killer took off with the serum. Or before he did anything to the group. Or Sabrina.

Sabrina. The person he'd been trying to avoid thinking about all morning. Bringing her back to his apartment the previous night had been an impulsive mistake. Nash hadn't worked this hard over the last few years only to let it all go by breaking such a cardinal rule. Sabrina was an FBI asset. Agents don't get involved with assets. He could and would be dismissed from the bureau if what happened that night ever came to light. He'd never had a problem sticking to this rule.

But Sabrina wasn't like anyone he'd met before. What was it about her that made it so difficult? From the moment their eyes first locked, he'd been hit with more than attraction. It was something more like awe. Or destiny. (Which Nash would never tell another living soul.) It was a feeling that the moment was bigger than just them. Part of him had hoped she wouldn't get selected for the program so he could find out if he was right.

As soon as she had been chosen, he shut those emotions off. He was good at compartmentalizing. If anyone knew how to separate emotionally, it was Nash. He'd learned that lesson early in life.

And yet, she kept surprising him. She was bolder than he'd realized. He loved — and hated — how fearless she was. He'd never seen someone face danger so easily, even among a group of trained FBI recruits. But it also made protecting her almost impossible.

The night before, when he'd pulled up and seen her smashed car, he'd feared the worst. Once he realized she was okay, he'd been flooded with relief — and that had made him capricious, reckless. He'd let his guard down.

He would need to get back to a level of total detachment. There was a serum that needed to be found, a murderer who needed to be caught and a very clean line with Sabrina he knew better than to cross again.

Patricia entered his office, her eyes on fire. "Do you have a suspect list? They'll be here any minute now."

"I've got it narrowed down," he answered. He looked up from his computer and blinked. He was about to propose something that he knew Patricia wasn't going to like. "I think it's a small enough number that you and I can take it from here. The five of them don't need to be involved. We don't want to put them in any more danger."

Patricia's look was offensive on its own, but she added, "You're being ridiculous. This is when we need them most."

"The suspect is a teacher at their school. You wouldn't send trained agents into the field without giving them weapons —"

"We did give them weapons. And the fact that it's a teacher is a gift. They can investigate right out in the open because there's nothing suspicious about them being at school. If we strolled in there questioning the suspects, it would be an automatic red flag. Whoever had the serum would bolt with it."

Patricia was solely consumed with the dangers the serum presented. Didn't she care if the group ended up dead as a result? Would they be just collateral damage in her mind?

"What if one of them gets careless *because* they're at school and they feel safe there?" Nash pointed out. "He knows about them. He was following Sabrina."

"We don't have nearly enough information to know what really happened with Sabrina. Z's paranoia with the van may have gotten to her, and Sabrina could have been chasing an innocent person who panicked." It was a possibility, Nash knew that. But they needed to assume the worst.

"We set up cameras around their homes just like you asked. That's more of a safety measure than we do for most assets. We'll make sure they stay safe," Patricia said in a tone that was the opposite of reassuring.

Nash had almost lost his chance to change her mind. "I think you're too close to this, Patricia. You're not seeing the kind of jeopardy you're putting them in." Regardless of his personal feelings for Sabrina, he had no doubts that he was being objective about his concern for her safety. For the entire group's safety.

"Perhaps *you're* too close to this case, Nash," she responded tautly. "Those five are the best set of assets the FBI has right now. The best chance we have of mitigating a disaster. This is a calculated risk. Besides, you know as well as I do that if an asset wants to continue their mission, it's ultimately up to them."

* * *

Andrew met the other Lost Causes in the Cytology parking lot. They wanted to have a word alone, without Patricia and Nash there. Once they entered that conference room, it would be straight to business. The only one missing was Sabrina, who had texted that she was running late. Andrew hoped she was okay after her car accident. Sabrina had assured them all by text that she was fine, but that was typical of her. Andrew couldn't imagine her ever admitting she needed to take a day off.

"I still can't believe it," Justin said, leaning his broad frame against the back of Z's Range Rover. "The person who stole the serum and murdered Devon Warner is one of our teachers? How is that possible? How was he right in front of our faces this whole time and we had no clue? Some psychics we are."

"Whoever he is, he's good at covering his tracks. We've known that from the start," Andrew said. "Remember the crime scene? No fingerprints, no one else's blood."

"How do you go from spending the day with teenagers to spending the night torturing and killing people?" Gabby asked warily.

Z shrugged. "How well do any of us really know our teachers?"

She was right. Outside the classroom, Andrew didn't have a clue who his teachers were or what they did with their spare time. But one of them was a killer.

"Think how many teachers got that windbreaker I saw in the vision," Gabby said. "It could be any of them."

"Not quite," Andrew cut in. He'd been glued to his computer since Gabby's discovery. Besides his desire to solve the case and get the serum safely back, he saw this as another opportunity to prove himself to Nash and Patricia, to cement his path toward a legitimate entry into the FBI. "I've been able to narrow the field down to six based on everything we already know about Devon's killer."

"Wow. How did you do all that in the last few hours?" Gabby asked.

One effect of the serum was that every time Andrew used his computer for research, he got a little faster, he could see a little further. He also had Nash's FBI passwords to thank. "Once I had their social security numbers, I could plug in different algorithms —"

"Who gives a crap how you did it?" Justin interjected. "It's pretty sweet you figured out how to get it down to six." Did Justin just give him a compliment?

Andrew could barely absorb it, though, because Sabrina had just pulled up in her rental car. His eyes went wide when he saw her. The bruise on her forehead was the size of Andrew's fist.

"Andrew, I'm okay. I promise," she said before he could say anything. "It looks worse than it feels."

"Did you go to the hospital?" Gabby asked.

"No, but the cop on the scene checked me out. He said I'm fine."

"And the accident happened because the white van was following you, right?" Z asked, chewing on one of her nails.

"Yeah," Sabrina said. "I was trying as hard as I could to see the guy driving. Nash said Devon Warner's white van was never returned. Obviously there's no way to be sure, but I think whoever killed Devon was the one driving it."

"Wait … if Devon's killer *is* the one driving around in that van … that means it was one of our teachers who was following you, Sabrina," Gabby said, the words getting caught in her throat.

Sabrina's eyes widened. "It would explain why he was racing away from me so fast." Then she thought of something else. "He's probably been stalking us at school, too, and we never even knew it."

"I don't get how he knows about us in the first place, though," Z pointed out.

The question lingered in the air.

"What are we going to do?" Gabby asked, her eyes darting from face to face. Justin draped a protective arm around her. "Patricia and Nash aren't going to want us to go to school now, knowing that ... are they?"

Her question startled Andrew. Sure, he intellectually understood the dangers of walking on to a campus with a murderer ... who seemed to have the five of them on his radar. But he had never considered that Patricia and Nash would hold them off at this point, right when they were getting so close. How would he be able to prove himself from the sidelines?

"Let's see what Nash and Patricia say about it all," Andrew said, breaking the silence.

Sabrina pushed the buzzer, then turned to Z. "What were you going to tell me last night? You texted that you had a crazy story."

"It was something I heard. But compared to all this, it doesn't seems so crazy anymore," Z said.

"Did you hear Principal Walters thinking about being horny again?" Justin asked. He'd laughed for at least twenty minutes when Z told them that story last week.

"Worse," Z replied.

Andrew scoffed. "No way. What could be worse?"

"My boyfriend wants to bone my brother."

"*You* have a boyfriend?" Justin said.

Z was unfazed. "Ex-boyfriend."

* * *

Andrew was on the edge of his seat as Nash brought up the images of Cedar Springs High faculty members on the projection screen, waiting to see if Nash's suspect list would match his own. Maybe then Nash and Patricia would realize how valuable the Lost Causes were in the field.

"There are forty teachers currently at Cedar Springs High," Nash began. "Now we know one of them has the serum. One of them has been leading a double life. Whoever it is, it's someone who not only has the capacity to commit murder but who had knowledge of the serum's existence and wanted it enough to kill for it."

He let the words sink in before turning back to the photos. "Of these forty teachers, twenty-four of them are female, so we can put them on the back burner for now. Gabby feels confident the assailant she saw was male."

Nash touched the board, swiping the entire cluster of female teachers to the right side of the screen.

"That leaves us with twelve male faculty members when we account for age, build and health." Andrew studied the faces on the screen. So far his list of suspects was right on track.

"We were able to eliminate seven more after pursuing further intel, like cell phone calls and credit card statements that established alibis for the night the medical examiner had determined that Devon Warner was killed."

Andrew watched intently as Nash slid several more teachers away. He put his hand up, confused. "Wait. Why did you move Coach Colfax over?" Andrew hadn't found any credit card activity or cell phone calls to indicate that Coach Colfax had an alibi for Devon's murder. Plus, the guy was in perfect shape, physically able to take a victim down.

"All the PE teachers were at a retreat in Denver the night Devon Warner was killed. Cell phones were banned for most of the conference, but we confirmed with the hotel that Colfax had a room and was accounted for the whole time."

Andrew shrank down. At least Nash hadn't said checkmate. Nash emphatically tapped the remaining photos on the left side of the board. "These five men are our strongest group of suspects."

Minus Colfax, it was the same as Andrew's list.

There was Mr. Wincott, the English lit teacher with a British accent that somehow made him attractive to every girl in school. Dr. Fields, his and Gabby's chemistry teacher, notorious for being one of the most demanding teachers at school. Computer science and technology teacher Mr. Manzetti, or Sweaty Manzetti, as he was widely known. Mr. Schroeder, the soft-spoken Spanish teacher with no sense of humor. And finally, Mr. Greenly, who obviously was a sociopath. He was the only one Andrew thought seemed capable of killing someone.

"So far we haven't found any major direct links between any of these teachers and Lily, Devon or the FBI," Nash said. "We know from Gabby's vision that Devon considered one of these men a friend."

"His only friend, he said," Gabby added.

"Andrew, you start digging into any connections that haven't come to light yet."

Andrew nodded. "Already on it."

"We're also trying to find the cracks in these five teachers' facades," Nash continued. "Who would have had the opportunity to hear about the serum? Did any of them ever speak to Lily — even if it was just in town at the farmers' market? Which of them has a compelling motive? A reason why they'd think this serum was worth killing for? Do they have criminal backgrounds or ties to an international government?"

"Our teachers?" Justin asked in disbelief.

"Things aren't always what they seem," Patricia reminded him, moving to the other side of the projection screen. "We found more than a few facts about these five teachers that you might not expect." She pointed to an old photo of Andrew's chemistry teacher, Dr. Fields. Andrew had never seen him without his lab coat on, so his suit and tie looked almost like a costume. She didn't need to state the obvious — that a chemistry scholar might be the only one of the bunch to come close to understanding the science behind the serum. "Before Fields moved to Cedar Springs, he was working in research and development at one of the world's largest biochem firms. I recognized his name the minute I saw it. Lily went to a conference where Dr. Fields was the keynote speaker. I remember because she raved about it for weeks afterward."

"A connection to Lily. That's huge," Andrew responded.

"Yes and no. The conference was at least fifteen years ago. But another thing worth noting is that Dr. Fields quit his job at the biochem firm unexpectedly three years ago and took up teaching high school chemistry. He moved to Cedar Springs within the same year as Lily."

It was a highly unusual move to quit and become a high school teacher with credentials like his. If Dr. Fields really felt a burning passion to teach, he could've been a college professor. His move to Cedar Springs was odd … and the timing of it was also a bit too coincidental.

Nash pointed to Mr. Schroeder. "We discovered that Schroeder has a sealed juvenile record."

Sabrina frowned. "A juvenile record for what? The guy barely speaks above a whisper in class."

Nash paused, probably debating whether to admit he'd broken into sealed records. Andrew was jealous he didn't have that kind of access himself. "He was in juvenile hall for two years," Nash finally told them. "For aggravated assault. I'm still getting more details, but he almost killed a man with a baseball bat when he was sixteen."

Andrew was shocked. It was hard to believe the gentle teacher who had never once given Andrew a hard time for his multiple absences was capable of violent assault … but then again, everyone had secrets. Look at the enormous one Andrew and the others were keeping from the rest of the world. Who would ever guess they were working with the FBI?

Andrew put a star next to Schroeder. Regardless of his outward temperament, a history of violence was a definite red flag. "What about Greenly?" he asked, hoping he didn't sound too eager. Now that was a guy he wouldn't be surprised to hear had a sordid past.

"Nothing major, nothing criminal," Patricia answered, and Andrew tried not to look too disappointed. "We know that he grew up and went to school in Albuquerque, the same city Lily used to live in, though that could be just a coincidence. There's no indication yet that they knew each other at all."

"What about Sweaty" — Justin stopped himself — "I mean … Mr. Manzetti. That dude's always creeped me out."

"Nothing specific has jumped out with him yet either," Nash said. "But like the others, he's the right age and build, with no alibi as far as we can tell for the night of Devon's murder."

"I found something that jumped out," Andrew piped up. He tried to tone down the gloating. "Manzetti has a ton of debt. I had to dig because he's constantly moving money around to different credit cards and bank accounts. But when I added everything up, he's in debt over thirty thousand dollars."

"Just because he has no money doesn't mean he's a killer," Justin snapped.

"I know. My point was that if he's desperate for money, it makes sense he'd want to steal the serum. He could sell it for billions, right?"

"Oh," Justin said. "Yeah, good call."

Nash wrote this information down, which meant he hadn't discovered that little tidbit yet. Minor victory for Andrew.

"What about Mr. Wincott?" Gabby asked, studying his face on the screen as though she was seeing him for the first time.

"Wincott is at the top of my list," Nash answered.

Z perked up. "What did he do? I mean other than walk around like we should all be making shrines in his honor."

"It's more what his father did, not him," Patricia answered. "His British father was briefly jailed fifteen years ago for contact he had with Wo Shing, a triad society in Hong Kong. They're incredibly powerful and fully armed, so to say they're dangerous is putting it lightly. They also have factions everywhere from London to Jordan to Australia. They're believed to be behind several successful and unsuccessful assassinations within the Chinese government."

"Sounds like the serum would be right up their alley," Z said. "Can you imagine a group of assassins who could hear thoughts like I can? We'd be leaking information to them without even knowing it."

"Both of Wincott's parents have been on Interpol's watch list for years," Nash added. "And the couple was being closely observed by England's version of the CIA."

Andrew made a mental note to ask Nash about access to international records.

"So when are you going to question them?" Z asked. "Am I going to sit in like I did with Sadie?"

"You can't," Justin responded. "All these teachers know who you are. They'd never talk in front of a student, right?" He looked at Patricia and Nash for confirmation.

"The situation is too delicate for a formal questioning right now," Patricia replied.

"What do you mean?" Andrew probed. "You're not calling any of them in?" Nash gave Patricia a pointed look. Yeah, Andrew thought he was definitely detecting some friction between them.

"We're not questioning them for several reasons. One, we don't have a shred of real evidence," Patricia replied, speaking more quickly. "We can't just bring somebody in on a psychic hunch."

"Maybe you should've thought of that before," Z mumbled just loud enough to be heard.

Patricia didn't pause to acknowledge her. "And two, we can't risk tipping our hand. One of these men has the serum. If he gets wind that we're bringing other teachers in for questioning, he could run — and the serum would run with him."

"So what are we going to do?" Gabby asked. "Have Andrew see what he can find online? And what do we do about school? Are we staying home?"

There was a brief silence. "No," Patricia finally replied. She looked at Nash, as if hoping he'd step in, but he remained silent. "The five of you are on the inside in a way Nash and I can't be."

"You want *us* to narrow the suspect pool?" Sabrina asked. "At school?" A nervous energy surged through Andrew. He hadn't wanted to back away from the case right when they were getting close to solving it … but now that he knew more of these teachers' histories, the extent of the danger was beginning to feel more real.

"But one of these five teachers is a killer — who knows exactly who the five of us are," Gabby protested nervously.

"Not necessarily," Patricia said. "We're not sure who was driving that van. But even if that was the case, and he was the one, then he was also driving the van around Z's house last week. He's known about you for a while."

"How is that better?" Gabby asked, sounding frantic.

"If he does actually know about the five of you, then as of now, he's only been keeping tabs on you, not trying to engage you in any way. If you suddenly don't show up at school, don't you think that will be a bigger red flag than sticking to your normal routines? Sudden unexplained absences — of the five people he's been tracking — could tip him off more, change his agenda."

Andrew instantly realized she was right. He looked around the room and saw Z and Sabrina nodding. They were damned if they did, and damned if they didn't. At least at school they might be able to discover something important.

"Let's be clear. However we proceed, we need to keep you safe," Nash cut in. His eyes stayed on Sabrina a bit longer — probably because she was the one who had just been followed by the van. "No one is asking you to apprehend anyone in the hallway. None of you should make any direct contact with these teachers if it's out of the ordinary. If they're not your teachers, don't talk to them. Is that clear?" Andrew and the others nodded.

"But within those parameters, we're relying on you for intel," Patricia said. She shot Nash an unreadable look. They were having so many private conversations that it was like being front row at a Charlie Chaplin movie. "It may take longer to draw him out, but it's the best way we can think of to find the serum."

Z squinted at the screen. "Why do you think this guy is still here? It doesn't make sense to me that he'd stick around when he knows we're on to him."

Patricia took a breath. "The only reason I can think of is that whatever he's planning to do with the serum, he's planning on doing it here."

CHAPTER THIRTY-THREE

Right next to the teachers' parking lot was a statue of a bulldog, the school mascot, sitting on top of a granite pedestal. Three months ago, Justin, Hindy and some other guys were wasted and snuck onto campus late one night to climb on top and stream themselves live. That felt like three years ago at this point. Justin remembered it now as he and the others stood behind the statue, using the spot as a lookout. They had a perfect view of the teachers' lot, but the teachers wouldn't be able to see them.

"I think we should try not to be alone today," Sabrina said.

A life-or-death buddy system, Justin thought grimly

"Are you guys sure we should be doing this?" Gabby asked, squeezing his hand tightly. "What if we're in over our heads this time? He's got to know we're on to him if he was driving that van."

"We're totally in over our heads," Z answered. Justin was surprised to hear fear in her voice, too. "But we're also the ones who have the best shot at figuring out who has the serum."

Sabrina nodded. "We have to finish this. I don't know about you, but I don't want to imagine a group of terrorists who have Andrew's brainpower or Justin's psychokinesis."

Gabby was practically cutting off the circulation in Justin's hand. "That's what I mean, though. If he's already killed people to get it, what's he going to do to us if we try to stop him? He could have a plan in place already. He doesn't even have to follow us. He knows exactly where we are all day."

"That's why we're not getting too close," Andrew responded.

Justin wrapped his arms around Gabby's waist. "You don't have to do this, Gabby. If you don't want to be here, I can take you home right now," he told her. He didn't realize until this moment, when it all suddenly became real, that he hoped she would bow out. He could handle himself, but what about her? If something happened to Gabby, he didn't know what he would do. He'd never felt like this about a girl —

"Can you please think about Gabby when you're not around me?" Z asked.

Justin's cheeks fired up. "You promised to stay out of my head, Z."

"I know, but it's hard to control when I'm nervous."

He had more to say to her, but Dr. Fields pulled up in his car. Justin had him for chem two years earlier, and all he remembered was that his class almost killed his GPA and Dr. Fields didn't give a crap about it. Justin would've gotten kicked off the football team if that nerd from the science club hadn't let him cheat off him.

"Did Dr. Fields always have a Mustang?" Justin asked, noticing for the first time how shiny his car looked.

"I don't think so. That car looks brand-new," Andrew answered. "It still has the plates from the dealer on it."

"What if he sold the serum and is already starting to spend the cash?" Justin asked, eyeing Dr. Fields as he got out of the car.

"I think you're reaching," Z responded. "It's only a Mustang."

Justin shot her a look. "Only a Mustang? Sorry, Z, we can't all have rich dads who buy us Range Rovers." When Z winced, he wished he could take it back. It wasn't her fault her parents had money and his mom didn't.

Fields was talking on his cell phone as he slammed his car door shut.

"He looks mad," Gabby whispered. They couldn't hear him, but Justin agreed. He was making the kinds of faces and hand gestures that you do when you're pissed at somebody. Fields still couldn't see them as he passed by the front of the bulldog statue.

"I told you why I was there," Fields seethed into his phone. "It's not my fault he didn't show up to the meeting."

"I wonder what meeting he's talking about," Gabby said.

"We need to get his phone," Justin responded, already strategizing how he could do it without getting caught. He looked down at Gabby, who watched Fields's every move as he walked away.

The bell was going to ring in ten minutes. "Should we head to class?" Sabrina asked, looking at Gabby.

"Do you think we can really do this?" Gabby asked. Something in her voice had shifted, though, as if she was looking for assurance instead of a reason to back out.

"Yes. We can," Sabrina said definitively. She turned to face them all. "If you were asking me if Hannah Phelps or Hindy or any of the cheerleaders or Mathletes could do this, I'd say no … but us? We were chosen for a reason. We're Lost Causes. That's exactly what makes us strong. We've been beaten down in life — and we've gotten back up. We can handle anything."

Justin wasn't going to lie. It was a pretty damn good speech. He was suddenly feeling more fired up than before a game. Maybe they should bring in Sabrina to do the football team pep talks from now on. But as he looked back at Gabby, he still felt protective. He didn't want her to feel peer pressured into this. It was too dangerous a situation to walk into if she really didn't think she could deal with it. If she started acting too freaked out in front of any of the suspects, it would be a bigger red flag than anything.

"If you don't want to do this, you don't have to," Justin told her again. "You could go home on your own, and Nash would make sure you were safe. The four of us would stay. I'm sure that won't look as suspicious."

Gabby shook her head. "No. It has to be unanimous." After a beat, she looked at them decisively. "I'm not giving up now. I'm in."

* * *

Wincott was lecturing about something as he sauntered around the classroom, but Sabrina couldn't pay attention to a word of it. As much as she knew the Lost Causes could handle this, the reality of sitting a few feet away from a teacher that might be a murderer was more daunting than she'd realized when she was trying to pump the others up near the parking lot. Instead of taking notes on Fitzgerald's use of war imagery in *Tender Is the Night*, she was picturing Wincott tracking her in the white van, and when that image faded away, she pictured him burying Devon's body at the Springs. She wasn't sure what kind of intel she was supposed to get just by sitting in class. Patricia said to look for anything unusual, even if it was slight, but Wincott was acting the same way he always did. Yet Sabrina was sitting there wondering whether Wincott had tortured Lily with a blowtorch. It didn't help that she remembered Nash saying that he felt Wincott was at the top of the suspect list.

She jumped when the bell rang and quickly packed up her books.

"Sabrina?" Her stomach dropped as she looked up to find Wincott standing directly over her. "Can you stay for a minute?"

The last few students were walking out. She knew she shouldn't stay in the room alone with him.

"I've got to get to physics."

"This will only take a minute."

"What's up?" she asked quickly, but it wasn't fast enough. The last student left and Wincott closed the door behind him. Now it was just the two of them.

"I just wanted to ask if you're okay?" He took a few steps toward her. "That was a pretty big accident you got into on Saturday night."

He looked at her evenly. Was this just concern or was he messing with her?

"How did you know …?"

"I was there." She must've given him an odd look because he quickly added, "I mean, I was headed to dinner nearby. I was going to stop, but it looked as though you had someone helping you."

Nash. "Right. My … friend was just a few blocks away when it happened …"

"You were lucky he was close," Wincott said. He sounded sympathetic, but his words had a double meaning Sabrina didn't like.

And he was watching her so closely. Too closely. "I've got to get to physics." Sabrina lunged for the door and threw it open. She started breathing again only when she was back at her locker. With shaky hands she texted the others to keep Wincott at the top of the list.

* * *

As Z walked to Dr. Fields's class, she decided the best way for her to get intel from him was to provoke an incriminating thought. But that would mean talking to him directly, and Nash had said not to do anything out of the ordinary. Z had never struck up a casual conversation with a teacher before. Plus, if Z was being honest, she was too scared to put herself right in his crosshairs.

As soon as she saw Jared idly walking toward Dr. Fields's classroom, she had a stroke of genius that even Andrew would appreciate. It might be a little painful, but it would be fine. Like jumping into a cold swimming pool.

"Jared!" she called out. He stopped and turned, surprise registering on his face when he realized it was Z. They hadn't spoken since their breakup, but Z wasn't angry with him anymore. Yes, he'd been using her, but hadn't she been using him, too? She kept him around mostly because she was bored and too apathetic to break up with him. Each had served a purpose for the other.

"Hey," Jared said so enthusiastically that Z felt guilty about using him yet again. "How are you?"

"I need a favor." It was unfortunate that she had to be so blunt, but she didn't have much time.

"Um, okay," he answered cautiously. "What is it?"

"I need you to ask Dr. Fields something for me."

"Why can't you ask him?"

"I just can't. Will you do it?"

Jared pulled on the straps of his backpack, watching her carefully. "If you tell me why you dumped me out of nowhere."

The first bell was going to ring any second, and she needed him to agree before they walked into class.

Z did what she had to do. She lowered her voice. "I dumped you because I know you're not attracted to me."

"What are you talking about? That's not true." He probably sounded halfhearted even to himself.

"Jared, I know you like dudes." His face paled so quickly that it was as if a vampire had sucked his blood out. "So will you ask Fields or not?"

* * *

Dr. Fields smoothed down his white lab coat while Z eyed it closely for traces of blood. He wore that thing so much that she wouldn't be surprised if he murdered someone in it.

"The lab we'll be doing tomorrow consists of six stations," Fields explained in a patronizing tone. "We'll be working with magnesium ribbon and a few moderately sized pieces of mossy zinc."

She locked eyes with Jared and he returned her pointed look with a grudging nod. She'd repeated over and over exactly what to say and how to phrase a follow up if necessary.

"Every station will have crucible tongs," Fields continued, "a flint striker and a Bunsen burner."

A Bunsen burner, could that have made those burn marks on Lily and Devon? Suddenly she had an image of Fields standing over Devon, searing his skin with that bright blue flame.

At the end of class, students scrambled out of their seats, but Z stayed in hers, methodically packing up her books. Out of the corner of her eye, she watched Jared walk over to Fields.

"Hey, Dr. Fields," Jared said. "How did you like that John Lennon biography?"

"What are you talking about?" Fields asked, erasing the whiteboard. Z knew Jared's constant questions annoyed Fields. She was counting on it, in fact.

"The John Lennon biography. I thought I saw you at the book sign ing for it in Pueblo two weeks ago. A Friday night?"

It was the night the medical examiner had determined as Devon Warner's time of death. She'd been able to narrow it down to a four-hour window that evening.

"No, you didn't. Couldn't have been me."

She'd never been so happy to hear the ringing in her ears.

Why the hell is he snooping into my personal life?

It wasn't a specifically incriminating thought, but it wasn't one she was about to dismiss.

Jared shifted his weight from one foot to the other. "Are you sure? Two Fridays ago. I swear I saw you there."

"I'm sure. Friday nights, I stay in with my wife."

He couldn't have seen me that night. No one saw me.

Where had he been that he needed to lie about it? At the Springs with Devon?

Z slipped out of the room, surreptitiously wiping the blood from her nose so Jared didn't see.

"So, are you, like, blackmailing me now?" Jared asked, once they were back in the hallway.

"Of course not," Z answered, a little offended. "I don't get why you're hiding it, though. You shouldn't be embarrassed."

"I just …" he trailed off. "I'm just not ready yet."

Z had never voluntarily given anyone a hug in her life, but for a split second she wanted to give Jared one. She didn't actually do it, but still. The sentiment was there.

"You going to tell me why I had to say that to Dr. Fields?" he asked.

"Nope. But I'll give you twenty bucks if you say it to Mr. Schroeder, too."

"How about a coffee sometime instead?"

"Done."

Jared reprised his performance next period. Schroeder's thoughts informed Z that he went to AA meetings on Friday nights in Castle Pines. Then Schroeder started thinking that he didn't realize there was a new John Lennon biography out and he couldn't wait to order it. Those didn't exactly sound like the thoughts of a guilty man. Maybe getting sober had resolved the violence issues in his past.

Z texted Nash and the others.

Move Schroeder to the bottom of the list. Keep Fields at the top with Wincott.

CHAPTER THIRTY-FOUR

Andrew entered Greenly's class, his sense of purpose diluting his underlying fear. He may have had a hard time picturing some of the other teachers as potential murderers, but he didn't have that problem with Greenly. Like most other sociopaths, he was missing the compassionate sensitivity chip.

"Andrew," Greenly said, handing him back a quiz. Andrew looked down and smiled. He hadn't gotten over the novelty of seeing an A at the top of anything that had his name on it. "I wouldn't look so excited. You still got one wrong."

Andrew bit his tongue. He'd purposely written in an incorrect answer for one of the questions to make his sudden improvement look a bit more realistic. Now, seeing Greenly's triumphant face, he wished he hadn't.

Class started and Greenly put a long problem set up on the board. As the class worked busily at their desks, Greenly sat at the front of the room, flipping through his black planner. Andrew had noticed that Greenly carried it with him constantly. What he wouldn't give for the chance to take a peek inside. Who knew what secrets could be buried in there? Suddenly, an idea formed in his head, but he needed Justin's help. Andrew slowly slid his phone out of his bag and under his notebook. They were supposed to keep their phones off during school, but most people ignored that rule and kept them on vibrate. He quietly tapped out the text.

Have an idea. Come outside room 306 when the bell rings. I want to see if you can move Greenly's planner from his desk into my bag.

A moment passed before Justin's reply came.

Dude. Really? Won't he notice his planner magically moving? I thought you were supposed to be a genius.

Greenly looked up just then, and Andrew slid his phone under his notebook just in the nick of time.

"Five more minutes," Greenly told the class. When Andrew saw his head go down again, he resumed his texting.

I'll ask him a question after class to distract him. My backpack will be open and right next to the desk.

Justin's reply came quickly.

All right. It's worth a try.

When the bell finally rang at the end of class, Andrew took his time gathering his books, his heart beating fast. They were actually going to try this. If he ever wanted to be in the FBI one day, he'd have to get used to putting himself in jeopardy. As he reached the front of the room, he saw Justin through the open door, standing against the wall in the hallway as dozens of other students scurried around him. Andrew gave a slight nod to the black spiral-bound planner that was on the desk. Justin gave him a thumbs-up.

"Was there something you needed, Andrew?" Greenly asked sharply.

"Uh, yeah," Andrew said, his hands clammy. "I was wondering if you could review graphic exponential growth?"

Greenly smirked. "But I thought all this was so easy for you now."

Most teachers were thrilled when a student of theirs suddenly made strides, but Greenly had taken Andrew's newfound success as a personal affront. Probably because taunting Andrew had been his primary form of classroom entertainment. With Andrew as the resident genius now, he had limited material.

"I want to double-check that I understand this. It sounded like you were saying that if the base was greater than one, it's exponential decay, not growth?" Greenly had, in fact, said the opposite. This was a better way to egg him on, though.

"I didn't say that." Greenly was instantly defensive. He turned away from the desk and to the board to illustrate his point. As he wrote out a sample function, Andrew turned to the open doorway and gave Justin a signal.

Justin laser-focused in on the planner.

"If the base is less than one, the graph decreases from left to right," Greenly said as he drew an axis. Andrew's eyes darted between the board and the planner.

"If the base is greater than one, the graph *increases* from left to right …" Andrew knew Greenly was reaching the end of the explanation. Out of the corner of his eye, he spotted the planner moving. He shifted his body to better block the activity from Greenly's view.

"So I *was* saying that a base greater than one proves exponential growth. Not decay." He looked at Andrew expectantly.

The planner was at the edge of the desk. A few more inches and it would slide into Andrew's bag. He had to get Greenly to turn back to the board so Justin could finish the job.

"What about a population growth model, though? How does that work?" he asked.

"We're not covering that in this course. That's calculus."

"Oh. Okay. If you don't know, I can ask Ms. O'Reilly at Mathletes …"

"Of course I know," Greenly huffed, turning back to the board. Andrew had correctly assessed his weak point.

Justin got back to work. Within seconds, the planner slipped over the edge of the desk and into the bag with a small thump. Andrew faked a cough to cover it.

"I think I get it now," Andrew said to Greenly quickly.

"I haven't even finished the explanation," Greenly said, eyeing Andrew suspiciously.

Andrew wanted to hightail it out of there before Greenly realized his planner was missing, but he could only think of one way to do it. He doubled down on the coughing.

"Sorry, the air in here is making it so I can't breathe. I think I need to see the nurse."

Greenly rolled his eyes and waved Andrew off.

Andrew smiled as he walked away. Sometimes it was hard to break old habits.

* * *

"Let's see it," Justin said, when he and Andrew met up right outside the building.

Andrew opened the planner, the smile fading from his face. The little black notebook was more of a lesson planner than a life planner. The contacts section remained totally blank. Like the rest of the world, Greenly probably kept his contacts in his phone. The calendar section was chock-full, but only with items related to school.

"That was all for nothing?" Justin asked.

Andrew turned the last few pages, reluctant to admit defeat. He reached a section titled Notes. It, too, was empty except for three lines. Each one held a different ten-character combination of letters and numbers.

Andrew's heart rate picked up.

Maybe this wasn't going to be as futile as he thought.

He had a feeling he knew exactly what those were.

CHAPTER THIRTY-FIVE

For the first time in recent memory, Sabrina ditched her last-period class and went straight home after school, while the rest of her friends were working through the list of teacher suspects. Her neck and shoulders had been throbbing all day from the residual pain of the car accident.

She took two ibuprofen and slipped into the shower. As the hot water cascaded over her, she imagined it washing away the stress. The white van. The accident. The strangely terrifying conversation with Wincott that morning … *Nash*.

She'd replayed the memory of their kiss many times since then, each time reminded of a new detail. The unexpectedly gentle way he'd touched her cheek just before he kissed her, the smooth skin her fingers had grazed under his shirt, the way their bodies had come together as if by gravitational force.

But what was the point of experiencing something so perfect only to have it snatched away?

Nash had been strictly professional in the meeting, as she'd expected. Sabrina understood the position he was in, but couldn't help feeling a bit stung. He could've given her a sign … a look … *something* that showed he was feeling the same way she was, even if he couldn't act on it. Was staying away as hard for him as it was for her? Or was he actually able to turn off his emotions as easily as it seemed?

And would there ever be a point where they *could* be together? If they solved the case and found the serum, he would no longer be constrained by FBI protocol ... and they would be free to do whatever they wanted. It was yet another good, if not completely unselfish, reason to try to find the serum as quickly as possible. Sure, saving the world from any number of terrifying scenarios was the top priority, but getting a chance to be with Nash was a close second in Sabrina's mind.

A *chance* to be with him. It wasn't a given. Solving the case could also mean that he would move on to his next one, wherever that took him, and forget all about her. Sure, he had admitted he cared about what happened to her ... and that he'd saved her phone number in case she wasn't picked ... but how much did that actually mean?

Suddenly, the lights went out in the bathroom. She stiffened, on high alert. Was this a sign a ghost was about to appear?

Then the water turned cold, so icy cold that it sent a shiver up her spine. She tried to adjust the faucet, but no matter how she turned it, the temperature remained freezing. Goose bumps erupted on her skin as she reached outside the shower and grabbed her towel, but she didn't see anything at all. *Strange.*

As she stepped off the mat, she slipped on a huge puddle of water, catching herself right before she slammed to the ground. Water was all over the floor. Sabrina sighed. The shower must have some kind of leak. Something with the pipes, which would explain why the water went cold. Here she was thinking this was some kind of sign from a ghost, when really it was just another sign of this house falling apart. The power had probably gone out, too. Had her father even remembered to pay the last bill? As many changes as the serum had brought about for Sabrina, it couldn't change her miserable family situation. Talk about lost causes.

She pulled a few towels from under the sink and started mopping up the mess, wondering how was she going to get a leak fixed on top of everything else she had going on in her life. The lights came back on and she breathed a sigh of relief. Now she only had the pipes to worry about and not the electric bill.

When she finally stood up and looked in the mirror, she gasped.

There, in the condensation, someone had written a name.

Amy Hanson.

CHAPTER THIRTY-SIX

Andrew was sprawled on his bed later that afternoon when the call from Nash came through.

"I'm letting you know we're crossing Manzetti off our list," Nash told him.

"Why?" Andrew had thought that Sweaty Manzetti's major credit card debt could have indicated desperation.

"I had a little time today to hack into his home security cameras. He has a totally hooked-up smart house, cameras throughout." It didn't surprise Andrew that technology teacher Manzetti had set up such a state-of-the-art system. Maybe that's what he blew all his money on. "The feed is automatically uploaded and stored to the cloud for six months before it deletes."

"You went back to the date of Devon's murder," Andrew guessed. He knew the medical examiner had given them a four-hour window to work with.

"Correct," Nash replied. "Manzetti has a camera at every entrance to his house — and then some. I was able to track him arriving home that day, eating dinner with his wife —"

"Sweaty Manzetti has a wife?"

"Focus. After they ate, they had a beer on their porch together and went to bed."

"Another one bites the dust." It was both exciting and terrifying each time the suspect field narrowed, bringing them that much closer to the true killer.

"What are you working on right now?" Nash asked.

"Just doing some recon," Andrew replied vaguely.

It wasn't that he didn't trust Nash — that was Z's department — but he didn't want to let on what his plans were for the rest of the afternoon.

Because Andrew was about to hack into Greenly's email.

He didn't want Nash offering to take over the job himself. Andrew was relishing the chance to take Greenly down once and for all.

He hung up with Nash and turned back to his laptop. He'd already entered the email address Greenly had given to his students at the beginning of the year.

Now, the cursor clicked, awaiting the password.

Andrew carefully typed in one of the ten-character combinations from the back of Greenly's notebook. He clicked enter, holding his breath to see if his earlier hunch would prove to be correct.

Invalid.

He typed in the second one.

Bingo.

Greenly's inbox filled his screen.

The good news was that it appeared he was the type of person who rarely deleted an email. The bad news was that it meant there were over ten thousand messages to sift through.

Andrew skimmed through the first few pages of Greenly's emails quickly. He was surprised to find dozens of personal email addresses, indicating Greenly had actual acquaintances he corresponded with, though it seemed to be mostly about Rockies baseball. The teacher was involved in two different fantasy baseball leagues.

After he'd gone through hundreds of emails, nothing jumped out at him. Andrew rubbed his eyes, trying to relieve the tension. The headaches had been getting worse lately, but thanks to a few medical journal articles, he now knew it was due to eyestrain and not a resurgence of his hypochondria.

He returned to the screen, switching tactics and jumping to the emails right around the dates of Lily Carpenter's murder and then Devon Warner's. There was nothing to suggest an alibi for either of the dates … no parties, no events. However, there was nothing suspicious either.

Growing impatient, he clicked on the Search Emails field. He typed in "serum." No emails found. That was a long shot, anyway.

He typed in "Devon Warner." No emails found.

He typed in "Lily Carpenter."

One email popped up.

However, it wasn't from Lily Carpenter. It was from a man named Frank Jenkins and it had been sent to Greenly and thirty other people. It was flagged because one of the other recipients of the email had the last name Carpenter.

Robert Carpenter.

It was the name of Lily's ex-husband. The one she kept in touch with before her death, if the picture on her mantel gave any indication.

Could it be the same Robert Carpenter? And if so, did that mean Greenly knew him?

Andrew clicked to the body of the email.

Hey, guys, can you believe it's been 30 years since we all lived in Hoover Hall? Who's going to the UNM reunion this weekend? Would love to see some old faces. Literally.

Frank had attached a photo that looked to be about twenty years old, according to the clothing — a bunch of guys crammed into a dorm common room.

Andrew immediately recognized one of the guys as a young Greenly.

His eyes traveled across the photo and his pulse picked up.

Robert Carpenter, easily identifiable from the photo on Lily's mantel, was standing next to Greenly.

So Greenly had a connection to Lily Carpenter through her ex-husband. He and Robert Carpenter had gone to college together at the University of New Mexico.

Was Robert Carpenter just an old acquaintance of Greenly's? There were no other emails between them to suggest a relationship. But wouldn't Greenly have deleted incriminating correspondence?

What if Greenly had learned about the serum through him? Then he had worked in tandem with Devon Warner and killed him for the serum later?

Which made him think of something else — was one of these men in the photo Devon Warner? He scanned the faces quickly before realizing that the timeline didn't add up. Devon was in his late twenties. These men were a few decades older than that.

Andrew was startled by the sound of his phone ringing.

"Andrew, where are you?" Sabrina asked, clearly agitated.

"Home. Why? Are you okay?"

"I need your help with something."

CHAPTER THIRTY-SEVEN

Nash was at his desk at Cytology, relieved that the day was over. He hadn't felt right about the decision to send the group to school today knowing that one of their teachers was a killer who could be on their trail. Way too risky.

However, Patricia had pulled rank, and the only thing Nash could do was periodically check the grainy camera feeds he'd placed around Cedar Springs High to try to catch a glimpse of each of them through-out the day. Unfortunately, the cameras were sporadically placed.

"You're still watching them?" Patricia had asked at one point earlier that day when she'd poked her head in.

"Just keeping an eye on things," he maintained coolly. "Protecting our assets."

"They're fine," Patricia said with a dismissive wave. Was she too emotionally involved with the case, causing her to put lives in jeopardy because she wanted it solved? Or did she see the five of them as merely tools? Either way, her lack of precaution alarmed him. Though he could admit the amount of intel the group had funneled to them by the end of the day was impressive, it didn't ease his nerves.

He turned his eyes away from the school security feed and back to his laptop. Robert Carpenter. That's the one he needed to concentrate on right now. Andrew had just called him to report the connection between Greenly and Carpenter — they were old college friends. Robert had an airtight alibi for the evening of Lily's murder. But if he, Greenly and Devon Warner were working together, Robert could have covered his tracks that night. Suspicion would naturally fall to an ex-husband, particularly an ex-husband aware of the serum's value. Greenly and Devon could've done all the dirty work while Robert was the brains behind the operation.

Now Nash was attempting to piece together an accurate time line for Robert during the time frame of Devon's murder. Robert may not have been as careful to secure an alibi that night as he had been for Lily's. Nash was also keen to get a better idea of why Lily and Robert's marriage had dissolved and what level of acrimony it had reached — and not necessarily from Patricia, who had been too close to Lily to be objective on the matter. Of course, it was possible that Robert hadn't been involved in any murders at all. Greenly could have learned about the serum from Robert and acted on his own accord with Devon.

Either way, it was a big find from Andrew. So why was Nash having such a hard time focusing on it?

There was something blocking him. A feeling that there was more danger he had missed. Or that there was something else hurtling toward them that he hadn't anticipated. It was only an instinct, but he never ignored his instincts. Not only had they saved his life and others in the field, they were what had led him straight into the FBI in the first place. It was rare to be recruited right out of high school, but the FBI had been watching him since he was ten years old.

Ever since they killed his father.

Nash had been just a toddler when his father left, and his subsequent visits over the years were rare. Random drop-ins that made Nash, his mother and his stepfather increasingly uncomfortable. Nash's father was always ranting about something new — secret wars, government robots, apocalyptic notions. Nash might not have understood the bizarre theories, but even as a child, he knew the thinking behind them was flawed and inaccurate.

On his father's last visit to Nash, they met on his mom's front porch and Nash made no move to hug him. For one thing, they rarely had physical contact. But his father smelled acrid this time, like motor oil.

He asked Nash what grade he was in and if he still played soccer. After a few more routine questions, his father circled back to soccer.

"You still play over at Woodley Park?"

"Sometimes," Nash answered.

"When?"

"On the weekends."

"Never after school?"

Nash told him no. There were too many lowlifes, junkies and cops hanging around the park on weekdays because of the courthouse right next to it. His father made a few comments about how the government was responsible for the mass addiction problems of the poor in this country and how the wrong people were being tried in that courthouse.

Later that night, Nash replayed the conversation in his head, something telling him not to let it go. His father had kept asking him about soccer. Why? He'd never been interested in any sports. Why had he suddenly taken such a keen interest in where and when Nash played?

When Nash woke up the next morning, it hit him all at once. The leading questions to confirm that he wouldn't be at Woodley Park on a weekday … the stench of motor oil emanating from his father's body as if he'd bathed in it …

Nash had never been more certain of anything in his life.

His father was going to blow up the courthouse.

He barged into his mother and stepfather's room and begged them to call the FBI. He was so insistent that they finally did. Agents found his father in the basement of the courthouse that day; he'd already killed two guards to gain access. He was moments away from detonating his homemade bomb, but the agents shot him dead right before he flipped the switch. Ten-year-old Nash had saved hundreds of lives … though he would never forget that it had been at the expense of his father's life.

When an agent questioned Nash later that day, he was impressed with the boy's deductions. He gave Nash a few games and puzzles to play with while he waited. At the time, Nash had thought it was to distract him from his father's death, but now he understood they were tests. The same agent checked in on him every year until he finally realized he was being vetted.

And his performance in the FBI had apparently been as impressive as they had hoped. There were only a select few in the FBI who knew who Nash's father was, but he still worked doubly hard to distance himself from that infamy. Step by step and year by year, he had built a name for himself within the agency, and he wasn't about to break his streak now.

He'd never been on a case with so much at stake. Was this imminent danger he sensed something that was right in front of him or something that had yet to show its face?

Nash turned back to his screen.

Time to focus on Robert Carpenter.

CHAPTER THIRTY-EIGHT

The original Cedar Springs Public Library was basically empty when Sabrina entered it later that afternoon with Andrew. It was the oldest building in Cedar Springs, one of those places where you felt that you were entering another world as soon as the massive oak double doors slammed shut behind you. Once you were in the ancient building, the sun could be blindingly bright outside and you'd never know it.

"Why did we need to come here?" Sabrina asked as Andrew led them to an antique wooden table in the back corner. "I thought we were looking for Amy Hansons's obituary online." She'd told Andrew about the name scrawled across her mirror — and that she suspected it belonged to the ghostly girl who kept appearing. Andrew was her best shot at confirming her identity and discovering why she kept visiting Sabrina. She had debated asking Nash for help as well, but her gut told her to leave him and Patricia out of it for now. After all, the girl had warned her about Nash and Patricia in the first place.

"I want to hack into the library's server," Andrew told her. "A lot of these obituary databases make you pay if the death was more than a few years ago. If we do it here, I can use the library's passwords so we can get it for free and we won't leave a virtual footprint."

While Andrew settled into his seat and pulled out his laptop, Sabrina considered what he'd just told her about the connection between Greenly and Robert Carpenter.

"It's weird Greenly never said anything about knowing him. Like after Lily was murdered, in the news or something," she said.

"I said the same thing to Nash," Andrew told her. "The newspaper was doing stories on this woman every day for a month. They would have loved a quote from someone who once knew her ex. Especially at the beginning, when Robert was still a suspect."

"Right. Why wouldn't he have mentioned that he knew the guy? If he had nothing to hide."

Andrew pulled up a local database. "What's the girl's name again?"

"Amy Hanson." Little goose bumps raised on her arms again at the mention of it.

His hands flew across the keyboard. "I'm not seeing a local match."

Sabrina's heart sank. "Don't worry," Andrew told her. "I'm just getting started."

He clicked on a few different search engines, broadening the parameters in the hope that that would yield something more conclusive. The hits started popping up, one after another. "Now we're getting somewhere. I've got at least ten deceased Amy Hansons here!" He reddened as the librarian looked over at him, realizing he shouldn't sound quite so excited about a bunch of dead women.

Sabrina suddenly felt a chill in the air. If there was any place for spirits to hang out, it was in an ancient library like this one. Her eyes darted around the room and she sucked in her breath when an elderly man hobbled by their table. He looked so pale ... was it possible he was ...

"I can see him, too," Andrew whispered.

She smiled sheepishly. "Sorry. Habit now. Okay, look for an Amy

Hanson who died as a teenager. So far, these ghosts seem to appear to me at the age they were when they died."

It took him about ten seconds to check the first six obituaries. Then, "Got it."

She scooted her chair closer to look at the grainy yearbook photo Andrew pointed at.

Instantly, she recognized the face.

Amy's black hair was swept over one shoulder, her almond eyes boring into the camera. She wasn't smiling for the photo — she looked as if she'd just seen something she didn't approve of.

"That's her," Sabrina whispered.

"She's from New Mexico, died in 2007," Andrew said. "She was a senior at North Valley High School, survived by her mom, aunt and uncle. There was a memorial service at school held two days later but no information about a church service."

Sabrina read the obituary herself, disappointed. "It doesn't say how she died. It barely says anything."

Andrew opened a new window and ran several more searches on Amy Hanson now that he knew where she was from. When archived articles came up from the local newspaper, he clicked on the first one, adjusting his laptop so Sabrina could read it, too.

February 5, 2007

North Valley — A tragic car accident took the lives of five North Valley High School students late last night amid one of the worst flash floods the city has seen in years. Amy Hanson, Catherine Freeman, Christopher Jarvis, Kevin Beswick and Danielle Wenkie were crossing the Rio Puerco Bridge around 11 p.m. when Hanson apparently lost control of her car. Though the families of the teens don't believe any foul play was involved, others who knew the deceased are not as certain. An administrator at North Valley High, who prefers to remain anonymous, suggested drugs or alcohol might have been involved. "All five of these kids were troubled. We're talking clinical depression, social anxiety. I'm not saying they weren't good kids. There was just something off with all of them. They were loners. It was news to me they even knew each other." Another student, who was on the varsity baseball team with Kevin Beswick, concurred. "I wouldn't be surprised if this little get-together had something to do with drugs," he noted. "Why else would these five be together?"

Sabrina was filled with unexpected sadness, her connection to Amy having more impact on her than she'd thought. "She died in the water. That's why she's always sopping wet when I see her." She looked at Andrew, who was practically jumping out of his seat. "What is it?"

"I think I know why she's coming to you. And it's not because of Lily or Devon." He glanced at the screen again, as if part of him didn't want to say it out loud. "Five teenagers, all troubled, all loners, who hadn't previously been friends."

It finally clicked for Sabrina.

"Just like us," she whispered.

"And this girl keeps showing up, telling you not to trust Patricia and Nash."

Sabrina locked eyes with him. "They can't be …"

"Another group of Lost Causes."

CHAPTER THIRTY-NINE

The sun had already set that night when Gabby and Justin were buzzed through the massive wrought-iron gates of Z's house. Sabrina and Andrew had called an emergency meeting.

"Do you think they found something with one of the teachers?" Gabby wondered as they wound up the long, curved drive to Z's mansion. The suspect field had been narrowed down to three, which made her more nervous about going to school. With each passing day, the chance increased that whichever teacher they were after would lash out at one or all of the Lost Causes.

"We know we've got Schroeder and Manzetti out of the equation now," Justin said. Soft-spoken Mr. Schroeder had been cleared once Z discovered he'd been at an AA meeting (and officially eliminated after Nash had confirmed the time and place of it). Nash had also eliminated Manzetti after checking out his home security camera feeds.

Of the three that were left — Greenly, Wincott and Dr. Fields — Gabby knew Greenly was the top suspect in Andrew's mind. He'd sent them all an email about Greenly's connection to Robert Carpenter earlier that afternoon. Gabby couldn't help agreeing that that pushed him to the top of the list, especially given his temperament. Anyone who could be as cruel as he'd been to Andrew had a major character flaw. "Maybe Andrew found out more about Greenly and that's why he called us here."

"Maybe. But I still think Dr. Fields is the one we should be looking into," Justin said. He'd had a bad feeling about him ever since Fields pulled up in his flashy new car that morning. "He's the one who has the actual connection with Lily, anyway. They could have met at that science conference Patricia said Lily went to years ago. Greenly only knows Robert, and he may or may not have even talked to him in the last twenty years. They could just be two dudes who once lived in the same dorm."

"What about Wincott?" Gabby asked as Justin parked in front of the five-car garage. Sabrina had gotten a weird vibe from Wincott earlier and so far nothing had come up to clear him, so he remained a suspect as far as she knew. After hearing about Sabrina's run-in with him, Gabby was relieved that she had a different English teacher this year.

"Wincott's a dark horse," Justin said. "He's pervy with all the girls at school. His dad's a Chinese spy —"

"*Alleged* Chinese spy," Gabby interrupted.

Justin looked at her, amused. "You really do give everyone the benefit of the doubt, don't you?"

He gave her a quick kiss before they exited the car.

"Hey, this way." Z opened the gigantic front door and motioned for them to come in. "You're the last ones."

* * *

Inside Z's room, Gabby and Justin perched on the large bed, while Z settled herself on the ottoman next to Sabrina. Andrew was across from them in an ornate antique desk chair that was way too small for a guy as tall as he was.

"So, what's going on?" Z asked.

Sabrina and Andrew exchanged a look.

"I know this is going to sound crazy …" Sabrina started.

"But that doesn't mean it isn't true," Andrew interjected.

Sabrina nodded. "Because we do have proof —"

"Just tell us!" Justin interrupted.

Andrew took a breath. "We don't think we're the first group of Lost Causes. There may have been another group just like us."

"And they're all dead," Sabrina added.

It was the absolute last thing Gabby had expected them to say.

Z and Justin looked up, equally in shock.

A group of teens like them who were now all dead? There were so many questions swirling in Gabby's mind that it took a second before she could formulate one and get it out of her mouth. "How did you find this out?"

"You know that ghost I keep seeing?" Sabrina said. "The teenage girl who warned me not to trust Nash and Patricia?" Everyone nodded. "I finally got her full name this afternoon. Amy Hanson. Andrew and I looked her up and we found this."

She pulled up the article on Z's iPad and passed it to the group.

Gabby read through the article slowly, certain phrases jumping out at her. "Tragic accident … all five of these kids were troubled … clinical depression, social anxiety … lost control of her car."

Justin was the first to speak. "This is all you got? I think you guys are reaching. It sounds like those kids were just a bunch of losers who all became friends."

Z raised an eyebrow at him. "Sounds familiar."

Gabby wasn't surprised that Z had instantly latched on to this second Lost Causes theory. But Gabby wasn't convinced. "You mean you think this group was recruited by Patricia ten years ago?" she asked carefully.

"Right," said Sabrina. "Just like us ... given the serum, maybe to solve a case."

"It's about a thousand times more likely that they were just a group of random friends," Justin said. "That Amy chick didn't know how to drive in the rain and they went off the bridge. Accidents happen. End of story."

Sabrina shook her head. "Think about it. Why does Amy keep coming to me? More than any other ghost. Three times already. There's something she wants me to know."

"And look at where they lived," Andrew added. "North Valley is in Albuquerque. Where Patricia and Lily are from. Patricia said they developed the serum at the FBI field office there."

"Is it possible these are all coincidences, though?" Gabby asked. Only Justin nodded.

"It's a lot of coincidences," Sabrina said. "Patricia said she developed the serum ten years ago. That's when these teens were killed."

"But Patricia and Nash also said they never used it on anyone before," Gabby pointed out.

Z gave her a pitying look. "Exactly. That's the point. They lied to us! If these five kids *were* Lost Causes, that means that ten years ago, Patricia — and probably Lily — gave them the serum and then somehow they all wound up dead."

"In a car accident," Justin said. "It's not like they were poisoned or something. Even if in some fantasy world, you're right about them being another group of Lost Causes, the way they died had nothing to do with the serum."

"That we know of," Z responded quickly.

"And why did Amy Hanson tell me not to trust them?" Sabrina asked. "If they were Lost Causes and everything was great until they all accidentally died in a rainstorm, why is Amy warning me about Patricia and Nash? Doesn't that mean there has to be some kind of connection?"

Gabby didn't have an answer for that.

Sabrina continued. "Here's the most important question: Are we putting ourselves in more danger than we think by helping Patricia and Nash with this case?"

"We knew from the start that this was dangerous," Justin said, growing exasperated. "I don't think we should stop investigating Greenly, Wincott and Fields just because there's a tiny chance Patricia and Nash may have lied to us about something unrelated."

Andrew nodded quickly. "Agreed. Regardless of this, the threat of the serum is too big to be put on the back burner. We should for sure keep investigating the teachers. We can't just let this person off the hook. Especially if they're on to us somehow."

Even though Gabby had been the most scared that morning — the one who thought they should take a step back from the case — she agreed with Andrew. The danger of the serum getting out was too high. And they were all way too invested to walk away now. At least she thought they were. Sabrina and Z still looked conflicted.

Andrew spoke again. "If Nash and Patricia can't be trusted, that's even *more* reason for us to stay on this case. To stay a step ahead of them."

Sabrina's and Z's eyes met, and Gabby knew Andrew had just found their common ground.

"That's true," Sabrina agreed. "But we should be careful how much we tell Patricia and Nash from here on. At least until we can find out more about Amy Hanson and the other kids in that car."

"How are we going to do that?" Justin asked.

"I think we should go to New Mexico," Sabrina said firmly. "Talk to Amy's family."

"I'm down to go," Z said. "Maybe we could ditch and do it during school tomorrow. It's only a three-hour drive."

Justin shook his head. "What are you going to do? Ask these dead kids' parents if they were ever tricked by the FBI into getting psychic powers?"

Something suddenly occurred to Gabby. "And if they really were Lost Causes like us, then their parents won't know anything anyway." For a moment, she felt a flash of kinship to Amy and the others. If they were actual Lost Causes, she knew their lives hadn't been easy.

"Look, I admit this whole idea about another group of Lost Causes could be a total delusional road we've gone down. I actually hope it is," Sabrina said, sounding sincere. "But what if we're right? The only way to protect ourselves is to find out the truth. We'll know more if we ask some questions. We need to get a sense of who these kids were, at least. And if their death really was an accident."

Andrew suddenly straightened up. "If they were Lost Causes, then Patricia and Lily probably gave them the serum to help solve a case, right?"

"Probably," Z agreed.

"So what if they were on the trail of someone, just like we are right now ... and what if the person they were after is the one who killed them all?"

It struck a chord with Gabby. Hadn't she been worried for her own safety?

Sabrina said exactly what Gabby had been thinking. "If someone killed *them* for being Lost Causes, what's to say the same thing won't happen to us?"

"What if this is even bigger than we thought?" Z ventured, the room eerily silent around her. "What if the person that they were after is the same person *we're* after?"

CHAPTER FORTY

If Sabrina had to guess, she probably got three hours of sleep, but she somehow had the jittery energy that came from too much coffee. She grabbed the keys to the rental car and texted Z that she was on the way. She was glad Z was the one headed to New Mexico with her.

Justin might be skeptical about another group of Lost Causes, but Sabrina kept coming back to it. Why else would Amy keep showing up to her? It seemed too strange to be just a coincidence.

The thought dancing around in her mind all night, though, was that if another group of Lost Causes really had existed, that meant Patricia had flat-out lied to them about never using the serum. More important for Sabrina, did that mean Nash had lied, too?

She wanted to believe that he had nothing to do with it. Obviously, even if there had been another group of Lost Causes, he wouldn't have been involved in giving them the serum. He was only twelve at the time of Amy's death. But he was running this case with Patricia. Wouldn't he have seen every file there was on the serum? Was it just wishful thinking on her part to think he was out of the loop? It was yet another reason why she was desperate to get down to New Mexico and find some answers.

Rocket's bark snapped her back to attention. He was peering out the living room window, barking his head off at something — or someone.

Her heart thumped and she took the pepper spray out of her purse. She kept her back against the wall and peeked outside the window just enough that she wouldn't be seen by whoever was outside.

It was Nash.

He was getting out of his car. What the hell was he doing here? Did he somehow know that she and Z were about to embark on a trip down to New Mexico?

She needed to act completely normal. The last thing she wanted to do was tip him off.

She met him on the sidewalk in front of her house. His five o'clock shadow made him look more rugged than usual. How was it that part of her still wanted him to throw her up against the car and make out with her even while she was conflicted about whether she could trust him?

"What did I do?" he asked as soon as she walked up. Then she followed his gaze to her hands. The pepper spray. She'd forgotten she was still holding it. He was actually making a joke. It was so unexpected that she found herself smiling.

"Nothing. Just being cautious, like you suggested."

"That's good."

"What are you doing here?"

"The security cam we put in the back of your house is going in and out. I want to reinstall it." He paused and their eyes locked. She thought he would look away quickly, just as he'd done every time they'd made eye contact at Cytology the day before, but instead he kept his gaze steady. Sabrina felt her body moving toward his — a magnetic pull she couldn't resist. Were they going to kiss? *Should* they kiss? Never mind, she knew the answer to that and she really didn't care.

But instead of moving closer, he abruptly looked away and took a very deliberate step back from her.

Her cheeks flushed at the rejection. "Was there anything else you needed?" she asked shortly. "I've got to go."

Taken aback by her tone, he asked, "Is everything okay?"

"I'm just confused which version of you showed up today," she replied. "It's like you're two different people sometimes. There's Nice Nash, and then there's Agent Nash, who doesn't always answer my questions and won't even look at me."

The tiniest of smiles appeared at the corners of his lips. It was the opposite reaction than she'd expected.

"Nice Nash?" He took one step closer to her. Her pulse instantly started racing. "He sounds boring."

Nash's jade eyes searched hers, glowing with an intensity so fierce that for the first time she realized he was having an equally difficult time figuring her out as she was him. "You sure everything is okay, Sabrina? I'm being serious."

Part of her wished she could tell him everything — fill him in on Amy, on New Mexico — but she couldn't let her attraction to him get the upper hand. Wasn't she the one lecturing everyone else last night about being careful?

"Yeah. Everything is fine," she said in what she meant to be an upbeat tone. "I mean, as okay as it can be right now." She let out a laugh that sounded super weird to her, but hopefully he didn't notice. "I better get to school, then." Sabrina's attempt at sounding casual was just plain awkward. Nash knew something was up. He wasn't moving.

"Are you nervous about Wincott's class after yesterday? Is that what this is about?"

Perfect. He'd just handed her an excuse for her weirdness. "Yeah, it was pretty awful. I can't stop thinking about it."

He looked at her seriously. "Skip his class today if it doesn't feel right. Greenly's, too." He grabbed her hand fiercely and caught Sabrina by surprise. She was even more surprised when he didn't let go. "Promise me you'll do whatever you can to stay safe today."

"I will," she said, though she had no idea what the day would hold. "I just want to get closer to some answers."

That part was at least the truth.

As soon as she drove away, a pit formed in her stomach. It really did seem that Nash cared about her — at least about her safety. Or was it possible that he was on to her, and his entire visit had been designed to reel her back into trusting him?

Instead of driving to Z's, Sabrina drove in the direction of Cedar Springs High. She pulled over to dial Z.

"Where are you? You're late," Z said.

"Meet me at my locker instead."

Twenty minutes later, she found Z in the designated spot.

"What's with the change of plans?" Z asked impatiently. "We're still going, right?"

"Yeah, but we need to leave our phones at school. Nash and Patricia can use them to track us."

"And I thought I was supposed to be the paranoid one," Z mumbled as she followed Sabrina back out to the parking lot.

* * *

The traffic on the way to New Mexico was more brutal than Sabrina had anticipated. It had already taken them an extra hour, and the only stop they'd made was to buy disposable phones.

A police car cruised by them and Sabrina stiffened.

"I'm glad I'm not the only one who doesn't think having a badge means you can be trusted," Z said. She flipped to a new song on the road-trip playlist she'd made the previous night when she couldn't sleep.

"So if there really was a group of Lost Causes before us, do you think the reason Patricia didn't tell us is because she didn't want us to know that the first group all died?"

"All died *together*. In the same place, at the same time," Z emphasized.

"What if they didn't tell us because the FBI knows it really was just a freak accident that had nothing to do with their case?" Sabrina fully knew this could be her feelings for Nash talking, but after seeing him earlier, she couldn't help making one last rationalization. "If the FBI did a whole investigation into Amy's crash off the bridge and realized that it definitely was an accident, I can kind of understand why Patricia wouldn't bring it up. If she had told me that everyone in the last group who helped the FBI had died, I don't know if I would've signed on to help with Lily's case. Even if they said it was a car accident."

Z didn't even pause to think about it. "It had to be something from their case that got Amy and the others killed and *that's* why they didn't tell us. And I'm really starting to wonder if it connects to our case. I don't believe in coincidences. Plus if it was just a freak crash, why did Amy tell you not to trust Patricia and Nash?"

Sabrina sighed. Somehow she'd allowed herself to forget about that part of it. "Maybe Amy's family can give us some kind of clue about the case they were trying to solve."

A gas station popped into view on the horizon, surrounded by nothing but dry desert. "Finally," Z said. "We're running on fumes."

Sabrina sent a status update text to the others, then she joined Z in the tiny convenience store.

Z was headed to the cash register holding three sticks of beef jerky. "Want one?" she asked.

"Beef jerky? Seriously?"

"I used to eat it just because I knew it grossed my mom out and then I got addicted. It's a comfort food."

"Mac and cheese is a comfort food. Beef jerky is just gross."

Sabrina handed her soda to the man at the cash register. He was so old that she was worried he was going to keel over before he rung them up. Instead, he just stared at her as if he couldn't believe he had a customer.

"I'll just get this, please," she told him, trying to hurry the transaction along.

Z gave Sabrina a weird look. "Who are you talking to?"

Sabrina looked back at the cash register and the old man was gone. But right behind where he'd been standing was a framed photo of him holding up a dollar bill. Sabrina pointed to the photo. "That guy."

A young clerk walked up and saw Sabrina pointing at the photo. "That's my dad. This place was his life. He was here every single day from open to close. Even died here."

Z and Sabrina exchanged a look. Sabrina had just asked a ghost to ring up her soda.

Z raised an eyebrow at her. "Beef jerky?"

Sabrina rolled her eyes and grabbed it.

* * *

It took another hour before they finally got to Taos. Amy had grown up near Albuquerque, but according to housing records Andrew dug up, her mom moved here several years earlier. Taos seemed like a peaceful place to live, with New Age stores and mineral galleries in the place of coffee and fast-food chains, and a Native American influence everywhere.

Z pulled off the commercial street and onto a residential one, if you could call it that. They were basically in the middle of the desert, and the houses were built at least a half mile or more away from each other. The views of the mountains were amazing, but living here had to be lonely.

"We're good with the cover story?" Sabrina asked.

"I guess. But I still think saying we're doing a report for school is lame."

"Let me know if you come up with something better in the next thirty seconds because we're here." Sabrina pointed to the small adobe house with a bright turquoise door in front of them. A large dream catcher made of woven vines dangled from the doorway, and the red, white and black feathers attached to the bottom swayed in the breeze. "So you'll do the talking and I'll do the listening?" Z asked.

"Hopefully Amy's family will do all the talking."

CHAPTER FORTY-ONE

On the way to weight training, Justin met Gabby at her locker. She had PE with Coach Colfax at the same time, so they could walk together — something they'd been trying to do as much as possible since they'd realized it was a teacher who'd killed Devon Warner — and most likely Lily Carpenter.

"Any word from the Scooby-Doo crew?" he asked. He still thought it was insane for Sabrina and Z to have trekked down to New Mexico in the hopes of finding out more about Amy Hanson.

"All I've heard so far is that Sabrina is apparently now a fan of beef jerky."

He guided her down the hallway, where a group of sophomore cheerleaders was staring at them as though they were on a freaking red carpet.

"Hey, Gabby!" Hannah Phelps exclaimed. "How are you?"

"Um, good," Gabby replied, fidgeting.

Justin slung a protective arm around her. As if she was going to go back to being friends with Hannah after the girl had ditched her years ago? And why was she suddenly talking to Gabby now? Because he, a football player, was walking down the hall with her? As odd as Z and Sabrina could be, Justin at least knew they were real friends.

He dodged the crowded flight of stairs inside the hall, instead opening the door to the secluded back steps outside of the building. It was the longer route to the gym, but at least it gave them a little privacy.

"How was Fields's class? Anything come up?" Justin asked her. Besides the chemistry connection and the conference he'd been at with Lily, Z heard him lying about where he was the night Devon was killed.

He couldn't have seen me that night. No one saw me.

Dr. Fields was hiding something. If he had killed Devon, those thoughts made perfect sense.

"There was one small weird thing," Gabby answered. "Nothing major. Maybe I'm reading too much into it, though."

"What?"

"He wasn't wearing his lab coat."

"That is strange," Justin said. Gabby looked at him as if she couldn't tell whether he was kidding. "I'm being serious. I've never once seen the guy not in it."

"It was more than that, though," Gabby said. "He seemed frazzled. Off his game somehow."

They walked down the stairs hand in hand, passing the faculty parking lot.

Justin slowed as Dr. Fields's shiny new red Mustang came into view. It bugged him as much as it had the day before. What was the school chemistry teacher doing with that car? He looked around. No one was in sight.

"What are you thinking?" Gabby asked nervously.

He inched closer to the car, stretching to look inside the window. A gym bag sat on the passenger seat. What was that peeking out of the side pocket? He took a step closer. It was a cell phone.

An old Nokia phone, though … not the iPhone Justin saw him talking on the day before. Strange. Why did he have two phones?

"Justin," Gabby warned. He looked up. A few students walked by and he moseyed closer to Gabby as they passed.

"There's a cell phone in there." He raised an eyebrow at her.

"Patricia and Nash said not to do anything out of the ordinary. You want to do what they explicitly warned us not to do?" Gabby asked. She was nervous, but a hint of amusement played around her eyes. "Why am I not surprised?"

"In and out. I've gotten so much better. It will take me ten seconds to unlock that door, I bet," he said.

Gabby looked around them. It was still quiet. The bell was about to ring, and most students had already made their way into class. "Okay. Try for a few seconds, then. If anyone comes, we'll stop."

Justin grinned and positioned himself in front of the door, focusing on the car lock. He beat his own record. It took only a few seconds for the lock to pop up with a click.

Quietly, he pulled on the handle and opened the door, sliding the cell phone out of the bag as fast as he could.

"Let's go," he said, pressing the lock back down as he shut the door.

He and Gabby speed-walked over to the back of the bleachers, partially hidden from the rest of campus.

"Take a look," he said, tossing the phone to her. "I'll make sure no one's coming."

A moment later he heard a shriek from Gabby.

He swiveled around. "Are you okay?"

She dropped the phone as if it was radioactive. "Oh my God, oh my God …"

"What?" he said. "What did you see? Something that ties him to the murders?"

Gabby shook her head. "Boobs," she squeaked.

He couldn't have heard her right. He picked up the phone and was assaulted by the same image Gabby had seen. A selfie of a woman flaunting her cleavage in a bathing suit and attempting to look at the camera seductively. But not just any woman.

Dr. Pearl. The school psychologist who'd awarded all of them demerits when Gabby and the others tried to tell her about that first group-therapy meeting with Patricia and Nash.

He gagged, only half kidding. "Why did you let me look at that?"

"There are hundreds of texts between the two of them, too. Planning what motels to meet at. What to tell their spouses about where they were going …"

It all made sense. That angry phone call they'd overheard yesterday? Probably his wife wanting to know where he'd been. The brand-new midlife crisis sports car. The secret phone he used just to talk to Dr. Pearl. Dr. Fields wasn't a murderer … he was just a sleazeball having an affair.

Justin quickly pulled out his own phone and tapped out a text about it to Nash. Sabrina and Z thought they couldn't trust him, but Justin figured they should keep him in the loop.

Then he quickly sent another text out to the rest of the Lost Causes.

Fields is boning Dr. Pearl. Don't vomit up your beef jerky, Sabrina.

CHAPTER FORTY-TWO

Z dodged the dream catcher as she and Sabrina approached the turquoise door. Z knocked twice. No answer. She hadn't considered that no one would be home. They'd wait all day, though, if they had to. She was about to knock again when the door suddenly cracked open just enough for a woman to pop her head out. She pushed her long, disheveled black hair out of her face so she could get a good look at Z and Sabrina. Her eyes were sunken and hollow, and the puffy purple bags underneath them looked like bruises on her dark skin.

"What do you want?" she growled, exposing a few cracked teeth. "If you're selling something, you're wasting your time."

"Mrs. Hanson?" Sabrina asked with much more confidence than Z could've mustered.

"Yeah, who are you?"

Z wasn't sure whether she was relieved or disappointed that they had the right woman. Although now that she really looked at her, the similarities to Amy Hanson were obvious. The same skin tone, the same long, straight nose and the same pronounced eyelids.

"My name is Sabrina. This is Z," Sabrina explained calmly, ignoring the woman's withering look. "We'd really appreciate if we could talk to you about your daughter, Amy."

Mrs. Hanson's face went slack. Z felt almost ashamed. Maybe they hadn't thought this completely through. What mother would want to have a conversation with two strangers about her dead daughter?

"Nina?" A soft, female voice came from inside the house. "Who are you talking to?"

The door suddenly swung open and another woman joined Mrs. Hanson. This woman looked like Mrs. Hanson might have if she were to take a shower and get some sleep. And maybe a little dental work. As opposed to the loose clothes that were hanging off Mrs. Hanson, the dress this woman was wearing hugged her curvy body.

"Can I help you?" the woman asked, toying with the lapis crystal pendant around her neck. She sounded suspicious but not rude.

"We're sorry to show up unannounced like this," Sabrina began again. "I know it's an incredibly difficult subject, but we were hoping to talk to Mrs. Hanson about her daughter, Amy."

The woman put her arm protectively around Mrs. Hanson's gaunt body. "Nina, go inside. I'll handle this." Amy's mother shuffled away, and the woman turned back to them. "I'm Nina's sister. Amy's aunt. What do you need to know about Amy?"

Their auras are fascinating. Such a bright yellow. And the one with the buzzed-off hair is a darker blue than I've ever seen.

As soon as Z heard the thought, she knew exactly how they'd get the answers they needed.

Z stepped forward. "My friend here keeps seeing Amy's ghost."

Sabrina shot Z a look she didn't need to interpret because Z heard her next thought.

Z, if you are listening, what the hell are you doing?

But Sabrina's annoyed look shifted to surprise as soon as the woman opened the door wider.

"Please come in."

Sometimes the truth actually worked.

* * *

"Do you both have the gift?" Kaya Hanson asked.

Z and Sabrina were sitting on a velvety pale blue couch across from the woman in her living room. A distinctive scent hung in the air — apparently she had just finished her weekly ritual of burning sage before they'd arrived. She was probably the type of person who thought meditation was the answer to everything.

"Just me," Sabrina answered.

That explains the bright yellow, Z heard Kaya think.

She continued trying to listen to Kaya's thoughts as she looked around the strange room. The antique walnut bookshelf housed no books but instead was brimming with multicolored crystals and candles. The couches and chairs were various shades of purple and blue, and with the dim light in the room, the ambience was almost ethereal. Z could imagine someone holding a séance there.

"And you saw Amy?" Kaya asked Sabrina, not a hint of doubt in her silvery voice. Her fingers toyed with the small box of Amy's keepsakes that she'd brought out for Sabrina to look through.

Sabrina nodded. "I've seen her a few times. I haven't been able to speak to her much, though, so I guess that's why we're here. I was hoping if I learned a little more about her, I could figure out why I keep seeing her."

"When she appears to you, what does she seem to want?" Kaya asked.

"It's like she wants me to understand something about her. Something no one else but me can understand," Sabrina answered honestly. "Was there anything strange about the way she died?"

Kaya paused for a second. "I always thought so, but no one else seemed to."

Z's pulse quickened. "We read about what happened. It was a car accident?"

"Yes. Amy was driving a few of her classmates one night. They were new friends of hers. Amy didn't have a lot of friends, so it was nice that she suddenly found this group." She rummaged through the box and pulled out a strip of three photo-booth pictures of Amy with two other girls. In each photo, the girls were in a different pose, making funny faces at the camera.

"Danielle and Catherine were in the car with Amy and the two boys that night. That's Danielle," Kaya said, pointing to a punk-looking girl in the middle. She had short bleached hair with streaks of blue and a gold hoop through her nostrils. Even through the silly face she was making, there was something tough about her, as if she could handle anything. In one photo, she had her arm around Amy, like a protective big sister.

Kaya pointed to the other girl in the photo. Out of the three, she was hamming it up for the camera the most, holding up a chubby middle finger in one photo and flashing her bra in another. "That's Catherine. She was quite a handful, according to Nina — Amy's mom."

"A handful how?" Z asked.

"From what I gathered, she didn't have much of a filter," Kaya answered. "Nina tried to throw her out of the house once when Catherine said some derogatory things to her about her addiction. When I brought it up to Amy, though, she was immediately defensive. She told me everything Catherine said to Nina was true and it was nice to have someone honest around. Amy made it very clear that these new friendships were not up for discussion."

Were the three of them Lost Causes or just three girls who became fast friends? "Do you know where they were going the night of the accident?" Z asked.

"I'm not sure. Neither is her mother. There was a storm that night and the streets were flooding. That's part of why I thought it was strange. Amy would've known better than to get on that bridge. I used to live down in those parts years ago. Everyone around there knew how slick that particular bridge would get in the rain, and everyone knew alternative ways to get around it."

"The police said that's what happened?" Sabrina asked. "That the car skidded and went over the bridge?"

"That's what they said, but there wasn't much of an investigation. It took them two weeks to find the wreckage, and even then, it was just" — Kaya steadied her voice — "parts of bodies. They weren't able to test for drugs or alcohol in Amy's system, which they assumed was one of the reasons it happened. But she never touched that stuff. Not with her mother the way she is. It had to have been something else. Maybe that's why Amy is appearing to you. She wants you to know the truth."

Sabrina was nodding effusively, but Z knew they still had zero in the proof department. "Was there anything different about Amy leading up to the accident?" Z asked, trying another angle.

Kaya cocked her head at Z curiously. "A few weeks before Amy died, Nina went to rehab and I stayed with Amy at their house. And yes, there was something different. Amy's aura had always been reddish brown. Some days it was cloudy, some days it was clear. But when I saw her then, her aura was bright white like it was beaming off her."

Z inwardly groaned. A change in Amy's spiritual aura wasn't the hard evidence they were searching for. She was getting impatient but tried not to be rude. "What about the way she was acting? Was there something different about that?"

"Yes, her behavior mirrored her aura. She was always dark. Troubled. Western medicine might diagnose her as bipolar. And usually when Nina went to rehab, Amy was despondent. But when I was down there, there was a lightness to her. Like I said, she suddenly started hanging out with a new group of friends. But it was more than that. It was a bit like she was looking at the world through different eyes."

Sabrina leaned forward. "So, she suddenly seemed less depressed? Like it almost happened overnight?"

Kaya paused, thinking it through. "Sort of. The depression might have faded, but something melancholy still lingered inside her. She became obsessed with this news story about a missing girl from Albuquerque."

Something stirred inside of Z. A missing girl?

"It was all incredibly morbid, but Amy wouldn't stop talking about it. So much so that I had to ask her to please stop bringing it up because it was so upsetting. Every word out of her mouth was about finding this little girl. Sam something-or-other."

Z's heart stopped. "Sam Carpenter."

CHAPTER FORTY-THREE

Nash sat at his desk at Cytology and checked the feed from the security cameras around Cedar Springs High just as school was letting out. His unease over sending the five of them in to gather intel had only increased on day two of this operation. He searched for a glimpse of Sabrina, whom he hadn't spotted all day. Which didn't necessarily mean anything, considering the scattered camera placement around the school.

But Nash was worried. She was acting strangely that morning, and Nash couldn't figure out what to make of it. Was she cracking under the pressure? It didn't seem likely. Nothing seemed to break her.

Maybe she realized he had lied to her.

No. It was impossible for her to know the cameras outside her house were working perfectly. Telling her he needed to adjust them was the only plausible excuse for a random visit, other than telling her the truth — which he was having a hard time admitting even to himself.

The truth was that he just wanted to see her.

But instead of leaving her house with relief that she was safe, he was more unsettled than ever. There was something Sabrina wasn't telling him. Something was worrying her more than just the obvious.

That intuitive feeling he'd had before flared up again. Some dangerous piece of the puzzle was still hidden, waiting to show its face when they were least expecting it. Did Sabrina have that same feeling? Is that why she was acting strangely?

He turned his eyes away from the school security feed and back to his laptop. Wincott and Greenly were the remaining suspects, but Greenly was at the top of the list because of his connection to Robert Carpenter. Patricia was headed to meet the flight attendant who had confirmed Robert's alibi on the night Lily was murdered. Maybe she was Robert's girlfriend and was lying for him, or maybe she was just someone Robert paid to lie for him about being on that plane. Patricia wanted to see for herself.

A call from FBI Albuquerque field director Carl Plouffe rang through on his computer, interrupting his thoughts.

"Agent Nash," Plouffe said, his icy blue eyes almost piercing the screen.

"Yes, sir," Nash replied. "Patricia isn't back yet."

"Yes, I know. I wanted to get a read on how you thought the case was going. Patricia seems quite certain you're close to locking it down and finding the serum." Nash understood the subtext: Plouffe wanted Nash to verify that Patricia wasn't sugarcoating their results.

Nash nodded. "I hope so. We've vetted all the teachers and administrators. The ones who were at the retreat and received the windbreaker. And since then, our suspect pool has significantly narrowed. We're extremely close to homing in on who has the serum so we can get it safely back to FBI hands."

"Patricia updated me on how you whittled it down. That's the other reason I'm calling." Plouffe shifted in his chair. "I assigned a few Albuquerque agents to back you up on the investigation of Wincott and Greenly."

Nash knew this was the type of thing that other agents hated, convinced that the extra "help" was a slap in the face, affecting their ability to solve the case or at least get the credit for it. But Nash had never been ruled by his ego that way, especially now when his five assets could potentially be in danger. "Did they find anything else on either suspect?"

"Nothing substantial yet. But they did discover three part-time staff members who were also at the teachers' retreat that you never accounted for."

"Really?" said Nash. That meant that there were three more people than he'd originally thought who had received the green jacket. Three more suspects to add to the pool, just when they were getting so close.

"I'm sure most will alibi out, but I wanted to let you know," Plouffe added. "I'll email you the list. We'll keep looking on our end, too."

"Thanks for the help," Nash said.

"Like I said, I'm sure it's nothing. The Greenly lead you managed to dig up sounds extremely promising."

"That one wasn't me," Nash replied honestly. "The five assets are responsible for most of our leads." Nash was astounded at how far they'd come in such a short time. He had to hand it to Patricia.

Plouffe's forehead creased in confusion. "What assets?"

It took a half second for Nash to understand. Plouffe had no idea that the five of them existed. He had never authorized any of it.

"How did Patricia tell you we got the lead about the windbreaker?" Nash asked carefully.

"The two eyewitnesses you found who were camping near the Springs. She said their accounts of that night matched up with the evidence."

"So you don't know anything about the five kids?"

Plouffe's look remained blank and Nash's anger at Patricia flared. From day one Nash had thought this assignment was inordinately bizarre and irresponsible. But his training, steeped in the philosophy of rank and hierarchy, had kept him from questioning it. He'd been assigned other cases with ethical boundary issues before. Now he could kill his former self for not asking more questions. Patricia had put the group in even more danger than he possibly imagined.

"Five kids?" Plouffe narrowed his eyes. "Why don't you enlighten me?"

CHAPTER FORTY-FOUR

Andrew's brain was spinning like a hamster on a wheel ... if the hamster had just ingested amphetamines. Sabrina and Z had come directly to his house from their road trip and filled him in on what they found out from Amy's aunt, Kaya.

"So you're both absolutely convinced that Amy was a Lost Cause now?" Andrew jumped up from his bed and started pacing. Theories were bouncing around his head like pinballs.

"Definitely," Z replied. "First of all, she was bipolar but all her symptoms went away almost overnight. Second, she had no friends until all of a sudden she was inseparable from these other four people from her class —"

"All who had some kind of mental or behavioral issue, according to that newspaper article," Sabrina interjected. "And if that's not enough proof that they were another group of Lost Causes, Amy keeps appearing to me and telling me not to trust Patricia and Nash."

Sabrina was looking through the box of Amy's possessions. She'd asked Kaya if she could hold on to it for a few days if she promised to send it back. She wanted all of them to check through it — especially Gabby.

Hopefully Gabby would have a vision from something of Amy's and make sense of everything once and for all.

"Okay. So the working theory is that Amy and her friends were another group of Lost Causes," Andrew said. "Patricia and Lily gave all of them the serum to help the FBI solve a case."

"But not just any case," Z cut in. "The Sam Carpenter case. Amy was obsessed with her disappearance. I looked back to that article about Amy's car accident to check the date. Her car went over that bridge the day after Sam's body was found. Their assignment from the FBI must have been to try to find her."

Sabrina nodded. "But we know they didn't actually find Sam because her body was discovered in the mountains by those hikers."

"So the big question now is whether it was a crazy coincidence that the other group of Lost Causes died that day or whether that accident wasn't really an accident," Z said, though Andrew knew it was no question in her mind.

"Let's say their death wasn't an accident," Andrew proposed. "Who would want them dead?"

"The person who abducted and killed Sam, for one," Sabrina answered. "If Amy and the others were getting close, he could've been trying to stop their investigation."

"I'm not letting Patricia off the hook for this either, though," Z replied. "It could've been the FBI who killed them and made it look like an accident."

"Why would the FBI want the five of them dead while they were working on this case?" Andrew asked.

Z responded with a morbid tone to her voice. "Maybe once Sam's body was found, they felt like they didn't need them anymore."

"So they killed them?" Andrew asked, incredulous.

"Yeah. Maybe they thought it was cleaner that way. So that no one could expose the program. That could've always been the FBI's plan," Z answered.

The theory momentarily paralyzed Andrew. He didn't want to believe the FBI was behind all of this. They couldn't be. He'd already spent the last few nights teaching himself coding so that he'd have a leg up when he took the entrance exam to become an analyst. The FBI had changed his life.

He'd never stopped to wonder if it was all too good to be true.

He looked at Sabrina and Z in a daze. "If the FBI is behind the death of the other group of Lost Causes, what does that mean for us?"

The fear in Sabrina's eyes was a reflection of his own. "Where are Justin and Gabby? I thought they were supposed to be here by now."

"Justin had to pick up some game film from Coach Brandt," Andrew answered. "They should be here any second."

"You still have our phones, right?" Sabrina asked. Andrew nodded and took them out of his desk drawer. He'd grabbed their phones from their lockers after school and brought them to his house. That way, if Patricia and Nash were tracking them, they would think Sabrina and Z were at Andrew's and not in Taos.

Z started rummaging through the box with Sabrina. She pulled out a yearbook and flipped through it. "Looks like this is from Amy's junior year, the year they all died. There's a memorial section in the back. There's a page for each one of them."

Andrew sat next to Sabrina and Z on the floor to take a look. There was a short blurb underneath Amy's photo that said she played the piano and did her school community service at a nearby animal shelter. The last thing on the page was a Margaret Atwood quote. Underneath it, a small caption explained that it was the quote Amy had chosen to go along with her photo in last year's yearbook. It took Andrew a second for the sad realization to sink in that they all must've died before they could turn in their quotes for this yearbook.

Sabrina flipped the page and pointed to the girl in the next photo,

Catherine Freeman. "She was one of the girls Kaya told us about. Supposedly she had no filter."

"The only thing it says about her is that she won the science fair in sixth grade," Andrew read. "They couldn't come up with anything more recent that she did? It doesn't even list her interests."

"According to Kaya, it didn't sound like she was an easy person to be around," Z answered.

Like me before the serum, Andrew thought.

"Me, too," Z said to him. "Sorry, your thought just popped into my head loud and clear."

Kevin Beswick was the next photo, and he looked like a stereotypical meathead. Andrew wondered what exactly made him a lost cause. It listed his interests as basketball, football and hockey. His yearbook quote was a lyric from an Eminem song that Andrew had never heard of.

On the next page, Danielle Wenkie stared back at them, her multiple facial piercings glinting from the flash of the camera. She had punk rock hair and bright pink lips. There was a Ramones quote underneath her photo about how life was an adventure.

"She looks like someone I would be friends with," Z said sadly.

The last photo was Christopher Jarvis, an overweight guy with an army-style buzz cut who stared defiantly at the camera. Something about his face made Andrew pause. He scanned Christopher's minimal interests — ATVing, camping — then got to his quote.

Andrew's throat went dry as he read it: "Nature teaches beasts to know their friends."

"You guys," he croaked out and pointed to the quote.

"No way," Sabrina said, jaw dropped.

It was the same Shakespeare line that Devon Warner's ghost had repeated to Sabrina.

Z jumped up. "Holy crap. Do you think Christopher Jarvis is related to Devon Warner? Could they be brothers?" Even she had to know it was a stretch. But how could this be a coincidence?

Andrew studied Christopher's face again.

Then he finally saw it.

He snatched the yearbook from Sabrina's hands so he could get a better look. He was right.

Above Christopher Jarvis's left eye was a small scar.

"What?" Z pressed. "What do you see, Andrew?"

"That's not Devon Warner's brother." Andrew finally looked up at them. "That's Devon Warner."

Sabrina looked at him as if he'd lost his mind. "What are you talking about? That's not possible. This guy was in the car with Amy. He died just like she did." She grabbed the yearbook back to look closely, and Z practically climbed on top of her.

But Andrew, who had spent so many hours looking at Devon Warner's face when he researched the driver's licenses, knew he was correct. "Take fifty pounds off Christopher Jarvis, age him ten years and give him shoulder-length hair."

Andrew pulled out the ID photo he'd printed of Devon Warner. "See the scar?"

"He's right," Z whispered. "That's Devon Warner as a teenager."

This was the Devon Warner whose body they found in the Springs. The Devon Warner who assaulted Sadie Webb. The Devon Warner who killed people and took their identities. All so he could hide who he really was. Christopher Jarvis.

Sabrina rubbed her eyes. "That doesn't make sense. I've seen Amy, I know she's dead. And they found parts of the car in the river, too, and the bodies."

"But not all of their bodies, remember?" Z broke in. "Kaya said they only found parts of bodies. He must have survived somehow. And no one realized."

Sabrina nodded, slowly accepting the explanation. "If Devon — Christopher — was an original Lost Cause, that would explain his connection to Lily. That's how he knew she had the serum. And how he knew the value of it."

As his eyes ran over the other four photos, a gruesome thought entered Andrew's head. "We know Devon's a killer. Could he have killed the other four? Maybe he was the one who caused the accident."

A crazy sound escaped from Sabrina that made Andrew think she must have seen a ghost. But she was staring at the memorial photo a few pages before Christopher's, her face frozen. "Kevin Beswick."

Andrew looked at the meathead with the Eminem quote. "What about him?"

"He's still alive, too." Sabrina jumped to her feet and lunged for her phone. There was panic in her eyes. "Andrew, where did you say Justin is right now?"

CHAPTER FORTY-FIVE

"Sorry I'm late, Coach," Justin said to Coach Brandt.

Gabby stood next to him, anxious to get to Andrew's house, but it was also nice to meet the famous Coach Brandt at last. He wasn't exactly what she'd expected. With his towering height and broad shoulders, he seemed intimidating, but then he smiled this huge smile and it was like looking at a completely different person.

"My head's been all over the place," Justin added.

"I wouldn't know it from the way you've been playing lately," Coach Brandt said, smiling. "Sometimes when life is going good with one thing, it helps you get focused on everything else. Something tells me we have you to thank for that, Gabby?"

Gabby exchanged a quick look with Justin. If Coach Brandt only knew.

He handed Justin an iPad. "This is my personal one. I downloaded all the practices and games to it. Take it for the next few weeks."

"Are you sure?" Justin asked.

"Absolutely. I want you to be ready when that scout comes," Coach Brandt answered. "Which reminds me. There's one more thing I have to give you."

He walked over to a desk awkwardly set up in the middle of the living room as if he hadn't known where else to put it. The small bungalow was the kind of bachelor pad that needed a woman's touch. All the furniture seemed mismatched and out of place, and the real deer head protruding from the wall made Gabby pretty sure no wife or girlfriend lived there.

Coach Brandt pulled out a Florida State pendant from the desk drawer. "Why don't you hold on to this for Justin, Gabby? I have a feeling he's going to need it in a few weeks."

Justin beamed as Coach Brandt handed her the pendant. Gabby's fingers grazed the ring on his bear-size hand.

Her eyes twitched, then fluttered shut.

She was outside, but it took her a second to adjust her eyes in the darkness.

I know this place.

Everything about the moment felt familiar. The biting chill in the air, the complete isolation as though there was no one around for miles. When had she been here?

And then she looked down and saw him.

Devon Warner, lying in the dirt, blood pooling under his body as he desperately gasped for air.

She was right. She'd been in this exact place, in this exact *moment* before, but she'd been in Devon's body. Now she was in his killer's.

She felt herself gingerly kneel down beside Devon.

Devon whispered, "'Nature teaches beasts to know their friends.' You were my only one."

"I'm sorry it had to end like this." Gabby braced herself. She remembered that right after Devon spoke those words, the killer took the serum.

Right on cue, her hands — the killer's hands — reached out to grab it from Devon's pocket. That's when she saw it. The ring on his right hand.

Gabby's eyes flew open, her mouth agape, as she looked at the ring on Brandt's hand. The same ring.

"Gabby?" Justin asked worriedly. "What's wrong?"

She tried to speak. She wanted to run. She had to tell Justin.

"Isn't it obvious, Justin? She just had a vision about me," Brandt said, his voice eerily calm.

Justin stepped in front of her protectively. "How the hell do you know about that?"

Something suddenly beeped, and it took Gabby a moment to realize it was coming from her hand. She was still clutching her cell phone. She looked down and saw the text from Z. Her knees buckled as she read it.

"Because he was a Lost Cause. He was in that car with Amy Hanson," Gabby whispered. She looked back up at Coach Brandt in disbelief. "Kevin Beswick. That's your real name."

Brandt nodded, his face still eerily calm, though Gabby noticed his shoulders tensed.

"There really was another group of Lost Causes?" Justin asked, as shell-shocked as Gabby was.

Brandt exhaled as if he'd been holding his breath for a year. "Patricia, or whatever she's calling herself now, does she know you're here?"

"She can track us with our phones," Justin answered uncertainly.

"You can't trust her," Brandt said gravely. "And you won't after I explain everything to you."

He wasn't hovering over them or threatening them in any way, but that didn't mean they could trust him, either. She just watched him kill Devon Warner — or Christopher Jarvis, according to Z. And he had something to do with Lily's murder, whether he pulled the trigger or not. What kind of explanation could he have for murdering two people?

"I don't understand," Justin stammered. "If you were in that car with Amy —"

Brandt held up his hand to stop him. "Text Sabrina, Z and Andrew back and ask them to come here. Then turn your phones off. I'll tell you all everything."

Gabby quickly typed out the text under his watchful eye. Though every bone in her body told her not to do it, she powered off the phone. Justin did the same.

Brandt took three strides toward them, towering ominously over Gabby. When he spoke again, his voice was deep and harsh. "Now sit down and don't move."

CHAPTER FORTY-SIX

Nash had been sitting alone at the conference table at Cytology for a half hour, stewing and waiting for Patricia to return. She was on her way back from interviewing the flight attendant who alibied Robert Carpenter the night of Lily's murder.

Finally, he heard the beeping sounds of numbers being plugged into the keypad upstairs. Patricia was back. Nash clenched and unclenched his fists. He needed to stay levelheaded through this conversation if he was going to get anywhere with her.

"The woman stuck with her story that Robert was on the flight, but I still think we need to step up the surveillance on him," she announced upon entering. She sounded jittery and frazzled, her clothes rumpled from the drive back. "Andrew really pulled through on that lead."

Nash steadied his voice as best he could. "Why doesn't Plouffe know about them?"

She stared right at him, frozen in place as though she'd been turned to stone. "Did you speak to him?"

"Yes."

"Does he know about them now?" She asked the question slowly, as

313

if she was trying to prolong the time until she had to hear the answer.

"No," Nash lied. He had no idea how Patricia would react if she knew Plouffe had a team en route to deal with her. Or that it was Plouffe who was running the case now. "Unless you give me a very good reason why Plouffe is in the dark, I'm picking up the phone right now and telling him everything."

She ran her tongue along the top row of her teeth nervously. "It's not what you think."

"You have no idea what I think. Start talking. Now."

Patricia sighed and dropped into the chair across from Nash. When she finally started speaking, her voice was strained. "I didn't tell Plouffe about the five of them because I wasn't authorized to use the serum again."

He tensed. "What do you mean, 'again'?"

She avoided his gaze, staring down at her hands. "Lily and I used this serum on a group once before. Ten years ago, around the time we first developed it."

"Why wasn't I briefed on that?"

She paused as if trying to decide whether she was going to divulge everything. The look he gave her made her realize she didn't have a choice.

"We had a fair amount of leeway whenever we were pioneering a new experiment back then, so we were able to move forward without getting official approval from anyone above us."

"In other words, you weren't authorized to do this the first time, either. What on earth made you and Lily think it was a good idea?"

"We didn't have time. We were desperate for answers." She stood up and looked at him, her eyes pleading. "Don't you understand? Lily and I recruited that group to help us find Sam."

* * *

The cold leather of Brandt's couch crinkled underneath Sabrina as she sat between Gabby and Z. Justin and Andrew were perched on the arms of the couch on either side of them, as Brandt had instructed as soon as they'd entered his house. He'd immediately confiscated their phones, refusing to tell them his story until they handed them over. He said they couldn't trust Patricia and they couldn't risk her tracking them to Brandt's. Sabrina hadn't wanted to do it, of course. Whatever kinship she felt to Brandt as a fellow Lost Cause didn't change the fact that he was a guy they now suspected of multiple murders. Was he really trying to protect the Lost Causes from Patricia? Or was he planning on doing the same thing to them that he did to Devon Warner, Lily Carpenter and whomever else he'd killed? But they needed answers and this was the only way they were going to get them.

She fidgeted in her seat and Brandt turned to her, icily. "Don't move, Sabrina. None of you."

He sat down on the ottoman across from them, though it didn't make him any less menacing, with his huge frame taking up the entire cushion.

"If I learned one thing from Patricia, it's not to trust anyone," he told them. "And you're the only five people in the world who know who I really am."

"We won't tell anyone," Andrew quickly said.

"I want to believe that, Andrew," Brandt said as a weird smirk crossed his face. "I do. But I don't know if I can ..."

He let the sentence hang and Sabrina shivered. What would he do to them if he decided he couldn't trust them? Would he kill them?

Justin's eyes flickered and Sabrina could tell he was debating hurtling Brandt across the room. They wouldn't get the answers they were after, but at least they'd be alive. She sat forward, preparing herself to run if need be.

But Brandt suddenly growled, "Don't even think about it, Justin."

Justin looked up at him with an innocent shrug. "What?"

"You're not the only one with special abilities," Brandt warned him in a low voice. "And I've been living with mine a lot longer than you. You have no idea what I'm capable of."

Sabrina's realization that they were completely trapped was tempered only by her surprise. She hadn't considered the fact that Brandt still had his ability from the serum. Was it psychokinesis, like Justin? Or something more dangerous? And deadlier.

Brandt surveyed the group. "I did promise you some answers, though. And unlike Patricia, I'm not a liar." It was an odd point of pride, considering he was now holding them captive, but Sabrina wasn't about to argue it.

Instead she decided to appeal to the common ground that the Lost Causes shared with Brandt. If she could convince him they were all on the same team, maybe he would be sympathetic toward them. "We think we're in the same boat you were in," she told him. "We didn't ask for this to happen to us. But it did, and now we're trying to understand it."

Brandt was silent and Sabrina took it as permission to continue. "You were part of the group Patricia and Lily first gave the serum to ten years ago. You, Amy Hanson and the other three people in the car that night."

"I'd be surprised you were able to piece it together if I didn't know firsthand the abilities the serum can bring you." Brandt turned to Gabby. "I knew you were having a vision earlier when I saw your eyes flutter like that. Amy used to have them, too."

He gave an odd smile to Gabby as if to let her know that he understood her experience. Sabrina took it as a good sign. Maybe he was softening.

"And the case you were assigned was Sam Carpenter's disappearance," Sabrina pushed forward.

"That's right. Except that in all Patricia and Lily's explanations of how the serum worked and what the case was, they never once mentioned that the girl we were trying to find was Lily's daughter. Which wasn't surprising since they really didn't tell us anything about themselves."

For a brief second, Sabrina allowed herself to think about Nash. What did she really know about him?

"Before we knew the truth, we were all into helping them," Brandt said. "It was better than the alternative. For me, it was either meet up for the case after school or go home, where my stepdad would beat the crap out of me if I gave him the wrong look." He met eyes with Justin. "I wasn't lying when I said I could relate to you. I've always wanted to help you, Justin."

Justin looked down silently.

"Anyway, I think what we liked the most was that we mattered when we were working on the case," Brandt continued. Patricia and Lily needed us. They wanted us there. The case gave us purpose. A little girl was counting on us to save her." Brandt's eyes became so haunted that Sabrina got the chills. "And then we found Sam's body."

"Wait," Andrew said. "*You guys* found Sam? I thought hikers did."

"Well, you thought wrong," Brandt snapped quickly, a wild look suddenly in his eye that set Sabrina on edge. After a beat, he looked away and began speaking again, his voice grim. "Patricia and Lily came up with some story afterward about hikers, but that was a lie like everything else. *We* led them there. The five of us. I was sixteen at the time. To find the dead body of an eight-year-old girl while her mother stands right beside you was …" He trailed off, lost in the moment, until he shook his head suddenly, as if trying to remove the image from his mind. "We didn't know at the time who'd done it. It took the police a few years to trace the prints to that handyman. A serial child predator. But even back then, as soon as we saw Sam's body, we all knew it was the work of a monster. Plain and simple."

"The car accident that you all got in happened the day after Sam's body was discovered ..." Andrew began. "Was it really an accident?"

Brandt shook his head, his face reddening in anger. "It was not."

Sabrina's stomach lurched. He might be a murderer, but she knew in her bones he was telling the truth. Even though she wasn't so sure she wanted to hear it now.

"What really happened?" Z dared to ask.

Brandt stood up, leaving a massive imprint in the threadbare ottoman. He stretched his legs and stared out the window into the darkness. The only sound for a moment was his knuckles cracking. It wasn't hard imagining him overpowering Lily or even Devon.

"We were all pretty messed up after we found Sam. It's like it finally hit us just how screwed up this entire situation was. We were a means to an end to the FBI and they didn't give a damn about what happened to us along the way."

Sabrina looked over at Z. It was as they'd suspected. Were they to be just as easily discarded as Brandt and company had been? Sabrina had been so caught up in what she was gaining from the serum — getting her old self back — that she didn't think about what part of herself she was giving up in the process. What bargain had she struck by agreeing to this? Brandt's experience with the case had clearly messed him up. When Sabrina and the others had time to process all this, would they become as damaged as Brandt?

If they even made it out alive.

"We met with Lily and Patricia the day after Sam was found. All five of us wanted out. We weren't going to be their lab rats anymore. But Lily and Patricia wanted us to keep going, to find whoever did this to Sam. We said no, that we'd go to the police or the papers and tell them what was going on if they didn't leave us alone."

"Why didn't you just take the antidote?" Z broke in. "Would they not inject you with it or something?"

Brandt tore his eyes away from the window in a cold stare that made Sabrina's breath catch in her throat. "What antidote?"

He glared at Z, motioning for her to speak. "Patricia told us she had one," Z said, her hands clutched tightly in her lap. "That we could take it at any time."

Brandt eyed them all suspiciously, as if he was making some kind of decision, then abruptly took his eyes off of Z. "She didn't have one back then," he finally said. "Not that she told us about, at least. She sure wouldn't have wanted us to take it, anyway." He moved away from the window, walking toward the deer head on the wall, its eyes frozen in fear and shock, the exact emotions Sabrina was feeling at that moment.

"After we told Lily and Patricia they could go to hell, we all drove away in Amy's car. It was pouring outside, coming down in sheets. After we'd been driving for a few minutes, Amy saw that Lily's car was right behind us. Patricia was in the passenger seat." His eyes became black, like bottomless pits. "It wasn't until we got on the bridge that they rammed our car for the first time. But it was after the third time they hit us that we finally went over the railing."

"But why?" Andrew gasped. "Because you wouldn't help them find Sam's killer?"

"I think they were petrified we were going to expose them. Killing us made more sense. For all I know, that was the FBI's plan from the start. Get us to solve the case, then eliminate us. Probably why they picked five kids whose parents didn't care enough to do a lot of digging around about their deaths."

Sabrina felt her whole body go numb, her limbs tingling as if tiny pins were pricking her skin. Patricia and Lily had killed the other group of Lost Causes. Or at least had tried to. How long would it be before Patricia tried to kill them?

* * *

Nash was starting to put the pieces together and did not like the shape this mental puzzle was taking. "What happened to the first group you gave the serum to?"

Patricia looked away, retreating into her own thoughts for a moment. Her voice was thick when she spoke again. "They died in a car accident. It was awful and tragic, but it had nothing to do with the serum. Lily and I were devastated. They'd made so much headway on Sam's case and then we were back at square one."

Nash finally realized Patricia wasn't just intense about her job. She was delusional. "That's why you were devastated? Because you were back at square one? You experimented on a bunch of kids for your own benefit. You didn't even use them for an FBI case."

"Trust me, it did a lot for those kids," she replied indignantly. "It gave them a purpose, the same way it did with this group. And anyway, we paid the price, too. Lily blamed herself, left the FBI and quickly spiraled downward after that. New supervisors came in and I was ordered to shut down the serum project and destroy whatever was left of it."

"Which you didn't even do." This was unbelievable.

"I knew I'd need it again one day. And I was right." Patricia gave him an oddly triumphant look. "The only way to solve Lily's murder was to use the serum again."

Nash was about to say that if she'd just destroyed the serum, she wouldn't have a murder case to solve right now, when his laptop dinged with a new email.

It was the list of those extra faculty members from Director Plouffe. The ones they needed to vet and possibly add to the suspect pool.

"What's that?" Patricia said, walking toward him and looking at the screen.

Nash ignored her and opened the email. Now that he knew what Patricia had done, the urgency to find the killer was that much greater, and he had three more suspects to vet.

He clicked on the attachment and looked at the three names and photos of the possible suspects. He scrolled down slowly. Right off the bat, two were female. They could be eliminated. But the last one, a broad-shouldered man who was the right age and build, could be added to the list.

Billy Brandt. Defensive coordinator of the Cedar Springs High football team.

Patricia looked at him questioningly. "Who is that?"

"A football coach we never originally put on our list. He received the green Windbreaker, too."

Patricia looked at the photo more closely, her eyes blinking quickly. "Zoom in on that."

There was something in her voice that made Nash oblige. Her eyes widened as the rest of her face sagged, aging her twenty years in five seconds.

"It can't be ..." she murmured so quietly that Nash barely caught it.

"Can't be what?" he asked.

"That looks like ... no."

"Looks like who? Who is it?"

Patricia walked back to the chair and sank down as if her legs had suddenly given out on her. "Kevin Beswick."

* * *

Patricia and Lily were murderers. Sabrina repeated it over and over in her head, her fear escalating each time. She didn't know who made her more afraid now. Brandt or Patricia.

The other Lost Causes were silent, trying to wrap their heads around the story, too. Gabby looked as if she might pass out.

"How did you and Devon — I mean Christopher — survive that car accident?" she asked. The more she could keep him talking about his past as a Lost Cause, to keep reminding him of that unique shared experience, the better chance they had at getting out alive. Or was that just wishful thinking? Was he going to kill them no matter what?

Brandt's eyes darkened at the memory. "Luck, I guess. If you can call it that." He laughed bitterly. "It all happened so fast. It was an old car with one of those crank windows. I was able to open the window and swim out before the waterline hit it and messed up the pressure. Chris and Catherine were next to me and got out, too. Catherine …" He swallowed, his face bleak. "She ended up drowning. I tried to help her to the shore, but I lost her in the current at one point. I swam back down for her, but it was too late. Chris said he saw Amy and Danielle in the front seat before he got out. They were both already dead from the impact."

Sabrina pictured Amy, Catherine and Danielle in that photo-booth strip, bonded like sisters through their shared experience, laughing and mugging for the camera. Sabrina blinked back tears. This whole time, Amy had been trying to save Sabrina from the same fate as her.

"Chris and I had no clue what to do next. I mean, the FBI had tried to kill us. But it's not like we could tell anybody. No one would believe the word of two punks over the FBI. And we were scared the FBI would just take us into custody and finish the job they started."

"So you guys decided to go on the run," Andrew said, his voice quavering.

"Yeah, once we realized everyone thought we died in the accident. They'd found enough body parts so they assumed Chris's and my remains had gone down river. We had nothing to stay home for anyway. Chris was in a group foster home. He was lucky if he ate once a day. And I'm sure my stepdad was happy as hell that I never came home."

"How did you guys survive without any money or anything?" Justin asked.

"They stole people's wallets," Gabby responded quietly. "I saw them do it."

Brandt gave her a withering look. "I assume you all understand we had to do what we had to do."

"Like stealing people's identities," Z said, unable to control the hostile edge in her voice.

Anger flashed in Brandt's eyes. Sabrina flinched. "What would you have done to survive?" he asked.

"I probably would've tried to be more resourceful than murdering people for their names," Z muttered.

Brandt punched the coffee table in front of Z so hard that a glass fell off it and shattered. Z's eyes widened in fear. "How could you of all people judge me? That was the life Lily and Patricia forced on us. As far as I'm concerned, that blood is on the FBI's hands. That's why we came here. We needed to get what was owed to us."

"The scrum?" Sabrina asked, clasping her hands to stop them from shaking.

"No," Brandt answered, his eyes glowing. "Justice. Chris and I were running out of money again in Alaska. We thought if we could find Patricia or Lily, we could blackmail them for cash to keep us quiet. It was the least they owed us. But we had no clue how to find them. When you work for the FBI, your name doesn't exactly come up in search engines."

"So how did you end up finding Lily?" Andrew asked. "That must have been close to impossible." He was stroking Brandt's ego, Sabrina realized. *Smart.*

"It was," Brandt replied, with a note of arrogance. "But I have a good memory. When Sam disappeared, the cops searched a cabin in Cedar Springs that Lily's dad owned. It was a long shot that we'd find Lily there, and we didn't even know exactly where the cabin was. But we needed a new place to live and Cedar Springs worked as well as any other place, so we figured we'd give it a try. We were here a few months and were pretty much convinced we wouldn't find Lily when, miracle of miracles, I open the paper one day and she's staring back at me."

Z's eyes flashed in comprehension. "That article. The news report that Lily was refusing to sell my father her property for his development."

"That's right. Chris and I decided to pay Lily a visit. Like I said, we were going to blackmail her. Get what was ours. When we showed up, though, she was so surprised to see us, she accidentally told us she had the serum. So we changed course. We wanted the serum."

"Why?" Gabby asked without making eye contact with Brandt.

"At first it was to prove our point. The evidence we had always needed. But then we realized there could be a market for this kind of serum. With prices that meant we'd never have to work again."

Sabrina remembered Nash saying as much. Were they too late? Had Brandt already sold it?

"But why did you kill Devon — Chris?" Justin asked.

"It was me or him. Chris was always impulsive and violent, and the last thing I wanted was for him to get us on the cops' radar right before we sold the serum. We were so close to getting the money and ending this nightmare. He knew he had a problem, too. Little did I know, he stole a bunch of meds from Lily and started taking them, thinking it would mellow him out and keep him under control. Instead he got a hundred times crazier and so paranoid he stopped sleeping. He was convinced I was going to double-cross him."

"Which you did." Sabrina couldn't help cutting in. Could Brandt admit to any accountability?

Brandt glared at her and suddenly, inexplicably, a red-hot flame shot at her feet, creating a small fire. Sabrina screamed, jumping out of the way, as Justin quickly ran over to stomp it out.

"What the hell just happened?" Justin demanded, looking at Brandt with the rest of the Lost Causes, in utter shock.

Brandt's lips turned into a rueful smile. "Pyrokinesis. The little gift Patricia gave me. Sometimes I can control it better than others."

His voice chilled Sabrina despite the heat still radiating around her.

"The burn marks …" Andrew realized. "That's what you did to Lily. And Chris."

Then it clicked for Sabrina. "It was you in the van. I saw a flame in there. I knew I did. You were following all of us."

"I realized you guys were involved when I went to clean out Chris's apartment and I saw some FBI lackey going in and out of his place." *Nash.* "I knew they'd be trying to solve Lily's murder, but I didn't think they'd ever pin it on us. I had no clue how they were even on Chris's tail. We weren't amateurs. We'd covered our tracks perfectly. Then the next night, while I was still waiting, I saw the five of you show up to 'Devon Warner's' apartment. And I understood it was happening all over again. They'd given another five kids the serum."

"I knew someone was watching us that night," Gabby said softly. "I could feel it."

"You'd think that knowing we had taken the serum would have made you sympathetic instead of trying to run me off the road," Sabrina shot back at him.

"You decided to follow me!" Before she even realized it was happening, another flame erupted, this one on her arm. She fell, clutching the searing burn. Gabby rushed to her side.

An errant ash landed on the floor, igniting a small fire along the edge of the curtain hem. Justin turned to stomp it out when Brandt stopped him.

"Don't move, Justin." Justin met his eyes, the two of them testing each other, before Justin ultimately sat back down, the flame on the curtain growing even higher, slowly beginning to consume the thin fabric.

"You had what you wanted. Why didn't you just leave with the serum?" Z asked Brandt.

"How could I? I was in the middle of selling it."

"Couldn't you do that from anywhere?"

Before he could answer, though, Nash and Patricia burst through the front door, the cold air fanning the flames on the curtain.

Sabrina locked eyes with Nash as he entered. Obviously he'd had nothing to do with the original Lost Causes. Still, she wondered how much of this he had actually known about before he'd helped recruit them.

"Patricia," Brandt said, inching closer to her. "It's been a while. About ten years, right?"

Patricia held her ground, her gun leveled at him. Beside her, Nash had his gun raised as well. "We thought you were dead, Kevin. We can make this right."

"Really?" Brandt asked. "Because it looks like you're trying to kill me. Again."

It was just a small flash — Nash's eyes darting from Brandt to Patricia for a brief second, his jaw flexing — but it made Sabrina wonder if this part was news to him.

"We didn't do anything," Patricia insisted. "Lily and I never meant for that to happen that night."

"Don't lie," Brandt beseeched her.

"I promise. We just wanted to talk. You guys ran out so quickly. There was so much at stake. We needed to make you understand. We never intended for that car to go over the bridge."

Sabrina locked eyes with Nash. The way he looked at her told her everything. Nash had no idea Patricia had killed, or tried to kill, the other group of Lost Causes.

"Like hell you didn't send that car over. You were on our asses. And in that rain? Like you didn't know something was going to happen. You forced us right off the bridge —"

"We were horrified when the car went over. We were the ones who called the cops," Patricia protested.

"Anonymously. Once you thought we were all dead and your secret was safe. How many times did you ram the car? Was it three or was it four?"

He turned to face Justin, and out of the corner of her eye, Sabrina saw Patricia begin to shift the gun in her hand.

"Put it down!" Brandt demanded, swiveling back around. Before Patricia could, a flame burst in her hand, forcing her to drop the weapon as she screamed in pain.

"You too," Brandt said to Nash. "Now." Brandt twisted toward Sabrina as if he was about to unleash another flame and Nash dropped the weapon instantly.

Brandt circled closer to Patricia, who clutched her blistered hand. "Did that hurt? That little special ability you bestowed upon me? My *gift*," he spat out mockingly. "It felt so good to kill Lily, you know. You ruined our lives, you two."

Patricia's eyes seared into his. "Your lives were ruined before you met us. What great things were you doing? I gave you a chance. You ruined that chance, too, though."

"You gave me this!" Brandt bellowed, releasing another flame at her, pinning her between the couch and the wall. In quick succession, three more flames burst forth, the whole room filling with smoke.

It was in that moment Sabrina finally understood that Brandt didn't care if any of them got out alive. He was focused only on getting revenge on Patricia.

"Run!" Nash yelled to the Lost Causes. As they scrambled up, he used the fleeting instant of diversion to dive for his gun on the floor.

But Brandt was expecting it, igniting Nash's weapon into a bouquet of flames before he could grab it. "Go!" Nash called from the floor, his eyes meeting Sabrina's for the briefest of seconds before he leaped up and charged toward Brandt.

Sabrina turned toward the front door, but the fire along the curtain had erupted into a towering blaze, blocking almost the entire threshold, the heat already assailing them from across the room.

"This way!" Andrew hissed, smoke strangling his vocal cords as he charged to the kitchen door. The kitchen table burst into flames, seemingly out of nowhere. Fire crackled through the wooden legs as if they were logs in a fireplace. The exit was blocked. Sabrina turned abruptly, looking for another way out, when she saw the hallway leading toward bedrooms on the other side of the living room. If they could just reach it, she was sure there was a window they could pry open.

But first they needed to be able to pass Brandt and the gauntlet of fire in the living room. Luckily, his back was to them, so Sabrina grabbed Z's hand, pulling her as she charged forward, the rest of the Lost Causes following as the room blurred around her.

"Kevin, put it down!" Patricia yelled. Sabrina turned to see that Brandt had managed to grab Patricia's gun, training it directly at her and Nash.

Nash caught Sabrina's eye. *Keep moving*, he mouthed to her.

"Kevin, put the gun down. I'm sorry," Patricia begged, a sob escaping. "We can work this out. I swear."

Sabrina pushed forward, gray smoke surrounding her like a thick fog, making it next to impossible to see the hallway just feet ahead of her.

Then the sound of a gunshot blasted through the room.

She dared to look behind her and could make out Patricia on the floor, blood seeping from her temple. Brandt, standing directly over her, discharged another bullet for good measure. *Where is Nash?*

Brandt was looking for him then, too, and began to shoot almost blindly into the smoky room.

Gabby screamed, "Justin!" Then she clutched her hand and Sabrina could see one of the bullets had grazed her.

Justin turned and saw her wound, too. Before Sabrina even understood what was happening, the deer head had ripped off the wall and was hurtling through the gauzy air straight at Brandt. The sharp point of an antler struck him, impaling his throat.

Brandt staggered backward, dropping the gun to clutch at his neck before he fell to the floor.

"We have to get out!" Z cried.

But Justin was frozen, watching Brandt suck in his last breath, until Z started pushing him forward.

"Stay low!" Sabrina heard Nash bellow through the raging flames.

"Smoke rises," Andrew choked out. He dropped to his knees and began crawling around the couch, the rest of the Lost Causes following him. They crept along the edge of the room, the fire from the kitchen now blazing into the living room behind them, almost at their heels.

"Hurry!" rasped Sabrina, who was at the tail end of the group. *Where is Nash?*

As they reached the doorway to the hall, the smoke thinned for a second and Sabrina caught sight of him, pinned down by a heavy wooden armoire that had fallen on his right leg. The edges of the armoire were burning while Nash attempted to push it off himself with one hand. The whole thing would be ablaze in less than a minute.

"Nash!" Sabrina yelled.

"Go ahead!" he implored her.

But Sabrina couldn't leave him there.

"Justin!" she called out. If he could just move the armoire out of the way, Nash could free himself. But Justin had already disappeared down the hall with the others, too far to hear her through the deafening roar of the fire.

Sabrina reversed course, crawling back across the room toward Nash.

"Get out!" he thundered. "I'll be okay."

But Sabrina continued toward him, smoke coating her throat in a thick layer. She pushed her shirt over her mouth, which helped a little, as she reached the armoire.

Together with Nash, she tried to push it back, but it wouldn't budge. "Go back!" Nash told her. "Please!"

"No!" The fire burned on, weakening the timber, and suddenly a large flame burst out of the upper cabinet, causing it to fall off and set the sofa ablaze. That was the piece of luck they needed.

"Now!" Nash boomed, he and Sabrina pushing the small remainder of the armoire off his leg. "Let's go!" Nash pushed her toward the hall doorway through which the other Lost Causes had gone.

Sabrina navigated the smoky corridor until she reached a bedroom. There had to be a window in there somewhere.

"Sabrina!" she heard Andrew calling in the distance. She moved toward his voice, wheezing as she crept through the room on her hands and knees, her chest threatening to explode as a coughing spasm rattled her body.

Pointing up, Nash nudged her leg. A few feet ahead was a window. Air. The thought of it made her gasp, sending her into another choking frenzy. She couldn't breathe as she clawed her way forward, vaguely aware of Nash's hands pushing her body upward, through the dense cloud of smoke, and thrusting her through the opening.

She fell through the window, more hands — Justin's, maybe? — helping her outside, ferrying her away from the house, the oxygen plunging through her lungs as if she were coming up from a deep-sea dive.

In the distance, she heard sirens, as the hands — yes, they were definitely Justin's, she could see him now — laid her down on the ground with the other Lost Causes. Z grabbed her hand, her deep blue eyes looking directly into Sabrina's. "You're okay," she said. "We're all okay."

CHAPTER FORTY-SEVEN

"So, what do I do now?" Andrew asked nervously, tiny beads of sweat forming along his hairline.

"Ask her out!" Gabby said excitedly.

It had been a little over a week since the fire at Brandt's house, and Sabrina and the other Lost Causes were sprawled on lawn chairs at the Cedar Springs campground, thousands of stars twinkling above them. The case might be over, but their friendship had survived.

The campsite was completely deserted, summer too long gone for tourists and fall too chilly for locals. But it was perfect for the Lost Causes, who pulled right up to a cozy spot by the creek in Z's Range Rover and popped open the trunk, which they'd stocked with snacks and drinks.

As soon as they got there, Z informed them she had big news she'd been waiting to drop on Andrew. Earlier that day, when Ali Hanuman had approached their lunch table to remind Andrew about a Mathletes meeting, Z had heard her thoughts. Apparently, Ali had a major crush on Andrew. Sabrina tried not to laugh watching Andrew hear the news and go from shock to excitement to panic all because a girl liked him.

"Ask Ali out? H-how?" Andrew stammered, as if he'd never heard of the concept before.

Justin raised an eyebrow. "Seriously, Foreman? You're a genius and you need us to spell this out?"

In some ways, when they were all like this, laughing together, the night of the fire already seemed forever ago to Sabrina. But then she would look down at the burn mark on her arm or the bandage on Gabby's hand where the bullet had grazed her and remember just how recent it actually was.

In the haze of those first few days, they'd all been debriefed by Nash and his boss, Carl Plouffe. Since then, they'd gotten sporadic updates. The serum was presumed to have been burned in the flames at Brandt's house. A story had been spun to explain the fire to the media, completely omitting the Lost Causes' presence there at the time.

But the biggest news Sabrina and the others had received was that Patricia had kept both Lost Causes programs a secret from her supervisors at the FBI. Brandt had been right. Patricia and Lily had rammed Amy's car over that bridge to keep their secret from being exposed. Nash had also been kept in the dark about everything. Even though he and Sabrina had barely spoken in the days since the fire, it was a relief to know he hadn't been lying to her. He'd been looking out for her from the start. She allowed herself to wonder if maybe now that the case was over, there was still a chance for her and Nash to be together (whatever that meant …).

Not likely, she told herself. Though he was no longer off-limits per se, Nash hadn't reached out to her personally since the night of the fire, outside of the briefings and updates he conducted with the Lost Causes. She knew he'd been busy since the showdown at Brandt's house, even traveling down to Albuquerque for a few days, but his absence still stung. She had started wondering if, in his mind, now that the case was over, so was whatever they had shared, but that idea was so painful, she couldn't quite let herself believe it yet.

Sabrina turned her focus back to the group.

"I just meant there are lots of different ways to ask a girl out," Andrew was saying, his cheeks still red. "Am I supposed to call or text?"

"Call!" Sabrina said in unison with Gabby.

Z shook her head. "No way. Calling feels so formal. Like we're our grandparents worrying about courting rules. Calling makes you seem desperate."

"I second that," Justin agreed. "Go for the text."

"If you want some intel before the date, I'm happy to keep listening in on what she's thinking," Z said. She threw a chocolate candy in the air and was about to catch it in her mouth when it suddenly zipped across the campfire and into Justin's hand. Z shot him an unimpressed look. "Not funny, Justin."

"Don't do anything like that in front of Nash," Andrew said. "I don't want to give him any more reasons to inject us with the antidote."

Nash had texted them all a few hours earlier saying he had to speak to them that night, and for the past hour, they had been debating the reason for his urgency. Though Andrew held out hope that perhaps the FBI had a new case they wanted the Lost Causes' help with, the theory they settled on was that Nash planned to tell them that they needed to be injected with the antidote. Now that they knew the Lost Causes program had never been officially authorized, it made sense that the FBI would want to eliminate all traces of the serum and its effects. Nash had already told them Patricia had been ordered to destroy it a decade ago, which was why Patricia and Lily had hidden it in the first place. The question the Lost Causes kept circling back to was what that would mean for all of them.

"It's not like he can tie us down and force us if we don't want it," Justin said.

"They're the FBI. They totally can," Z replied.

"What if he lets us choose?" Sabrina asked. "Would you want it?"

Sabrina knew Z had been slightly worried by the nosebleeds she kept getting whenever her ability was put to good use. Between her nosebleeds and Andrew's headaches, they'd all been talking about whether new side effects from the serum would pop up over time. Not to mention how delusional Beswick and Jarvis had become. Was that some kind of long-term result the five of them were yet to experience? It was a reason to think about taking the antidote.

"Take the antidote and give up my special gaydar skill? No way," Z told her. It didn't matter that she masked it with sarcasm, Z was worried about her depression returning in full force. Justin and Gabby had already said earlier that they would fight not to take the antidote. Gabby had felt liberated, free of the constraints of her OCD, and the trade-off of having visions was one she'd take any day. Justin said it was a no-brainer, too. The serum made him more dominant at football and he wasn't angry at the world all the time.

"Obviously, I don't want it," Andrew said. "What about you, Sabrina? If he gives you the choice, what will you do?"

"I think I want it." She hadn't made up her mind for sure until right this second. Saying it aloud assured her even more it was the right decision. The person she was now — the person who she'd been for the past two weeks — that was who she really was. Not the self-medicating stranger she'd transformed into. Serum or not, there was no way she would let herself become that girl again.

Andrew interrupted her thoughts. "Hey! Maybe we're all wrong. Maybe Nash wants to meet because we're getting some kind of medal." A smile slowly formed on his face. "Like the FBI version of a Purple Heart or a Bronze Star."

"We should get something," Justin agreed. "We saved their asses."

"We were pretty awesome," Z responded. "We basically saved the world."

Sabrina held up her cup. "To us. For being awesome."

They had just clinked their cups when the sound of a car silenced them. Nash pulled into the park area.

Sabrina wished her heart wasn't racing in her chest at the thought of seeing him, but apparently it was out of her control. As he reached the group, the knots in her stomach tightened. He managed to give them a quarter of a smile as a greeting, then launched into business mode. Some things never changed. "I wanted to give you all an update in person."

Before he could continue, Andrew blurted out, "Are you here to inject us with the antidote?"

The muscles in Nash's jaw tensed. "No."

Andrew grinned and Sabrina gave his shoulders a squeeze. Gabby, Justin and Z relaxed. Everyone was going to get what he or she wanted.

Nash cleared his throat. "Because I don't have one."

Sabrina let herself pretend for one second that she hadn't heard him right. Then her heart sank. "What do you mean? Patricia told us we could use it whenever we wanted."

"I know. But she never told me where she kept it. And to be honest, I'm not sure if it ever existed." Nash was looking at everyone except her.

She was silent, trying to wrap her head around the fact that she would be seeing ghosts for the rest of her life. When she looked up, the Lost Causes were staring at her, devastated on her behalf.

"But Sabrina —" Gabby started to say something to Nash, but Sabrina cut her off. She didn't want a pity party.

"Guys, it's okay. I wasn't sure I wanted it anyway," she lied.

"I'm sorry." Nash finally locked eyes with her when he said it. "As you all know, I was kept in the dark about a lot, as was my boss. But we're working on creating an antidote as we speak. Patricia didn't leave any kind of blueprint behind for how she isolated the compound, but there's a team in the lab working on it. These people are the best in their field."

"But we don't have to take it if you do get one. You can't force us, right?" Gabby asked nervously.

"Let's cross that bridge when we come to it."

"That's not an answer," Z replied.

Nash's face softened for the briefest of seconds. "Let's put it this way, I will be pushing for you to be able to make whatever choice you want."

"I'm not doing anything until I at least take the FBI entrance exam," Andrew huffed.

"There's one more thing," Nash said. His expression darkened and Sabrina's stomach clenched. "I thought you all deserved to know. We had believed the serum burned with the house, but it looks like we were wrong."

"Looks like? What the hell does that mean?" Justin asked.

"We initially thought we found the compound in the wreckage. Now that we've tested everything, we could find no trace of it. Either it's hidden somewhere else or Kevin Beswick managed to sell it before we caught up to him."

Sabrina and the other Lost Causes met eyes. The serum was still out there.

"And now you want our help to find it," Andrew supplied giddily.

Nash shook his head. "No. As much as I know firsthand how helpful you all would be, that's not an option. There are too many risks for the FBI to authorize that type of program." As if he sensed the dimming mood of the group, he continued, "That being said, due to you five, we actually have a shot at finding it. You led us to Beswick. I know we'll find something in the clues he left behind."

"So, what now?" Sabrina wondered.

"I'll be sticking around Cedar Springs to follow whatever leads we can get on the serum. My boss is sending a few more bodies up to help with the investigation."

"But what about us?" Andrew asked.

"You guys can get back to your normal lives now. Or as normal as they can be under the circumstances. Until we get this antidote problem remedied, I'll be checking in with you weekly."

It was the only bit of good news Sabrina held on to as Nash walked away. He wasn't leaving her life forever. He would still check in with them. Even if he had absolutely no desire to be with her, she couldn't handle the thought of not seeing him again.

"Who do you think Beswick was trying to sell it to?" Gabby asked the group once Nash had driven off.

"I'm sure once the FBI found out that Brandt was actually Beswick, they retraced every step he took for the past few months," Z said. "They could probably pull tapes from the NSA. They're already recording every conversation we've ever had anyway."

As they all got into a debate with Z about how much access the NSA really had into their lives, Sabrina was dragged away from the conversation by a text.

Her pulse quickened when she saw who it was from.

Nash.

We need to talk.

* * *

Sabrina reached up to knock on the door, but it opened before she had a chance.

"Sabrina." Nash's voice was softer than it had been when he addressed them a few hours earlier, and she had to consciously remember she needed to breathe. He was still wearing the same dark jeans and charcoal sweater, adhering to his usual palette of black, blue and gray. She followed him into his apartment and stood awkwardly in the living room across from him.

The entire drive there, she'd contemplated what it was that Nash wanted to talk to her about, and she thought she had a good idea. He was going to personally apologize to her for the lack of an antidote. No one took his job more seriously than he did. He must have felt solely responsible for not knowing anything about it. Once he'd seen that Sabrina was the only disappointed one out of the five of them, he figured he owed her a better explanation.

"About earlier …" he began.

She decided to start talking to avoid whatever apology speech he probably had planned. He would be as uncomfortable giving one as she was hearing one. Sympathy wasn't what she wanted from him anyway.

"I don't blame you. It's not your fault," she said quickly.

"What's not my fault?"

"Not knowing about the antidote. And for me having to deal with ghosts popping up in my face for the rest of my life —" He looked confused. "Isn't that what you wanted to talk to me about?"

"No," he answered, frowning. "But you're right. I should've questioned Patricia more, seen something sooner. I am sorry."

Sabrina should've kept her mouth shut. She'd been trying to avoid an apology exactly like that one and instead she'd forced it out of him. "So, what then? Why did you want to talk?"

He turned more serious. If that was possible. "You saved my life, Sabrina. I wanted to thank you."

"Oh," she said. She definitely hadn't been expecting that. "Well, if I'd known you were going to disappear right after, I might not have done it."

A hint of a smile managed to break through his seriousness. Her heartbeat always picked up when she got a glimpse of that other side of him. Maybe she was the only one who could draw it out.

"There's one more thing I needed to tell you." He paused for a moment before looking up at her. "Technically, you're no longer an asset."

Sabrina nodded. "Yeah, I know. You already told us the FBI won't let us help you find the serum."

"Right. Which means technically I'm no longer your boss."

Was this his way of saying goodbye? "Okay. Got it."

He didn't take his eyes off hers. The look was so intense she almost wanted to look away. Almost.

He finally spoke. "Don't you think we should celebrate that fact?"

For a split-second she was completely lost. And then it clicked. Nash was no longer her boss. There were no FBI rules holding him back anymore.

He must have seen the realization fall into place for her because that small smile tugged at the corners of his mouth again.

"You're right," Sabrina said, taking a step toward him, bringing their bodies close, but not quite touching. "I do think a celebration is in order …"

He raised a single eyebrow. "What did you have in mind?"

Everything she'd been feeling for weeks burst through her as she wrapped her arms around him, her lips hungrily meeting his. He gripped her waist tightly and his warm hands sent sparks charging through her body.

"Wait," Nash said after a second, pulling away. Sabrina looked at him questioningly. Was he changing his mind so quickly?

"I've been thinking about this for way too long. I don't want to rush." His eyes never leaving hers, he cupped her face toward his and just looked at her. She basically stopped breathing, transported back to when he'd first appeared in front of her. That visceral feeling that he could see parts of her she didn't even know existed. But now as she looked at him, his green eyes smoldering, she could see those parts of him, too.

He finally kissed her again, pulling her body toward his, and she realized he was right. They could take their time. They had all night.

* * *

Z rolled into the kitchen the next morning a bit earlier than usual, surprised to find her father was the only one present until she realized it was a Saturday. That meant her mother was still sleeping off the effects of the double sedative she'd no doubt taken the night before, and she vaguely remembered Scott discussing plans to go helicopter-skiing in Telluride with some of his friends.

Relishing the quiet, Z took her cup of espresso to the table where her father sat reading the paper.

"You're up early," her father commented, surprising Z. She hadn't realized her movements through the house ever registered on his radar.

Z shrugged as she grabbed a muffin from the plate Louise, their housekeeper, had left out. She'd had a hard time sleeping since Nash had informed them all the previous night that the serum was still out there somewhere. It was killing her not to be part of the investigation. How were they supposed to go back to their "normal lives" when some psycho had the serum and could unleash it at any time?

Her father put down the *Wall Street Journal*, moving on to the local Cedar Springs paper, whose front page was still dominated by the Brandt story.

As was no surprise to Z, the FBI had intervened immediately to control and whitewash the news flow. There was no mention, of course, of the Lost Causes past or present, the serum or Brandt's true identity as Kevin Beswick. Instead, the official story as reported by the police and FBI was that evidence had been found in Brandt's house implicating him in the murder of Lily Carpenter. Patricia was being hailed as the FBI agent who'd tracked him down, sacrificing her life as she attempted to bring him into custody. After Brandt fatally shot her, it was explained, he set fire to his house in an apparent suicide.

Z had to hand it to the FBI — they'd managed to tie up all the loose ends in a neat-enough bow, though the frenzy for information still hadn't slowed. Every time she saw a new article speculating on why the fire had started or how Patricia had tracked Brandt down, it was tantalizingly difficult to refrain from revealing all she knew. Even now, as her father skimmed the front page, she found herself wanting to skate around the issue.

"Have they figured out why that guy killed Lily Carpenter?" she asked innocently.

"Their best guess is a robbery gone bad. Sounds like this guy was unstable to begin with."

Z had to literally bite her tongue as she reached for her blueberry muffin. But the ringing in her ears jerked her head up. It was the first time she had heard a thought from her father. It came through loud and clear the way all the others usually had.

But this one shook her to the core.

She froze, clutching the underside of the table as if it was a life raft. Her father's expression remained impassive as he flipped through the pages, but Z knew what she'd just heard.

Feeling her gaze, her father looked up at her, taking in her wide-eyed stare.

"Zelda, are you okay?"

She could call him out right this second. The words tingled in her throat, eager to escape. But who knew how he would react?

Instead, she nodded demurely, dropping her eyes to the floor. "I, uh, forgot something. Upstairs."

Her legs shaking, she took the back staircase up to her room, two steps at a time.

Only when she was firmly ensconced in her bedroom, the door assuredly locked behind her, did she take out her phone and call Nash.

"I know who bought the serum. I was just eating breakfast with him."

ACKNOWLEDGMENTS

First, we want to thank our readers, especially the ones who loved this book enough to even read the acknowledgments. We hope living in the world of the Lost Causes was as much fun for you as it was for us.

This book wouldn't have been possible without the following people lending us their minds and hearts:

The world "brilliant" gets thrown around a lot but in the case of our editor, Kate Egan, it is not only true, it's the best word to describe her. Kate, thank you for making us better writers. You helped us shape this book into everything we hoped it could be.

Huge thanks to Holly Root, our tenacious literary agent at Waxman Leavell, who instantly got this book when it was still an idea in our heads and never stopped fighting for it.

To the team at Kids Can Press and KCP Loft, we cannot thank you enough for your support and enthusiasm for this project.

A shout-out to Melanie Downing, whose early thoughts gave us the motivation to push forward.

(And speaking of shout-outs, thank you to whoever invented leggings, which you can write in all day and sleep in, too.)

We want to thank the co-presidents of our fan club (our mothers), as well as our entire families for being an endless source of love and support for us always.

And finally, the biggest thank you of all to Josh and Dan who never doubt us even when we doubt ourselves. We're publicly admitting that sometimes you guys are right. Thank you for taking over everything and not blinking an eye when we were in our writing cocoons. You guys are our therapists, cheerleaders, best friends and the most amazing husbands in the world.